RATKING

RATKING

Michael Dibdin

BANTAM BOOKS
TORONTO · NEW YORK · LONDON · SYDNEY · AUCKLAND

RATKING
A Bantam Book / February 1989

Book design by Jeffrey L. Ward

Library of Congress Cataloging-in-Publication Data

Dibdin, Michael.
  Ratking.

  I. Title.
  PR6054.I26R3 1989   823'.914   88-47832
  ISBN 0-553-05337-X

Bantam Books are published by Bantam Books, a division of Bantam Doubleday
Dell Publishing Group, Inc. Its trademark, consisting of the words "Bantam Books"
and the portrayal of a rooster, is Registered in U.S. Patent and Trademark Office and
in other countries. Marca Registrada. Bantam Books, 666 Fifth Avenue, New York,
New York 10103.

PRINTED IN THE UNITED STATES OF AMERICA

WAK   0 9 8 7 6 5 4 3 2 1

Agli amici di quel tempo

Hello?"

"*Hello? Who is it?*"

"Who's calling?"

"*I want to speak to Senator Rossi.*"

"Speaking."

"*Ah, it's you, Senator? Forgive me! These phones make everyone sound like anyone, or rather no one. This is Antonio Crepi.*"

"Commendatore! What a pleasure! Are you here in Rome?"

"*In Rome? God forbid! No no, I'm in Perugia. At home, at the villa. You remember it?*"

"But of course, of course. Of course."

"*When my eldest boy married.*"

"Exactly. Precisely. An unforgettable occasion. A wonderful couple. How are they both?"

"*I don't see that much of them. Corrado's moved to Milan and Annalisa's seeing some footballer, or so they tell me. Our paths don't cross very often.*"

"Ah, what a shame."

"*These things happen nowadays! I don't really give a damn anymore.*

1

At our age it's absurd to go on pretending. Let them do what they like. Just as long as I've got my vines and my olives, and one or two friends I can still talk to. People I understand and who understand me. You know what I'm talking about?"

"Of course, of course! Friendship is the most important thing in life, I always say. No question about that."

"I'm glad to hear you say so, Senator. Because the fact is I'm phoning to ask for your help on behalf of a friend. A mutual friend. I'm talking about Ruggiero Miletti."

"Ah. A tragic business."

"Do you know how long it has been now?"

"Shocking."

"Nearly four and a half months. A hundred and thirty-seven days and nights of agony for the Miletti family and for all their friends. To say nothing of Ruggiero himself."

"Horrible."

"A man as old as you or I, Senator, chained up in some shack in the mountains, in this bitter weather, at the mercy of a gang of callous bandits!"

"Dreadful. Scandalous. If only one could do something to help . . ."

"But you can help! You must help!"

"In any way I can, Commendatore! I am only too ready, believe me. But we must be realistic. Kidnapping is the scourge of society today, a plague and a peril in the face of which we are all equally vulnerable, equally powerless, equally . . ."

"Bullshit! Excuse me, but when something happens to one of you politicians the whole country is put into a state of siege! Nothing is too much trouble then, no expense is spared. But when it's an ordinary, decent law-abiding citizen like our friend Ruggiero, no one even takes any notice. Business as usual! 'It's his own fault. Why didn't he take more precautions?'"

"Commendatore, do not let us fall into the trap of deluding ourselves that any responsible person might presume to deny the gravity of . . ."

"Save that stuff for the press, Senator. This is Antonio Crepi you're talking to! Don't you try and tell me we are all equal. If you got kidnapped, God forbid, you would get the crack units, the top men. Well, that's what I want for Ruggiero."

"Of course, of course! Naturally!"

"I'm not blaming the people here in Perugia. But let's face it, if they

were the best they wouldn't be here, would they? They would be in Rome, looking after you politicians."

"One should perhaps avoid exaggerating the effectiveness of the measures to which you refer, Commendatore."

"Listen, if you get a pain in the chest you go to a specialist, right?"

"Our specialists couldn't save Aldo Moro."

"Spare me the platitudes, Senator! God knows we've had enough talk. Now I want action, and that's why I'm phoning. I want a top man sent up here to shake up the whole operation. A new face, a fresh approach. You can arrange that in a second, with your contacts."

"Well . . ."

"Or is it too much to ask?"

"It's not . . ."

"Don't you think Ruggiero deserves the best?"

"Naturally."

"Senator, I wouldn't have bothered to call you if I thought you were one of those people with short memories. There are enough of them about, God knows! But no, I thought, Rossi's not like that. He hasn't forgotten what the Miletti family has meant to him. Senator, I beg you, think of them now! Think what they are going through. Think what it will mean to them to know that thanks to you one of the top policemen in Italy has been sent to Perugia to inspire the hunt for their beloved father! And then think that you can arrange all that with a single phone call, as easily as ordering a taxi."

"You overestimate my power."

"I hope not. I sincerely hope not. Because I have always thought of you as a friend and ally, and it would sadden me to feel that I could no longer count on your support. And you on mine, Senator, and on that of the Miletti family and their many friends."

"For heaven's sake, Commendatore! What are you talking about? Please do not allow ourselves to be misled into imagining that—"

"Perfect! There is no more to say, then. When can I expect to hear?"

"Well, in a situation of this type one would perhaps be wise to avoid imposing rigid deadlines. Nevertheless, broadly speaking, I would by no means rule out the possibility of being in a position to—"

"I'd like to know by this afternoon. Or perhaps you have more important business to attend to?"

"Look here, Crepi, it's no good your expecting miracles, you know! Excuse me saying so."

"I'm not asking for miracles, Senator. I'm asking for justice. Or does that take a miracle in this country?"

"Lapucci."
"Did I wake you, Giorgio?"
"Who's this?"
"Gianpiero Rossi."
"Ah, good morning, Senator! No, I was working in the other office. No one ever believes it, of course, but we do work here at Central Office."
"Listen, Giorgio, I have a little problem I think you may be able to help me with."
"Consider it done."
"You know about the Miletti kidnapping?"
"The tire king from Modena?"
"Modena! What do you mean, Modena? Would I give a damn if he was from Modena? Miletti, Miletti! Radios, televisions!"
"Ah, of course. Excuse me. From Perugia."
"From Perugia, exactly. And that's my problem. Because some people there, friends of the family, feel that not enough is being done. You know how it is, everyone wants special attention. And these are people who are difficult to refuse. Do you follow?"
"Perfectly."
"Like they say, the poor pray for miracles, the rich think they have a right to them. Now I'm not trying to justify what cannot and should not be justified. I neither condone nor condemn. But the fact remains that I'm in a difficult situation. You see what I mean?"
"Of course. But what exactly do they want, these people? If you don't mind my asking."
"They want a name."
"A name? Whose name?"
"That is entirely up to you. It must be someone presentable, naturally. Don't make me look like an idiot. If he's well known, so much the better."
"And what is this person to do?"
"Why, go and sort things out."
"Go to Perugia?"
"To Perugia, of course!"
"A police official?"
"Exactly. Can you help me?"
"Well, I must say that this is a particularly difficult moment, Senator. Since the Cabinet reshuffle the party's relations with the Ministry have been—"

"When you've been around as long as I have, Giorgio, you'll know that it's always a particularly difficult moment. That's why I rang you instead of some other people whose names came to mind. Now, can you help me?"

"Well, despite the changes I've just referred to, we do have various contacts, of course. There's one in particular I'm thinking of who may well be able—"

"I'm not interested in the details, Giorgio. I just want to know if you can help me. Or should I ring someone else? Perhaps you could recommend someone?"

"You must be joking, Senator. Anything that can be done, I'll do for you. By this time tomorrow you'll—"

"By this time tomorrow I'll be in Turin. Make it this afternoon. I'll be here till seven."

"Very well."

"Excellent. I knew I did right to call you. I've got a nose for these things. Giorgio's a man who can make things happen, I said to myself. A million thanks. I'll be expecting your call."

"Yes?"

"Enrico?"

"Who's that?"

"Giorgio Lapucci."

"Christ, I thought it was his royal highness. Excuse me while I change my trousers."

"Why the panic?"

"He's at a conference in Strasbourg, and every so often he phones up and demands a complete update on the situation here. All part of this new managerial style you've been reading about. Keeps us on our toes, he says. Anyway, what can I do for you?"

"I suppose this line is safe?"

"Giorgio, this is the Ministry of the Interior you're talking to. Any phone tapping that goes on around here, we do it. So what's up?"

"Well, it's the old story, I'm afraid. Someone's leaning on someone who's leaning on me."

"And you want to lean on me."

"Isn't that what friends are for? But this shouldn't be too difficult. It's a question of getting a senior police official transferred temporarily to Perugia to take over a kidnapping case."

"That's all?"

"That's all."

*"No problem. I can lose it in the routine postings and bang it through
at departmental level. No one ever looks at that stuff. The only headache
could be finding someone. When are we talking?"*

"Now."

"Shit. Look, I'll have to think a bit. Let me get back to you."

"Today, though."

"I'll do my best."

"I appreciate it, Enrico. Give my regards to Nicola."

*"And mine to Emanuela. Listen, why don't we all get together
sometime?"*

"Yes, we should. We really should."

"Personnel."

"Mancini. I need someone we can send up to Perugia on a
kidnapping. Who do you suggest?"

"No one."

"What do you mean, no one?"

"I mean there isn't anyone available."

"What about Fabri?"

"In Genoa on that bank job."

"De Angelis?"

*"Sardinia. Where there were three kidnappings last week alone, in
case you haven't seen the papers. This weekend we've got the visit of the
President of France plus an English football team, God help us. Are you
getting the picture? If not, I can go on."*

"Calm down, Ciliani. I know things are difficult. But there's
always somebody. Look harder."

"There's no one except Romizi, and he's going on leave."

"Well, tell him he'll have to put it off."

*"Excuse me, dottore, but you tell him! He's booked a flight to
America."*

"What's he doing going to America?"

"How should I know? Got relatives there or something."

"Well, what about people outside Criminalpol?"

"You said this was operational."

"We could always stretch a point. Isn't there anyone who's had
some experience? Couldn't stand the sight of blood and requested a desk job, that sort of thing. Use your head, Ciliani! I
mean we're talking about a gesture here, not a new chief for the
fucking Squadra Mobile. What about what's-his-name, the one
we've got doing Housekeeping?"

"Zuccaroni?"

"No, the other one."

"Zen?"

"That's it."

"But surely he's . . ."

"What?"

"Well, I thought there was, you know, some problem about using him."

"Really? I haven't heard anything."

"I don't mean anything official."

"Well, as long as it's not official I can't see that there's any problem. A kidnapping, too! Wasn't he something of a specialist? Couldn't be better."

"If you say so, dottore."

"It's perfect. Ideal from every point of view. The only thing that would ruin it is delay. And that's why I'm going to leave it in your lap, Ciliani. I want Zen and the relevant paperwork in my office within the hour. Got that?"

"Uh."

"Caccamo?"

"Uh."

"Ciliani. You seen Zen?"

"You tried his office?"

"No, I'm too stupid to think of that. Of course I've tried his fucking office."

"Hang on, isn't he away somewhere? Treviso?"

"Trieste. He was due back this morning."

"Did I ever tell you about that girl from Trieste I met the time I was doing beach duty down at Ostia? She was sunbathing totally nude behind a dune, and when I—"

"Fuck off, Caccamo. Christ, this is all I need. Where has that son of a bitch Zen got to?"

o! I don't believe it! It isn't possible!"

"It isn't possible, but it happens. In short, it's a miracle!"

"Just a few hundred meters away from the station and they stop! This is going too far!"

"Not quite far enough, I'd say!"

"For the love of God, let us out of this damned train!"

"'And yet it does *not* move,' as Galileo might have said. Ah well, let's be patient."

"Patient! Patient! Excuse me, but in my humble opinion what this country needs is a few people who will no longer be patient! People who refuse to suffer patiently the bungling and incompetence with which we are surrounded! There! That's what I think!"

"It's better to travel hopefully than to arrive, they say. It should be the motto of the state railways."

"You choose to joke about it, signore, but in my humble opinion this is no joking matter. On the contrary, it is an issue of the very highest importance, symptomatic of all the gravest ills of our poor country. What does one expect of a train? That it goes reasonably fast and arrives within five or ten minutes of the time stated in the timetable. Is that too much? Does that require divine intervention to bring about? Not in any other country in the world! Nor did it used to here."

"You can always move to Switzerland, if that's how you feel."

"But now what happens? The railway service, like everything else, is a disaster. And what is the government's response? To give their friends in the construction business billions and billions of lire to build a new railway line between Rome and Florence! And the result? The trains are *slower* than they were before the war! It's incredible! A national disgrace!"

The young man sitting near the door, Roman to his elegant fingertips, smiled sarcastically. "Ah yes, of course, everything was better before the war," he murmured. "We know all about that."

"Excuse me, but you know nothing about it," replied the vigorous, thickset man with the shock of silver hair and the Veronese accent. "Unless I am very much mistaken, you weren't even born then!"

He turned to the third occupant of the compartment, a distinguished-looking man of about fifty with a pale face whose most striking feature was a nose as sharply triangular as the jib of a sailing boat. There was a faintly exotic air about him, as though he were Greek or even Levantine. His expression was cynical, suave, and aloof, and a distant smile flickered on his lips. But it was his eyes that compelled attention. They were gray with glints of blue, and held a slightly sinister stillness which made the Veronese shiver. A cold fish, this one, he thought.

"What about you, signore?" he demanded. "Don't you agree that it's a disgrace, a national disgrace?"

"The train was delayed at Mestre," the stranger observed with a deliberate courtesy that somehow seemed mocking. "That has naturally upset the schedules. There were bound to be further delays."

"I know the train was delayed at Mestre!" retorted the Veronese. "You don't need to remind me that the train was delayed at Mestre. And why, may I ask, was the train delayed at Mestre? Because of an unofficial stoppage by the local section of one of the railway unions. Unofficial! As if we didn't have enough official strikes, we are also at the mercy of any local gang of workers with a grievance, who can throw the whole transport system of the nation into total chaos without, needless to say, the slightest fear of any reprisals whatsoever."

The young Roman slapped the leg of his trousers with a rolled copy of a glossy news magazine. "Certainly it's a nuisance," he remarked. "But don't let's exaggerate the inconvenience. Besides, there are worse things than chaos."

"And what might they be?"

"Too much order."

The Veronese made a contemptuously dismissive gesture. "Too much order? Don't make me laugh! In this country too much order wouldn't even be enough. It's always the same. The trains are late? Build a new railway! The South is poor? Open a new factory! The young are illiterate delinquents? Hire more teachers! There are too many civil servants? Retire them earlier on big pensions! The crime rate is soaring? Pass new laws! But for the love of God don't expect us to make the railways or the factories we *have* run efficiently, or make the teachers or bureaucrats do an honest day's work, or make people respect the existing laws. Oh no! Because that would smack of dictatorship, and of tyranny, and we can't have that."

"That's not the point!" The young Roman finally gave up his pose of ironic detachment. "What you want, signore, this famous 'order' of yours, is something un-Italian, un-Mediterranean. It's an idea of the North, and that's where it should stay. It's got no place here. Very well, so we have a few problems. There are problems everywhere in the world! Just look in the newspaper, watch the television. Do you think this is the only country where life isn't perfect?"

"It's got nothing to do with perfection! And as for this beautiful Mediterranean myth of yours, signore, permit me to say that . . ."

The man at the window looked at the blank wall of the Campo Verano cemetery beside the tracks. Neither this further delay nor the argument to which it had given rise seemed able to touch the mood of serenity which had been with him since he had awakened that morning. Perhaps it had been the dislocation of routine that had done it, the shock of finding himself not back in Rome but inexplicably stalled at Mestre, 560 kilometers farther north. For a moment it had seemed as though reality itself had broken down like a film projector and soon everyone would be demanding their money back. After a blind tussle with his clothes in the cramped darkness of the sleeping compartment he had stepped out into the misty early-morning air, laden with the salty stench of the lagoon and the acrid odors of petroleum and chemicals from the heavy industry he could hear murmuring all around, and wandered along the platform to the bar, where he pushed his way into a group of railwaymen, ordered an espresso laced with grappa, and discovered that no trains would move out of Mestre until further notice due to a dispute regarding manning levels.

I could go, he had thought. I could have gone, he thought now, simply by boarding one of the orange buses which passed the station with illuminated signs bearing that magic combination of letters. VENEZIA. But he hadn't, and he'd been right. His mysterious mood of elation had been one to float on, gliding lightly as a shallow-bottomed skiff across the inlets and channels of the lagoon whose melancholy topography he had explored as a boy. At his age such gifts came rarely and should be handled with care. His reward had been that the mood proved unexpectedly durable. Neither the delay at Mestre nor subsequent holdups at Bologna and Florence had been able to touch it, and despite the weather, gray and unseasonably cold for late March, even the return to the capital hadn't depressed him as much as usual.

He would never learn to like Rome, never be at ease with the weight of centuries of power and corruption there in the dead center of Italy, the symbol and source of its stagnation. How could he ever feel at home in the heaviest of all cities when he had been born and formed in its living antithesis, a city so light it seemed to float? Nevertheless, if he were forced to take sides between the old Veronese and the young Roman there could be only one choice. He had no wish to live in some miserable northern land where everything ran like clockwork. As if that was what life was about! No, it was about those two lads out there in the corridor, for instance, typical Roman working-class toughs in jeans and leather jackets staring into the first-class compartments as they strolled along the corridor with an easy, natural insolence which no degree of poverty could touch, as if they owned the place! The country might have its problems, but as long as it could go on producing that burning energy, that irresistible drive and flair . . .

In a second, the door was closed again and the taller of the two youths was inside, a plastic sports bag in one hand and an automatic pistol in the other.

A brief smile flashed across his face. "Don't worry, I'm not a terrorist!" The bag landed on the floor at their feet. "All the goodies in there! Wallets, watches, rings, lighters, lockets, trinkets, bangles, earrings, silk knickers, you name it. Foreign currency in major denominations only, all major credit cards accepted. Move it, move it!"

The snout of the automatic jabbed out toward each of the three passengers in turn.

"You piece of shit." It was hardly audible, a shiver of pent-up loathing finding its release.

The pistol swung toward the silver-haired man. "You said *what*, grandpa?"

The gray-eyed man by the window cleared his throat conspicuously. "Don't shoot me, please," he said. "I'm just getting my wallet out."

The pistol swung away from the Veronese as the man at the window took from his pocket a large brown leather wallet from which he extracted a plastic card.

"What's that?" the youth snapped.

"It's no use to you."

"Let me see! And you two *move it* for fuck's sake, or do you want to get kneecapped?"

Expensive leather and precious metals began to hit the bottom of the plastic bag.

The youth glanced at the plastic card and laughed briefly. "Commissioner of Police? Eh, sorry, dottore, I didn't know. That's okay, keep your stuff. Maybe one of these days you can do me a favor."

The Veronese forgot the threatening pistol and turned furiously toward the man at the window. "You're a police official?" he demanded as the carriage jerked violently and the train started to roll forward.

But before the gray-eyed man could reply, the door opened and the other youth beckoned urgently to his companion. "Haven't you fucking finished yet? Let's go, for Christ's sake!"

"Well, do something!" shrieked the silver-haired man as the pair scooped up the bag and vanished. "If you're a policeman, do something! Stop them! Pursue them! Shoot them! Don't just *sit* there!"

The train was now rolling slowly past the San Lorenzo goods

yard. A carriage door slammed nearby. The police official opened the window and looked out. There they were, haring away across the tracks toward the safety of the streets.

The Veronese was beside himself with rage. "So you refuse to reply, do you? But that won't do! I *demand* an answer! You can't get out of it that easily, you know! Do you feel no shame, Commissioner? You calmly allow innocent citizens to be robbed under your very nose while you hide behind the power of office and do precisely damn all about it! Mother of God! I mean, everybody knows that the police these days are a bad joke that makes us the laughingstock of every other country in Europe. That's taken for granted. But dear Christ, I never in my worst moments expected to witness such a blatant example of craven dereliction of duty as I have seen today! Eh? Nothing to say for yourself? Very well. Excellent. We'll see about this. I'm not just some nobody you can push around, you know. Kindly give me your name and rank."

The train was rounding the curve by the Porta Maggiore and the terminus was now visible up ahead.

"So, your name?" the silver-haired man insisted.

"Zen."

"Zen? You're Venetian?"

"What of it?"

"But I am from Verona! And to think you disgrace us like this in front of these Southerners!"

"Who are you calling a Southerner?" The young Roman was on his feet.

"Ah, ashamed of the name now, are you? A few minutes ago it was your proudest boast!"

"I'm ashamed of nothing, signore! But when a term is used as a deliberate insult by someone whose arrogance is matched only by his stupendous ignorance of the real meaning of Italic culture—"

"Culture! What do you know about culture? Don't make me laugh by using big words you don't understand."

As the carriage jarred over several sets of points and began to run in alongside the platform, Zen left the compartment and squeezed through the line of people waiting in the corridor.

"In a big hurry, eh?" remarked a sour-looking woman. "Some people always have to be first, and just too bad for everyone else."

The platform was packed with passengers who had been

waiting for hours. As the train slowed to a halt they stormed it like assault troops, intent on winning a seat for the long haul down to Naples and beyond. Zen struggled through them and out to the station concourse. The phones were all in use. At the nearest a tired-looking poorly dressed woman was repeating, "I *know* . . . I *know* . . . I *know*," over and over again in a strident, unmodulated country voice. Zen waved his identity card at her.

"Police. This is an emergency. I need to use this phone."

He took the receiver from the woman's unresisting hand and dialed 113.

"This is Commissioner Aurelio Zen. No, Zen. Z-E-N. No *O*. That's right. Attached to the Ministry of the Interior. I'm calling from the Stazione Termini. There's been a train job. They ran off toward Via Prenestina. Get a car off now and then I'll give you the descriptions. Ready? The first was about twenty, height five ten or eleven, short dark hair, military cut so possibly doing his service, dark green leather jacket with twin zippered flaps, faded jeans, dark brown boots. The other slightly taller, longer lighter hair, mustache, big nose, brown leather jacket, new jeans, red, white, and blue running shoes, carrying a green plastic sports bag with white lettering: 'Banca Populare di Frosinone.' He's got a small automatic, so be careful. Got that? Right, I'll leave a full report with the railway police."

He hung up. The woman was gazing at him with an air of cautious fascination.

"Was it a local call?" he asked.

Fascination was replaced by fear. "What?"

"Were you speaking to someone in Rome?"

"No, no! Salerno! I'm from Salerno."

She started rooting in her bag for the identity card which was her only poor talisman against the dark powers of the State.

Zen looked through his change until he found a telephone token, which he handed to her. "Here. Now you can dial again."

The woman stared at him suspiciously. He put the token down beside the phone and turned away.

"It's my sister," she said suddenly, gripping his arm. "She works for the Pope. At the Vatican! She's a cleaner. The pay's rotten, but it's still something to work for the Pope, isn't it? But her husband won't let me in the house because of what my brother found out about him, the dirty bastard. So I phone her whenever I come up to see my grandson. She hasn't got a phone, you see, so I phone from the station. They're stingy bastards, those priests. Still it's better than packing anchovies, at least your fingers don't stink. But listen, can that criminal do that? Forbid me to see my own sister? Isn't there a law against that?"

Mumbling something about emergencies, Zen pulled away from the woman's grasp and crossed the concourse toward the distant neon sign reading POLIZIA FERROVIARIA.

"Welcome home," he muttered under his breath. His earlier mood already seemed as remote and irrelevant as a childhood memory.

The heavy front door closed behind him with a definitive bang, shutting him in, shutting out the world. As he moved the switch, the single bulb which lit the entrance hall ended its long wan existence in an extravagant flash, whisking him back forty years and leaving him in the dark, just back from school. Once he had kissed his mother he would run out to play football in the square outside. Astonishingly, he even seemed to hear the distant sound of lapping water. Then it faded and a didactic voice began pontificating about the ecology of the Po delta. Those liquid ripples overlaying the constant rumble of traffic came not, of course, from the backwater canals of his childhood, but from the television.

He moved blindly along the passage, past pictures and furniture which had been part of his life for so long that he was no longer aware of their existence. As he approached the glass-paneled door, the noise of the television grew louder. Once inside the living room, it was deafening. In the dim mix of video glare and twilight seeping through the shutters he made out the frail figure of his mother staring with childlike intensity at the flickering screen.

"Aurelio! You're back!"

"Yes, Mamma."

He bent over her and they kissed.

"How was Fiume? Did you enjoy yourself?"

"Yes, Mamma."

He no longer bothered to correct her, even when her mistakes sent him astray not just in space but in time, to a city that had ceased to exist a third of a century earlier. Fiume was now Rijeka, and officials of the Italian State were no longer partic-

ularly welcome there since it was part of Yugoslavia. His
mother's world was as meticulously inaccurate as an old atlas.

"And what about you, Mamma? How have you been?"

"Fine, fine. You needn't worry, Maria Grazia is a treasure. All
I've missed is seeing you. But I told you when you joined! You
don't know what it's like in the services, I said. They send you
here and then they send you there, and just when you're getting
used to that they send you somewhere else, until you don't know
which end to sit down on anymore. And to think you could have
had a nice job on the railways like your father, a nice supervising
job, just as secure as the police and none of this roaming
around. And we would never have had to move down here to
the *South!*"

She broke off as Maria Grazia bustled in from the kitchen.
But they had been speaking dialect, and the housekeeper had
not understood.

"Welcome home, dottore!" she cried. "They've been trying to
get hold of you all day. I told them you hadn't got back yet,
but . . ."

At that moment the phone started to ring in the inner
hallway. It'll be that old fascist on the train, Zen thought. That
type always has friends. But "all day"? Maria Grazia must have
exaggerated. He moved past the housekeeper to the phone.

"*Zen?*"

"Speaking."

"*This is Enrico Mancini.*"

Christ almighty! The Veronese had gone straight to the top.
Zen gripped the receiver angrily.

"Listen, the little bastard had a gun and he was standing too
far away for me to jump him. So what was I supposed to do, I'd
like to know? Get myself shot so that the Commendatore could
keep his lousy watch?"

There was a crackly pause.

"*What are you talking about?*"

"I'm talking about the train!"

"*I don't know anything about any train. I'm calling to discuss your
transfer to Perugia.*"

"What? Foggia?"

The line was very poor, with heavy static and occasional
cutouts. For the hundredth time Zen wondered if it was still
being tapped, and for the hundredth time he told himself that
it wouldn't make any sense, not now. He wasn't important

anymore. Paranoia of that type was simply conceit turned inside out.

"*Perugia! Perugia in Umbria! You leave tomorrow.*"

What on earth was going on? Why should someone like Enrico Mancini concern himself with Zen's humdrum activities?

"For Perugia? But my next trip was supposed to be to Lecce, and that's not till—"

"*Forget about that for now. You're being reassigned to investigative duties, Zen. Have you heard about the Miletti case? I'll get hold of all the documentation I can and send it round in the morning with the car. But basically it sounds quite straightforward. Anyway, as from tomorrow you're in charge.*"

"In charge of what?"

"*Of the Miletti investigation! Are you deaf?*"

"In Perugia?"

"*That's right. You're on temporary secondment.*"

"Are you sure about this?"

"*I beg your pardon?*" Mancini's voice was icy.

"I mean, I understood that, you know . . ."

"*Well?*"

"Well, I thought I'd been permanently suspended from investigative duty."

"*First I've heard of it. In any case, such decisions are always open to review in the light of the prevailing circumstances. The Questore of Perugia has requested assistance and we have no one else available, it's as simple as that.*"

"So it's official."

"*Of course it's official! Don't you worry about that, Zen. Just concentrate on the job in hand. It's important that we see results quickly, understand? We're counting on you.*"

Long after Mancini had hung up Zen stood there beside the phone, his head pressed against the wall. At length he lifted the receiver again and dialed. The number rang for a long time, but just as he was about to hang up she answered.

"*Yes?*"

"It's me."

"*Aurelio! I wasn't expecting to hear from you till this evening. How did it go in wherever you were this time?*"

"Why did you take so long to answer?"

"*I've got my lover here. No, actually I was in the bath. I wasn't going to bother, but then I thought it might be you.*"

He grunted, and there was a brief silence.

"Look, something's come up. I have to leave again tomorrow and I don't know when I'll be back. Can we meet?"

"*I'd love to. Shall we go out?*"

"All right. Ottavio's?"

"*Fine.*"

He looked round the hallway, confronting the furniture which, having dominated his infancy, had now returned to haunt his adult life. Everything in his apartment had been moved there from the family house in Venice when his mother had finally agreed, six years earlier, to leave. For many years she had resisted, long after it had become obvious that she could no longer manage on her own.

"Rome? Never!" she cried. "I would be like a fish out of water."

And her gasps and shudders had made the tired phrase vivid and painful. But in the end she had been forced to give in. Her only son could not come to her. Since the Moro affair his career was nailed down, stuffed and varnished, with years of dreary routine to go before they would let him retire. And there was simply no one else, except for a few distant relatives living in what was now Yugoslavia. So she had moved, avoiding the fate she had feared by the simple expedient of bringing all her belongings with her and transforming Zen's apartment into an aquarium from which she never emerged.

But if she was thus protected from suffocation, the effect on Zen was exactly the reverse. He had never particularly liked his apartment, located on a drab, pompous street just north of the Vatican, but in Rome you had to take what you could get. The nearest he had come to a personal feeling for the place had been an appreciation of its anonymity: it had been like living in a hotel. But his mother's arrival had changed all that, swamping the sparse furnishings provided by the landlord with possessions laden with dull memories and obscure significance. At times Zen felt that he was choking, and then his thoughts would turn to the house in Venice, empty now, the rooms full of nothing but pearly light, intimations of water, the cries of children and gulls. One day he would retire there, and in the meantime he was often so intensely there in spirit that he wouldn't have been in the least surprised to learn that the place was believed to be haunted.

From the kitchen came a clatter of pans supplemented by Maria Grazia's voice alternately berating the ancient stove, encouraging a blunt knife, singing snatches of the spring's big hit, and calling on the Madonna to witness the misery to which her life was reduced by the quality of the vegetables on offer at the local greengrocer. He would have to eat something here before sneaking out to meet Ellen. His mother's birthday was in a week, he realized. He would almost certainly still be away. In any event, he would have to tell her about the change of plans, which meant hearing once again how he should have got a nice job on the railways like his father. Did she really not realize that she told him this every single time he returned? Or was she, on the contrary, having a fine old laugh at his expense? That was the trouble with old people, you could never be sure. That was the trouble with living with someone you loved more than anyone else in the world, but had nothing in common with now but blood and bones.

"But I don't understand. Surely you're not a real policeman? I mean, you work for the Ministry, don't you? As a bureaucrat. That's what you told me, anyway."

Ellen's implication was clear: she would never have had anything to do with him if she had thought he was a "real" policeman.

"And it's the truth. Ever since I've known you that's what I've been doing. Going the rounds of provincial headquarters checking how many paper clips are being used, that sort of thing. Inspection duty, popularly known as Housekeeping, and just about as glamorous. The nearest I got to real police work was smashing the great stolen-toilet-roll racket at the Questura in Campobasso."

She didn't smile. "And before that?"

"Well, before it was different."

"You were a real cop? A police officer?"

"Yes."

There was so much shock in her look that he could not tell what else it might contain. "Where was this?" she asked eventually.

"Oh, various places. Here, for example."

"You worked in the Questura, here in Rome?"

"That's right."

"Christ! Which department?" She was looking hard at him.

"Not the Political Branch, if that's what you're worried about."

It was, of course. Ellen's circle of expatriate acquaintances already regarded it as rather bizarre that she was involved with an official from the Ministry of the Interior, just as Zen's few friends were clearly at a loss to know what to make of his liaison with this American divorcée, a classic *straniera* with her bright little apartment in Trastevere filled with artistic bric-a-brac and books in four languages and her Fiat 500 illegally parked in the street outside. The only answer in either case had been that whatever it was, it worked for both of them. It had seemed to be the only answer necessary. But now, without the slightest warning, Ellen found herself facing the possibility that her official had once been an active member of La Politica: one of those who routinely beat up demonstrating students and striking workers and pushed suspects out of windows, while protecting the neofascists responsible for the indiscriminate bombings of public squares and cafeterias and trains.

"I asked you what you did do," she insisted, "not what you didn't."

Her manner had become that of the tough brutal cop she perhaps assumed him to have been, bullying a statement out of a suspect.

"I was in the section concerned with kidnappings."

At this her features relaxed slightly. Kidnappings, eh? Well, that was all right, wasn't it? A nice uncontroversial area of police work. Which just left the question of why he had abandoned it for the inglorious role of Ministry snooper, spending half his time making exhausting trips to dreary provincial capitals where his presence was openly resented by everyone concerned, and the other half sitting in his windowless office at the Viminale typing up unreadable and no doubt unread reports. But before Ellen had a chance to ask him about this, Ottavio appeared in person at their table and the subject changed to that of food.

In pained tones, Ottavio outlined his opinion that people were not eating enough these days. All they ever thought about was their figures, a selfish, shortsighted view contributing directly to the impoverishment of restaurateurs and the downfall of civilization as we know it. What the Goths, the Huns, and the Turks had failed to do was now being achieved by a conspiracy of dietitians who were bringing the country to its knees with all this talk of cholesterols, calories, and the evils of salt. Where were we getting to?

Such were his general grievances. His more particular wrath

was reserved for Zen, who had told the waiter that he did not
want anything to follow the huge bowl of spaghetti carbonara
he had forced himself to eat on top of the vegetable soup Maria
Grazia had prepared at home.

"What are you trying to do?" Ottavio demanded indignantly.
"Put me out of business? Listen, the lamb is fabulous today. And
when I say fabulous I'm saying less than half the truth. Tender
young sucklings, so sweet, so pretty it was a sin to kill them. But
since they're dead already it would be a bigger sin not to eat
them."

Zen allowed himself to be persuaded, largely to get rid of
Ottavio, who moved on to spread the good word to other tables.

"And how have you been?" Zen asked Ellen, when he had
gone.

But she wasn't having that. "Why haven't you told me this
before?"

"I didn't think you'd be interested. Besides, it's all past history
now."

"When did all this happen, then?"

He sighed, frowned, rubbed his forehead, and grimaced.
"Oh, I suppose it must be about . . . yes, about four years ago
now. More or less."

Surely he had grotesquely overdone the uncertainty? But she
seemed satisfied.

"And now they're suddenly putting you back on that kind of
work? This must be quite a surprise."

"It certainly is."

There was no need to conceal that, at any rate!

"So it was 1979 you quit?"

"The year before, actually."

"And you got yourself transferred to a desk job?"

"More or less."

He tensed himself for the follow-up, but it failed to materi-
alize. Fair enough. If Ellen didn't appreciate how unlikely it was
that anyone in that particular section of the Rome police would
be allowed to transfer to a desk job in 1978 of all years, he
certainly wasn't going to draw her attention to it.

"What made you do that?"

"Oh, I don't know. I suppose I was just fed up with the work."

The food was brought to their table by Ottavio's youngest
son, a speedy little whippet who, at fourteen, had already
perfected his professional manner, contriving to suggest that he

was engaged on some task of incalculable importance to humanity carried out against overwhelming odds under near-impossible conditions, and that while a monument in the piazza outside would be a barely adequate expression of the debt society owed him, he didn't even expect to get a decent tip.

They ate in silence for several minutes.

"So, like I said, what have you been up to?" Zen repeated. "How's business?"

"Very quiet. There's a big sale on Tuesday, though."

Ellen made a living as representative for a New York antiques dealer, but it was a case of profiting from a lifelong hobby, one that she had tried in vain to get him to share. Zen had had his fill of old furniture!

"How long will it be altogether?" she queried.

"Not long, I hope."

"Do you know Perugia?"

Perugia, he thought. Chocolates, Etruscans, that fat painter, radios and gramophones, the University for Foreigners, sportswear. "Umbria, the green heart of Italy," the tourist advertisements said. What did that make Latium, he had wondered, the bilious liver?

"I may have been there on a school trip, years ago."

"But not for work?"

"Not a chance! There're two of us on Housekeeping. Zuccaroni is better regarded than me, so he gets the soft jobs, close to home."

"Will it be very difficult, the job?"

He pushed away his plate and topped up their glasses with the bland white wine.

"There's no way of knowing. A lot depends on the magistrate who's directing the investigation. Some of them want to make all the decisions themselves. Others just want to take the credit."

She also finished eating and at last they could smoke. He took out his packet of Nazionali. Ellen as usual preferred her own cigarettes.

"Can I come and visit you?" she asked with a warm smile.

"It would be wonderful."

She nodded. "No mother."

He suddenly saw which way the conversation was heading.

"Don't you think it's ridiculous, at our age?" Ellen continued. "She must know what's going on."

"I expect she does. But as far as she's concerned I'm still

married to Luisella and that's that. If I spend the night with you it's adultery. Since I'm a man, that doesn't matter, but one doesn't mention it."

"It matters to me." Her tone hardened. "I don't like your mother thinking of me as your mistress."

"Don't you? I quite enjoy it. It makes me feel young and irresponsible."

The remark was deliberately provocative, but he had long ago decided that he was not going to be talked into matrimony a second time.

"Really?" she retorted. "Well, it makes me feel old and insecure. And angry! Why should I have my life dominated by your mother? Why should *you*, for that matter? What's the matter with Italian men, letting their mammas terrorize them their whole life long? Why do you give them such power?"

"Because we've found over the centuries that they're the only people who can be trusted with it."

"Oh, I see. You can't trust me? Thanks very much!"

"I can't trust anyone in quite that way."

It seemed perfectly obvious to him. Why was she getting so angry?

"Not because my mother's a saint," he explained. "It's just that mothers are like that. They can't help it, it's biological."

"Oh, that's wonderful! Now you've insulted both of us."

"On the contrary, I've complimented both of you. My mother for being what she is, and you for being everything else. And above all for being so understanding in what is a very difficult situation for both of us, but one that won't last forever."

She looked away, disarmed by his allusion, and Zen seized the opportunity to signal Ottavio for the bill.

The air outside was deliciously cool and fresh after the small, stuffy restaurant. They walked in silence toward the roar of traffic on Viale Trastevere. In Piazza Sonnino a burned-out office building was being refitted, and the hoarding put up by the builders had attracted the war paint of rival political clans. The Red Brigades' five-pointed star was the most conspicuous, but there were also contributions from Armed Struggle (*"There's no escape—we shall strike everywhere!"*), the Anarchists (*"If voting changed anything they'd make it illegal"*), and the neofascist New Order (*"Honor to our fallen companions—they live on in our hearts!"*).

To Zen, the clash of slogans seemed eerily appropriate.

Because if the events of 1978 had had a secret center, and part of their horror was that he would never be sure, then in a sense it had been here, at the terminus of the 97C bus and the San Gallicano hospital opposite. If there had been an unspeakable secret, then one of the two men who had guessed it had died here. And since that moment, day and night, whatever else he might be doing or thinking, Zen had remained uneasily aware that he was the other.

2

he entire resources of the Questura of Perugia are at your disposal. Eager to obey, my men await only your commanding word to spring into action. Your reputation of course precedes you, and the prospect of serving under your leadership is an inspiration to us all. Who has not heard of your brilliant successes in the Fortuzzi and Castellano affairs, to name but two? And who can doubt that you will achieve a no less resounding triumph here on Umbrian soil, earning the heartfelt thanks of all by succeeding where others, less fortunate or deserving, have failed? The city of Perugia has a long and historic relationship with Rome, of which your posting here is a concrete symbol. My men will, I am sure, wish to join with me in bidding you welcome."

There was a feeble flutter of applause from the group of senior officials assembled in the Questore's spacious top-floor office, all discreetly modern furniture, rows of law books, and potted plants. Aurelio Zen stood in their midst like a Siamese cat dropped into a cage full of stray dogs: tense and defiant, his eyes refusing to meet those fixed on him with expressions of

more or less successfully concealed mockery. They knew what
he was going through, poor bastard! And they knew that there
was absolutely nothing he could do about it.

Salvatore Iovino, their chief, a corpulent, vivacious fifty-year-
old from Catania, had given a masterly performance. Fulsome
and vapid, laden with insincere warmth and hidden barbs, his
introductory speech had nevertheless left no legitimate grounds
for complaint. He had spoken of Zen's "reputation," without
actually mentioning that his abrupt departure from the Rome
Questura in 1978 had been the subject of the wildest rumors
throughout the force. The two cases he had mentioned dated
from the midseventies, underlining Zen's lack of recent operational experience. He had referred to the transfer as a
"posting," thus emphasizing that it had been imposed on him by
the Ministry, and had called it a symbol of the historic relationship between Rome and Perugia, a relationship consisting of
two thousand years of bitterly resented domination.

"Thank you," Zen murmured, lowering his head in a proud
and melancholy gesture of acknowledgment.

"And finally," the Questore continued, "let me introduce
Vice-Questore Fabrizio Priorelli."

Iovino's bland tone did nothing to prepare Zen for the glare
of pure hostility with which he found himself transfixed by the
Vice-Questore. The Questore's next words followed an exquis-
itely judged pause during which the silence in the room
assumed a palpable quality.

"Until today Priorelli was handling the Miletti case for us. To
be perfectly frank," Iovino continued, "that's one of the many
problems your unexpected arrival has caused us. It's a matter of
protocol, you see. Since Fabrizio outranks you I can't very well
make him your second-in-command. Nevertheless, should you
wish to consult him, he has assured me that despite his numerous other duties he is in principle at your disposition at all
times."

Once again Zen murmured his thanks.

The Questore barely seemed to hear. "Right, lads, lunch!" he
called briskly. "I expect you're about ready for it, eh?"

As the officers filed out, Iovino picked up the phone and
yelled, "Chiodini? Get up here!" Then he turned pointedly away
and stood gazing out the window until there was a knock at the
door and a burly man with a bored, brutal face appeared, at

which point the Questore suddenly appeared to notice Zen's existence again.

"I'll leave you in Chiodini's safe hands, dottore. Remember, whatever you need, just say the word."

"Thank you."

As they walked downstairs Zen studied his escort: hair closely cropped on a head that looked muscle-bound, ears cauliflowered, no neck to speak of, shoulders and biceps that formed one inflexible block, the "safe" hands swinging massively back and forth. Chiodini would be the one they sent for when old-fashioned interrogation methods were required.

At the third-floor landing the man jerked his thumb to the right. "Along there, room three-five-one," he called without turning or breaking his stride.

Zen just managed to stop himself from intoning another "Thank you."

Yes, it had all been consummately handled, no question about that. Iovino's speech had been a brilliant set piece, systematically exploiting all the weaknesses of Zen's position. Words are not everything, however, and the Questore had by no means neglected other opportunities of making his point, such as the contrast between the bombastic formality with which he had rolled out the red carpet and the perfunctory way he had then dismissed Zen into the "safe hands" of the local third-degree specialist. The message was clear. Zen would be offered the moon and the stars, but if he wanted a coffee he'd have to fetch it himself.

He opened the door of the office and looked around warily. Everything seemed normal. On one wall hung the mandatory photograph of the President of the Republic; facing it on another was the inevitable large calendar and a small crucifix. There was a gray metal filing cabinet in the corner, the top two drawers empty and the bottom one stuffed with plastic bags. In the center of the office, dominating it, stood a desk of some sickly looking yellow wood which had seemingly been grown in imitation of one of the nastier synthetic materials. Like every other piece of furniture in the room, down to the metal rubbish bin, this carried a tag inscribed MINISTRY OF THE INTERIOR and a stamped serial number. Screwed to the back of the door was a list itemizing every piece of furniture in the room, down to the metal rubbish bin, together with its serial number. It was not that the Ministry did not trust their employees. They were just tidy-minded and couldn't sleep at night unless they were sure that everything was in its place.

Zen walked over to the window and looked out. Down below was a small parking lot for police vehicles. Facing him was a windowless stone wall with a heavy gate guarded by two men, one in gray uniform with a cap, the other in battle dress and a flak jacket. Both carried submachine guns, as did another guard patrolling the roof of the building. So that was it: they had given him an office with no view but the prison. He smiled sourly, acknowledging the hit. Sicilians were notoriously good at this kind of thing.

And the phone? He would never forget those first months at the Ministry, sitting in a windowless office in the basement, his only link to the outside world a telephone which was not connected. The repairmen were always just about to come, but somehow they never did, and for more than three months that telephone had squatted on his desk like a toad, symbol of a curse that would never be lifted. And when it finally was repaired Zen knew that this was not a token of victory but of total defeat. They could let him have a phone now. It didn't matter, because it never rang. Everyone knew about his "reputation." He had broken the rules of the tribe and been tabooed.

Here in Perugia his phone worked all right, but the same logic applied. Whom was he going to call? What was he going to do? Should he fight back? Call Iovino's bluff and start throwing his weight around? The Ministry had sent him and they were bound to back him up, if only as a matter of form. With a bit of effort and energy he could soon bring the Questore and his men to heel. The problem was that at heart he just didn't care enough about these provincial officials and their petty pride. He didn't even care about the case itself. Nine kidnappings out of ten were never solved anyway, and there was no reason to think that this one would be any different. In the end the family would pay up or the gang would back down. As a spectacle it was as uninspiring as an arm-wrestling contest between two strangers.

Outside the Questura he found the driver who had brought him there, a young Neapolitan named Luigi Palottino, still standing attentively beside the dark blue Alfetta. The sight of Palottino merely increased Zen's humiliation by reminding him of the scene at his apartment that morning when he'd returned, having spent the night with Ellen, to find Maria Grazia and his

mother trying to organize his packing while the driver stood
looking on with a bemused expression and everyone had to
shout to be heard above the cheery chatter of the television,
which had apparently turned itself on so as not to be left out of
things.

"What are you doing here?" Zen snapped at him.

"Waiting for you, sir."

"For me? I'm not in the mood for company, frankly."

"I mean waiting for your orders, sir."

"My orders? All right, you might as well take me to my hotel.
Then you can go."

The Neapolitan frowned. "Sir?"

"You can go back to Rome"

"No, sir."

Zen looked at him with menacing attention. "What do you
mean, 'no'?"

"My orders are to remain here in Perugia with you, sir.
They've allocated me a bed in the barracks."

They want to keep tabs on me, thought Zen. They don't trust
me, of course. *Of course!* And who could say what other orders
Luigi Palottino might have been given?

Half an hour later Zen was sitting in a café enjoying a late
lunch, when he heard his name spoken by a complete stranger.
The café was an old-world establishment quite unlike the usual
chrome-and-glass filling stations for caffeine junkies, a long,
narrow burrow of a place with a bar on one side and a few seats
and small tables on the other. The walls were lined with tall
wooden cabinets filled with German chocolates and English jam
and shelves bending dangerously under the weight of undrink-
ably ancient bottles of wine. There were newspapers dangling
from canes and waiters in scarlet jackets who seemed to have all
the time in the world, and faded pastoral frescoes presided
amiably from the vaulted ceiling. Zen took the only free table,
which was between the coat stand and the telephone, so that he
was continually being disturbed by people wanting to get at one
or the other. But he paid no particular attention to the other
clients until he was jarred into it by hearing his name being
laboriously spelled out.

"Z-E-N. Yes, that's right."

The speaker was in his early sixties, short but powerfully
built, with an almost aggressively vigorous appearance that

suggested a peasant background not many generations earlier. But this man was no peasant. His clothes and grooming betrayed wealth, and his manner was that of a man used to getting his own way.

"So I've been told. Perhaps he hasn't arrived yet? Ah, I see. Listen, Gianni, do me a favor, will you? When he comes back, tell him . . . No, nothing. Forget it. On second thought I'll call him myself later. Thanks."

The receiver was replaced, and the man glanced down.

"Sorry for disturbing you, eh?"

He walked slowly away, greeting various acquaintances as he went.

The elderly cashier seemed to have no idea how much anything cost, and by the time the waiter who had served Zen had told her and she had manipulated the Chinese box of little drawers to extract the right change, the man had disappeared. But as soon as Zen got outside he almost bumped into him, standing just to the left of the doorway chatting with a younger, bearded man. Zen walked past them and stopped some distance away in front of a glass case displaying the front page of the local edition of the *Nazione* newspaper with the headlines circled in red ink.

TRAGEDY ON THE PERUGIA–TERNI: ATROCIOUS DEATH OF YOUNG COUPLE UNDER A TRUCK. He could see the two men quite clearly, reflected on the glass surface in front of him, the younger protesting in a querulous whine, "I still don't see why I should be expected to deal with it." BUSES IN PERUGIA: EVERYTHING TO CHANGE—NEW ROUTES, NEW TIMETABLES. "It's agreed, then?" exclaimed the older man. "But not Daniele, eh? God knows what he's capable of!" FOOTBALL: PERUGIA TO BUY ANOTHER FOREIGNER?

Zen scanned the newspaper for some reference to his arrival. Rivalries within the Questura usually ensured that an event which was bound to be damaging to someone's reputation would be reported in the local press. But of course there would have been no time for that yet.

When he next looked up, he found that the two men had separated and the older one was walking toward him.

"Excuse me!"

The man turned, suspicious and impatient. "Yes?"

"I couldn't help overhearing your telephone call in the café. I believe you wish to speak to me. I am Aurelio Zen."

The man's impatience turned first to perplexity and then embarrassment.

"Ah, dottore, it was you, sitting there at the table? And there I was, talking about you like that! Whatever must you have thought?"

His voice drifted away while he seemed to be rapidly searching his memory, no doubt trying to recall what exactly he had said. Then with an apologetic gesture he went on, "I am getting old, dottore! Old and indiscreet. Well, what's done is done. Forgive me, I haven't even introduced myself. Antonio Crepi. How do you do. Welcome to Perugia! Will you allow me to offer you a coffee?"

They returned to the café, where Crepi hailed the barman familiarly.

"Marco, this is Commissioner Zen, a friend of mine. Anytime he comes in I want you to give him good service, you understand? No, nothing for me. You know, dottore, they say we must be careful not to drink too much coffee. I'm down to six cups a day, which is my limit. It's like a bridge, you know. You can reduce the number of supports up to a certain point, depending on the type of construction, nature of the soil, and so on. After that the bridge collapses. For me the lower limit is six coffees. Fewer than that and I can't function. Anyway, how do you like Perugia? Beautiful, eh?"

"Well. I've only just . . ."

"It's a city on a human scale, not too big, not too small. Whenever I go to Rome, which nowadays is almost never, I feel like I am choking. It's like putting on a collar that's too tight, you know what I mean? Here one can breathe, at least. A friend of mine once told me, 'Frankly, Antonio, the moment I set foot outside the city walls I just don't feel right.' That's the way we are! Provincial and proud of it. But listen, dottore, I want to be able to talk to you properly, not standing in some bar. Can you come to dinner this evening?"

Zen avoided a reply by taking a sip of coffee. He still hadn't the faintest idea whom he was talking to!

"I'm sure this is very different from the way you do things in Rome," Antonio Crepi went on. "Maybe you even think it's a bit strange, but I don't care! The only thing that interests me is getting Ruggiero released. The *only* thing! Do you understand? It is wonderful that you're here, your arrival gives us all new heart. Come to dinner! Valesio will be there too, the lawyer who's been handling the negotiations. Talk informally, off the record. Say what you like, ask any question you like. Be as indiscreet as I am, if you can! No one will mind, and when you start work in earnest tomorrow morning you'll know as much about the case as anyone in Perugia. What do you say?"

This time there was no way out.

"I'll be delighted."

Crepi looked pleased. "Thank you, dottore. Thank you. I'm glad you understand. We Umbrians are just simple, forthright country folk. Rome is another world. If at first you find us a bit rough, a bit blunt, that's just our way. After a while you'll get used to it. We lack polish, it's true, but the wood beneath is sound and solid. But you're not from Rome, surely? Excuse my asking."

"I'm from the North."

"I thought so. Milan?"

"Venice."

"Ah. A beautiful city. But Perugia is beautiful too! I'll send someone to collect you at about eight. No, I insist. It's easier than trying to give directions. You need to have been born here! Until this evening, then."

As Zen walked back to his hotel he noticed several people staring at him curiously, but it was not until he caught sight of his reflection in a shop window that he realized that he was wearing one of those annoying little Mona Lisa smiles which makes everyone wonder why you're so pleased with yourself. It was just as well that no one knew him well enough to ask, for he had no idea what he would have replied.

Whatever the reason might have been, by eight o'clock the smile had definitely faded.

He had spent the afternoon and early evening reading the background material he had been given on the Miletti case. Like most police drivers, Luigi Palottino clearly considered himself a Formula One contender manqué, and his relentless high speeds and succession of near misses had brought on a mild attack of the car sickness from which Zen often suffered, so that he just hadn't been able to face the pile of documents Enrico Mancini had sent round with the Alfetta. Not that he needed them, of course, to know who Ruggiero Miletti was. To any Italian of his generation the name was practically synonymous with the word *gramophone*. Ruggiero's father, Franco, had started the business, first repairing and later constructing the newfangled machines in a spare room at the back of the family's furniture shop on Corso Vanucci, the main street of Perugia. That was in 1910. Ruggiero had been born the preceding year. By the time he left school, Miletti Phonographs had become a flourishing concern which had outgrown the original premises and moved to a site convenient to the railway line down in the valley.

Although by no means cheap, the Miletti instruments had enjoyed from the first the reputation of being well made, durable, and technically advanced, "combining the ancient traditions of Umbrian craftsmanship with an irresistible surge toward the Future," as the advertisements put it. Old Franco had a flair for publicity, and before long such notables as D'Annunzio, Bartali the cycle ace, and the composer Respighi had consented to be photographed with a Miletti machine. Franco's greatest coup came when he persuaded the Duce himself to issue a typically bombastic endorsement: "I declare and pronounce that your phonographs are truly superior instruments and represent a triumph of Fascist civilization." Meanwhile the radio age had arrived, and the Miletti company was soon producing the massive sets which formed the center-piece of every wealthy family's sitting room, around which friends and hangers-on would congregate on Sunday after-noons to listen to the program called *The Four Musketeers,* which eventually became so popular that the football authorities had to delay matches until it was over.

The family's good fortune continued. Although Ruggiero's elder brother Marco was killed in Greece, the Milettis had a relatively easy war. Having sacrificed one son, it was easy for Franco to convince influential friends that Ruggiero's brains were too valuable a commodity to be put at risk, and hostilities ended with them and the Miletti workshops intact. Both were quickly put to work. The postwar economic boom, artificially fueled by the Americans to prevent Italy from falling to the Communists, provided ideal conditions for rapid growth, while Ruggiero soon proved that he combined his father's technical genius with even greater ambition and vision. In the next decade the company steadily expanded and diversified, though often in the teeth of considerable opposition from Franco Miletti. When his father died in 1959, Ruggiero found himself at the head of one of the most successful business concerns in the country, producing hi-fi equipment, radios, televisions, and tape recorders, exporting to every other country in Europe as well as to many in South America, and often cited as a glowing example of the nation's economic resurgence. In 1967 the firm became the Società Industriale Miletti di Perugia, or SIMP for short, but this fashionably ugly acronym changed nothing. The Miletti family, which in practice meant Ruggiero himself, remained in absolute and sole control.

The kidnap itself was described in a few pages of material copied over the teleprinter from Perugia. The contents proved to be highly predictable, but at least Zen discovered who Antonio Crepi was: the retired director of a construction company with whom Ruggiero Miletti was in the habit of spending every Sunday evening of the year playing cards, with the exception of August, when he went to the seaside. One week Crepi would motor over to the Miletti villa, the next Ruggiero would drive down to his friend's place overlooking the Tiber valley. On the last Sunday in October, four and a half months earlier, it had been Ruggiero's turn to visit Crepi. He had left home as usual at eight o'clock and arrived at Crepi's twenty minutes later. The two had played cards and chatted until about quarter past eleven, when Ruggiero left to drive home. He had never arrived.

The alarm had been given by Silvio, one of Ruggiero's three sons. It was rare for Ruggiero not to be back by midnight, and since there was a hard frost Silvio began to worry that his father might have had an accident. He therefore phoned Crepi, who had already gone to bed, and learned that Ruggiero had set out on his return journey an hour earlier. But, as so often, no one thought of a kidnapping. Daniele, the youngest son, arrived home while his brother was speaking to Crepi, and instead of alerting the police the two decided to search the road themselves. When they arrived at Crepi's villa without having found any trace of Ruggiero, the police were finally informed. It was 12:37 A.M.

Perugia is blessed with a crime rate among the lowest in Italy, and at that hour only a skeleton staff was on duty at the Questura. It took another quarter of an hour to call out the men on standby, and it was 1:20 before a complete set of roadblocks had been set up. Meanwhile, the route Miletti had taken was thoroughly examined, revealing evidence of a struggle. Ruggiero's hat, tie, and shoe were found lying on the verge, and not far away lay a muslin wad soaked in ether. But it wasn't until daybreak that the burned-out shell of the car Ruggiero had been driving, one of a fleet of leased Fiat Argenta sedans used by both the family and the senior management of SIMP, was finally spotted by a helicopter in an abandoned quarry some eleven miles north of the city. The front bumper was dented and one of the headlamps cracked, indicating that the gang had front-tailed Ruggiero from the villa, then deliberately braked hard on a bend to cause a minor collision, immobilizing his car. They would have got out to examine the damage, all smiles and apologies. At the last moment their victim must have realized what was happening, for he had fought and kicked and struggled. But by then it was much too late. You could defend yourself against kidnappers only *before* they struck, by persuading them to strike somewhere else.

The remainder of the report on the Miletti kidnapping set out the investigators' provisional conclusions. The gang had had about two hours in which to seize Miletti, dispose of his car, and make good their escape. Assuming the first two stages took about thirty minutes, that left an hour and a half before the roadblocks went up. It was more than enough.

If they had continued north they could have been on any one of a dozen remote roads high up in the Apennines within an hour. It was quite possible that the kidnappers had gone to ground there, in some isolated farm or mountain hut. Or, on the other hand, they might well have left the area altogether, taking the link road west to the motorway and spending the rest of the night driving south. By dawn they could have reached the Aspromonte mountains behind Reggio di Calabria, a territory fifty times the size of San Marino and considerably more independent of the Italian State.

In short, it had been a typical professional kidnapping: well planned and well executed. The victim had been carefully chosen to combine the maximum potential return with the minimum possible risk. Like many others, Ruggiero Miletti had regarded kidnapping as something that happened to other people in other parts of the country, in the industrial cities of the North and the harsh countryside of the South. He must have known what was going on, of course. You couldn't open a newspaper or watch the television news without hearing about another family which had been shattered by the experience of having a son or daughter or parent torn from them. There was an average of one kidnapping every week, and many of the victims had never returned. Sometimes their bodies turned up on refuse dumps or in makeshift graves, sometimes they were cut up and fed to pigs. Even when they were released alive, the psychological scars never entirely healed. A few victims had spoken of their months spent bound and gagged, ears stuffed with cotton wool, eyes covered with plastic tape, lying in a concrete trench under the floor of a garage, knowing that any moment could be their last. Most preferred to remain silent, to try to forget. But everyone knew what was going on. Many families had become virtual prisoners of their own wealth, ferried from bunker to bunker in bulletproof cars, guarded by squads of private security men, unable ever to make an arrangement to be anywhere at any fixed time. The glamorous and romantic nightlife which so many tourists dreamed of seeing had become almost a thing of the past. The rich no longer dared show their faces after dark. No one with real money could afford to stroll along the Via Veneto these days, or take midnight dips in the Trevi fountain. They stayed at home watching television and playing computer games, and bars and restaurants closed early.

Ruggiero Miletti had known all this. But the places where these things happened would have seemed almost as foreign to him as Beirut or Ethiopia, and he would have read about the goings-on there with a sigh and a shake of the head. What was the world coming to? Thank goodness such things were unknown in gentle, rural, provincial Umbria.

But he had been wrong. For months, Zen thought, his movements must have been logged and analyzed until the kidnappers knew more about his way of life than he did. They had taken him at the weekend. By Monday morning the snatch squad would be back at the garages or factories or bars where they worked. Their companions would laugh as they yawned their way through the day and made crude jokes about their wives being too much for them. They wouldn't mind. They would be getting paid soon, their job over.

Meanwhile, the central cell of the gang would be in touch with the family to get the negotiations moving. They wouldn't be too impatient at first, although they would sound it, phoning up with bloodcurdling threats about what would happen to their victim if they weren't paid by the day after tomorrow. But they had timed the operation for the autumn precisely to allow themselves the long winter months in which to break any resistance to their demands. By now, though, in late March, they would be starting to grow restless, wanting to see some return on their considerable investment. Summer was just around the corner, and they wouldn't want to risk missing their month at the seaside. Criminals have the same aspirations as everyone else, Zen mused. That's why they become criminals.

More recent details were skimpy in the extreme. The gang had apparently contacted the family soon after the kidnapping and it was understood that a ransom had been agreed upon. The family had refused to disclose the sum, but it was thought likely to have been in the region of ten billion lire. Payment was assumed to have taken place toward the end of November, but the hostage had not been released, and a local lawyer named Ubaldo Valesio was now believed to be negotiating on behalf of the family. This last snippet was dated mid-December, and unless someone had filleted the file before it was put on the teleprinter it was the most recent piece of information the police in Perugia had. The message was clear: ". . . *was understood that a ransom had been paid . . . remained unknown but was thought to have been in the region of . . . was assumed to have taken place toward the end . . . believed to be negotiating . . .*" Whoever had drafted the report wanted no one to be in the slightest doubt that the Miletti family had not been cooperating with the authorities.

There was nothing unusual in this, of course. The trouble with the authorities' line on kidnapping was that it sounded just too good to be true. Free the victim, punish the criminals, *and* get your money back! Most people were happier doing business with the kidnappers, whose motives they understood and who like them had a lot to lose, than with the impersonal and perfidious agencies of the State. If Zen was unpleasantly surprised to discover how little the Milettis had been cooperating, it was because it put paid to the theory he'd evolved to explain his sudden recall to active duty.

The explanation Enrico Mancini had given him was obviously false. In the first place, provincial detachments never requested intervention of this kind. A local Questura might ask for an expert from Criminalpol to advise them on some technical problem, but that was a very different thing from handing over control to someone from Rome. Such a procedure was always imposed by the Ministry and was regarded as a humiliating

reprimand for inefficiency or incompetence. But an even more
serious objection to Mancini's story was simply that Mancini was
telling it. Enrico Mancini was a very big fish indeed, whose
natural habitat was the wider ocean of political life. At the
moment he chose to swim in the local waters of the Ministry of
the Interior, where indeed he had survived an abrupt change in
the political temperature which had proved fatal to several of
his species. But tomorrow he might well be sighted in one of the
other branches of government, between which he moved as
effortlessly as a porpoise moves from the Tyrrhenian to the
Adriatic and back again. Indeed, according to some observers,
this rather too evident ease, together with Mancini's brashly
confident manner, might prove to be his downfall in the long
run.

The likes of Mancini, Zen reflected, did not concern themselves with such normal everyday matters as staff movements.
The implication was clear. Despite appearances, this particular
staff movement was neither normal nor everyday. When you
got a personal phone call from an assistant undersecretary to
the Minister and were told you were leaving the next morning,
someone had been pulling strings. The obvious candidates had
been the Miletti family, but if the Milettis were not cooperating
with the authorities they would hardly run to the Ministry
complaining that those authorities weren't doing enough. So
what was going on?

Zen read and reread the material, scribbling a few notes and
a lot of convoluted designs in the margins. But it was no good.
There were too many faceless names, or, what was worse, names
which had somehow acquired a totally misleading set of features
and characteristics. Thus, Pietro, Silvio, Cinzia, and Daniele
appeared as "The Miletti Children," a quartet of child enter-
tainers in matching outfits, and this despite Zen's knowledge
that the youngest, Daniele, was twenty-six years old, while
Pietro was already in his late thirties, married and living
somewhere abroad. As for Cinzia, she could hardly be a
winsome little prepubescent charmer since she already had two
children of her own, the eldest eleven years old.

Meanwhile it was getting late, and the full implications of
accepting Crepi's invitation were becoming clear to Zen. He'd
acted without thinking, purely on reflex, paralyzed by his
ignorance of who Crepi was. But after what had happened at
the Questura he could be in no doubt as to the weakness of his

position in Perugia. To survive he must armor himself in authority, surround himself with as many of the signs and symbols of office as he could muster. Instead of which he foolishly had agreed to venture out onto dangerously ambiguous ground, half-social and half-official; a treacherous no-man's-land where all manner of elaborate games might be played at his expense, where any points he scored would count for nothing but the slightest slip might compromise his position forever. Well, at least he would go in style. He had phoned the Questura and arranged for Palottino to meet him outside the hotel. They could follow Crepi's chauffeur back to the villa.

The call came at ten past eight.

"There's someone here to collect you. He says he's expected."

"I'll be down at once."

The lobby was empty except for a bearded man reading a newspaper and a French couple hotly disputing some item on their bill with the receptionist. Zen had almost reached the revolving door when he was called.

"Excuse me!"

Suddenly Zen had an unpleasant sense that events were getting out of hand. It was the bearded man Crepi had been talking to outside the café earlier that afternoon.

"You are Commissioner Zen?"

"Yes?"

"I'm Silvio Miletti. How do you do?"

"I had no idea that you would be coming in person to fetch me," Zen murmured in some confusion. "You shouldn't have bothered."

"It was no bother."

The way this was said made it quite clear that exactly the opposite was the case. For a moment Zen was tempted to refuse to go, invent some last-minute engagement. But they were outside now, and Silvio Miletti was pointing across the street.

"My car's over there."

Palottino saved Zen. The Neapolitan had parked the Alfetta right in front of the hotel, practically blocking the entrance, and was now leaning in a nonchalantly heroic posture on the driving door, receiving the homage of the passersby. As he caught sight of the superior from whom flowed his power to flaunt, dazzle, and ignore the parking regulations, he snapped smartly to attention.

"And mine's right here," Zen replied.

"No, no, dottore," Silvio Miletti insisted fussily. "You're traveling with me. That's why I've come, after all."

"Signor Miletti, my driver gets so little work he's almost going crazy as it is. But if you would permit me to offer you . . ."

"No, no, I insist!"

"So do I."

Zen softened the words with a pale smile, but there was nothing soft about his tone.

Silvio Miletti sighed massively. "As you wish, dottore, as you wish. Perhaps you would have the goodness to wait just one moment, however, if it's not too much to ask."

He walked across the street to a large blue Fiat sedan and spoke to the driver. Zen stood watching, his brief triumph draining away. He had not only been rude, he had been uselessly rude. His petty insistence had demonstrated his weakness, not his strength. I've lost my touch, he thought bleakly. Then the blue sedan drove off and Zen saw that the driver was a woman. That made it perfect. He had succeeded in insulting not only Silvio Miletti but also his female friend.

"I'm sorry, I didn't realize you were with someone," he remarked as the two men took their places in the back of the Alfetta.

Miletti shrugged. "It's only my secretary. I don't drive."

They followed the blue Fiat through a wedge-shaped piazza and down a steeply curving street. At the bottom it turned sharply right and disappeared through a narrow archway. Numerous scratches on the brickwork showed where drivers had misjudged the clearance, but Palottino revved up and took it like a lion going through a blazing hoop, almost crushing two pedestrians in the process.

Out of the corner of his eye, Zen studied Silvio Miletti. Up close, Ruggiero's second son looked like an overweight ghost, at once corpulent and insubstantial. His features, which might have been strong and full of character, had sagged like paint applied too thickly. His gestures were oddly prim and fussy for his sturdy frame, and his voice was high and slightly querulous, with an underlying whine of self-pity.

Superficially there was nothing of the man of power about him, nothing to suggest the might and influence of the Miletti family. But Perugia was not Milan, still less Dallas. Those who had it didn't flaunt it. They didn't need to. Everyone who counted already knew who they were, what they were capable of. The Milettis would not show off their power or their wealth for the same reason that a champion boxer doesn't go around picking fights in bars: they had nothing to prove. But Zen could sense it just the same. To him, the heavy miasma of melancholy and fatigue that surrounded Silvio Miletti was as visible as the expensive green overcoat he wore. It was an exhalation of unquestioned and unquestioning power, the choking vapors of privilege neither relished nor rejected. But there was something else too, some personal note of lethargy and disgust with everything and everyone, himself most of all. Silvio Miletti had the air of someone who had never really reconciled himself to what he saw in the mirror every morning.

As suddenly as in a medieval fresco, the city ended and the countryside began. One moment they were driving down a densely inhabited street, the next they were on a country road that dropped so steeply Zen felt his ears aching. A yellow sign flashed by: ALL VEHICLES USING THIS ROAD FROM 1 NOVEMBER TO 31 MARCH MUST CARRY SNOW CHAINS ON BOARD. Palottino kept the Alfetta tucked tightly in behind the slowly moving Fiat, like a dog worrying a sheep.

"Tell me, when did your father's kidnappers last make contact?" Zen dropped the question idly, just to test the water.

"The negotiations are being handled by Avvocato Valesio." Silvio Miletti's tone was uncompromising.

"Presumably he keeps you informed."

"No doubt he tells us everything he feels we should know," Miletti replied with a fastidious quiver, rearranging the folds of his coat. "On the other hand, he fully understands how difficult this experience is for us, and I'm sure that he would avoid distressing us unnecessarily."

He made it quite clear that the negotiator's tact and consideration could well serve as a model to other, less thoughtful people.

As the road bottomed out in the valley, Palottino swung out and booted the accelerator, leaving the Fiat behind in a burst of speed.

"For Christ's sake!" Zen exploded. "We're supposed to be following that car!"

"Oh, fuck. Sorry, sir, I forgot."

"I'll tell you when to turn." Silvio Miletti sighed. The world, his sigh seemed to suggest, had once again demonstrated its limitless capacity for stupidity, vulgarity, and total insensitivity to his needs and desires. Not that this surprised him; on the contrary, he had long resigned himself to the unremitting awfulness of life. Nevertheless, each reminder was another pebble thoughtlessly tossed onto the already intolerable burden which he was expected to bear without complaint or even comment. It really was too bad!

"So when did the gang last make contact, to the best of your knowledge?" Zen continued relentlessly.

There was a rustle of clothing as Miletti changed position with a wriggle of his hips. "I'm afraid I really can't discuss this. I'm sure you understand why."

"No, as a matter of fact I don't understand at all. I'm aware that the Miletti family has not been cooperating with the police up to now, but since you have agreed to meet me tonight I assumed that you must have decided to change that attitude. I certainly can't imagine what we're going to talk about otherwise."

The sigh emerged again in all its glory. "As far as cooperation goes, I think the fact that I was prepared to come and pick you up from your hotel is sufficient proof of my personal goodwill. Precisely what Antonio's purpose may be in bringing us together like this, I have no idea. But in any case, during my father's absence decisions are being made jointly by the whole family, and the decision which has been made is that all dealings with the authorities are to be handled by our legal representative, Ubaldo Valesio. He will be present this evening and you will have ample opportunity to put your questions to him."

The road ran along between two ridges, beside a small stream. The moon was almost full, and by its light the scenery looked flat and unconvincing, depthless shapes blocked out of black cardboard. Even the few clouds in the sky were as neat and motionless as a backdrop. To one side, on the crest of the ridge, a row of cypresses and cedars led up to a ruin with a tall tower.

"In other words, Valesio will be acting as intermediary not just between you and the gang but also between you and me?"

Zen made no attempt to conceal his irony, and Silvio's reaction was to flare up.

"Yes, dottore, that's exactly what I mean! Despite what some people seem to think, I'm made of flesh and blood like everyone else and there's only so much I can stand. I just can't cope with anything more! I can't be expected to!"

He broke off abruptly to tell Palottino to turn left up a narrow dirt track.

"For over a month we have heard nothing," he continued in the same self-pitying tone. "Nothing!"

The headlights swept over rows of neatly pruned vines as the twists and turns of the steeply climbing track succeeded one another.

"Before, they used to make threats, to rant and rave and say God knows what. That seemed bad enough at the time, but now I almost miss their threats. They seem almost reassuring in retrospect, compared with this terrible silence."

The track became a driveway lined with cedars and cypresses and suddenly the house was there before them, a fantastic affair of mock-medieval turrets and towers with fishtail embattle-ments and coats of arms embedded in the walls, which Zen realized with a slight shock was the ruin he had caught sight of from the road below. With a satisfying spray of gravel, Palottino brought the car to a halt beside a white Volvo parked in the forecourt.

Antonio Crepi must have been on the lookout, for when Zen got out he found his host at the door to welcome him.

"How do you like my little fortress? It's mostly fake, of course, but nowadays such things have a charm of their own. No craftsman alive could do those moldings. There's even a roman-tic story behind it. Years ago, before the war with Austria, my grandfather met his future wife up here during a summer outing. There was nothing here then but the ruins of an old watchtower. Later he bought the land and had the ruins turned into this place as a present for their silver wedding anniversary. Look, this wall is original, over three meters thick! Pity you can't see the view. The Tiber's just down there, and on the other side the hills stretching away toward Gubbio. Better than any painting in the world, in my opinion. Silvio, my boy, how are you?"

As they passed down a long hallway Zen had a confused impression of ancient furniture, elaborate paintwork in poor condition, of musty smells and frigid, immobile air. Crepi opened one of the three sets of double doors in an anteroom at the end of the corridor and ushered his guests through into a large sitting room with a high frescoed ceiling. As they entered, a woman of about thirty moved quickly forward, her hand held out to Zen. She had a skier's tan and long honey-blond hair and was wearing tawny leather slacks, a hazel-brown silk blouse, and masses of gold everywhere.

"Cinzia Miletti, dottore, pleased to meet you, so glad you could come. Wonderful, really. We're counting on you, you know, please tell us there's hope. I'm sure there is, I don't know why but something tells me that Father will be all right. Are you religious? I wish I were. And yet sometimes I feel I am. I don't go to church, of course, but that's not what religion is really about, is it? Sometimes I think I'm more religious than all the priests and nuns in Assisi. I have these tremendous feelings."

Crepi broke in to introduce the other person in the room. Gianluigi Santucci, Cinzia's husband, was a wiry little man in his late thirties, with carefully sculpted, thick black hair, a neat mustache, and something almost canine about his sharp, wary features. Zen sensed hostility in the brief glance and minimal nod with which he acknowledged his greeting without budging from where he stood in front of the log fire. Silvio, he noted, had ostentatiously turned his back on his sister and brother-in-law, and was apparently studying a lugubrious oil painting which occupied most of one wall. But Cinzia immediately swept Zen away again.

"Where are you from? You're not Roman, are you? I can't stand Romans, arrogant, pushy people, think they still rule the world. Of course we have masses of friends in Rome. But your name, it reminds me of that book I keep meaning to read, a classic, by what's-his-name, about the man who's trying to give up smoking. Do you smoke? I really should stop, but I've been to the doctor and he told me to take pills, which I simply refuse to do, it's worse than smoking. You read these horror stories in the magazines, years later your children are born deformed, though there's nothing wrong with my two, thank God. Have you got any children? But where are you from? No, let me guess. Sicily? Yes, you've got Norman blood, I can sense it. Am I right?"

"Not quite, my dear," Crepi put in with heavy irony, and corrected her.

"Venice?" she said lightly. "Well, it's the same thing, isn't it, an island."

Just then another woman came in from the hallway, closing the door quietly behind her. She was tall and extremely plain, about forty years old, with mousy-brown hair twisted up in a bun, and was dressed in a trouser suit made from some synthetic material which reminded Zen of beach fashions at the Lido back in the fifties. It was clearly meant to look stylish, but somehow succeeded in being both brash and drab at the same time. No one took the slightest notice of the newcomer. Gianluigi Santucci was saying something to Crepi in an intense whisper, while his wife wandered distractedly about, asking everyone if they had seen her handbag and discussing how much easier life would be if handbags didn't exist but how could you survive without them although of course her friend Stefania had given up using hers completely, just thrown it away one day, and she still managed so perhaps it was possible, with time all things were possible.

"Are your brothers coming?" Zen asked Silvio, who shook his head briefly.

"Pietro's in London. And Daniele is not interested in this sort of thing."

But Zen remembered hearing Crepi tell Silvio that afternoon: "But not Daniele, eh? God knows what he's capable of!" So whatever sort of thing it was, the youngest Miletti was being deliberately kept out of it.

Gianluigi Santucci's raucous voice suddenly cut loose, as if someone had flicked the volume control on a badly tuned radio.

"Well, that's his tough shit, in my opinion! If people arrive late they can't expect everyone else to wait for them. It's not as if he's the head of the family or an honored guest!"

Crepi explained to the others that they had been discussing whether to wait any longer for Ubaldo Valesio.

"What's the point in waiting?" Cinzia's husband demanded. "These lawyers are always stuffing themselves, anyway. Lawyers and priests, they're the worst!"

"Yes, let's get on with it!" Silvio agreed. Judging by his tone, he meant, "Let's get it over with."

Crepi turned to Zen. "Dottore, you're the neutral party here," he said with exaggerated heartiness. "What do you say?"

Fortunately, Cinzia saved him. "Oh, I'm sure the Commissioner feels just the same as the rest of us!" she cried, stepping forward. "Let's eat, for heaven's sake! I'm starving, and you know Lulu's digestion is always a problem. Standing around waiting just gets the juices going, you know, eating into the stomach lining. Horrible, disgusting. But he bears it like a lamb, don't you, Lulu?"

The dining room was cold and smelled damp. It was lit by a

large number of naked bulbs stuck in a chandelier whose supporting chain ran up several meters to an anchorage planted with surreal effect in the midst of the elaborate frescoes which covered the ceiling. Zen had plenty of time to study these buxom nymphs and shepherds disporting themselves in a variety of more or less suggestive poses as the meal proceeded at a funereal pace, presided over by an elderly retainer whose hands shook so alarmingly that it seemed just a matter of time before a load of food ended up in someone's lap.

The tagliatelle were homemade, the meat finely grilled on a wood fire, Crepi's wine honest and his bottle-green oil magnificent. Nevertheless, the dinner was a disaster. Ubaldo Valesio did not arrive, and without the lawyer, by tacit consent, the kidnapping of Ruggiero Miletti could not be mentioned. There was nothing to do but be relentlessly bright and superficial. Cinzia Miletti thus came into her own, dominating the table with a breathless display of frenetic verbiage which might almost have been mistaken for high spirits. Antonio Crepi punctuated her monologues with a succession of rather ponderous anecdotes about the history and traditions of Umbria in general and Perugia in particular, narrated in the emphatic declamatory style of university professors of the pre–1968 era.

Silvio sat eating his way steadily through his food, casting occasional glances at the others with an expression midway between a squint and a scowl, as though he were looking at something repulsive through the wrong end of a telescope. Gianluigi Santucci contributed little beyond occasional explosive comments that were the verbal equivalent of the loud growls and rumbles emanating from his stomach. The woman in the grotesque trouser suit, who was apparently Silvio's secretary, said not one word throughout, merely smiling ingratiatingly at everyone and no one, like a kindly nun watching children at play. As for Zen, he studied the ceiling and thanked God that time passed relatively quickly at his age. He could still remember half hours from his childhood which seemed to have escaped the regulation of the clock altogether and to last forever, until for no good reason they were over. Crepi's dinner party made the most of every one of its 113 minutes, but shortly after half past ten its time was up and they all filed back into the other room.

But the situation remained a stalemate. There was continued speculation about what could have happened to Valesio, whose thoughtlessness in not phoning to apologize and explain was universally agreed to be typical. The origins of the problem were traced to his mother, a Swede who had fallen in love first with Perugia and then with a Perugian, and who as a foreigner could not be expected to know how to bring up her son properly. But Zen was beginning to suspect that Crepi had been outmaneuvered, that Valesio was staying away deliberately under orders from the Milettis to prevent any discussion of the kidnapping.

What was quite clear to Zen was that he was no more than a pawn in whatever sophisticated games were being played. A family as secure in its power as the Milettis had no reason to fear a mere police official. Whatever strings might have been pulled to bring him to Perugia, and whoever was pulling them, Zen represented no possible threat to their policy of noncooperation with the authorities. If he was ill-advised enough to take any initiative of which they disapproved, they would simply have it blocked higher up the ladder of command, at a level inaccessible to him. No, what had brought them to dinner, he now felt sure, was a curiosity about Crepi's motives in inviting them in the first place, and Crepi was clearly in no mood to satisfy this curiosity.

So why didn't they all go, for God's sake? The farce had been played out to its bitter end and there was nothing to stop them from making a graceful exit. But the fact remained that no one appeared to have the slightest intention of doing anything of the kind.

At last the sound of a motor was heard outside, and everyone perked up.

"Ah, finally!" cried Cinzia. "He's impossible, you know, really impossible, and yet such a nice person really. My mother always told me whatever I did never to marry a lawyer. He'll be late for his own funeral, she used to say, and I must say Gianluigi for all his faults is always on time."

This paragon of punctuality exchanged a glance with Silvio. "That's a motorcycle engine," he remarked

Crepi got up and walked over to the window.

"Well?" Cinzia demanded. "Who is it?"

"There's nobody there."

"Exactly, there's nobody here!" a new voice exclaimed.

Six heads turned in unison toward the other end of the room, where the door had opened a crack.

"Or rather I'm here," the voice continued. "It comes to the same thing, doesn't it?"

"Stop playing the fool, Daniele!" cried Cinzia sharply. Her face was flushed. "You know what my nerves are like. What must you think of us, dottore? You must forgive him, he's a good boy really. It's my mother's fault, God rest her. A good woman, a wonderfully warm person, but she hadn't read Freud of course, I shudder to think how she must have toilet trained us all."

The door swung open, but Daniele remained standing on the threshold. The youngest Miletti was tall and shared his sister's good looks, which were set off by about a million lire's worth of casually elegant clothing: Timberland shoes, tweed slacks, lambswool sweater, and a Montclair ski jacket.

"What are you doing?" exclaimed Silvio in a tone of sullen irritation. "Come in and close the door!"

A contrived look of surprise and puzzlement appeared on Daniele's handsome features. "What do you think I am, some kind of gatecrasher? Someone who just barges into parties he hasn't been invited to? I wasn't brought up on a farm, you know."

Antonio Crepi gestured impatiently. "Oh, come along, Daniele! We haven't got time for this kind of thing. You know very well that I invited the whole family. If you couldn't be bothered to come, that's your business, but don't waste our time with these childish scenes."

"Oh, the whole family, eh? That's not what I was told."

He came in and closed the door, staring pointedly at Silvio.

"If you're so fussy about your manners suddenly, then you might at least greet Antonio's guest," chirped Cinzia. "This is Commissioner Zen, who's come up specially from Rome to help save Father. He's from Venice, lucky man. What a beautiful city! I'm just crazy about Venice."

Daniele swung around and peered at Zen with comically exaggerated interest, staring intently at his feet. He frowned.

"That's odd. I've always been told that the policemen in Venice have one wet shoe. You know, because when they've finished their cigarettes they throw them in the canal and . . ."

He mimed someone stubbing out a cigarette with his foot and started to laugh loudly.

"But Commissioner Zen's feet are perfectly dry!" he resumed.

"So clearly he can't be from Venice. Either that or he's not a policeman."

"Shut your face!"

The reprimand came not from Silvio or Crepi but from Gianluigi Santucci. Daniele continued to smile genially as though he had not heard him. He did not speak again, however. Neither did anyone else, and so silence fell.

In the end it was left to Silvio's secretary to save the situation.

"Well, I expect Commissioner Zen would like to get an early night," she remarked, standing.

It was the first thing Zen had heard her say all evening, and he realized with a shock that she was not Italian. Of course! With those clothes he should have guessed.

"That's very thoughtful of you, signora." He rose to his feet to ensure that her gesture did not go for nothing.

"She's not a signora," Cinzia corrected him. "She's not married. Are you, Ivy?"

It was a horrible and quite deliberate insult. Any woman of a certain age is entitled to be addressed as "signora" whether or not she is married. But the reaction came not from Ivy herself but from Silvio Miletti.

"How dare you?" he cried, his fist clenched as though he was about to strike his sister. "I won't have it! You have no right to say such things!"

It seemed an exceptionally violent intervention to make on behalf of someone who was supposed to be no more than an employee, but no one appeared surprised. Cinzia grinned maliciously and glanced at her husband, who banged his hands together loudly and stood. Daniele burst into hysterical, excessive laughter, and Antonio Crepi's eyes remained fixed meaningfully on Zen. As for Ivy, she just stood there like a statue, her plain face lit by the same beatific smile she had worn all evening.

"No, it's all right, Silvio," she replied evenly in her deep, chesty voice, enunciating every word with almost pedantic clarity. "What Cinzia says is perfectly true, after all. But the Commissioner hasn't been here long enough yet to know all these little details. However, I expect in a few days he'll know more about us than we do ourselves!"

It was a remarkable performance. The woman's foreignness made Zen think of Ellen, and so it was with genuine warmth that he replied, "Good night, signora," and received a beaming smile in return.

Everyone stood, except Daniele, who remained slumped on a sofa.

"I don't want to leave yet," he complained. "I only just got here."

Gianluigi Santucci strolled over to him and grabbed him by the ear. "Ah, these young people today!" he cried with vicious playfulness. "No energy, no initiative. It makes me sick!" With a mocking laugh he hauled Daniele to his feet and pushed him over to join the others.

At the front door, hands were shaken and formulas of farewell exchanged. At the last moment, however, their host plucked at Zen's sleeve, holding him back.

"Not you, dottore."

The Milettis exchanged a flicker of rapid glances.

"I thought he wanted to get an early night," Silvio objected.

"Don't you worry about Commissioner Zen." Crepi smiled, all cheerful consideration. "Mind how you go yourselves, that driveway of mine is quite dangerous in places. I keep meaning to have it resurfaced, but what with one thing and another I never get around to it."

"And if Valesio comes?"

"If Valesio comes he'll get a dish of cold tagliatelle and a piece of my mind! But we won't discuss the kidnapping behind your backs, if that's what you're worried about."

Gianluigi Santucci grimaced. "Worried? Why should I be worried? It's for others to worry, not me!"

A few minutes later the disparate noises of the Fiat, the Santuccis' Volvo, and Daniele's Enduro trail bike had all faded to a distant, intermittent drone that was finally indistinguishable from silence.

"Well, what did you think of them?" Crepi demanded the moment they returned to the living room. "But first let me offer you something to drink. Do you like grappa? I'm told this one is good. It's from your part of the world. My youngest girl married a dentist from Udine and they send me a bottle made by one of the uncles every Christmas. Actually, my doctor has forbidden me to drink spirits, but I haven't the heart to tell them that."

He handed Zen a glass of liquid as limpid as spring water.

"Now listen, dottore," Crepi continued. "You must be wondering why I should want to ruin your first evening in Perugia like this."

Zen sniffed the grappa appreciatively. "I'm even more curious to know why they agreed to come."

"The Milettis? Oh, they came because each thought that the others were coming and no one could bear the thought of being left out. This afternoon on the Corso, just before you and I spoke, I ran into Silvio. I mentioned the dinner and let him think that Cinzia and her husband were coming. Silvio didn't care for the idea of Cinzia and Gianluigi discussing matters with you behind his back, so he invited himself. Then I phoned Cinzia and told her that Silvio was coming, with the same result. Did you notice no one wanted to be the first to leave? If it hadn't been for that foreigner I might have had to throw them out!"

He did not make this prospect sound too displeasing.

"And Daniele?"

"Daniele's less predictable. But you can usually get him to do something by convincing him that you don't want him to do it. I told Cinzia not to mention the dinner to him, which is like asking someone to carry water in a sieve. He assumed he was being excluded and barged in trying to be as rude as possible to everyone. Little did he suspect that that was precisely what I wanted! But there you are, you see. They think they're so clever, these children, but once you understand how they work you can do anything you like with them. It's just a shame that Valesio couldn't make it. If only we'd been able to discuss the kidnapping you'd really have seen what we're up against."

Zen considered this for a moment. "I thought we were up against a gang of kidnappers."

"If only we were!" Crepi exclaimed. "How simple that would be. But that's why I invited you here this evening. Because if you're to help, really help, the first thing you have to realize is that this is no ordinary kidnapping, for the simple reason that the Milettis are no ordinary family. Let's start with Silvio. Of the whole brood, he's the one who resembles his father most, physically I mean. In every other way they couldn't be more different. Silvio hasn't the slightest interest in the firm, or in anything else except his stamp collection, and one or two nastier hobbies. Ruggiero has never understood him. For example, when the time came for Silvio to do his military service, everyone assumed that his father would make a few phone calls and get him exempted. Well, Ruggiero made the phone calls all right, but to make sure that Silvio not only did his full time but did it in some mosquito-ridden dump in Sardinia. He'd just begun to realize that his son was a bit of a pansy, you see, and he reckoned that was the way to make a man of him. I don't think Silvio's ever forgiven him for it. Not just the time in Sardinia, but above all the humiliation of having a father who thought so little of him he wouldn't even pull a few strings in Rome to get him off the hook."

Crepi stood, opened a small ceramic jar on the mantelpiece, and extracted a short cigar. He offered one to Zen, who shook his head and extracted one of his four remaining Nazionali. He realized with dismay that he had forgotten to bring a supply of those deliciously coarse cigarettes made from domestic tobacco, costing only a few hundred lire a pack but as difficult to find as wild mushrooms. In Rome he could count on getting them from a tobacconist to whose son he had once given a break, but in Perugia what would he do?

"I won't waste time on Cinzia," Crepi continued. "She's just a pretty child who's growing old without ever having grown up. There are only two important things about her. One is that husband of hers. I must admit to a sneaking admiration for Gianluigi, although he's undoubtedly one of the most appalling shits ever invented. He's not from round here, of course. You spotted those ugly Tuscan *c*s, like a cat being sick? Santucci's been on the make since the day he was conceived. Marrying Cinzia Miletti hasn't done his career any harm, of course, but he would have risen anyway, anywhere, under any circumstances."

Zen smiled slyly. "We have a saying in Venice. Whether the water is fresh or salt, turds rise to the top."

He immediately regretted the comment. What was he doing talking to Crepi in this familiar fashion? But his host's laughter sounded genuine enough.

"Quite right, quite right! I've been at the top myself, so I should know! Oh yes, Gianluigi has done all right for himself. With Silvio taking no interest and Pietro abroad, he's wormed his way into the senior management level at SIMP. But of course Ruggiero still makes all the final decisions, and there's no love lost between those two, needless to say. It must be quite a relief for Gianluigi to have the old man out of the way. But we mustn't forget the other important thing about Cinzia, which also applies to her little brother. It's simply that when Ruggiero passes on, God forbid, they'll each inherit twenty-five percent of

SIMP. A quarter of the company each! That's quite a thought, isn't it? Particularly when you realize that our foxy little Tuscan is married to one-quarter and has the other very firmly under his thumb. Daniele ignores me and treats Silvio like shit, but he obeys his brother-in-law."

Zen took another little sip of grappa, rolling it around his mouth. The rough, stalky taste burned down his throat and up into his brain. Why was Crepi telling him all this, he wondered.

"What about Pietro?" he asked. "Isn't it rather surprising that he's not here in Perugia during his father's ordeal?"

Crepi nodded. "He did come back at first, but when it began to drag out, he claimed that he had to go back to London to look after his business interests. He takes after his father in that. Silvio inherited Ruggiero's looks, Pietro got the brains. He's extremely sharp, but much too intelligent to let it show. Ruggiero has a slow country manner which has deceived a lot of clever Milanese into not reading the fine print. Pietro originally went to London ten years ago to organize the distribution of SIMP products there, then somehow talked his father into letting him set up a semiautonomous subsidiary to import a range of products. But that's just a cover. His real business is currency manipulation. He's organized a chain of more-or-less fictitious companies and shifts funds around between them, turning a tidy profit each time. Clever, eh? But Pietro *is* clever, and fiercely ambitious, although you'd never guess it from his manner. He acts like the model of an English gentleman, all vague and shy and diffident. But don't let that fool you. You could use his ego to cut glass."

Zen's head was beginning to swim. "I don't expect to have much to do with the family. They've made it quite clear that they're not prepared to cooperate with the authorities."

"I know. What bothers me is that they're not prepared to cooperate with the kidnappers either."

"But haven't they already paid up?"

Crepi shrugged. "They paid once, back in November. We all thought that was that. But instead of releasing Ruggiero, those bastards came back for more. That's when all the trouble started."

"How much more did they want?"

"The same again. Ten billion lire."

Zen made a face.

"God almighty, they've got it!" Crepi snorted impatiently.

"And if they haven't, there are a hundred ways they could raise it. But they decided they'd agreed to the first demand too easily, and that this time they should strike a harder bargain, argue over every last lira. Then there was the question of how to raise the money. More problems, more bickering. Exactly what should be sold? Or should they borrow it? Couldn't Pietro help out? And what about Gianluigi's idea of doing a deal with a foreign firm interested in acquiring a stake in SIMP? Et cetera, et cetera. I won't bore you with all the details."

"What about the police, the judiciary? Are they aware that Valesio is in regular contact with the gang?"

Crepi waggled his hands. "Yes and no. They know, of course. In Perugia everyone knows everything. But officially they've been kept out of it. You see, part of the problem all along has been that the investigating magistrate who's handling the case, Luciano Bartocci, is a Communist who's got it in for the Milettis on principle. Given half a chance, Bartocci would like to use the kidnapping as an excuse to pry into the family's affairs for political reasons."

"Couldn't he be replaced?"

After a moment Crepi gave another long, loud laugh. "My answer to that, dottore, is the same as a certain politician gave his wife when they went to the Uffizi to see that Botticelli which was cleaned recently. The wife is in raptures. 'I can just see it over the fireplace at home,' she says. 'Listen,' her husband replies, 'I can't do *everything*, you know!'

"Anyway, this is really beside the point," Crepi resumed. "If the Milettis were united, all the Bartoccis in the world couldn't touch them. As it is, they would starve to death for want of agreeing which sauce to have with their pasta if the cook didn't decide for them. And meanwhile Ruggiero's life is in the balance! He's over seventy years old, dottore, and his health is failing. Ever since the accident that killed his wife he has suffered from bouts of semiparalysis down one side of his body. Two years ago it looked as though he would have to give up working altogether, but in the end he pulled through. Who knows how he's suffering at this very moment, while we sit here warm and well fed in front of the fire? He must be brought home! The family must pay whatever is being asked, immediately, with no further haggling! That's what you must tell them, dottore."

To hide his look of dismay, Zen brought the glass to his lips and drained off the last drops of grappa. "What makes you think the family will listen to me?"

"I don't mean the family."

"Who, then?"

Crepi leaned forward. "Your arrival here in Perugia will be widely reported. I'll see to that! You'll be interviewed. They'll ask you about your impressions of the case. Tell them! That's all. Just tell them."

"Tell them what?"

"Tell them that you wonder how serious the Milettis really are about getting Ruggiero back! Tell them that the family gives no impression of having understood the extreme gravity and urgency of the situation. In a word, tell the world that you're not convinced that the Milettis are in earnest! Naturally I'll give you my fullest backing. We'll shame the family into paying! Do you see? Eh? What do you say?"

But at that moment the phone rang.

3

As the car leaned farther and farther into the curve he tensed for the inevitable smash. But there was no sound of screeching tires, of metal crunching. Cheated again! There was no getting used to it.

"If that's Valesio with his apologies I'll tell him what he can do with them!" Crepi muttered as he went to answer the phone. "Hello? Who? Oh. Yes? I don't understand. What? No! Oh, my God! Oh, Jesus!" He bent over, taking deep breaths.

"What's happened?"

Crepi was panting as though about to faint. Zen took the receiver from him.

"Hello? Who's there?"

The line went dead.

"Dottore? What's happened? Who was that?"

"They've killed him," Crepi murmured as he lurched toward the door, ignoring Zen's questions.

Zen dialed the Questura, but they didn't know anything. He told them to find out and call him back.

He walked over to the hearth, picked up a log, and threw it

onto the embers. Some dried moss and a section of ivy still clinging to the bark flared up. Gradually the wood itself took hold, first smoking furiously and then bursting into flame.

A ladybug appeared from a crack and began exploring the surface of the log, now well alight. Zen took a splinter from the hearth and lowered the end of it into the path of the little creature, which promptly veered away. Again and again he tried to tempt the ladybug to safety, until his hand began to ache from the heat. Just as he had finally succeeded, the phone rang again. The insect fell and flamed up on the glowing embers at the front of the grate.

"The Carabinieri are handling it and they're not giving much away," he was told. *"The gist of it seems to be that someone's been killed out near Valfabbrica."*

Crepi was nowhere in sight. Zen walked downstairs calling for Palottino, who emerged from the kitchen, where he'd been watching television. It wasn't till they were getting into the car that Crepi appeared, looking for the first time like the old man he was.

"I'm coming too."

The night was still mild and luminous, but a gusty southerly breeze had sprung up and was pushing the clouds along, and when they cleared the moon, the landscape was revealed, distinct and yet mysterious, in a way that made daylight seem as crudely functional as neon strip lighting. Then the clouds closed in again and it was night, the headlights punching holes in the darkness.

"There it is!"

Crepi's voice was uncomfortably close to Zen's ear. He just glimpsed the blue-and-white sign reading VALFABBRICA as they raced past.

The main street was dark and tightly shuttered. Outside the Carabinieri station three men in uniform were chatting beside a dark blue Giulietta. A burly individual with a sergeant's stripes on his sleeve responded to Zen's request for directions by jerking his head at the open doorway behind him, but before Zen could get out, Palottino leaned across him and started speaking in tongues. The sergeant said something in return and then got into the Giulietta.

"He's going to take us there," the young driver explained.

"Friend of yours?"

Palottino shook his head. "He's from Naples, I recognized the accent. Says this is the first interesting thing that's happened here."

"And what exactly *has* happened?"

Wonderful, Zen thought. I'm reduced to getting my information on the dialect grapevine.

"Somebody found shot in a car."

Crepi groaned as though knifed.

About a kilometer outside town they turned left onto a dirt road winding through a desolate landscape created by the floods of a nearby river. After a while the Giulietta slowed, lights appeared ahead, and the road was blocked by vehicles parked at all angles across it.

The scene was illuminated like a film set by a powerful searchlight mounted on a Carabinieri jeep. As they got out, Zen saw a group of men standing talking near a large gray car. Then everything disappeared as the searchlight went out.

"Till tomorrow, then!"

"Excuse me!" Zen called.

"Who is it?"

"I'm from the police."

The silence was broken only by the incomprehensible squawks and crackles of a shortwave radio.

"You're rather late."

Someone laughed.

"As usual!"

"It's gone."

"And we're off."

"Is it true, then?"

It was Crepi's voice, just in front of Zen.

"Is what true?"

"He's dead?"

"Who are you?"

"I am Antonio Crepi. Who are *you*?"

Someone drew in his breath sharply.

"Forgive me, Commendatore, I had no idea! For God's sake, Volpi, tell your men to put that light back on. Ettore Di Leonardo, Deputy Public Prosecutor. My apologies, I thought you said you were from the police."

"I'm from the police," Zen began. "Commissioner Aurelio—"

"Answer me!" Crepi rasped. "Is he dead?"

The searchlight burst back to life and they all covered their eyes.

"Unfortunately, Commendatore. Unfortunately."

Zen saw Crepi's body shudder, but the old man made no sound.

"The first murder victim I've ever seen," declared a young man with a full black beard. "And it wasn't a pretty sight, I can assure you."

"For Christ's sake, show a little respect!" Crepi burst out, his voice almost breaking. "The man was my friend!"

The young man shrugged. "Mine too."

"You, Bartocci?" Crepi's laugh was like a blow. "A friend of Ruggiero Miletti? God keep me from such friends as you!"

"Who said anything about Ruggiero Miletti?" asked the older of the two civilians.

"I was referring to the murdered man, Ubaldo Valesio," explained his bearded colleague.

Crepi looked at the third man, a major of the Carabinieri. "But I was told that it was Ruggiero who had been killed!" he exclaimed. "One of your men phoned me with the news."

"There was initially some confusion as to the identity of the victim," the officer replied smoothly.

The older civilian had turned his attention to Zen. He was short and stout, with a face as smooth and featureless as a bladder, and he glared at everyone, as though he knew very well how foolish he looked and had decided long ago to brazen it out.

"You're from the police? I'm Di Leonardo, Deputy Public Prosecutor. I'm by no means happy with the way this investigation has been handled. In my view the police have shown a lack of thoroughness bordering on the irresponsible, with the tragic results that we have seen tonight."

Zen shook his head vaguely. "Excuse me, I've only just arrived. . . . "

"Quite, quite. This is in no sense intended as a personal reflection on you, Commissioner. Nevertheless I find it quite incredible that no attempt has been made to exploit the dead man's contacts with the gang, really quite incredible. If his movements had been monitored, much might have been learned. As it is we now have a corpse on our hands without being any closer to tracing either the gang or Ruggiero Miletti's whereabouts. It is most unsatisfactory, really most unsatisfactory indeed."

Zen gestured helplessly. "As I say, I've only just arrived here, but I must point out that electronic surveillance of the kind you mention requires the cooperation of the subject. If no such attempt was made, it's presumably because the police were respecting the wishes of the Miletti family."

The Public Prosecutor waggled his finger to indicate that this wouldn't do. "The constitution states quite clearly that the forces of the law operate autonomously under the direction of the judiciary. The wishes of members of the public have nothing whatever to do with it."

"But the police can't be expected to contradict the wishes of the most powerful family in Perugia without specific instructions from the judiciary," Zen protested.

Major Volpi intervened, holding out his hand as though he were directing traffic. "I cannot of course speak for my colleagues in the police," he remarked blandly, "but I can assure you that in this case as in any other my men will at all times do whatever is necessary to ensure a successful outcome, regardless of who may be involved."

A fierce rivalry had always existed between the civil police, responsible to the Ministry of the Interior, and the paramilitary Carabinieri, controlled by the Defense Ministry. Indeed, it was deliberately cultivated on the grounds that competition helped to keep both sides efficient and honest.

"There you are, you see!" Di Leonardo told Zen. "You can't expect us judges to do all your thinking for you, Commissioner. We expect to see some initiative on your part too."

With that, he turned away to speak to Antonio Crepi. The Carabinieri officer went off to supervise a tow truck which had just arrived from the direction of the main road. Bartocci, the young investigating magistrate, was standing beside the car in which Valesio's body had been found, a gray BMW, almost new by the look of it. Zen walked over and looked down into the open trunk, but there was nothing to be seen except a small dark pool of blood held back by the edge of a plastic pouch containing an instruction booklet on the use of the jack.

"His wife's very close to my sister," Bartocci remarked. "She's only thirty-one. They've got three children."

Zen had enough sense to keep quiet.

"The worst of it is that this wasn't his line at all! Ubaldo was a labor lawyer. Union disputes, contracts, that sort of thing. A good negotiator, of course."

Luciano Bartocci provided the strongest possible contrast to his senior colleague from the Public Prosecutor's office. Both men had clearly been called out unexpectedly, but while Di Leonardo was turned out immaculately in a suit, lambswool pullover, and tie complete with gold pin, the younger man was wearing a ski jacket, open-necked shirt, and jeans. He was about thirty-five years old, athletic and vigorous, with a frank and direct gaze. His beard almost hid his one weakness, a slight facial twitch, as if he were constantly restraining an impulse to smile.

"Why should they do such a thing?" he murmured.

"Perhaps it was a mistake."

Zen was hardly conscious of having spoken until Bartocci swung around, glaring at him.

"You wouldn't say that if you'd seen him! They put the gun in his mouth, it blew the back of his head clean off. There was no mistake about it!"

"No, I meant . . ."

But before he could explain, Bartocci was called away by Di Leonardo. All the vehicles were revving their engines ready for departure. Without warning the searchlight went out again.

Zen hadn't been paying attention to his surroundings and at first he was afraid to move a step in case he walked into a ditch. But as his eyes adjusted he started to make his way toward the Alfetta, slowly at first, then with growing confidence. He was moving at almost his normal pace when he ran into someone.

"Sorry!"

"Sorry!"

He recognized Bartocci's voice.

"Is that the Police Commissioner from Rome?" the young magistrate asked.

"Yes."

"Listen, I'd like to see you tomorrow morning. Can you come to my office?" The voice was moving away. "I'll have to break the news to his wife," Bartocci continued, more and more distantly. "I don't know how long that'll take. Shall we say nine o'clock? If I'm late perhaps you could wait."

"Is there anything in particular you want?"

There was no reply. Zen walked forward cautiously, hands outstretched before him, but when the moon came out again he found that he was alone.

■   ■   ■

The Uncle of Italy, Sandro Pertini, looked down with his inimitable air of benevolent authority on Aurelio Zen, who stared blankly back. This apparent lack of respect was due to the fact that he was not looking at the President of the Republic but at the glass covering the photograph, which reflected the doorway open to the adjoining room, where his two assistants were sifting through the mound of documents that had been removed that morning from Ubaldo Valesio's home and office. Or rather, that is what they were supposed to be doing: the reflection on the presidential portrait revealed that in fact one of them was engaged in an intense whispered discussion with the other, punctuated by furtive glances in the direction of Zen's office.

Zen's face was even paler and more drawn than usual, and his eyes glittered from the combined effects of too little sleep and too much coffee. It was after three o'clock before he'd finally got to bed. He awoke four hours later with the taste of blood in his mouth, the tip of his tongue aching fiercely where his teeth had nipped it. That was a bad sign, a sign of tension running deep, of nerves out of control. He got out of bed and opened the window for the first time. The noise of traffic from the broad boulevard directly below rushed in along with the icy pure air. In the middle distance two churches marked the route of a street running out of the city through a medieval suburb. The nearer was a broad structure of rough pink stone with a solid rectangular belltower, squatting amid the cramped and jumbled houses with the massive poise of a peasant woman in the fields. The other, by contrast, was a complex conglomerate of buildings topped by a tall, slim spire. Far beyond them both, fifteen or twenty kilometers away, a mountain as round and smooth as a mound of dough rose from the plain. Zen had never seen it before, but he had the oddest sensation that he had known it all his life.

He had got up and searched through his luggage, still scattered untidily about the room, until he found the little transistor radio he took with him on his travels. The news had just begun, and he listened with one ear as he shaved. A minister had decided to respond with "dignified silence" to calls for his resignation following claims that his name appeared on a list of those involved in a kickback scandal involving a chain of construction companies. The leader of one party had described as "absolutely unacceptable" a statement made the day before by the secretary of another, whom he accused of "typical arrogance and condescension." A senior police officer in Palermo had been shot dead as he left a restaurant. The Pope had announced a forthcoming tour of ten countries. Flights were likely to be disrupted later that month by a planned strike by air traffic controllers. An accident on the Milan–Venice motorway had left three people dead and eleven more injured and had strengthened the calls for the building of an extra carriageway. The murder of a lawyer in Umbria had been squeezed in just before the weather forecast; the Carabinieri were said to be investigating, but there was no mention of Ruggiero Miletti.

Zen jerked back his chair, making it squeak loudly on the floor, and the two heads reflected in the rectangle of glass immediately bent over their respective piles of papers, each one covered with almost illegible notations in Ubaldo Valesio's minuscule handwriting. Zen shifted his gaze to the right, toward the small crucifix and the calendar showing cadets on parade at the training school at Nettuno. The calendar was still turned to February, although it was now March and his mother's birthday was in less than a week. He absolutely must not forget to get her a present.

On the desk in front of him lay the *Nazione* newspaper. The headline read BUTCHERED, THE MILETTIS' MOUTHPIECE: A MESSAGE TO THE "SUPERCOP" FROM ROME? Below it appeared a photograph of a scene which had become as familiar a part of Italian life as a bowl of pasta. Lying in a stiff and unnatural fetal crouch with a rather fatuous, lopsided grin on his face, Ubaldo Valesio made an extremely unconvincing corpse. But conviction was amply supplied by the pictures of the other side of the lawyer's head, which Bartocci had shown him earlier, the pulpy mass of the brain hollowed out like a watermelon seeded with bits of shattered bone.

But perhaps he had not died in vain! Thanks to this development Zen had been able to enforce payment of the blank check which the Questore had so boldly dashed off the day before. He had requested and obtained the services of two inspectors and a detective sergeant, together with an extra office and various communications and vehicle privileges which he had no reason to suppose he would need but had thrown in for good measure. But as the morning newscast had made clear, the Carabinieri had taken a stranglehold on the murder inquiry, and all that remained for the "supercop from Rome" was to check Valesio's movements on the previous day and sift through the material which had been removed from his home and office. Lucaroni, one of the two inspectors, was handling the first chore, while the other, Geraci, was at work next door on the second. He was being assisted, if that was the word, by Chiodini, whose services Zen had specifically requested. The sight of the big brute straining to decipher Ubaldo Valesio's finicky jottings was some small compensation for the way he had been treated the day before.

Zen had arrived at Bartocci's office promptly at nine o'clock. The courthouse occupied most of a rambling Renaissance palace situated in the inevitable Piazza Matteotti. The portal was surmounted by a lunette containing a statue of Justice flanked by two creatures apparently consisting of a vulture's head and wings attached to the body of a hyena, a motif repeated extensively elsewhere in the building. Zen had plenty of time to admire the architectural features of the place, since Luciano Bartocci did not put in an appearance until shortly after ten.

By day the young magistrate conformed rather more to the sartorial norm for members of his profession: a tweed jacket, lambswool pullover, checkered shirt, woolen tie, and corduroy trousers. He, too, looked haggard, having been up until almost five o'clock that morning dealing with the victim's widow. Patrizia Valesio, it seemed, had at first reacted with eerie calm to the news of her husband's death.

"She was still up when we got there," Bartocci explained, "still waiting for her husband to come home. I'd taken my sister along to help out. I think Patrizia must have realized what had happened the moment she opened the door, but she invited us in as though nothing whatever had happened. We might have been paying a normal social call, except that it was the middle of the night. I told her that her husband had been involved in an accident. 'He's dead, isn't he?' she replied. 'They've killed him.' I just nodded."

They were outside the courthouse, waiting for Palottino to bring the car. Bartocci had explained that he wanted Zen to accompany him to Valesio's home and office, where he planned to remove any documents which might have a bearing on the lawyer's murder or his contacts with the kidnappers. The street was brilliantly sunny and busy, with people going into and out of the market building, whose entrance was through an arcade beneath the courthouse.

"She stayed perfectly calm until I mentioned something about the car," Bartocci went on. "Then she went crazy. 'No, it's not possible!' she shrieked. 'It was brand new, I gave it to him for Christmas! Don't tell me it was damaged too!' Marisa and I just stood looking at each other. It sounded like the ultimate consumerist nightmare, a woman who accepts her husband's murder without blinking an eyelid and then breaks down because the car's been scratched. Then she started to get hysterical, snatching up things from the shelves and throwing them across the room. Marisa tried to calm her while I rang for a doctor. It took him forty minutes to get there. I'll never forget that time as long as I live."

A woman who looked like a barrel wearing a fur coat was waiting for the bus. Her son, perfectly dressed as a miniature man, was staring unbelievingly up at the balloon whose string he had just lost hold of, now floating away high above the arriving Alfetta.

"The calmness was all a façade, of course," Bartocci continued once they were settled in the car. "Patrizia had been so terrified by what her husband was doing that she had convinced herself that nothing could happen to him. But she'd forgotten to extend this magic immunity to the BMW, which is why she went into hysterics as soon as I mentioned it."

"Where is she now?"

"With relatives, under sedation."

The Valesios' house was one of a number of modern apartments forming an exclusive development on the lower slopes of the city, all pink brick and double glazing and concrete balconies dripping with greenery. In the absence of Patrizia Valesio the family interests were represented by her mother, a formidable woman who followed Bartocci and Zen from room to room, personally checking every single item that was removed while bemoaning the fact that the authorities were permitted to make free with the private papers of a man above suspicion, a pillar of the community and a repository of every known human virtue. Ubaldo Valesio himself made a ghostly fourth presence, smiling at them from photographs, haunting a wardrobe full of clothes, proclaiming his taste in books and records, even trying to lay claim to a nonexistent future by way of a scribbled note on his desk jotter reading "Evasio Thursday re plumbing."

It was not until they were driving back to the city center that Bartocci produced the photographs.

"Just in case you still think it was a mistake," he commented as Zen mutely studied the images of horror.

"No, I meant that Valesio may have accidentally caught sight of one of the gang," Zen explained. "These would have been the top men, don't forget. No one else would be entrusted with the negotiations. They might well have been worried that he would be able to identify them."

Bartocci seemed to be about to say something, but in the end he just turned away and looked out the window, leaving Zen to wonder once again why he had been invited along on this routine errand.

The offices which Ubaldo Valesio had shared with two other lawyers was in the center of the city, just behind the cathedral, in a street so narrow there was barely room for Palottino to park. It consisted of one wing of the first floor of the building, two huge rooms divided into separate work areas by antique screens and potted shrubs. Valesio's partners were both present. They were very correct, very polite, and very unhelpful. Yes, they had known that Ubaldo was acting for the Milettis. No, they had never discussed it. They watched discreetly but attentively as the two representatives of the State looked through diaries, memo books, files, and folders. Then they drew up an inventory of what had been taken, obtained a receipt, said goodbye, and went back to work.

"When may I expect your report on this material?" Bartocci asked Zen when they got back to the courthouse.

"Tomorrow, I hope. But if anything important comes up I'll phone you."

He turned back and started to get into the car, but Bartocci called him back.

"Listen, there are a few things I'd like to discuss with you. Off the record, as it were."

Zen gazed at him, his face perfectly expressionless.

"In fact I thought we might have lunch. That little restaurant down the street there is where I usually eat, the one with the neon sign and the awning."

"Today?"

"If that's convenient."

Bartocci's tone was polite, almost deferential. It scared Zen stiff.

"I'd be delighted," he replied with a ghost of a smile.

As Palottino drove him back to the Questura he saw that the

restaurant Bartocci had indicated was called The Griffin and displayed a sign with a beast similar to those he had seen at the courthouse.

Back in his office, Zen thought about griffins and Luciano Bartocci and Ubaldo Valesio. Griffins, he discovered from the dictionary kept in the desk drawer, were mythical creatures having the head and wings of an eagle and the legs and tail of a lion. He wondered why they had been carved above the entrance to the courthouse. Were they symbols of Justice? Certainly Luciano Bartocci seemed to be something of a hybrid. Zen had never been invited to lunch by a member of the judiciary before, and he found the prospect as unattractive as the invitation to Crepi's the previous evening. Once again he felt that he was being drawn into an area where the stakes were high and the rules not clearly defined. *"A few things I'd like to discuss with you, off the record."* What was Bartocci up to?

Almost with relief, his thoughts turned back to Ubaldo Valesio. Although they had never met, Zen felt he knew the dead man well: a successful and ambitious lawyer in a city which despite its recent growth was still a small town at heart, a place where rumors spread as silently and effectively as a virus. His partners had been telling the truth, Zen felt sure, and his assistants next door were almost certainly wasting their time going through the lawyer's records. People like Valesio, who knew everything about someone and something about everyone, not only stopped talking to others about their affairs, they very soon stopped talking even to themselves. Above all, they would never commit anything to paper unless it was absolutely necessary. Ubaldo Valesio would have kept the details of his dealings with Ruggiero Miletti's kidnappers in the only place he considered safe, his own head. With a shiver, Zen remembered the photographs Bartocci had shown him.

A clanging of bells suddenly rang out from churches near and far, calling the faithful to Mass and reminding the rest that their lunch was just an hour away. Zen fetched his coat and hat and walked into the next room. Geraci looked up at him with an expression of intense anxiety. His face was heavy and fleshy, and the two deep furrows running from the corners of his nose to the edges of his mouth gave him a hangdog look. His chin had a weak and skimpy look, as though the material had run out before the job was quite finished, while his eyebrows were absurdly thick and bushy, with a life of their own.

"Anything?" Zen inquired.

Geraci shrugged. Chiodini pretended to be so intent on his labors that he did not even notice Zen's presence.

Outside, the sun illuminated every surface with uncompromising clarity. The air seemed full of disquieting hints of summer, but the illusion lasted no longer than it took to turn the corner into a narrow alley sunk deep in shadow, where the wind whetted the cold edge of the air like a knife. Bare walls faced with crumbling plaster rose on both sides, pierced by the high, inaccessible windows of the prison, covered with heavy steel mesh. After going about a hundred meters Zen was beginning to feel he had made a mistake in turning off the broad avenue that led directly up to the city center, but he persisted, and was rewarded when the street widened out into a little square where the wind disappeared and a cherry tree was in sumptuous blossom in a garden high above. But at the next corner the wind was back, keener than ever. He turned left down a long flight of steps to get away from it.

In the grocery at the corner a sad pale pig of a girl, a greasy sliver of cooked ham dangling from her mouth, jerked her thumb at a set of steps opposite in response to his request for directions to the center. It was a staircase for mountain climbers; the steps seemed to get progressively higher as he climbed. The wall it ran up looked like the face of history itself. It was founded on massive blocks of rock whose dimensions were those of ancient days, presumably Etruscan. Above this layer came another, Roman work, where the blocks, though still large, had lost the epic scale. Then came a long stretch of small cubes of pinkish stone forming the wall of a medieval house, and finally an upper story tacked on in brick and concrete.

He stopped to catch his breath, leaning against one of the giant blocks which had weathered to form intricate niches and cavities. In several of them tiny plants had somehow contrived to put down roots in a trace of dust, in another someone had wedged an empty Diet Coke can. Below, a breathtaking view stretched away, line after line of hills rippling off into the hazy distance. He stepped carefully over a dead pigeon on the next step and clambered grimly to the top. The street in which he came out continued upward without respite through an ancient gateway, and still up, darkly resonant and noisy, past basement workshops where carpenters and furniture repairers and picture framers were at work. The air, fresh and cold and deli-

cately flavored with wood smoke, was a luxury in itself, an air
for angels to breathe.

On the wall of a nearby building a hoarding displayed two
posters. The one on the right featured a garish picture of a
woman in a bathing costume being pursued by a number of
eager fish with teeth like daggers. "For the first time in Italy,"
the caption exclaimed, "women and sharks in the same pool!!!"
The name of a circus appeared beneath, with the dates of its
upcoming visit to Perugia. The other poster showed a famous
footballer leering suggestively at a bottle of milk, but what
attracted Zen's attention was the top left-hand corner, where the
mass of posters accumulated over several months was starting to
curl back under its own weight, revealing a section of older
strata far beneath. In the corner, in large red letters, he read
LETTI. The protruding curl was almost a centimeter thick,
layered like plywood, and when Zen tugged at it the whole block
peeled off and fell to the ground at his feet. Now he could see
almost all the earlier poster, which was headed SIMP AND THE
MILETTI FAMILY. There were five short paragraphs of closely set
writing:

The arrogance and intransigence of the Miletti family,
amply demonstrated on innumerable occasions in the past,
are once again in evidence. Not content with shutting down
the Ponte San Giovanni subsidiary, or laying off more than
800 workers in Perugia—to say nothing of their continuing
exploitation of female piecework labor and well-known
antiunion policies—they are now reported to be planning
to sell off a controlling interest in the Società Industriale
Miletti di Perugia to a Japanese electronics conglomerate.

Having crippled a once-prosperous enterprise by a combination of managerial incompetence and ill-advised
speculation in the activities of such gentlemen as Calvi,
Sindona, and their like, the Milettis now intend to recoup
their losses by auctioning off SIMP to the highest bidder.

The company named in the takeover bid already owns
factories which are running well below their maximum
potential production level due to the world economic
recession and consequent shortage of demand. Their intention is to use SIMP as a means of eluding the EEC
quotas by importing Japanese-produced goods to which
nothing will be added in Umbria but a grille bearing one of

the brand names which generations of local workers have helped to make famous.

The Umbrian Communists totally condemn this example of cynical stock market manipulation. SIMP is not to be sold off like a set of saucepans. The future of our jobs and those of our children must be decided here in Perugia after a process of consultation between representatives of the work force, the owners, and the provincial and regional authorities.

Italian Communist Party
Umbrian Section

Zen turned away from the billboard and started to climb the ancient street paved with flagstones as smooth as the bed of a stream. An old woman lurched toward him, a bulging plastic bag in each hand, bellowing something incomprehensible at a man who was looking up at the scaffolding hung with sacking that covered a house being renovated. A gang of boys on scooters swooped down the street, slabs of pizza in one hand, horns groaning like angry frogs, yelling insults at one another. They missed the old woman by inches, and a load of rubble gushing down a plastic chute into a hopper made a noise that sounded like a round of applause for their skill or her nonchalance.

"Anything else?" The waiter perched like a sparrow beside their table, looking distractedly about him.

Bartocci shook his head and glanced at Zen. "Shall we go?"

At the cash desk the manager greeted Bartocci warmly. No bill was presented. Like the rest of the almost exclusively male clientele of the noisy little restaurant, the magistrate was clearly a regular who paid by the week or month.

"How about a little stroll before having coffee?" Bartocci suggested once they were outside. "I must warn you though that it's uphill, like everything in Perugia!"

It was a measure of Zen's state of mind that he found himself wondering whether the words had more than one meaning. Lunch with Bartocci had indeed proved very much like dinner with the Milettis, except that the food was even better: macaroni in a sauce made with cream and spicy sausage meat, chunks of liver wrapped in a delicate net of membrane and charred over embers, thin dark-green stalks of wild asparagus, strawberries soaked in lemon juice. But just as at Crepi's the evening before, the conversation had been dominated by what was *not* discussed. Bartocci had shown himself to be particularly interested in Zen's career and views on various items of news: a scandal about kickbacks for building permits involving members of a Socialist city council, reports that a Christian Democrat ex-mayor had been a leading member of the Palermo Mafia, allegations that the wife of a Liberal senator in Turin was involved in the illegal export of currency. Zen knew what was happening, of course, and Bartocci knew that he knew. It was all part of the process. How would this police official from Rome react to being sounded out "off the record" by a Communist investigating magistrate?

The magistrate led the way up a broad flight of steps which at first appeared to lead to someone's front door. At the last moment, however, they swerved to the left and continued into a tunnel burrowing underneath a conglomerate of interlocking houses, walls, gardens, and yards deposited there over the centuries by generations of people neither more nor less dead than Ubaldo Valesio. It was dark and the wind whined emptily past them. On the wall a soccer fan had spray-painted ROME ARE MAGIC, while a dustbin opposite was inscribed JUVENTUS HEAD-QUARTERS.

After about fifty meters the subterranean arcade widened out slightly into a concrete yard where six Fiat 500s were packed in so tightly that there was barely room to pass on foot. Bartocci led him on without a word, turning left and right without hesitation, always climbing, until they reached a small piazza in front of a church where the walls fell back to reveal a view similar to the one Zen had seen that morning from his bedroom window, centered by that strange mountain, full and rounded as a mound of risen dough.

Bartocci glanced around the square, which was empty except for a few parked cars.

"What were you saying about Di Leonardo?" he asked suddenly.

"Well, he implied last night that the police were at fault for not having exploited Valesio's contacts with the kidnappers. I wondered if you agreed."

"No, I don't see things in quite the same way. In fact I should have preferred to pursue a much more active line in this case from the very start. I tried to have the family's assets frozen, to prevent any possibility of a ransom payment. I also sought to have Ubaldo's phone monitored. But there was considerable opposition to these initiatives, notably from Di Leonardo himself."

"But you don't need higher authority to authorize those things," Zen pointed out.

"I don't need higher authority to sign a warrant for the arrest of President Pertini, either. But it would be the last I ever signed. If I'd frozen the Miletti account and had the phone tap put on, the net result would have been to destroy any chances I have of influencing the outcome of this case. Besides, people like the Milettis can always raise cash somewhere, and as for the phones, the gang must assume that they're all tapped anyway. We wouldn't have learned anything much without trying to follow Valesio, which would have been a very risky venture indeed. Di Leonardo tried to suggest that Ubaldo was killed because of my negligence. I was his real target, not you. But just imagine how he would have responded had there been the slightest evidence that Valesio's death was the result of my interference! No, that's not the way to handle these things."

Zen moved over to the parapet at the edge of the piazza, where stone benches were placed at intervals between trees giving shade on hot summer days. Here the wall dropped vertically away to the gardens of the houses far below. Beyond them rose a lengthy strip of high medieval city wall, then a valley cut steeply into hills dotted with modern villas, leading the eye away to the still more distant hills and the valley beyond, green and gray and brown beneath the azure sky, where the strange mountain rose. In the far distance, at the limit of vision, shimmered the snow-covered peaks of the Apennines.

Zen got out his packet of Nazionali. It contained only one cigarette, the last of the supply he had brought with him. As he lit up, a flicker of movement down below caught his eye. A girl in jeans and a red sweater was standing at an open window in one of the houses, looking out at the garden with its rows of vegetables running up to a chicken coop at the foot of the high retaining wall. She was clearly unaware of being observed.

"Valesio's death has changed everything, of course," Bartocci continued. "Your arrival at the same moment is extremely convenient. The whole investigation will have to begin again from scratch. We must be prepared to reexamine all our assumptions, even the most fundamental, without allowing ourselves to be influenced by the thought that some people might find our conclusions difficult to swallow."

Zen exhaled a long breath of the fragrant earthy tobacco. The girl moved and the window was empty again.

"That's why I asked to speak to you today," the magistrate went on in the same confidential tone. "It's very refreshing for me to deal with an outsider, someone free of any preconceptions. You have no ax to grind here, no interests to protect. One can consider every possibility."

The girl reappeared at the window. Her legs were now bare.

"About a month ago I received this," Bartocci said, handing Zen a sheet of paper.

Aren't the Milettis clever? They can turn their hand to anything—even kidnapping!!?? They've had plenty of practice in extortion, ask their workers! But if you are not in their pay too then know this. Old Miletti got himself kidnapped at just the right moment. With him out of the way the family can't sign any takeover papers which might let the Japs into the game. And what if the ransom ended up in the family's pockets into the bargain? Maybe then they could keep screwing us for another few years!

Think about it.

One Who Knows

Zen silently handed the letter back to Bartocci, who replaced it carefully in his pocket.

"Of course I get a lot of this sort of thing, and normally I would simply discount it as a hoax from someone with a grudge against the family. But in this case it seems to me that the writer knows what he's talking about."

The girl had moved again, so that only her bare legs and feet were visible. Then she disappeared completely.

"What's this about a takeover?" Zen asked. "I saw something about it on an old poster today, too."

"SIMP has been in financial difficulties for some time now. The root cause is that old Ruggiero has insisted all along on maintaining total personal control of every aspect of the business. But the company has diversified into areas he knows nothing about; the market has changed out of all recognition in the last ten or fifteen years. Above all he is no longer the man he was. The result has been a gradual running down of the whole operation. They've been forced to close one of their factories and lay off about a quarter of the work force at the other. But the real crunch came with the collapse of Calvi's financial empire. It seems that Miletti had foolishly sunk quite a lot of money in it. Since then the company has been living from one loan to another, under increasing pressure to improve their performance and efficiency. Finally, just before Miletti was kidnapped, a Japanese company made an offer to put up the money SIMP badly needs in return for a license to sell its products under the Miletti name. The old man wouldn't hear of it, of course."

"That's not what the PCI poster suggested."

"No, the Party quite correctly takes the line that unless prevented the family will do whatever makes sense from a financial point of view. Ruggiero's opposition is merely the sentimental stubbornness of an old man, and as such he cannot be depended on to protect the interests of the workers."

Again a flicker of movement below caught Zen's eye. The girl passed by the window, naked except for a yellow towel wrapped round her hair.

"I know this theory sounds fantastic," Bartocci continued. "But look at what else happens in this country. Look at Gelli, look at Calvi. Was that any more fantastic? When Michele Sindona got into difficulties with the law in New York he staged a fake kidnapping for himself so that he could go to Palermo and pressure people he thought might be helpful. What's to stop the Milettis doing the same thing? It's a scheme worthy of Calvi himself. Take Ruggiero out of circulation to prevent any takeover deals going through, and then use their own money, recycled through a faked payoff, to prop up the company's finances."

Zen tried to keep his eye off the window below and his mind on what Bartocci was saying.

"But that would mean that they also murdered Valesio."

Bartocci nodded. "It's precisely Valesio's death which has made me take the theory so seriously. You said that he may accidentally have caught sight of one of the members of the gang. But why should the kidnappers care if Valesio caught a glimpse of some Calabrian he'd never seen before and would never recognize again? But suppose that the person Valesio saw was *not* a stranger? Suppose it was someone he knew very well, someone anybody in Perugia would know well. Imagine his rage as he realizes the shameful game they have been playing on him and on everyone! And imagine the Milettis' horror as they face the certainty of a revelation which would smash the family's power forever and send many of them to prison for years to come. What are they to do? Either kill Valesio or admit that all these months we've been working tirelessly for Ruggiero Miletti's release he has in fact been comfortably holed up in some property of the family a few miles from here, perhaps even in his own house. Do you remember how long it took the family to get around to informing the police of his disappearance? They said it was because the idea of kidnapping never occurred to them, but it might equally be because they needed time to fake the accident and the evidence of the struggle, time to burn the car."

Again a movement at the window below caught Zen's eye. But this time the figure was that of a man, who reached for the shutters and banged them shut.

"So you really believe that there's a conspiracy?" Zen still wasn't sure whether the magistrate was completely serious.

"There's always a conspiracy. Everything that happens in society at a certain level is part of a conspiracy."

Zen noted the evasive reply. "If everything is, nothing is. If we're all conspirators then there's no conspiracy."

"On the contrary, the condition of this conspiracy is that we're all part of it," Bartocci retorted. "It's like a ratking."

"A what?"

"A ratking. Do you know what that is?"

Zen shrugged. "The king rat, I suppose. The dominant animal in the pack."

Bartocci shook his head. "That's what everyone thinks. But they're wrong. A ratking is something that happens when too many rats have to live in too small a space under too much pressure. Their tails become entwined and the more they strain and stretch to free themselves the tighter grows the knot binding them, until at last it becomes a solid mass of embedded tissue. And the creature thus formed, as many as thirty rats tied together by the tail, is called a ratking. You wouldn't expect such a living contradiction to survive, would you? That's the most amazing thing of all. Most of the ratkings that are discovered, in the plaster of old houses or beneath the floorboards of a barn, are healthy and flourishing. Evidently the creatures have evolved some way of coming to terms with their situation. That's not to say they like it, of course! In fact the reason they're discovered is because of their diabolical squealing. Not much fun, being chained to each other for life. How much sweeter it would be to run free! Nevertheless, they *do* survive, somehow. The wonders of nature, eh?"

He paused to let Zen's exasperation mature.

"Now a lot of people believe that somewhere in the wainscoting of this country the king of all the rats is hiding," he finally went on. "The toughest brute of all, the most vicious and ruthless, the dominant animal in the pack, as you put it. Some thought it was Calvi, some thought it was Gelli. Others believe that it is someone else again, someone above and beyond either of them, a big name in the government perhaps, or on the contrary someone you've never even heard of. But the one thing they all agree is that he exists, this super-rat. It's a message of hope and of despair. Hope, because perhaps one fine day we'll finally trap him, run him down, finish him off and rid this house of rats forever. Despair, because we know he's too shrewd and powerful and cunning ever to be trapped. But in fact that's all just a fairy story! What we're dealing with is not a creature but a condition. The condition of being crucified to your fellows, squealing madly, biting, spitting, lashing out, yet somehow surviving, somehow even vilely flourishing! That's what makes the conspiracy so formidable. There's no need for agendas or strategies, lists of members or passwords or secret codes. The ratking is self-regulating. It responds automatically and effectively to any threat. Each rat defends the interests of the others. The strength of each is the strength of all."

"I don't quite see what all this has to do with the present case," Zen said.

Bartocci glanced at his watch. "Quite right. I'm sorry, I got carried away. But the fact remains that whether or not there is a conspiracy in progress in the Miletti case, I believe that the investigation has reached a point where I can no longer continue to ignore such a theory. However, it would be fatal for me to announce my intentions. If I were to conduct this investigation like any other, the political repercussions would ensure that the truth never came to light."

"Which is where I come in."

The magistrate looked at him, a strange stalled smile straining away at the corner of his mouth. "If you are prepared to help."

Zen turned round, taking a deep breath. One of the first-floor windows of the houses was a painted dummy, but at the one next to it a portly silver-haired man in a plum-colored dressing gown stood staring down at them with undisguised curiosity.

"What do you want me to do?" Zen asked tonelessly.

"Just a few things that would be difficult for me to do without causing comment," Bartocci replied. "First of all I'd like you to check what firearms are registered to members of the Miletti family. Don't forget to include the Santuccis. I also want you to make discreet inquiries as to the whereabouts of family members yesterday."

"I can tell you where they were yesterday evening. They were having dinner with me at Antonio Crepi's."

Bartocci gave him a look that modulated rapidly from astonishment through alarm and respect to suspicion. Then he laughed.

"Well, well! You do get around, don't you?"

"Apparently Crepi wanted me to meet the Milettis. To 'see what we're up against' as he put it."

At the other end of the piazza a young couple were hungrily necking, bent over a parked car. The fat man at the window was still looking on, his thumbs tucked under the belt of his dressing gown.

"Did he say anything else?"

"Yes, quite a lot. In fact to some extent it seemed to tally with what you've been saying. Not that he suggested that the family had any complicity in the kidnapping . . ."

"Of course not! Anyway, he wouldn't know."

"But he feels strongly that the family are not doing enough to bring Ruggiero home. He asked me to make that plain to the press in an attempt to pressure the Milettis to pay up."

The young magistrate smiled sourly. "Typical. Anyway, one thing is certain. No additional pressure will be necessary now. Valesio's death will do more than any press conference to resolve this issue one way or the other. Within the next few days I expect the family to announce that they've received a demand for the full amount of the ransom to be paid at once and that they are going to comply. That's why we need to move fast. Once that money is handed over and Ruggiero is back, we'll never be able to prove anything. But we must be discreet above all! This entire matter is politically sensitive in the very highest degree, and if any word of it leaks out I shall be forced to—"

He broke off suddenly, looking past Zen. The young man had produced a camera and was taking photographs of his girl-friend posed in various positions against the landscape.

"Anyway, I must go. No time for coffee, I'm afraid."

As Bartocci hurried away, the man with the camera came striding purposefully toward Zen, his girlfriend following more slowly behind.

"Pardon me! Would you be as good enough to mind making of us two both a photograph?"

Foreign, thought Zen with relief. The young magistrate's sudden departure had been unnecessary. One thing at least was certain: the bastards would never employ foreigners.

4

That afternoon Aurelio Zen went boating.

After the shock of Valesio's murder and his almost sleepless night, lunch with Luciano Bartocci had really been the last straw. One thing he could have done without was an ambitious young investigating magistrate with a fierce political bias, a prefabricated conspiracy theory, and an itch to get his name in the news. At Zen's expense, needless to say, should anything go wrong.

Once upon a time magistrates had been dull stolid figures, worthy but uninspiring, above all remote and anonymous. But the combination of television and terrorism had changed all that. A new breed of men had emerged from the vague gray ranks of the judiciary to stamp themselves on the nation's consciousness: the glamorous investigating magistrates and Public Prosecutors who were to be seen on the news every evening leading the fight against political violence and organized crime. Now all their colleagues craved stardom too, and almost overnight the once faceless bureaucrats had blossomed out in trendy clothes and bushy beards, and an anonymous letter was enough to get them as excited as any schoolboy.

Since Bartocci had taken great pains to emphasize that his comments were "off the record," Zen could of course simply ignore them. But that would be rash. There were an infinite number of ways in which the investigating magistrate could compromise or embarrass a police officer, whereas having the judiciary on your side was an invaluable asset. No, he had to try to keep Bartocci happy. On the other hand, the inquiries he had been asked to make, although on the surface innocuous, were also fraught with risk. A great family such as the Milettis is like a sleeping bear: it may look massively apathetic and unimpressionable, but each hair of its pelt is wired straight into the creature's brain, and if you twitch it the wrong way often enough the thing will flex its tendons and turn on you, unzipping its claws. What was he to do? How was he to react? What was a safe course to take?

His immediate solution was to go boating. Not for long, of course. With all these new developments pressing in on him the last thing he could afford was an afternoon off work. But neither was there any point in trying to take action with his head in this condition. So having made his way back to the hotel he closed the shutters, took off his shoes, jacket, and tie, lay down on the bed, and cast off. The image of the long shallow craft gliding forward through the reeds in regular surges, propelled by the oarsman's graceful double-handed sweeps, was a powerful agent of calm. Just ten or fifteen minutes of it now would see him right, a short trip out through the islets and mudbanks where you could let the boat drift, lean over the stern and watch the inner life of the dirty green water, the shreds of seaweed and small branches and other shapes that sometimes proved to be alive, or focus on the surface, a depthless sheet of scum on which the pearly light shimmered in continual shifting patterns, or even look up to see a huge modern building, several stories high, going for a stroll along a neighboring island, the superstructure of a freighter putting out to sea along the deep-water channel . . .

But in fact when he looked up it was to find to his annoyance that he'd been away longer than he'd intended: it was twenty to five.

He got up and put the light on, shivering. Something was wrong. How could the room feel stuffy and cold at the same time? And it was totally silent, no distant murmur of traffic, no footsteps, no voices. Catching sight of the transistor radio, he clicked it on and fiddled with the tuner, encountering only heavy bands of static interspersed with the twittering gibberish of machines. He felt like the last person left alive.

"... *very much and you get a fabulous Radio Subasio T-shirt so keep those calls coming out there this one is for Adriana in Gubbio it's Celentano's latest coming to you at fifteen before five this Thursday morning courtesy of your friend Tullio who says ...*"

Zen silenced the radio, walked to the window, and opened the shutters. The deserted piazza glistened under the streetlights. He had slept all afternoon and right through the night.

Catching sight of his reflection in the window, he felt a surge of self-pity and suddenly realized that he missed Ellen very badly, and that it was only at moments like this, when he surprised himself, that he could admit how much he needed her. Why couldn't he tell *her?* That was what she wanted, after all, and he knew that she was right to want it. For a moment he thought of phoning her, right then, and telling her how he felt. But it would be ridiculous, of course. He imagined the phone ringing and ringing until it prodded her unwillingly out of sleep, and her uncomprehending response. "For Christ's sake, Aurelio, couldn't this have waited? Do you know what time it is? I've got a sale to go to at nine, and you know how difficult it is for me to get back to sleep once I've been woken." Instead he read a paper he'd bought in Trieste and forgotten to throw away, immersing himself in the debate over the council's delay in resurfacing the streets in an outlying zone of the city, until it was time to go to work.

A crowd of people of various races, clutching passports and sheaves of official documents, were clustered around an office in the foyer of the Questura. A sheet of paper attached to the glass partition read FOREIGNERS in crude lettering. Behind the glass an official from the Political Branch scowled at a worried-looking applicant.

"And I suppose it's my fault you haven't got it?" he demanded.

As Zen approached his office, the inspector who had been trying to trace Ubaldo Valesio's movements poked his head around the door of the next room.

"Just a moment, chief!"

Lucaroni was short and rather sleazy-looking, with narrow-set eyes and a broad jaw blue with stubble. His movements were quick and furtive and he spoke in a speedy whisper, as though every word were classified information.

"You've got a visitor," he muttered. "The widow. Rolled in about five minutes ago demanding to see you. We weren't sure what to do with her."

He looked doubtfully at Zen, who nodded. "Turn up anything yesterday?"

Lucaroni shook his head. "He phoned his office at nine to cancel all appointments. It was obviously unexpected. There were two clients waiting who had to be sent away."

Zen looked into the inspectors' room. Chiodini was poring over a sports paper. Geraci was staring fixedly back at Zen, as though he was trying to remember whether he'd turned the gas off before leaving home.

"How about you two?" Zen asked.

Geraci's eyebrows wiggled briefly. "Just a lot of stuff about his house and taxes and kids."

"And those marks in the diary," Chiodini put in without looking up from his paper.

"They're nothing," Geraci commented dismissively.

"What marks?" asked Zen.

Chiodini took the desk diary from the pile of documents on his desk and showed him where the lawyer had marked several pages during the previous three months with a red asterisk. The last asterisk had appeared two days earlier. Zen walked over to the door that opened directly into his office, taking the diary with him.

"What do you want us to do now, chief?" Geraci asked. He sounded slightly panicky.

"Nothing, for now."

He should never have asked for three assistants, Zen realized. Now he would always have them hanging about, making him feel guilty, getting in his way. Moreover, one of them was bound to be reporting back to the Questore, and since there was no way of finding out which, he would have to keep them all busy if he was to do what Bartocci had asked.

The spare chair in his office was occupied by a woman of about thirty-five dressed in an elegant black outfit. Her face was large and round and slightly concave, with a long sharp nose.

"You're the man they sent up from Rome?" she asked. "I am Patrizia Valesio."

"I'm very sorry. . . ."

She waved dismissively. "Please, don't let's waste time."

Zen took out a notepad and pencil and laid them on the desk. "Very well. What can I do for you?"

Patrizia Valesio took a deep breath. She clearly had a task to perform and had convinced herself that she possessed enough strength and control to see it through. But she might be wrong about that, Zen thought as he watched the widow's left hand compulsively sweeping and smoothing the fabric of her coat.

"I've come to make an accusation. You may find it bizarre, even unbelievable. I simply ask you to listen, and not to judge what I say until I have finished. My husband did not usually discuss the negotiations for Ruggiero Miletti's release with me, but on one occasion about a month ago, while we were having dinner . . ."

She paused. The strain of what she was saying showed on her face. Then she finished quickly.

"He suddenly blurted out, 'Someone is going behind my back.'"

The phone rang.

"Excuse me," Zen said, and lifted the receiver.

"Good morning, Commissioner. This is Antonio Crepi. I'm just phoning to make it quite clear that our discussion the other night is no longer . . . er . . . relevant. Pietro has flown in from London and he's assured me that as soon as the gang makes contact the matter will be resolved without further delay. I don't need to tell you to keep what I said to yourself, of course."

"Of course."

"Incidentally, I hear you had lunch with young Bartocci yesterday."

Zen watched Patrizia Valesio's hand picking invisible hairs off her coat. Please don't let her break down again, he thought. Not here in my office.

"I don't want to interfere, dottore, but remember what I told you about him. Bartocci's a good lad at heart, but he's got a bee in his bonnet when it comes to the Milettis. You know how these lefties are, they read Marx and stop seeing reality. Now that's a dangerous attitude for an investigating magistrate, in my opinion. Still more so for a policeman. See what I mean? Just a friendly word of advice, from one who knows."

Zen put down the phone. *". . . from one who knows."* Where had he heard that phrase before?

Patrizia Valesio was staring at him with the expression of one who is determined not to be put off by interruptions or delays.

Her face reminded Zen of an old-fashioned candlestick: a shallow dish with a spike in the middle.

"I'm sorry, he murmured. "You were saying that . . ."

"Ubaldo told me that someone was going behind his back," she repeated. "He said that every time he went back to the kidnappers to present a carefully prepared offer, worked out after lengthy discussions with the family, claiming that this was the absolute maximum the Milettis could afford to pay, the gang accused him of lying. 'Have you forgotten the villa at Punta Ala? And what about the olive grove at Spello? Why haven't you sold the shares in such and such a company?' And when Ubaldo asked the Milettis, lo and behold there *was* such a villa, such an olive grove, such shares! It was a negotiator's nightmare!"

Zen stared hard at the pad. He had been doodling obsessive boxlike designs, a nest of interlocking right-angled lines locking out all possibility of error or surprise.

"What about Ruggiero himself?" he suggested gently. "He knows more than anyone about the family assets, and he's totally in the kidnappers' power. It wouldn't be difficult for them to make him talk."

"That's what Ubaldo thought at first. But the gang knew about financial developments which had taken place *since* the kidnapping, things Ruggiero couldn't possibly have known about. Eventually my husband became convinced that someone in the family circle was supplying the gang with information on a day-to-day basis. Which means that my husband was the innocent victim of some hideous double dealing within the Miletti family! That's why I have come. I want his murderers punished. Not just the ones who pulled the trigger but also the ones who stood behind them, in the shadows!"

She broke off, taking quick shallow breaths.

"This is all very interesting, signora. . . ."

"I haven't finished!" she snapped. "There's something else, a vital clue. The gang always used the same procedure when they wanted to make contact. The telephone would ring at one o'clock, just as we were sitting down to lunch. Only two words were spoken. The caller gave the name of a football team and Ubaldo had to reply with the name of the team they were playing the following Sunday. He kept the schedule by the phone. Then he hung up immediately, phoned his office, and canceled his afternoon appointments. That was the procedure, and it never varied. But on Tuesday . . ."

She broke off again, fighting for control.

"On Tuesday the call came not at lunchtime but early in the morning, about seven forty-five. I heard Ubaldo give the password and then say 'Now?' in great surprise."

She held Zen's eyes with hers. "When did you arrive here in Perugia, Commissioner?"

"On Tuesday."

"At what time?"

"About half past one."

"And who knew you were coming?"

He frowned. "Various people in the Ministry and here at the Questura."

"No one else?"

"Not as far as I know. Why?"

Was that a sound from the next room, from behind the closed door?

"Then how do you explain the fact that the kidnappers phoned urgently, demanding to see Ubaldo in person, at a time when you were still in Rome and no one supposedly knew you were coming except the authorities?" Her voice was triumphant, as though this clinched the matter.

Zen deliberately allowed his frown to deepen. "I don't see there's anything to explain. What connection is there between the two events?"

She snorted indignantly. "The connection? The connection is obvious to anyone who can put two and two together. Do you really believe that the first contact after weeks of silence just happened by sheer coincidence to fall on the same day as your arrival here? I'm sorry, but that would be just a little too convenient. But how could the kidnappers have known about your arrival in Perugia five hours *before* it happened? Because their contact in the family tipped them off!"

"But how did the Milettis know, for that matter?"

"Because it was they who had you sent here, of course! You don't think that things like that happen without someone pulling strings, do you?"

Zen looked away. He had just remembered where he'd heard the phrase with which Crepi had rung off. It was the signature of the anonymous letter Bartocci had received suggesting that the kidnapping of Ruggiero Miletti was a put-up job. He found himself writing CREPI??? in block capitals on the pad in front of him. He hastily crossed it out, then covered the whole area with tight scribbles until all trace of the name was obliterated.

"I don't quite understand, signora. First you claim that the family is collaborating with the kidnappers, then you say they must have used their influence to have me sent here. Surely that is a contradiction?"

With a convulsive movement, Patrizia Valesio got to her feet.

"Don't you dare speak to me of contradictions! That whole family is a living contradiction, consuming anything and anyone that comes within its reach, one of them smiling in your face while another stabs you in the back. My poor husband, who wanted only to help, ended up as their victim. Be careful you don't share his fate!"

Zen also rose. He kept his voice soothing.

"Anyway, since this case is under investigation by the judiciary, the proper person to inform is the magistrate in charge, Luciano Bartocci."

His visitor scooped up her gloves and handbag. "Oh, I *shall* inform him, don't worry! And I shall inform him that I've informed you. And then I shall inform the Public Prosecutor's department that I've informed both of you. Do you know why I'm going to inform so many people, Commissioner? Because I am expecting there to be a conspiracy of silence on this matter and I intend to make it as difficult as possible for the Milettis and their friends. If there is to be a conspiracy, at least everyone will see that it exists and will know who is involved. That will be some poor consolation, at least."

At the last moment Zen remembered the diary. He showed it to Patrizia Valesio and asked if she knew anything about the asterisks which Chiodini had pointed out. The sight of her husband's writing was clearly a great shock, but she held herself together.

"Those are the days on which Ubaldo had a meeting with the kidnappers," she replied in a dull voice. "He marked the diary as soon as they phoned. He thought it might be useful later."

Well, perhaps it might, Zen thought when she had gone. But he couldn't see how.

He opened the door to the other room. Lucaroni was standing almost immediately inside, studying a notice concerning action to be taken in the event of fire breaking out in the building. Geraci was sitting at his desk, a paperback edition of the Penal Code open in front of him. Chiodini had fallen forward on his newspaper and seemed to be asleep.

"Well, I've got some work for you, lads," Zen exclaimed breezily. "From what Valesio's widow has told me, it's clear that her husband's contacts with the gang began with a telephone call that was simply a signal for him to go to some prearranged meeting place. The chances are that it was a bar, somewhere not too far away. I want you to find it. Draw up a list and visit each in turn. Take a photograph of Valesio along. It shouldn't be too difficult. A smart young lawyer driving a BMW will have been noticed."

When they had gone, Zen went back to his office and dialed an internal number.

"Records."

"I want a check run on any firearms licenses issued to the following persons. Family name Miletti, first names Ruggiero, Pietro, Silvio, and . . ."

Again that sound next door. Zen put down the phone, got up, and went over to the door to the corridor. He looked out. The corridor was empty, but the door to the inspector's room was slightly ajar. Zen walked softly along the corridor and pushed it wide open. Geraci was standing by his desk. He whirled round as the door hit the rubbish bin with a loud clang.

"Forgot my notebook," the inspector explained hastily.

Zen nodded. "Listen, Geraci, I want you to keep an eye on the other two for me."

Geraci stared uncertainly at Zen. "Keep an eye on them?"

"That's it. Just in case."

He winked and tapped the side of his nose. "Better safe than sorry. Know what I mean?"

Geraci clearly didn't have the slightest idea what Zen was talking about.

"Better get going," he muttered nervously.

"Good thinking. Don't want to make them suspicious."

He watched Geraci walk all the way down the corridor before going back to his office, leaving the connecting door open so that if anyone came in he could see them reflected on Pertini's portrait. Then he picked up the receiver again.

"Hello?"

"So far I've got Miletti Ruggiero, Pietro, and Silvio."

"Right. Also Miletti Daniele, Santucci Gianluigi, and Cinzia née Miletti."

"Who's speaking?"

Zen seemed to see again that glare of hostility and hear the Questore murmur, "Until today he was handling the Miletti case for us."

"Fabrizio Priorelli."

"I'll call you straight back, dottore."

"Eh, no, my friend! Sorry, but you'll do it now, if you please. I'll hold."

"Of course, dottore! Right away."

There was a *clunk* as the receiver hit the desk, followed by receding footsteps. While he waited, Zen looked round his office. Something about it was slightly different today, but he couldn't decide what it was.

The footsteps returned.

"There are three cards, dottore. A Luger 9mm pistol in the name of Miletti Ruggiero, issued 27 04 53. Then Santucci Gianluigi registered a rifle on 19 10 75. Finally Miletti Cinzia, a Beretta pistol, 4.5mm, dated 11 01 81."

Zen noted these details in the margin of his earlier doodles.

"Shall I send a written copy up to your office, dottore?"

"No! Definitely not. I've got what I wanted. Much obliged."

He hung up, studying the information. Ruggiero's Luger would be war loot, belatedly registered once the menace of an armed Communist insurrection had faded. That might possibly have done the damage to Valesio's head, at close range. So might Gianluigi's hunting rifle, for that matter. But he didn't really believe any of it, not for a moment.

He got an outside line, dialed the courthouse, and asked to speak to Luciano Bartocci. While he waited, he looked round his office with a deepening frown, trying to track down the detail which had been altered. What *was* it? The filing cabinet, the coat stand, the rubbish bin, that big ugly crucifix, the photograph of Pertini, the calendar? Of course, the calendar! Someone had thoughtfully turned the page to March and now the glossy color photograph showed the Riot Squad drawn up in full battle gear in front of their armored personnel carriers.

"Yes?"

"Dottor Bartocci? It's Zen, at the Questura."

"Finally! I've been trying to get hold of you since yesterday afternoon! Where have you been?"

"Well, I was—"

"Listen, there've been developments. Come and see me at once."

"Patrizia Valesio has been here. She claims that—"

"*I've already seen her. This is something else. Be here in twenty minutes.*"

Outside, the weather was hazy and dull. In the parking lot between the Questura and the prison Palottino had taken a break from polishing the Alfetta to chat with a pair of patrolmen. He looked hopefully at Zen, who waggled his finger and walked off up the street.

It was market day, and the wide curving flight of steps leading up to the center was lined with flimsy tables covered with kitchenwear and watches and clothing and tools and toys. Music blared from a stall selling bootleg cassette tapes. The traders called like barnyard cocks to the women moving from one stand to the next, uncertain which to mate with.

". . . at prices you simply won't believe . . ."

". . . never before in Perugia . . ."

". . . thanks to the miracle of American technology . . ."

". . . ever wears out I will pay you twice the . . ."

"*Socks! Socks! Socks!*"

". . . one for thirty thousand, two for fifty . . ."

A man sitting on a three-legged stool emptied a dustpan full of rubbish over his suit and then removed it with a battery-powered mini-vacuum cleaner. On the wall behind him the name UBALDO VALESIO appeared over and over again in large black capitals. It was a notice board devoted exclusively to funeral announcements, and the lawyer's death was well represented. There were posters signed by his partners, by the local lawyers' association, the Miletti family, various relatives, and of course his wife and children. The wording changed slightly, depending on the degree of intimacy involved, but certain formulas recurred like the tolling of a bell:

". . . *an innocent victim of barbarous cruelty* . . ."

". . . *tragically plucked from the bosom of his loved ones by a callous hand* . . ."

". . . *a virtuous and well-respected life extinguished by the criminal violence of evil men* . . ."

The morning session at the courthouse was in full swing, and the halls and corridors were crowded. Luciano Bartocci's office was tall and narrow, with bookshelves that seemed to lean inward like the sides of a chimney as they rose toward the distant ceiling. Two lawyers were facing the magistrate across a desk that occupied most of the floor space. One was clearly asking some favor on behalf of a client: bail or a visitor's pass or access to official files. Meanwhile the other lawyer was growing impatient with Bartocci for allowing himself to be imposed upon in this way by his pushy and unscrupulous colleague instead of attending to *his* utterly reasonable request for bail or a visitor's pass or access to official files. In the end Bartocci solved the problem by shooing both of them out of the office and leading Zen downstairs.

"There's something I want you to hear."

He took him to a room in the cellar of the courthouse where phone taps were carried out. A bank of reel-to-reel tape recorders lined the wall. A policeman wearing headphones was monitoring one of them. He jumped slightly as Bartocci touched his shoulder.

"Morning, Aldo. Can you play us that recording I was listening to earlier?"

"Right away." He selected a tape from the rack and threaded it onto a spare machine.

"This was monitored late yesterday afternoon on the Milettis' home phone," the magistrate explained to Zen. "That's why I've been trying to get hold of you."

The technician handed Zen a pair of headphones and started the tape. There was a fragment of ringing tone and then a voice.

"Yes?"

"Signor Miletti?"

"Who is this?"

"Go to the bottom of the hill, on the corner of the main road. There's an empty bottle lying in the gutter. Smash it open. Go quickly, before the cops beat you to it."

The caller had a thick, raw Calabrian accent.

"The time for games is over. You have three days to do what we say, otherwise we'll do to your father what we did to Valesio. Only more slowly."

The tape ended there. Zen removed the headphones. "What was in the bottle?"

"A letter."

"What did it say?"

"That's what we're about to find out. Thank you, Aldo!"

As they walked back upstairs Bartocci went on, "Pietro Miletti has agreed to see me. I'm expecting him shortly and I'd like you to be present. We've just time for a coffee."

They went to a tiny bar in Piazza Matteotti. The only other person in the bar was a woman eating a huge cream-filled pastry as though her life depended on it.

"I had a phone call from Antonio Crepi," Zen remarked casually.

"Really?" Bartocci's voice, too, was carefully expressionless.

"He knows we had lunch."

"I'm sure he does. In fifteen minutes he'll know we've had coffee, too."

"What did you make of Patrizia Valesio's story?" Zen asked.

The magistrate shrugged. "It doesn't get us anywhere. A hostile Public Prosecutor would make mincemeat of her. The distraught widow trying to assuage her grief for her husband's death by carrying out a vendetta against the Miletti family, that kind of thing. But this letter is another matter."

It took Zen a moment to see what Bartocci was getting at. "If they try to fake a letter from the kidnappers, you mean?"

Bartocci nodded between sips of coffee. "They can't fake it well enough to fool a forensic laboratory. I'm surprised they haven't realized that. So this meeting with Pietro Miletti may well prove decisive. That's why I want you to be there."

The eldest of the Miletti children seemed as unlike the others as was possible. Short and plump, with receding hair and a perpetually peeved expression, Pietro looked at first sight like an English tourist who had come to complain about his belongings being stolen from his hotel room, full of righteous indignation about Italy being a den of thieves and demanding to know when the authorities proposed to do something about it. From his tweed jacket to his patterned brogues he looked the part perfectly: not the usual designer mix from expensive shops in Milan or Rome, but the real thing, as plain and heavy as Zen imagined the English climate, character, and cuisine to be.

Bartocci introduced Zen as "one of the country's top experts on kidnapping cases, sent here specially by the Ministry to oversee the case."

Pietro Miletti was politely dismayed. "I understood this was to be a private meeting."

"Nothing which is said in this room will go any further," Bartocci assured him. "We are here simply to discuss what measures to take in the light of recent developments. Please be seated."

After a moment's hesitation Pietro leaned his rolled umbrella and leather briefcase against the desk and sat down. Bartocci took his place on the other side of the desk. There was no other chair, so Zen remained standing.

"Now then," the magistrate continued smoothly. "I understand that in the course of a telephone call yesterday afternoon the kidnappers informed you of the whereabouts of a letter from them, and that this letter was subsequently recovered. You've brought it with you, I take it."

"Not the original, no."

Bartocci glanced at Zen before replying, "A copy of the letter is of very little use to our scientific experts."

"I haven't brought a copy."

Bartocci gestured impatiently. "Excuse me, dottore. You haven't brought the original letter, you haven't brought a copy. Would you mind very much telling me what you *have* brought?"

Pietro Miletti opened his briefcase and took out a sheet of paper, which he offered to the magistrate. "I've brought a memorandum prepared from the original letter, itemizing every relevant piece of information it contained."

Bartocci made no attempt to take the paper. "Dottore, I strongly resent the assumption that anybody is in a position to dictate to me what is or is not relevant to a case I am investigating. If you are not prepared to let me see the original letter, then this pretense of cooperation becomes a farce and I see no point in continuing it."

Pietro Miletti's short laugh sounded unpleasantly arrogant and mocking, although it might equally well have been nervous in origin. "I'm afraid that's impossible."

"Impossible? Allow me to remind you that you are head of the family in your father's absence. Nothing is impossible if you want it."

"No, no, I mean it's literally impossible. The letter no longer exists."

Bartocci shot Zen a triumphant glance. So the Milettis *had* realized the threat to their schemes which the fake letter would pose and had no intention of letting them see it!

Pietro balanced the sheet of paper on his knees. "I should explain that although part of the letter was dictated by the kidnappers, most of it was written by my father. It was a personal letter addressed to his family, and like any personal letter it was not intended to be read by outsiders. It was, besides, a very long, rambling, and really rather distressing document.

Distressing for the evidence it provided of my father's state of mind, I mean. The strain and anguish of his long ordeal has clearly had a terrible effect on him. Naturally no reasonable person would wish to hold him accountable for what he wrote, but certain passages nevertheless made very disturbing reading."

Zen gazed up at the shelves loaded with rows of books as uniform as bricks.

"He accused you of having abandoned him," he said. "He recalled the innumerable sacrifices he has made on your behalf and reproached you for not being prepared to help him in his hour of need. He compared your behavior unfavorably with that of his kidnappers."

Pietro Miletti looked round in amazement. "How do you know that? It isn't possible! Unless . . ." An idea flared up in his eyes for a moment and then went out.

"Such letters resemble one another," Zen explained. "Like love letters."

"Ah, I see." Pietro had lost interest again. "Yes, he said all that. And more."

Bartocci was staring angrily at Zen, who suddenly realized that he had made the mistake of speaking as though the letter really existed, as if the kidnapping was genuine.

The magistrate rapped on his desk. "What became of the letter?" he demanded.

"We burned it."

"You *what?*"

"My father specifically forbade us to communicate any of the information it contained to the authorities, or to cooperate with them in any way whatsoever. That position received the strongest support from various members of the family, and it was only by strenuous and prolonged efforts that I have been able to persuade them to let me bring you this memorandum, which contains, as I've said, all the relevant items in the letter."

Zen suddenly understood that Bartocci had some move in mind, something which he was keeping up his sleeve for the moment.

"And what are these 'relevant items' you mention?" the magistrate asked, deliberately postponing this initiative.

Pietro Miletti picked up the paper again and began to read in a calm, confident voice, a voice that was accustomed to being obeyed, that had never needed to make a fuss. The full ten billion lire, in well-worn notes, not consecutively numbered, was to be made ready for delivery immediately. An untapped telephone number was to be communicated to the gang, who would use it to pass on further details, identifying themselves by the same method they had used with Valesio. The police were not to be informed of any of these arrangements or to be involved in the payoff in any way. Failure to comply with these instructions would result in the immediate death of the victim.

"And what do you intend to do now?" Bartocci asked when Pietro had finished.

"We shall obey, of course. What else can we do?"

"What you've been doing for the past four months! Stalling for time, crying poor, haggling over every lira."

Pietro Miletti replaced the sheet of paper carefully in his briefcase. "That'll do, Bartocci. We already know what our enemies say about us."

An effortless hardening had taken place in his tone. He got to his feet and looked at both of them in turn.

"Do you know why kidnapping flourishes here in Italy? Perhaps you think it's because we're saddled with a corrupt and inefficient police force directed by politically biased career judges lacking any practical training whatsoever. That is certainly a contributing factor, but similar conditions exist in other countries where kidnapping is almost unknown. No, the real reason is that in our hearts we admire kidnappers. We don't like successful people. We like to see them brought low, made to suffer, made to pay. They used to call Russia an autocracy moderated by assassination. Well, Italy is a plutocracy moderated by kidnapping."

"How do you propose to raise the money when for the past months you've been claiming that it just wasn't possible?"

But Pietro Miletti had no further interest in the exchange. "That's our affair."

"There's always SIMP, of course," Bartocci insinuated.

Miletti's eyes flicked over the magistrate contemptuously. "Yes, there's still SIMP left to bankrupt. And no doubt some people would be very glad to see that happen. But if our company ever does go under, those are the very people who are going to moan loudest."

"What about this untapped telephone number the kidnappers have asked for? How are you going to communicate it to them?"

"If I told you that, I doubt whether the number would remain untapped for very long. We're paying an extremely high price to get my father back. We have no intention of putting the success of that operation at risk because of the usual bungling by the authorities."

"I take it you've asked for guarantees," Zen put in quietly.

Pietro Miletti turned at the door. "What guarantees?"

"How do you know your father is still alive?"

"We just got a letter from him!"

"But how do you know *when* he wrote it? You should make it a condition of payment that the gang supplies a Polaroid photograph of your father holding the morning's paper on the day the drop is made. That will incidentally also establish that the people you're dealing with have still got possession."

"Possession of what?"

His tone was reasonable and polite, a senior manager seeking specialized information from a consultant.

"The negotiations for your father's release have been very drawn out," Zen explained. "It may well be that the original kidnappers couldn't afford to wait so long. It would depend on their financial situation, how the other jobs they're involved in are going. If they need some quick cash, they may have sold your father to another group as a long-term investment."

Pietro Miletti repeated his short laugh. "My God, are we talking about a business in secondhand victims?"

Luciano Bartocci had been shuffling papers about noisily on his desk in an attempt to disrupt this exchange in which he had no part to play. "There is just one other thing . . ." he began.

But Pietro Miletti cut him off. "But what does it matter, after all? We don't care who we pay as long as we get my father back."

"But you wouldn't want to pay one gang and then find that they'd sold your father to another, would you?"

"There is just one other thing," the magistrate repeated impatiently. "When the payoff is made, one of the people present will be Commissioner Zen."

Bartocci might previously have had some difficulty in making himself heard, but now he instantly had the total attention of both men. It was so still in the room that it seemed the three had suspended their dealings by mutual consent in order to catch the barely audible undulations of a distant ambulance siren.

"You must be crazy," Pietro Miletti said at last.

The young magistrate did actually look slightly mad. His eyes were bright with determination, his face flushed with a sense of the risks he was taking, and the stillborn smile twitched away at the corner of his mouth.

"Should you refuse to cooperate," he went on, "I must warn you that as of this evening each member of your family and household staff will be under surveillance twenty-four hours a day by a team of Commissioner Zen's men from Rome."

Bartocci gave Zen a long, level look, daring him to deny it.

"Naturally this flurry of police activity will get into the newspapers. The kidnappers will quite possibly call off the whole operation."

"How dare you, Bartocci?" Pietro Miletti's voice was quiet and curious. Despite its rhetorical form, the question seemed to have real meaning. "How dare you make my father a pawn in your games?"

The investigating magistrate steepled his fingertips judiciously. "Dottore, we are all here in our official capacities. You represent your family. Commissioner Zen and I represent the State. As such, our duties are clearly laid down in the Criminal Code. They are to investigate crimes, prevent them from being carried out, discover the guilty parties, and take any further steps to uphold the law. In our official capacities that is *all* that we need do. But we are not simply judges or police officials, we are also human beings, and as human beings we sympathize deeply and sincerely with the terrible situation in which the Miletti family find themselves, and wish to do everything possible to bring it to a swift and satisfactory conclusion. At the same time, we cannot ignore our duty. And so, after long and careful deliberation, we have arrived at a compromise between the action we must take in our official capacities and our natural wish to avoid hindering your father's release in any way. It is this compromise which I have just outlined to you. I believe that you would be well advised to accept it."

Pietro Miletti shook his head slowly. "How can you even consider putting my father's safety at risk in this way?"

"There is no risk," Bartocci assured him. "No risk whatsoever. Isn't that so, Commissioner?"

Zen's mouth opened and closed soundlessly. *You bastard,* he was thinking. *You shifty little bastard.*

But Pietro Miletti was not interested in Zen's opinion.

"The kidnappers have just given us quite explicit instructions not to involve the police in any way, yet you claim that we can send a senior officer along on the payoff itself without there being any risk!"

Bartocci waved the objection aside. "They won't know that he's a police official."

Pietro Miletti stood staring intently at the magistrate. "Why, Bartocci? You're going to put my father's life at risk, alienate half the city, all for what? What's in it for you? Why are you prepared to play such a desperate game, to put your whole future in jeopardy like this?"

"How dare you threaten me?" Bartocci shot back.

After a moment Pietro shrugged and turned away. "I shall have to discuss the whole matter with the rest of the family."

"Since when has the Miletti family been run as a cooperative?" Bartocci jeered.

"I shall contact you tomorrow morning."

"You'll contact me by three o'clock this afternoon," the magistrate insisted. "Otherwise I shall have no alternative but to allow Commissioner Zen to put his men in position."

Bartocci made Zen sound like a mad dog he was managing to restrain only with the greatest difficulty.

Pietro Miletti turned in the doorway. "Needless to say, if we do agree to a police presence at the payoff, the responsibility for the consequences of that decision will be on your heads. You might like to think about that before committing yourselves to this course of action."

"I tell you there isn't the slightest risk!"

"That's what they told Valesio."

As the door closed, Zen let out a breath he realized he had been holding for a long time. And to think he'd been agonizing about what line to take on Bartocci's conspiracy theory! No need for that now. Henceforth, as far as the Milettis were concerned, Zen was Bartocci's accomplice, the henchman whose men were to be used to enforce their enemy's will.

"You're prepared to go, I suppose?" The magistrate spoke with a studied casualness Zen found insulting.

"It's my job. But I would have preferred to know you were going to do it."

Bartocci laughed boyishly. "I didn't know I was going to do it myself until it happened!"

He walked over to one of the shelves on the far wall and took down a large file box. Zen thought he was going to be shown some decisive new piece of evidence, but Bartocci simply reached through the space left vacant on the shelf and with a grunt of effort manipulated a lever. There was a loud metallic click and the whole section of wall swung outward.

"It was this business about the letter that decided me," the magistrate continued as a widening slice of the outside world appeared in the gap. "Clearly the reason they claim to have burned it is simply that they realize it would be too risky to let us examine it."

The view expanded as he pushed the twin doors fully open. There was a small balcony just outside the hidden window, now inaccessible and covered with pigeon droppings.

"So according to the Milettis, what have we got?" Bartocci asked rhetorically, counting off the points on his fingers. "One telephone call which could easily have been faked from any pay phone, a letter which no one outside the family has seen, and a payoff which will supposedly take place once arrangements have been made over a secret telephone number. If I hadn't insisted on your going along on the drop, we would have absolutely no proof that it had ever taken place! It's a conjuring trick! The money which has suddenly and mysteriously become available simply vanishes into thin air and Ruggiero Miletti magically reappears. And from that moment on there would be absolutely no way of ever proving that the whole thing had been faked. No, this payoff is our last chance, and one that I wasn't prepared to let slip."

They stood gazing out at the few early swallows looping around in the hazy fragrant air.

"It's all coming together!" Bartocci muttered excitedly, as though to himself. "So many separate bits of evidence all pointing in the same direction. Yes, it's coming together!"

Despite his lingering feeling of resentment, Zen watched the young magistrate with an almost fatherly tenderness. He knew that he was feeling what Zen himself had felt often enough in the past, on one fateful occasion in particular: *This time the bastards are not going to get away with it.*

5

Smiling! Everyone was smiling
and applauding! The chubby balding presenter was smiling, the
blond starlet was smiling, the famous politician was smiling, the
best-selling journalist was smiling, while the clean, well-drilled
young people dancing around them were smiling hardest of all.
Even the balloons they released as they gamboled about seemed
to have a sleek benevolent look about them as they rose, passing
a shower of confetti as dense and continuous as the applause on
its way down.

"Make me a coffee, will you?"

The barman dragged himself away from the knot of men
deep in conversation about the price fetched by a piece of land
across the road.

"And not even big enough to have a decent crap on!" he
hurled over his shoulder before turning to jab a finger at Zen.

"Coffee?" he demanded accusingly.

Zen popped two motion-sickness pills out of their plastic nests
and put them in his mouth. One to two, the box said. Better safe
than sorry.

On the way back to his conversation the barman punched a button on the television and suddenly they were in Texas, where folk lived and loved fit to bust and discussed it all in idiomatic but poorly synchronized Italian. When the call finally came, it took Zen several moments to realize that the phone wasn't ringing in Sue Ellen's en suite boudoir but in the dingy poolroom at the end of the bar, where a pack of the local rogue males was playing pool. He just managed to beat one of them to the receiver.

"*Avellino.*"

He had the list of the First Division schedules ready. The Avellino team were at home to the champions.

"Juventus."

There was a loud clack behind him as one of the players sent the white hurtling down the table, scattering the colors.

"*Take the Cesena road. Stop at the sign 'Sansepolcro one kilometer.' At the base of the pole.*"

The line went dead. A moment later he heard the characteristic click as the interception machinery disengaged.

Outside it was pitch dark and spitting with rain. The Fiat sedan parked in the piazza looked ridiculous with a yellow child's cot strapped to the roof, but this had seemingly been stipulated by the gang to make it easier for them to identify the car.

Zen climbed into the front seat on the passenger side. "Take the Cesena road," he instructed.

The faint light from the dashboard caught a gold filigree earring spelling *Ivy* in flowing script. The earring was typical of its wearer's taste, he thought. It was presumably real gold, yet it somehow contrived to look brash and cheap, like junk jewelry trying to make up in flash what it lacked in value.

When the Fiat had emerged from the gateway of the Miletti villa at five o'clock that afternoon, Zen had been astonished to find that his driver for the ransom drop was to be Silvio's secretary, Ivy Cook. He had been waiting there since hearing from Bartocci less than an hour earlier that the kidnappers had been in touch and the car would be leaving as soon as it got dark. Pietro had finally agreed to Zen's presence, on condition that there was no contact until the payoff actually began, so during the intervening forty-eight hours he had had nothing to do with the case beyond arranging for the ransom money to be photographed and finalizing the arrangements for collecting

Ruggiero when he was released. The family's passive resistance continued right up to the last moment: Zen was not permitted to set foot on Miletti soil but had to wait for the Fiat in the street, beyond the imposing wrought-iron gates. He'd had plenty of time to speculate about who else would be in the car. He thought he had covered every possibility, but the Milettis had amazed him.

But if the Milettis had scored a point with their choice of driver, Zen felt that he got one back when Ivy named their destination: the country bar, unearthed by Lucaroni, where Ubaldo Valesio had gone to receive the phone calls from the gang. On the assumption that the kidnappers might use the same initial rendezvous, Zen had informed Bartocci, who had authorized a wiretap. The resulting tapes would be voiceprinted and compared with existing samples.

The headlights of the Fiat swept from one side of the narrow winding road to the other, picking out an area of plowed field, a thicket of scrub oaks with last year's brown leaves still clinging to the branches, an ancient wooden cart fitted with modern truck tires, an abandoned barn covered with posters for a dance band called "The Lads of the Adriatic," a dirt track leading off into the hills. Ivy drove steadily but not too fast, and thanks to the pills he had taken Zen was not worried about the prospect of nausea. He even felt a rather pleasant sense of detachment from what was going on, almost as though everything around him were happening on television and the barman might switch to another channel at any moment. Perhaps it was just due to the way he'd been sleeping lately—restless, shallow sleep full of dreams which never seemed to work themselves out properly, leaving him half-enmeshed in their elaborate complexities even after waking. In the morning his head felt as if the cast of a soap opera had moved in uninvited during the night, and the effort of following their interminable dreary intrigues left him mentally soiled and worn, less refreshed than when he'd gone to bed.

Or was it simply fear? For he was acutely aware that Ubaldo Valesio had waited in that bar, used that phone, and then walked out of that door, got into his car, and never returned. Bartocci might be convinced of his conspiracy theory, but Zen just couldn't take it seriously, much as he would have liked to. He had never taken part in a ransom drop before, but he knew what an extremely delicate moment it was. In a way it mirrored the original kidnapping itself, and carried almost equal risks for everyone concerned. It was a time when nerves were tense and misunderstandings costly or even fatal, a time when anything and everything might go wrong.

He turned slightly so that he could see Ivy out of the corner of his eye. She didn't look frightened, but neither did she look as though she was faking anything. There was tension in the lines at the corners of her mouth, but also determination and a sense of great inner strength. Ivy Cook wouldn't crack easily, he was certain of that.

"Is it far now?" he asked.

"About ten minutes."

Her strange deep voice pronounced the words like a parody of someone from the Trento area, where the warm and cold currents of Italian and German meet and mingle.

"What are we supposed to do when we reach the Cesena road?" she went on.

It seemed to take him an age to remember. "We have to find a sign beside the road reading 'Sansepolcro one kilometer.' I suppose they've left another message there."

"It's like a treasure hunt."

When he had met Ivy at Crepi's dinner party her appearance had struck him as so willfully bizarre that he had written it off as a freak effect, as though all her luggage had been lost and she'd had to raid the oddments put aside for collection by the missionary brothers. But evidently her appearance that first evening had constituted a rule rather than an exception. Tonight's color scheme was more somber but just as tasteless: chocolate-brown slacks, a violet pullover, and a green suede jacket.

"You're English, then?"

The association of thought was clear only to him, luckily!

"My family is. I was born in South Africa. And you're from Venice, I believe?"

"That's right. A district called the Cannaregio, near the station."

A fine rain blurred the view.

"Have you lived in Italy for long?"

Ivy turned on the wipers. "Years!"

"How did that happen?"

"I was on a tour of Europe. People take a couple of years off, buy a camper and explore the world, then they go back home, get steady jobs, and never leave South Africa again. I just didn't go home."

A patch of lights off to the right revealed the presence of a town which slowly orbited them and disappeared into the darkness again. Side roads came and went, labeled with the names of famous cities: Arezzo, Gubbio, Urbino, Sansepolcro. Then the road stretched away before them again, bare and gleaming and straight and dark, like a tunnel. . . .

"What?"

Ivy was looking at him with a peculiar expression. He realized that he had just murmured something under his breath.

"Nothing."

Jesus, what was in those capsules? He hadn't even needed a prescription to buy them. Surely they were just like aspirin? The government should step in, warn people, ban the things.

He had said, "Daddy?"

Then reality moved so fast that by the time he caught up it was all over and they were parked on the curb. Replaying the sequence, he realized that Ivy had braked hard, the car swerving slightly on the slick road, then backed up. Now she was looking at him expectantly.

"Yes?" he said.

She pointed out of the window. "Isn't that it?"

He looked out and saw the sign.

Outside, it was cold and blustery. Droplets of water gusted against his face. The base of the sign pole was concealed in a clump of long brown grass. A large spider's web strung between the base of the sign and the pole bellied back and forth in the wind, the spider itself clinging fast to it.

Beneath the strands of dead grass his fingers touched something hard. He pulled out an empty pasta box sealed at one end with industrial adhesive tape. The damp cardboard showed a picture of a smiling mother serving a huge bowl of spaghetti to her smiling husband and two smiling children. *"Get this fabulous apron absolutely free!"* exhorted a slash across the corner of the packet.

"Is everything all right?" Ivy had the door open and was leaning out, looking impatient.

"I'm just coming."

He tried to strip off the tape, but it was too tough and his fingers were numb and he couldn't find where it began. When he got back to the car, Ivy took it from him and opened the other end. Why hadn't that occurred to him?

She pulled out a cassette tape and pushed it into the car's tape deck. After a short hissy silence there was the usual voice.

"Play this tape once only, then put it back where you found it. At the Sansepolcro turn-off take the road to Rimini. When you reach the crossroads beyond Novafeltria stop and wait."

There was the sound of a car behind them and it suddenly became very light. Then a figure appeared on Ivy's side and rapped on the window. She opened it.

"See your papers?"

The Carabinieri patrolman had the raw look of a recruit freshly dug up from one of the no-hope regions of the deep South and put through the human equivalent of a potato-peeling machine. The uniform he was wearing seemed to have been assembled from outfits designed to fit several very different people: the sleeves were too long and the neck too wide, while the cap was so small it had left a pink welt around his forehead. He scrutinized the documents as if they were a puzzle picture in which he had to spot the deliberate mistakes. Then he looked suspiciously around the car.

"Having problems?"

"Just stopped for a look at the map," Ivy told him.

"It's illegal to park on the curb except in case of emergency."

"I'm sorry. We were just leaving."

The patrolman grunted and walked back to his vehicle. Ivy started the engine.

"The tape," Zen reminded her. "We've got to put it back."

They sat and waited. Fifteen seconds. Thirty seconds. The headlights behind showed no sign of moving.

Zen palmed the cassette and got out. He walked to the verge and made a show of urinating. After a few minutes the Carabinieri vehicle revved up and screeched off down the road. Zen slipped the tape back into its nest of grass at the foot of the pole and hurried back.

It was only when they reached the turning to Sansepolcro that he felt something hard underneath his foot.

"Damn! I forgot to put the box back."

"Does it matter?"

There was no telling, that was the problem. *"The responsibility for the consequences will be on your heads,"* Pietro Miletti had said. All along Zen had been haunted by the idea that he might make some blunder which would hang over him for the rest of his life, yet here he was behaving like a dope addict. He felt an overwhelming desire for a cigarette, but Ivy was a nonsmoker and he had agreed not to smoke in the car.

The road to Rimini bypassed the town and in a few moments they were out in the wilds again, laboring up a steep, tortuous medieval track on which modern civilization had done no more than slap a layer of asphalt and a route number. The ascent was arduous and prolonged, twisting and turning upward for more than twelve kilometers to the pass, almost a thousand meters high. The starkness of the landscape revealed by the headlights penetrated the car like a draft. Zen sat there unhappily taking it all in. He didn't much care for nature in the raw: it was messy and wasteful and there was too much of it. This was a fertile source of incomprehension between him and Ellen. The wilder and more extensive the view, the better she liked it. "Look at that!" she would exclaim, indicating some appalling mass of barren rock. "Isn't it magnificent?" Zen had long given up trying to understand. It all came of her being American, he supposed. Americans had more nature than anything else except money, and they got pretty excited about that too.

To take his mind off the scenery outside, he looked at his companion. Part of the oddness of her appearance, he realized abruptly, came from the fact that she didn't look like a woman so much as a rather inept female impersonator. Not that there was anything butch about her. On the contrary, it was precisely the excessive femininity, laid on with a trowel as it were, that created the effect of someone pretending to be a woman, someone in fact rather desperately hoping to be taken for one. But this desperation was perhaps understandable. Certainly her role in the Miletti household appeared to be anything but feminine. She was evidently their drudge, used for tasks which no one else was prepared to take on. Typically, it was Ivy, he'd learned, who had been sent to answer the gang's summons to collect the letter from Ruggiero.

"Are you married, Commissioner?" she asked suddenly.

It was the first remark she had volunteered all evening.

"Separated. And you?"

"What do you think?"

Zen had no idea what he was supposed to think. Eventually Ivy herself seemed to sense the need for an explanation.

"My association with Silvio rather precludes marriage."

They rounded yet another bend, the headlights sweeping over a bald expanse of stricken scanty grass. It had started to rain more heavily.

"If you really want a cigarette very badly I think on the whole I should prefer you to have one," Ivy told him crisply.

He gave an embarrassed laugh. "Is it that obvious?"

"Well, you keep fiddling with the ashtray and pushing the cigarette lighter in and out. Just open the window a crack."

"What about the rest of the Milettis?" Zen asked as he lit up. The wind burbled at his ear like frantic drumming.

"What about them?"

"How do you get on with them?"

She took a moment to think. "They find me useful, on occasion."

"I remember how Cinzia Miletti treated you that evening at Crepi's."

"Poor Cinzia!" murmured Ivy. "She's terribly unhappy."

"Isn't it a bit of a strain, though, living in the same house with them?"

"Oh, I don't. They would never stand for it. Ruggiero would have a fit!" She laughed gaily, as though Ruggiero Milietti's attitude was frightfully amusing. "No, I have a little flat of my own," she went on, "although I have been spending more time than usual at the villa since the kidnapping. But I'll be very glad when it's all over and things return to normal."

"But you and Ruggiero don't get on?"

That gave her pause.

"Ruggiero doesn't have a very high opinion of either foreigners or women," she said at last. "That places me at something of a disadvantage."

Zen didn't reply at once. He was at the honeymoon stage with his cigarette, listening to the nicotine marching through his blood.

"And yet you're looking forward to his getting back? I don't understand."

"It's a question of the lesser of two evils. At least we all know where we are when he's around. For the last few months everything has rather fallen apart. Ruggiero kept all the reins in his own hands, you see. So in a sense I'll be glad when he is back, despite his attitude toward me."

He decided to risk a shot in the dark. "Is it your relationship with Silvio that Ruggiero objects to?"

"Why do you say that?" she snapped.

Clearly this was a sensitive topic. Then she laughed, as if to cover her outburst.

"Anyway, you're quite right. Silvio is a very complex and tormented personality, someone who has great difficulty in coming to terms with the demands of life. I help to ease that burden for him. Ruggiero doesn't accept that, perhaps because it would mean accepting responsibility for the way his son has turned out."

"In what way is he responsible?"

The cigarette had suddenly turned bad on him.

"Oh, in all sorts of ways. He was responsible for Loredana's death, for one thing. Silvio has never really recovered from that."

"What happened?"

"Ruggiero was driving her back from Rome late one night, and somehow the car left the road and ended up against a tree. Loredana was killed instantly. Ruggiero's legs and collarbone were broken and he was trapped in the wreckage for almost seven hours, pinned beside her corpse. He was discovered the next morning by a boy on his way to school. People say he has never been the same since. Loredana moderated the violence of his personality, or at least sheltered the children from it. After her death they certainly took the full brunt, Silvio in particular. He was only thirteen and he'd been particularly close to his mother. Her death was a great blow to him, and I imagine Ruggiero handled it in exactly the wrong way, telling him to snap out of it, stop sniveling, that sort of thing. He's a man who has crushed all softness in himself, so why should his son be indulged, be allowed to cry and display his grief, be stroked and cuddled and consoled when *he* never was? Of course, Cinzia suffered terribly too. The others rather less, I think. Pietro was old enough to cope better, Daniele too young to understand."

Zen wound down the window and let his half-smoked cigarette be sucked out into the airstream. The conversation no longer kept the landscape at bay but intensified it, showing its desolation to be a reality not merely natural but also human.

Eventually the car slowed to a halt. The rain was now pelting down, covering the windows with a coat of water as thick and opaque as glycerine. The headlights created a luminous swath ahead of the car, but nothing was visible except a variety of shapes which obstinately refused to become more than that. Ivy turned off the engine. Nothing moved outside, and the only sound was the steady metallic drumming on the roof of the car.

"Why did you ask if I was married?" Zen asked.

She glanced at him briefly. "I don't know. To break the silence, I suppose. Why does one ask anything?"

He leaned closer to the window, but his breath fogged the glass and he saw even less.

"Well, in my case it's usually to get information out of people," he said. "Then after a while it becomes a habit, like those teachers who speak to everyone as though they're five years old."

"I suppose I was trying to make you seem more human. I'm frightened of the police, you see, like most people. Almost as frightened as I am of these kidnappers."

The minutes slipped away, their passage recorded with unnecessary precision by the digital clock on the instrument panel.

"They don't ever attack people, do they?" It sounded as though the reality of what they were doing had come home to her for the first time.

"Who, the police?" he joked.

She did not reply. Her expression showed that she no longer had any time for jokes.

"No, it's completely unheard of," he assured her. "All they want from us is the money that's in the trunk. We won't even see them, probably."

The rain ceased abruptly, as if it had been turned off.

"I think I'll just stretch my legs a bit," Zen announced.

The whole night was in motion. Gusts of wind almost knocked Zen off his feet, but they were mere glancing blows. The serious punches were being thrown somewhere in the clouds swirling about overhead.

The visibility had improved slightly. What he had taken to be a gate turned out to be a wall, the hump on the ground nearby a heap of gravel, and the massive bulk on the other side of the road a barn whose gable end still bore the faded icon of a helmeted Mussolini and the slogan, "*It is important to win, but still more important to fight.*"

At first the sound might have been thunder, or an animal. Next a light appeared, and a moment later a shape swept out of the night, big as a centaur, its blinding eye striking him, along with something solid. Then it was gone, leaving a weighted envelope lying on the wet black asphalt at his feet.

Back in the car, he showed Ivy the black-and-white Polaroid photograph the envelope contained.

"That's Ruggiero," she confirmed.

The picture showed a stocky man with a shock of white hair and the typical Umbrian moon-face, wearing a checkered shirt open at the neck and holding up a newspaper. He looked resentful and slightly embarrassed, like an elderly relative who had grudgingly agreed to pose in order to keep the peace at a Christmas party. The photo might have been modeled on those sent by the Red Brigades during the Moro kidnapping, but where those middle-class intellectuals had used the center-left *Repubblica* to mark the date, Ruggiero Miletti was holding the *Nazione*, just the kind of paper which a bunch of good Catholic boys like the kidnappers would choose.

Ivy took the envelope from him, widened the opening, and extracted a small coil of blue plastic strip about a centimeter wide. A message had been punched out in capital letters with a labeling machine: *PUT PHOTO AND MESSAGE BACK IN ENVELOPE LEAVE HERE FOLLOW BIKE.* Zen slipped the photo and tape back into the envelope, opened the door, and let them drop out.

"Right, well, let's get on with it."

For the next three hours the motorbike led them a nightmare chase over more than a hundred kilometers of mountain roads that were often little more than channels covered by scree and loose gravel, furrowed by rainwater and ridged by surfacing strata of rock. All they ever saw of their guide was a faint distant taillight, and then only rarely, at irregular moments after long periods of doubt when it seemed that they had lost the scent, made the wrong decision at some unmarked junction up in the stormy darkness.

Driving demanded constant attention. Only a narrow range of speeds was viable. Below that the car risked bogging down in the mud or grounding on an obstacle; above it the tires might lose adhesion on the continual twists and turns or clifflike descents, or one of the vicious potholes or rock outcrops might rupture the suspension or pierce the oil pan. They barely exchanged a word. Ivy had her hands full with the driving, and although Zen soon gave up trying to follow their route on the maps he had brought with him, which proved to bear only a partial and rather disturbing resemblance to the landscape, he kept up a pretense of poring over them to try to assuage his guilt at being a mere passenger, unable to share her burden. And still the faint red light up ahead came and went by fits and starts, leading them on across gale-swept open moorland, through massively still pine forests, up exposed dirt tracks and over passes whose names had vanished with the inhabitants of the farms where until a few decades earlier generation after generation of human beings had eked out lives of almost unimaginable deprivation.

It was after midnight when a set of headlights appeared behind them, flooding the interior of the car with light. Ivy squinted, trying to shut out the glare that made her task still more difficult.

"What's going on?" she asked edgily.

"They must be sandwiching us in."

Then everything happened at once. The motorbike slowed so that for the first time they could see the outlines of the rider, a derelict farmhouse appeared in its headlight beam, and the car behind them started flashing its lights. Figures appeared in the road ahead, waving them into the yard of the farmhouse. Their faces were black and completely featureless except for two oval eye slits, the heads hooded, the bodies shrouded in shiny waterproof capes. There were piercing whistles, then a thump as they opened the trunk, where the money was packed in cardboard boxes wrapped in plastic rubbish bags. With a series of dull thuds and strangely intimate bumps the unloading began, punctuated by more of the raucous inhuman whistles which finally blew away the remaining shreds of doubt in Zen's mind about the reality of the kidnapping. That eerie keening, like the cry of a great predator, was used by shepherds to communicate across the vast windswept spaces in which they lived and worked. No outsider, no amateur, could ever fake that sound.

The rain, which had been easing, suddenly began to pour down again, spattering in big gobs all over the glass around them. In the still warmth of the car, bathed in the calm green glow of the instrument panel, it was impossible to imagine what conditions were like out there. Inside and outside seemed so absolutely separate that once again Zen, drifting off into pleasantly dopey inattention, had the sensation of being a mere spectator of screen images, some television documentary about hardy men who did dangerous work for big money.

"What's happening?" Ivy whispered fearfully.

The activity at the back of the car had ceased and silence had fallen.

"They're probably checking the money."

He could make out nothing in the darkness around the car. The headlights revealed only the worn flagstones of the farm-yard, the archway into the cow barn on the ground floor of the house, the crumbling steps that had once led to the living quarters above. The door was staved in and torn half off its hinges in what looked to have been an act of senseless violence. At one of the gaping window frames, a bit of ragged cloth flapped spasmodically in the wind.

"Perhaps they've gone," Ivy whispered.

He didn't answer.

"Can't we go?"

"Not yet."

Even before he finished speaking, the driver's door was wrenched open and a powerful torch shone into their faces.

"Out! Out! Out!"

The next instant the door behind him opened too, transform-ing the interior of the car into a wind tunnel. A huge hand grabbed Zen's shoulder and dragged him outside, shoving him up against the side of the car. Light hit his face as hard as the stinging raindrops. Then it abruptly disappeared, and all he could see were entrancing colored patterns chasing one another about the glowing darkness like tropical fish.

The pain was so unexpected, so absolute, that he had no name for it and fell over without a sound, like a baby, too shocked to make any fuss.

"Fuckarse cocksucker of a cop!"

He could just make out the outline of the figure in front of him, sweeping its heavy cape to one side, then something smashed into the side of his head. They've shot me, he thought. They've shot me like they did Valesio. They're proving they exist, punishing us for not believing in them, like gods.

With a strange detachment he noted the final sequence of events: the roar of a car engine nearby, the hiss of a tire skidding past, the oddly painless blast which ended it.

Like Trotsky and the iceman, he thought. Of course! The solution was so obvious, so satisfying, that there was no need to try to understand it.

The cold was no problem, either. Obviously if it weren't cold the ice would melt. In fact some of it already had. The cold smooth surface pressed to his face was covered in water. As for the purposeful darkness tugging at his clothing, this must be the wind in the tunnel. The only question, in fact, was where his father had gone, why he had left him alone. Perhaps there was an answer to that, too.

Once again he called weakly, but as before there was no reply. He lay back, stretched out on the cold wet tracks, waiting for the express to Russia to come and chop off his head.

The telephone call could hardly have been vaguer.

"One of your men is by the farm up above Santa Sofia there, above the river, up there on the way to the church."

The voice was male, adult, uneducated, with a strong Calabrian accent. It was 1:43 A.M. and the duty sergeant wasn't quite sure whether he was dealing with a wrong number, a hoax, or an emergency. But the next words made sense all right.

"You'd better go get him before he dies."

The Carabinieri station was at Bagno di Romagna, a small town high up in the Apennines on the borders of Tuscany and Emilia-Romagna. The locals were a staid lot; the sergeant, who was Sicilian, privately thought them dull. They were not given to silly pranks at any time, let alone at a quarter to two on Sunday morning. So what the hell was going on?

He phoned his provincial headquarters at Cesena, who called regional headquarters at Bologna, who checked with their opposite numbers in Florence before confirming that no member of the force had been reported missing on either side of the Apennines. Better get out there and have a look just the same, Cesena told him with a hint of malice. Even down there in the coastal flatlands it was a wild night. They could imagine what conditions must be like up in the mountains, having done their stint in the sticks at one time or another.

Out *where*, though? Apart from the undisputed fact that the farm in question was "up," the sergeant knew only that it was near a village called Santa Sofia, above a river and on the way to a church. He pored over his 1:100000 maps and finally selected four possibilities. If none of them proved correct they would have to wait until dawn and call out a helicopter, by which time it would probably be too late. The wind howled about the building, driving rain against the shutters.

They had been at it for over two and a half hours before the searchlight finally picked out the slumped body in the yard of an abandoned farm at over a thousand meters on the slopes of Mount Guffone. The young private at the wheel let out a gasp of surprise.

"You see?" the sergeant exclaimed triumphantly.

His relief at not having been made a fool of was matched by his curiosity to find out who the devil he was, this man lying chest down on the wet flagstones, face turned to one side as though asleep. There were some quite nasty-looking cuts on his head, and the sergeant was a bit apprehensive about turning him over.

He would never forget that time when a corporal had been machine-gunned in an ambush on a country road near Palermo. He'd been found lying face down too, and the only sign of what had happened was a slight discoloration on the back of his jacket, as though some of the red dye from the trimming had leached onto the body of the black fabric. But when they had turned him over there was a sound like a fart and all his insides had spilled out, bits that weren't meant to be seen and which God accordingly hadn't bothered to finish off like the rest. Amazingly, nothing had seemed to take any notice! The sky was still blue, the sun still shone, somewhere nearby a lark gibbered away. Only he had watched, fascinated, as the pool of blood collecting around the spilled innards suddenly burst its confines and set off down the road, finding its way slowly and with difficulty, its bright fresh surface soon matted with dust and drowning insects.

"What we going to do?" asked the young private, a little concerned at the way his superior was acting.

"Do? Well, we've got to find out who he is, haven't we?"

In the end it was all right. There were no visible injuries at all, in fact. The man even mumbled something, and his eyelids flickered for a moment without opening.

"No wonder no one knew about him!" the sergeant exclaimed as he studied the identity card he had found in the man's wallet. "He's not one of ours at all. Stupid bastard didn't know the difference."

Or more likely didn't care, he thought. The glorious traditions of the Service meant nothing to scum like that.

The man lying at their feet mumbled something again.

"Did you hear what he said?" the sergeant asked.

The private made a face. "I'm not sure. It sounded like he said, 'Daddy.'"

Yellow light, stale warmth, a pervasive scent of chemicals: the contrast with his earlier dips into consciousness was total.

Zen was sitting on a stool under a bright light in a small white-curtained cubicle, thinking about Trotsky and the iceman. With his open-necked shirt, his air of dejected exhaustion, and the newspaper spread open on his knee, he might almost have been a kidnap victim waiting to have his existence confirmed by means of a Polaroid photograph. But in fact he was waiting for a different kind of photograph, a different kind of confirmation.

Trotsky and the iceman had been his attempt to solve the problem of why he was still alive despite having been shot in the head. Leon Trotsky protested with his dying breath that he had been shot, not stabbed, even though his assassin had been caught with the ice pick still in his hand. Zen's mistake was less excusable, since all he'd suffered were a few hard kicks to the head and shoulders.

Then the wind and the darkness and the sense of utter abandonment had unlocked a memory which had already put in a passing appearance earlier that night. It was a memory he hadn't known he had, and even now he knew very little about it beyond the fact that it involved him and his father and a railway tunnel. He didn't know where or when it had happened. There they were, the two of them, walking into the tunnel. It must have been on a main line, because there were two sets of tracks, and the mouth of the tunnel had seemed to him—he might have been five, six?—bigger than anything he had ever seen, bigger than anything he had known could exist.

They had gone a very long way into the tunnel. He hadn't wanted to, but since his father was holding his hand it was all right. When he looked round he found that the tunnel mouth had become a little patch of brightness, quite faint and very far away. The silence echoed with large drips falling from the invisible curved mass above. A dank wind poured past them, forcing them deeper into the solid darkness ahead.

Meanwhile his father, his voice reverberating in a way that hinted at the extent of the invisible spaces about them, told him about the tunnel, when it was opened and how long it was and how deep below the surface. He pointed out the sloping white stripes on the walls, whose incline indicated the nearest of the niches providing protection for tracklayers who otherwise might end up under the wheels of one of the expresses which thundered over these rails, bound for famous foreign cities.

Then, without warning or explanation, the warm grip on his hand disappeared and the soothing voice fell silent.

It was only for a moment, no doubt, as adults measure time. It must have been a joke, a little trick of the kind fathers like to play on their children, toying idly with their power, whimsical tyrants. Zen knew that it had been a joke, because when it was over his father laughed so much that the laughter echoed around them as they started back toward the light. It had sounded almost as though the tunnel itself were enjoying some deeper, darker joke whose significance not even his father had fully understood.

An unshaven young man in a white coat slouched into the cubicle and handed Zen three dark rectangular sheets of plastic.

"No fractures."

Zen held the X-rays up to the light. They looked as dubious as the photographs which are claimed to prove the existence of a spirit world: swirls and patches of white suspended in a gray mix.

"You're sure?"

It certainly hurt badly enough. But perhaps pain was no guide. Oddly enough, the worst was his shoulder, where the man had seized it to pull him out of the car.

"It's only bruised," the orderly insisted. "But next time take it easy, eh? I might be in the other car."

Zen had told them he'd been involved in a traffic accident, which had got a good laugh all around when it emerged that he was from Venice. For want of practice, Venetian drivers are proverbially considered the worst in Italy.

He left the hospital and began to walk slowly along the boulevard leading back to the center of Perugia. The morning was quiet and warm. The storm had blown itself out, leaving the sky pearly. There was a mild southerly breeze. A few people were about, returning from church or walking home with a newspaper or a neatly wrapped pastry. He was glad that he had dismissed Palottino, although the Neapolitan had made it clear that he strongly disapproved of this mania for walking. He had driven up to collect his superior from the Carabinieri post where he and his rescuers had returned as soon as Zen had recovered enough to assure the sergeant that he didn't need to call an ambulance. As soon as they'd reached Bagno di Romagna, Zen had phoned Geraci, whom he'd left holding the fort, and inquired about Ivy Cook. His greatest worry was that somehow his presence had compromised her, that he might have another corpse on his hands, another death on his conscience. But Geraci was able to reassure him: Ivy had arrived home three hours earlier, badly shocked but unharmed. The money had been taken but there had been no communication from the kidnappers.

While Zen had waited for his driver to arrive, his hosts had tried politely to find out who he was and what he'd been doing. But he had remained deliberately vague. Even with Palottino he had been discreet, not mentioning what the kidnapper had said to him. And when his driver had asked, "You don't think they knew?" Zen had pretended not to understand.

"Knew what?"

"That you were from the police."

"How could they?"

Palottino had no answer to that, any more than Zen himself, though the question had tormented him for the whole drive back to Perugia. How could they have known? But they had, that was certain. *"Fuckarse cocksucker of a cop,"* the man had said. So they knew that their orders had been deliberately disobeyed. These men had already killed for less. The thought of what they might even now be doing to Ruggiero Miletti took the sparkle and warmth out of the morning and made Zen realize how exhausted he was.

As he passed through a small piazza there was a shout and a boy appeared at a window holding a bulging plastic shopping bag which he let drop to a friend who stood in the street, arms raised to catch it. But it was immediately obvious that the bag was too heavy and was falling much too fast. At the last moment the boy below stepped back. The bag struck the pavement, bounced, and then the boy caught it and peeled away the bag to reveal a football, which he struck in a high curling shot which ricocheted off the wall slightly to the left of a priest who had emerged from the large church which closed off one end of the piazza. Through the open door Zen could just make out the huge ornate crucifix above the high altar.

"How could they?" he murmured to himself again.

6

Twenty-four hours later he was sitting out on the Corso. It was brilliantly sunny and the atmosphere was charged with vitality and optimism. One bar had even gone so far as to put a few tables outside, and on impulse Zen settled down to enjoy the sunlight and watch the show on the Corso. This broad flat street was the city's living room, the one place where you didn't need a reason for being. Being there was reason enough, strolling back and forth, greeting your friends and acquaintances, window shopping, showing off your new clothes or your new lover, occasionally dropping into one of the bars for an espresso or an ice cream.

For fifteen minutes he did nothing but sit there contentedly, sipping his coffee and watching the restless scene around him through half-open eyes: the tall bearded man with a cigar and a fatuous grin who walked up and down at an unvarying even pace like a clockwork soldier, never looking at anybody; the plump, aging idler in a Gestapo officer's leather coat and dark glasses holding court outside the door of the café, trading secrets and scandal with his men friends, assessing the passersby as though they were for sale, calling after women and making hourglass gestures with his hairy gold-ringed hands; a frail old man bent like an S, with a crazy harmless expression and a transistor radio pressed to his ear, walking with the exaggerated urgency of those who have nowhere to go; slim Africans with leatherwork belts and bangles laid out on a piece of cloth; a gypsy child sitting on the cold stone playing the same four notes over and over again on a cheap concertina; two foreigners with guitars and a small crowd around them; a beggar with his shirt pulled down over one shoulder to reveal the stump of an amputated arm; a pudgy shapeless woman with an open suit-case full of cigarette lighters and pirated cassettes; the two Nordic girls at the next table, basking half-naked in the weak March sun as though this might be the last time it would appear this year.

At length Zen lazily drew out of his pocket the three items of mail he had collected from the Questura. One, he found, was a letter stamped with the initials of the police trade union and addressed to Commissioner Italo Pompeo Baldoni. He replaced this in his pocket and picked up a heavy cream-colored envelope with his own name printed on it and a postcard showing the Forum at sunset in gaudy and unrealistic color with a message reading, *"Are you still alive? Give me a ring—if you have time. Ellen."*

Putting this aside, he tore open the cream-colored envelope. It contained four sheets of paper closely covered in unfamiliar handwriting, and it was a measure of how relaxed he was that it took him the best part of a minute to realize that he was holding a photocopy of the letter written by Ruggiero Miletti to his family three days previously.

My children,

If I address you collectively, it is because I no longer know who to address individually. I no longer know who my friends are within the family. I no longer even know if I have any friends. Can you imagine how bitter it is for me to have to write that sentence?

I remember one day, long ago, when I was out hunting with my father. He showed me a farmhouse, a solid four-square Umbrian tenant farm, surrounded by a grove of trees to break the wind. Look, he said, that is what a family is. Have many children, he told me, for children are an old man's only defense against the blows of fate. I obeyed him. In those days children did obey their fathers. But what has it availed me? For you, my children, my only defense, my protection against the cruel winds of fate, what do you do? Instead of sheltering me, you turn to squabbling among yourselves, haggling over the cost of your own father's freedom as though I were an ox brought to market. It is not you but my kidnappers who care for me now, who feed me and clothe me and shelter me while you sit safe and secure at home trying to find new ways to avoid paying for my release!

No doubt this tone surprises you. It is incautious, ill-advised, is it not? I should not permit myself such liberties! After all, my life is still in your hands. If you treat me like an ox to be bargained for, I should be the more careful not to annoy you. Swallow your pride and your anger, old man! Flatter, plead, ingratiate, and abase yourself before your all-powerful children! Yes, that is what I should do, if I wished to match you in devious cunning. But I don't. You have refused to pay what has been asked for my return, but if you knew what I have become, a fearless old man with nothing left to lose, you would pay twice as much to have me kept away! Whatever happens now, my children, we can never be again as we were. Do you imagine that I could forgive and forget, knowing what I know now, or that any of you could meet my eye, knowing what you do? No! Though the ox escape the ax, it has smelled the blood and heard the bellows from the killing floor, and it will never be fooled again. I know you now! And that knowledge is lodged in my heart like a splinter.

Nothing remains to me of the pleasures and possessions of my old life, which you now enjoy at my expense. I have been forced to give them all up. But in recompense I have received a gift worth more than all the rest put together. It is called freedom. You laugh? Not for long, I assure you! For I shall prove to you how free I am. Not free to indulge myself, to be sure. Not free to come and go, to buy and sell, to control my destiny. You have taken those freedoms from me. Losing them was bitter, and my only reward is that now I can afford the one thing which, with all my wealth and power, I've never been able to permit myself until this moment. I can afford to tell the truth.

I have paid dearly for it, God knows! More than a hundred and forty days and nights of anguish to soul and body alike! My leg, which never mended properly after the accident, has not liked being cooped and cramped and bound, and like a mistreated animal it has turned against its master, making itself all pain. Yes, I have paid dearly. So let me show you what I mean by freedom. Let me tell you what I know, what I have learned. Let me tell each of you the truth, one by one.

I shall start with you, Daniele, my youngest, the spoiled darling of the family. What a beautiful child you were! How everyone doted on you! Whatever happened to that little boy, all cuddles and kisses and cheeky sayings that set everyone in a roar? Back in the sixties, when the kids seemed to think of nothing but politics and sex, I used to pray God almighty that my Daniele would never turn out like that. It never occurred to me that he might turn out even worse, a vain spineless ignorant lout with no interest in anything but clothes and television and pop music, who would be rotting in jail on a drugs charge at this very minute if his family hadn't come to his rescue. But when his own father needs to be rescued little Daniele is too busy to lift a finger, like the rest of you.

Cinzia I pass over in silence. Women cannot betray me, for I have never made the mistake of trusting them. The worst she could do was to bring that Tuscan adventurer into the family, after which none of us has had a moment's peace. I can't claim to have had my eyes opened to your true character, Gianluigi, for they were wide open from the first. Ask my daughter what I said to her on the subject! However, she preferred to disobey me. You think you're so clever, Gianluigi, and that's your problem, for your cleverness gleams like a wolf's fangs. I at least was never fooled. Take this business of the Japanese offer, for example. Certainly the scheme you've worked out is very cunning. I really admire the way the structure of the holding company leaves you in effective control of SIMP through an apparently insignificant position in the marketing subsidiary. I suppose you thought that old Papa Miletti would be too stupid to spot that, wrapped up in a lot of technical detail about nonvoting share blocks and nominal investment consortia? Of course the kidnapping has given you an extra edge. All you had to do was to hold up the negotiations until I got desperate and then bully me into authorizing the Japanese deal on the pretext of raising money to pay for my release! In fact the kidnapping was very well timed from your point of view, wasn't it? It wouldn't even surprise me to learn that you set it up! Beware of in-laws, my father used to say, and when he's Tuscan into the bargain I think we can expect just about anything.

But none of this really bothered me, it was all piss in the wind as long as my eldest boy was true. Silvio I had already written off, of course. I realized long ago that the only thing he has in common with other men is the prick between his legs. God knows why—I made him the same way I made the rest of you—but there it is. There's nothing manly to be expected from Silvio, unless that English witch knows something the rest of us don't. Let him spit in her mouth and breed toads. He'll never breed anything else, that's for sure.

But Pietro made up for all that and for everything else, or so I thought. The rest of you, choke on this last gobbet of my scorn! If he had been loyal I should never even have mentioned these playroom plots and tantrums of yours. But what I didn't realize, and what has proved the gravest shock to me, is that Pietro is the worst of you all. What a superb role he has invented for himself, the English gentleman who stands disdainfully aside from the vulgar squabbles of this Latin rabble to whom he has the misfortune to be related! I've got to hand it to you, son, you're the only one who really managed to deceive me, the only one who could break your father's heart. And you have, you have. The others I could afford to lose, but you were too precious. I loved you, I needed you, and blinded by my love and need I never looked at you closely enough. But now I have, and I see what I should have seen a long time ago, the selfish, arrogant, unscrupulous fixer who has been quietly feathering his nest in London for the past ten years at our expense after turning his back on us as though we weren't good enough for him, who couldn't even be bothered to come home during this ordeal but just flew over on a weekend return when the mood took him, when he had nothing better to do, like the tourist he is!

Gianluigi likes to think he's clever, but you really are,

Pietro. You've inherited my brains and Loredana's morals, God rest her. You don't instigate plots, because you know that plots get discovered. Instead you manipulate the plots of the others to your own ends, playing one off against the others, letting them waste their energies in fruitless rivalries while you look on from a safe distance, waiting patiently for the moment to make your move, the day when I drop dead and you can come home and claim your own.

Well, there we are, I've had my say. How do you like yourselves, my children? When you lie down tonight in your soft warm beds, think over what I have said. Get up and look at yourselves in the mirror. Look hard and long, and then think of your father lying here tormented with cold and pain and fear and despair.

What follows has been dictated by my kidnappers. For some reason they seem to believe that you will obey them this time. First then, the full ransom of ten billion lire is to be paid immediately, in well-worn consecutively numbered notes. . . .

There, at the foot of a page, the photocopy broke off. Zen inspected the envelope. It was of distinctive hand-laid paper with a griffin watermark and had been posted in Perugia the previous Thursday.

"A personal and private family letter," Pietro Miletti had said. "A rather distressing document, not intended to be read by outsiders. Certain passages made very disturbing reading." Yes, it was easy to see why the family, who as Antonio Crepi had put it couldn't agree which sauce to have with their pasta, had found no difficulty in agreeing to burn Ruggiero's letter on the spot. But this made it so obvious who had sent this stolen copy that he was astonished that it had been sent at all. When Pietro Miletti thought Zen must have seen the letter, he'd burst out, "But that's impossible!" Then an idea had occurred to him, and he'd added, "Unless . . ." Now Zen knew what he had been thinking. If the letter had been burned in the presence of all the members of the family immediately after being read, then the copy could only have been sent to him before they received it, by the person who went to pick it up.

But that could wait. He tucked a two-thousand-lire note under one of the saucers on the tray and went inside the café to phone.

Luciano Bartocci wasted no time on small talk.

"Jesus Christ almighty, Zen, what the hell do you think you've been up to?"

Zen was too taken aback to reply.

"The family are absolutely incensed, and quite naturally so. How could you do such a thing? I thought you were an experienced professional or I'd never have let you go in the first place! Don't you realize the position this puts me in?"

"What are you talking about?"

"I'm talking about what happened at the payoff, when you were beaten up. The woman who drove you told us all about it. It's no use trying to cover up now."

"I'm not trying to—"

Another voice broke in: *"Maurizio? Maurizio, is that you?"*

"It's in use!"

"What? Who is this?"

"This line is in use, please put your phone down."

There was a grunt and a click.

"Hello? Hello?"

"I'm still here."

"The man who assaulted you called you a dirty cop, or words to that effect. So evidently they knew who you were. You must have given yourself away somehow. It's absolutely unforgivable."

"They didn't find out from me!"

"Then how did they find out? Eh?"

Zen decided to give him the only answer he had been able to come up with: "Perhaps one of the family told them."

"That's nonsense! Why should they do that?"

Zen put a hand out against the wall to steady himself. "How should I know? The last I heard, you thought they were behind the whole thing!"

"Now listen, that's enough! I don't want to hear any more talk of that kind. This is a very serious situation you've got us into. There's no telling what the gang may do now."

Zen lowered the receiver and stared at it, as though its expression might help him understand the words it was uttering.

"Hello? Hello?" Bartocci's voice emerged in a comically diminished squawk, like a character in a cartoon film.

The white-jacketed waiter scurried into the café carrying a tray on which a pyramid of empty cups and glasses was balanced. "Four coffees, two beers, one mineral water!" he called to the barman.

With a sigh Zen raised the receiver again. "Look, dottore, they knew I was there before I got out of the car, before they'd even had a glimpse of me."

"I'd like to believe you, Zen. But it's just not credible. If the gang knew you were coming, why did they allow the payoff to continue? Why didn't they just cancel the whole thing?"

"I don't know. All I know is that my presence was no surprise to them, but they decided to go ahead with the drop anyway. And afterward they went to the trouble of calling out the Carabinieri to make sure I didn't die of exposure. So there's no reason to suppose that they're going to do anything stupid now."

"You and the kidnappers seem to have a perfect understanding, Zen. They know what you're doing, you know what they're thinking. I just hope you're right. For all our sakes."

The line went dead.

A young man with a bad case of acne approached and pointed at the phone. "You finished?"

Yes, he had finished. There was no point now in telling Bartocci about the letter he had received. Now that his elaborate conspiracy theory had been proved false, the young magistrate had embraced orthodoxy with all the fervor of a recent convert. He was no longer interested in sensational revelations by anonymous informants.

As Zen turned away he glanced at the calendar hanging beside the phone and suddenly realized what day it was. After all these years it had finally happened! Come hell or high water, he'd always managed to get his mother a present and to send her some flowers and a card. But this time he had forgotten, and tomorrow was her birthday.

Then he remembered Palottino. Since arriving in Perugia, the Neapolitan's days had been spent slumped in the Alfetta in the parking lot beneath Zen's office window, reading comics and listening to the radio. Yet poor Luigi was not happy. He longed for action, yearned to be trusted with high responsibilities, to undertake prodigious feats requiring a cool head, a stout heart, and nerves of steel. Delivering a gift to Zen's mother didn't quite come into that category, but it was better than nothing. Besides, he could pick up some Nazionali from Zen's tame tobacconist as well. So it remained only to find a suitable present.

Forty minutes later Zen was not only still empty-handed but beginning to panic. He had to get something, and quickly, before the shops closed for lunch. It was at this point that he found himself face to face with Cinzia Miletti, stunningly somber in gray woolen slacks and a jacket of silver fox.

"Show me where they hit you!" she cried. "Oh, is that all? Surely it should be worse. But you must tell me all about it, I can't wait to hear. Come and have coffee, I'm just on my way home, you can help carry this. Gianluigi's away and if that woman thinks I'm going to wait one second longer . . ."

Zen murmured something about needing to find his mother a present, and Cinzia immediately took charge.

"Well now let's see, it should be something traditional, characteristic, typical of the region. Embroidery, for example, or does she collect ceramics? I know, chocolates! We'll get her a nice presentation pack, that one over there, local pottery."

Even once Cinzia had bullied one of the assistants into offering Zen a discount, the item she had selected came to about three times what he had reckoned to spend, but he paid up. A few minutes later the Deruta vase containing about half a kilo of assorted chocolates had been arranged on the rear seat of the Volvo and he was sitting in the front watching Cinzia tear up the parking ticket which had been tucked under the windshield wiper.

Cinzia Miletti drove as she talked, in a prolonged spasm characterized by unpredictable leaps and frenetic darts and swerves, serenely unimpressed by the existence of other traffic. The drive to her house just outside Perugia was littered with miraculously unachieved collisions. Cinzia naturally also talked as she drove. If anything, she seemed even more voluble than usual, which Zen put down to embarrassment. With her father's fate still undecided, he had caught her cruising the shops as though she hadn't a care in the world. She was therefore at some pains to explain that the only reason she had come into Perugia at all was that she had an appointment with Ivy Cook, of all people, who had telephoned her earlier that morning.

"I must see you urgently, she tells me, shall I come out there or could you meet me in town? So out of the kindness of my heart I agreed to come in."

The kindness of Cinzia Miletti's heart was a quality Zen had

considerable difficulty in imagining where Ivy Cook was concerned, but he found it easy enough to believe that in her
husband's absence Cinzia had been feeling bored and had
welcomed any excuse for going into Perugia.

"Did she say what it was about?"

"She didn't want to discuss it on the phone, that's all I know.
First of all I had the most awful trouble starting this thing. We
should never have got rid of the little Fiat we used to have which
started first time every time and if anything did go wrong you
could fix it with an elastic band or a bit of string Gianluigi used
to say, although personally I'm hopeless with machinery. Anyway, when I got to the café where we were supposed to meet
there's no sign of her! Well you can't get near her flat, they've
closed the street, they're turning the whole city center into a
museum, next thing they'll be charging admission and closing in
the afternoon. I had to walk all the way round there in these
shoes, they look good but believe me they're not meant for
walking, and in the end she's not even home. Have you ever
heard anything like it? I mean it's really just the most infuriating
thing conceivable, maddening, really."

They were driving through the suburbs in the valley far
below the ancient hill settlement forming the historic core of the
city. In the midst of a sea of concrete towers and slabs, the office
blocks and apartment buildings of the new Perugia, stood an
old stone farmhouse, squat and sturdy, with its attendant
chicken coops and vegetable garden, the walls dyed green by
years of sulfur sprayed on the vines running up to form a
pergola. Was this the one Franco Miletti had pointed out to his
son Ruggiero as an image of the family? If so, the protective
trees had gone, and the brutal buildings which had replaced
them would channel the wind more fiercely, not screen it.

They crossed the strip of wasteland underneath the motorway link that came tunneling and bridging its way through the
hilly landscape and entered a zone of fenced-off lots containing
warehouses and salesrooms, light industrial units and the offices
of small businesses. The whole area was no more that ten or
fifteen years old, straggling along either side of what had once
been a country road and ending messily with the shell of an
unfinished building of some indeterminate nature. Shortly
afterward Cinzia turned off to the left along a dirt road. High
fences marked the positions of villas hiding coyly behind rows
of evergreens. Guard dogs hurled themselves against the wire

and then chased the car the length of the property, barking frantically, while Cinzia told Zen how she had persuaded Gianluigi to buy a place in the country although he couldn't see the point but to her Nature was not a luxury but something fundamental, a source of sanity and order, did he understand what she meant?

They drew up in front of a pair of steel gates topped with spikes. While Cinzia searched the glove compartment for the remote control unit, Zen noted the heavy-duty fencing with angled strands of barbed wire at the top and electronic sensors at the bottom, and the video camera mounted on a pole just inside the gates. It was all brand new. The local security-equipment retailers had clearly done well out of Ruggiero Miletti's kidnapping. Bartocci should have noticed details like that, Zen thought. People don't go out and spend millions turning their homes into prison camps unless there is real fear in the air.

They were barely inside the front door when the elderly housekeeper appeared and told Cinzia that Signorina Cook had been looking for her.

"What?" shrieked Cinzia. "Here? But she must be mad!"

"She said you were supposed to meet her here. She waited about ten minutes and then left."

"What nonsense! Would I have bothered to go all the way into town if we had arranged to meet here?"

The housekeeper held up her hands in a conciliatory gesture and muttered something about a mistake. But Cinzia was not to be mollified.

"Oh no, she did it deliberately! Well, I'll teach her to play tricks on me!"

She strode to the telephone and dialed. After a moment or two she passed the receiver to Zen with an exclamation of disgust.

"Just listen to this!"

". . . *at the moment,*" Ivy's recorded voice said. "*If you wish to leave a message please speak after the tone.*"

"I'll leave her a message all right, when I see her," Cinzia exclaimed, slamming down the receiver.

She turned to Zen, her anger apparently gone. "I'm going to change. Look around, make yourself at home. Margherita, make us some coffee."

Zen stood there in the elegant and spacious sitting room,

listening to the insistent voices of the glass and steel coffee table supporting a spray of glossy magazines, the pouchy leather furniture over which a huge lamp on a curved stainless-steel pole craned like a vulture, the silver plates and the crystal bowls, the discreetly modern canvases, the shelves lined with works of literature, the expensive antiques, the handwoven rugs on the gleaming parquet floor, the baby grand piano with a Mozart sonata lying open on the stand, the fireplace piled high with logs. The view from the picture window showed a carefully landscaped garden, a swimming pool, a tennis court, and a field where a wiry old gardener in baggy peasant clothing and a felt hat was tending his master's vines and olives. Even nature was made to chatter.

"Ah, so you've found our little secret, with your policeman's flair!"

The room had as many entrances and exits as a stage set. Cinzia had appeared almost at his elbow. She picked up a small statuette which he hadn't been aware of before.

"But we didn't buy it from some grave-robber, you know. I mean that's totally wrong, taking the national heritage for your own selfish private use. But you see Gianluigi's cousin works in the museum and they've got so much stuff there they literally don't know what to do with it all, it just sits and rots in boxes in the cellar, no one ever sees it. At least here it's cared for, admired, which is what they would have wanted. Wonderful people, very sexual and full of life. I'm sure I have Etruscan blood in me."

She was wearing a short skirt with a big broad belt, a soft woolen pullover with a deep V-neck, and a double string of pearls. She had removed her shoes and stockings.

"This wood is magic," she exclaimed. "In winter it's warm and in summer it's cool, can you explain that? I can't, not that I want to. I hate explanations, they ruin everything. But you mustn't peek at my feet like that, poor horrible ugly deformed things."

She moved restlessly about the room, lifting and rearranging things without any evident purpose.

"Kant," she remarked, taking a book down from the shelf. "Have you read Kant? I keep meaning to, but somehow I never get around to it."

She curled up on the leather sofa that looked as comfortable as a bed and waved Zen into a matching armchair opposite.

"So your husband's away?"

"In Milan, lucky pig! Very urgent business which he'd been putting off until after the payoff. But there's no point in him being here anyway, as far as I can see. I mean there's nothing we can do, any of us. It's just a question of waiting."

Despite her alleged impatience to hear about his experiences on the night of the ransom drop, she made no attempt to refer to it again, launching instead into a blow-by-blow account of a film she had seen the preceding evening, going on to explain that she loved films, really loved them, that the only place to see them properly was the cinema, that her favorite was a wonderful old place in the center of town called the Minerva, and what a shame it was that no one went to the cinema anymore.

The housekeeper brought in the coffee on an ornate silver tray which she deposited on one level of the Scandinavian wall unit. *I've been in the family for generations*, said the tray, *so you can see that they're not just a bunch of jumped-up farmers like so many around these days. Quite so*, commented the wall unit, *but despite their solid roots these are modern progressive people with a truly cosmopolitan outlook.* Oh shut up, Zen thought. Just shut up.

"Is your husband's trip to Milan connected with this Japanese deal I've been hearing about?" he asked.

Cinzia's air of boredom deepened significantly. "He never discusses business with me."

And you would do well to follow his example, her eyes added, *because while I'm not very good at business there are other things that I am good at, very good indeed.*

A lanky girl with bad skin and a moody look walked in, strolled self-consciously over to the table, and took a tangerine from a bowl.

"Fetch me my cigarettes, will you, Loredana darling?" Cinzia asked her.

"Fetch them yourself. You could use the exercise."

Cinzia shot Zen a dazzling smile. "Do forgive her manners. It's a difficult age, of course. She'll start menstruating soon."

The girl flung the cigarettes at her mother.

"Much better talk openly about it!" Cinzia continued calmly. "There's no need for us women to be ashamed of our bodies anymore."

"It's not *your* fucking body," the girl shouted as she ran upstairs.

"She's a crazy mixed-up kid," exclaimed Cinzia, as though this were one of her daughter's main virtues. "At the moment she

keeps threatening to become a nun, if you please. My other
one's about somewhere too, little Sergio. He's a darling! Too
much so, in fact. I'm reading him the Greek myths at bedtime
and I just hope when we get to Oedipus the penny will drop. It's
perfectly normal at that age, of course. At least I haven't taught
him how to masturbate, like some mothers. Cigarette?"

As she leaned forward to offer them, her pullover bellied out
and he caught a glimpse of her breasts, almost adolescent in
size, but with large and prominent nipples.

"I've always tried to be an understanding parent," she continued serenely. "I treat my kids as friends and equals."

"Is that how your parents treated you?"

Cinzia appeared completely dismayed by this remark. "My
mother's dead!"

"I know, but what about your father? Did he treat you as an
equal?"

"Well, it depends what you mean. I suppose he does his best.
But take the business of Daniele's arrest, for instance. That was
typical. For years Father had been nagging away at him to take
some interest and prove he had the Miletti flair, yet as soon as
he tried to show a bit of initiative everyone got on their high
horse about it, Father especially, calling him a worthless junkie
and I don't know what else besides. It was so unfair, I thought.
I mean I suppose what the others were doing was illegal, but it's
not as if they were forcing anyone to take the stuff. If they
hadn't sold it, someone else would have. And as far as Daniele
was concerned it was just a business arrangement, nothing else.
He never actually took the stuff or got his hands dirty in any
way."

She rearranged herself in another pose, her legs curled
under her like a cat.

"As it was, the poor kid ended up losing everything. Not just
the money he'd invested but his allowance from Father as well.
Lulu's been helping him out, but it's still been very hard on him.
Now I don't call that being very understanding, do you? You'd
think people would be more tolerant with their own family."

Zen gulped down the rest of his coffee and announced that he
had to be going.

"Already?" Cinzia queried with a pout. "Why not stay to
lunch? Margherita's a wonderful cook."

Her disappointment appeared genuine, but he forced himself to phone Palottino. The family were absolutely incensed,

Bartocci had told him. If Zen had survived more or less intact all this time it was thanks to the instinct that was telling him to leave now.

"You still haven't told me about your adventure," Cinzia reminded him as they waited for Palottino to arrive. "It must have been terrifying. I think you're very brave. To sit in a car with that Cook woman for however many hours it was, I simply couldn't do it! Did you talk a lot? Did she talk about me? She must have. What did she say?"

"We didn't talk that much."

"Oh come on, I don't believe that! I know the woman. What did she say? Whatever it was I've heard worse. Tell me. What did she say about me?"

He looked away, out the window, then back at Cinzia. "She said you were terribly unhappy."

Her features abruptly slackened all over, making her look years older. "Unhappy?" It was a shriek. "She's crazy! I've suspected it for a long time, but now it's absolutely clear! Absolutely and totally clear, plain and evident for everyone to see."

She gripped Zen's arm tightly. "I ask you, do I look unhappy? Do I seem unhappy? Have I got the slightest reason in the world to be unhappy? Look at this house! Look at my husband and my children, look at my whole life. Then look at her! What has she got? Unhappy? What a joke!"

She walked away a little distance, then came back to him. "The truth is that she envies me," she went on more calmly. "She envies all of us, she's riddled with envy! That's the real problem. It's not me who's unhappy, it's her! She's projecting her problems onto me. I've read about it, it's a well-known thing that mad people do."

She shook her head and tried to smile. "I'm a little tense at the moment, with Gianluigi away and still no word about Father."

"I'm sure he'll be released very soon now," Zen said as reassuringly as he knew how.

But an oddly vacant look had come over Cinzia's features. Deafened by thoughts he couldn't begin to guess at, she hadn't even heard him.

Back at the Questura, Zen tried to put Cinzia Miletti out of his mind. He felt that a winning hand had been dealt him and that he had played it badly. In any case, it was too late now.

He stuck his head round the door to the inspectors' room. "Anyone know an officer called Baldoni?"

Geraci looked up. "Baldoni? He's in Drugs."

"Three-five-one," Chiodini chimed in without raising his eyes from his newspaper.

"Don't be stupid," Lucaroni told him. "This is three-five-one."

Chiodini stuck one fat finger thoughtfully up his right nostril. "Used to be three-five-one," he pronounced at last.

Lucaroni consulted the directory. "He's in four-two-five," he said. "Do you want me to . . . ?"

"That's all right," Zen replied. "I'll do it myself."

Baldoni was a pudgy balding man wearing a blue blazer with five silver buttons, a canary-yellow pullover, and a red tie. He was picking his teeth with a match while someone on the phone talked his ear off. When he hung up Zen handed him the letter.

"Fucking union." He frowned. "All they ever do is ask for money. The reason I joined was I thought they were going to get more money for me, not take it away."

"I'm on the Miletti kidnapping," Zen began.

Baldoni looked at him more warily. "Rather you than me."

"I understand that Daniele Miletti got himself into some trouble with your section some time ago."

Baldoni laughed briefly. "Got himself into it and got himself out of it."

He tried to sit casually on the edge of his desk, farted loudly, and stood up again.

"You know about the University for Foreigners?" he demanded. His tone was suspicious, as though the institution in question were missing and Zen was suspected of having stolen it.

"I've heard of it."

"Forget what you've heard. I know what you've heard. You've heard about this symbol of the brotherhood of man set in welcoming Perugia with its ancient traditions of hospitality, where every year bright-eyed bushy-tailed youngsters come from the four corners of the world to study Italian culture and promote peace and international understanding."

He looked intently at Zen. "You're not from round here, are you?"

Zen shook his head.

"In that case I can tell you that in my humble opinion this place is the meanest tightest little arsehole in the entire fucking country. International understanding my bum! Christ, the people in this dump are so small-minded they treat the folk from the village down the hill like a bunch of aliens. So why do they put up with the real foreigners? For one very simple reason, my friend. It's spelled m-o-n-e-y."

"And Daniele?" Zen prompted.

"Don't worry, I'm getting there. Now you also have to realize that the foreigners aren't like the ones you've heard about either. They used to come down from the North—German, Swiss, English, American. Girls, mostly. They came to read Dante, drink wine, sit in the sun, and get laid. But those days are long gone. Now the Arabs have moved in, because you-know-who in Rome has done a deal for oil rights, including a fat kickback for you-know-who, naturally. Meanwhile you and I get paid worse than his housekeeper, and the fucking union writes to ask *me* to send *them* money!

"So, anyway, all these Arabs start rolling up to learn engineering and dentistry and Christ knows what. Unfortunately the professors object to giving lessons in Arabic, so suddenly we've got hundreds of thousands of students who need to learn Italian. And where do they go? To the University for Foreigners, of course, right here in lovely medieval Perugia. Only these foreigners are a bit different from what we've been used to. Masculine like they don't make them anymore, don't give a fuck about Dante, don't touch alcohol, find it cold here after their own country, and are more interested in praying and politics than getting laid. Bright eyes and bushy tails are at a distinct premium among this bunch, and as for the brotherhood of man, their idea of that is that if someone disagrees with you, you kill him. Remember Ali Agca, the man who shot the Pope? He was here. Remember the Palestinian commando that murdered half the Israeli athletes at the Munich games? They trained at a farmhouse in the hills just outside Perugia. The Jihad Islamica suicide squads, the pro-Khomeini mob, the anti-Khomeini mob, KGB spies, Bulgarian hit men—you name it, it's been here. The Political Branch have installed a hot line direct to the Ministry's central computer in Rome and even so they can't keep up. At one time there were two and a half thousand Iranians alone in town. Their consul in Rome came up on an official visit last year and there was nearly a diplomatic incident when he got thrown out of the new university canteen he'd come to inspect. Turned out the last time the staff had seen him he was a student here and he'd made such an arsehole of himself they'd sworn they'd never let him back in!

"All right, so that's the new Perugia, crossroads of international terrorism. A big headache for the politicos upstairs, but what's it got to do with yours truly, you're no doubt wondering, or with Daniele Miletti for that matter. Well, terrorists need cash. The official ones get it from the government back home, the rest have to earn it. And there's no quicker way to make money than drugs, particularly if you happen to come from a country where the stuff is sold like artichokes. So we start to take an interest, and among other things we're passed the names of a couple of Iranians who make frequent trips back home by train. That's one hell of a way to travel to Iran, unless of course you want to avoid the screening procedures at the airports. The next time through we have them picked up and lo and behold they've got a suitcase full of heroin. So we get to work on them and forty-eight hours later we have the whole ring, including one Gerhard Mayer, twenty-nine, from West Berlin, their linkman into the local drug community. Which is where everything starts to fuck up, because the moment we turn our attention to Herr Mayer, he tells us that the money he used to pay the Iranians was put up by the son of a certain well-known local citizen."

"Daniele Miletti."

"You know the feeling? One minute I had a nice clean case busted wide open, stiff sentences all round, and bonus promotion points for yours truly. The moment that fucking kraut mentioned Miletti I knew I could kiss that sweet dream goodbye. We went through the motions and pulled him in, of course, but by the time the magistrate spoke to him Mayer had changed his mind. He'd never met Daniele Miletti, never seen him, never even heard of him. The kid was back home in time for lunch."

"And Mayer's statement?"

"Extorted under duress. Duress my bum! Mayer couldn't fucking *wait* to shop his rich young pal."

"What happened to Mayer?"

"He hopped on the first plane back to Germany."

Zen gazed at him, frowning. "They let him out? With a drug-trafficking charge hanging over him?"

Baldoni nodded. "Like I say, where the Milettis are concerned, rather you than me, my friend. Rather you than me."

■　■　■

By evening, Zen was beginning to feel rather like a hostage himself. He had spent the entire afternoon in his office, pacing from the desk to the window, from the window to the door, and back to the desk again. It was now over forty hours since the money had been handed over, but there had been no word of Ruggiero Miletti's release. Despite the fact that he was powerless to influence events in any way, Zen felt bound to remain on watch, like the captain of a ship. But in the end he could stand it no longer and went out for a walk.

The side streets through which he wandered at random were almost deserted. Occasionally his path crossed that of a couple walking home or a group of young friends going up to the center, and the brief appraising glances they gave him left Zen feeling obscurely ill at ease, underlining as they did his lack of purpose or direction. Thoughts flitted to and fro in his brain like swallows: phrases from Ruggiero Miletti's letter, an insinuation of Antonio Crepi's, something Ivy had said in the car, what Valesio's widow had told him, Luciano Bartocci's brisk new manner, Italo Baldoni's story, Cinzia Miletti's breasts. . . .

He felt simultaneously starved and stuffed, deafened and denied. It was the nature of the place, he thought, perched up there on its remote peak, its back turned to the world, all the more obsessed with its petty intrigues and scandals because it knew them to be of no interest whatever to anyone else. Nothing he had been told from the very first moment he had arrived in Perugia amounted to any more than salacious gossip, casual slanders, ill-informed rumors of no real value which elsewhere would never have reached his ears. But folk here were eager to let you into their neighbors' secrets, particularly if they thought it might distract your attention from their own. *"Mayer couldn't fucking* wait *to shop his rich young pal."* Yes, that was the style of the place. It was all a fuss about nothing, another example of the national genius for weaving intricate variations around the simplest event. Zen had always derived much amusement from Ellen's simpleminded approach to current affairs. Despite her intelligence, she could be quite amazingly naïve in her judgments. She seemed to believe that truth would prevail, so why waste time spinning a lot of fancy theories? Whereas Zen knew that truth prevailed, if at all, only after so much time had passed that it had become meaningless, like a senile prisoner who can safely be released, his significance forgotten, his friends dead, a babbling idiot.

But in the present case it was time to take a stand, to declare once and for all that this time at least the truth was as obvious and evident as it appeared to be. The crimes which had been committed were manifestly the work of hardened professionals who had no more to do with the incestuous dramas of this city than Zen himself. Any suggestion to the contrary was simply an excuse for the locals to settle a few scores with their neighbors.

Inevitably, his steps led him in the end to the Corso, where the evening promenade was in progress. People paraded up and down, displaying their furs and finery, hailing their friends, seeing and being seen, streaming back and forth continually like swimmers in a pool. Part of the street was thronged with teenagers, and more were arriving every instant on their mopeds. The males dominated, bold gangling youths in brightly colored designer parkas and jeans turned up to reveal their American-style chunky leather boots. They threw their weight about with boisterous nonchalance, while the girls, in frilly lace collars, tartan skirts, and colored stockings, looked on admiringly. One of the most prominent of them was a tall youth with the extravagant gestures and loud voice of an actor who knows his performance is going well. Only at the last moment, when he'd been recognized in turn, did Zen realize that it was Daniele Miletti.

"A very good evening to you, dottore!" Daniele called out in a bad parody of a Venetian accent. "So sorry to hear about your accident. Do try and take more care in future!"

He turned to explain the joke to his companions, who laughed loudly.

"Don't you dare beat me up, you nasty nasty man, I'm a policeman!" one of them shrieked in a mocking falsetto.

It was almost predictable. The young trendies of the soft Right, like their Fascist counterparts of half a century earlier, bragged about "not giving a damn." Nothing would do more to boost Daniele's status than to be seen showing off on the Corso while his father's life still hung in the balance.

Zen pushed on, understanding how Italo Baldoni must have felt when the young Miletti slipped through his fingers. Increasingly it seemed to him that there were people who needed to spend a few hours locked in a room with the likes of Chiodini. The trouble with the system was that they were the ones who never did.

When he reached the Questura, he had an irrational feeling

that something must have happened in his absence, simply because he hadn't been there, but he was wrong. He was back where he'd started, staring at the wall with nothing to do but wait. As his eyes fell on the crucifix he realized that he'd always loathed it, and in a small gesture of defiance he lifted it off its hook and set it down on top of the filing cabinet. Then he remembered the copy of Ruggiero's letter, and realized that there was something he could do after all.

"Seven double eight one eight."

"Good evening. This is Aurelio Zen. Am I disturbing you?"

"No, no. Not at all. Well, not really . . ."

Ivy sounded flustered. Had she already guessed why he was calling?

"I wanted to contact you this morning, but . . ."

"I was out. I'd arranged to meet someone."

"Yes, I know."

"You know? How?"

"I met Cinzia Miletti in town. She'd been waiting for you."

"Well I'd been waiting for her, too! We'd arranged to meet at her house."

"She told me that you phoned her and asked for a meeting in town."

"I really can't imagine why she should have said that, Commissioner. It's exactly the opposite of what happened. She phoned me and asked me to come straight over. She didn't say why, but obviously in my position . . ."

It occurred to Zen that while they were talking, any incoming call announcing Ruggiero's release would be blocked.

"Never mind about that," he said briskly. "There's something I want to discuss with you. It's about a letter I've received."

"A letter? What sort of letter?"

"I'd rather not discuss it on the phone. Do you think you could drop by my office? It won't take long."

"Well, it's a bit difficult. It's a question of the family, you see. I'm not sure they'd approve, just at present."

They'd approve still less if they knew what it was about, thought Zen.

"Perhaps later on, once this is all over."

"Very well."

He hung up, his hand hovering hopefully above the receiver. But the phone remained sullenly silent.

His suspicions were confirmed. The uncharacteristic fuss and fluster in Ivy's manner was surely a proof that she knew only too well which letter he was talking about and was in mortal dread of the family finding out.

He took out the letter and scanned the final lines again. That mistake was curious: "*. . . well-worn consecutively numbered notes . . .*" For a moment it had made him inclined to doubt the authenticity of the whole thing. But it was only a detail, and it didn't alter the fact that no one but Ivy could have done it. She must have taken the letter straight to a photocopy shop after breaking open the bottle which contained it, and then posted the copy to Zen immediately, before returning to the house, calculating that if the copy came to light, each of the Milettis would equally be under suspicion. But that calculation had gone up in smoke with the original letter, and since then she must have bitterly regretted her rashness. Why had she taken such a risk? Was it because she knew the Miletti family only too well and was determined that this time at least everything should not be conveniently hushed up? Had sending Zen the letter been her humble way of serving the great principle upon which Luciano Bartocci had now apparently turned his back, of not letting the bastards get away with it? At all events, she had committed no crime, so there was no reason for him to pursue the matter any further.

He sat there until his eyelids began to droop, then phoned the switchboard and told them that he would be at his hotel. There was no point in continuing his lonely vigil.

But why couldn't he rid himself of the eerie sensation that it had *already happened*, that everyone knew except him, that he was being deliberately kept in the dark?

He was in bed, in the room in Venice where he had spent his childhood, and he was still that child. A figure moved slowly through the uncertain light toward him, as faceless and monumental as Death in an old engraving. But he wasn't frightened, because he knew that it was all just a joke, a little comedy of the kind fathers like to play with their sons.

He'd always known his father would come back. Not that he'd ever admitted it before, even to himself. But nothing and no one could ever really convince him that a world where fathers just disappeared one day and never returned could be anything other than a pitiful sham, a transparent hoax. He had never been taken in, not really, not inside, but he'd known moments of doubt, so his delight and relief were unbounded now that he found his instincts had been right all along! For here his father was, sitting down beside him, hugging and kissing him, taking his hand again and laughing at the silly terrors his little game had aroused in his son.

The phone beside his bed rang. It was the duty officer on the intercept desk at the courthouse.

"We've just picked up a message on the Miletti family line, dottore. It was from the kidnappers. They've released Signor Miletti."

Thank God, Zen thought with obscure fervor. Thank God.

"Have you informed Dottor Bartocci?"

"Yes. The pickup arrangements are to be put into effect immediately."

"Where has Signor Miletti been released?"

"If you've got a pen I'll read the directions as they gave them to the family."

Zen scribbled the instructions on the back of an envelope. They were to take the road to Foligno, turn right just beyond Santa Maria degli Angeli, and drive until they saw a telegraph pole with a yellow mark. Here they were to turn left, then take the second right and go about a kilometer to a building site where Ruggiero Miletti was waiting, unable to move because of his bad leg. It was this problem which had led to the complex arrangements for picking up Ruggiero on his release. Normally kidnap victims are simply turned loose in the middle of nowhere and left to find their own way to the nearest house or main road. But since Miletti was immobilized it had been agreed that he would be fetched by a group consisting of Pietro Miletti escorted by Zen and Palottino in the Alfetta, with an ambulance in attendance in case Ruggiero required immediate attention.

After the events of Saturday night and Bartocci's angry phone call the previous day, Zen had half-expected to be rebuffed when he rang the Milettis. But Pietro, although cool, made no attempt to change the arrangements. Now that the family's fears had been proved groundless, the bungled payoff could be dismissed as just another example of clumsy incompetence on the part of the police, the latest in a long list of blunders.

Twenty minutes later the convoy set out. It was brilliantly sunny, as though summer had leapt forward a few months. People were moving more slowly and nonchalantly, without the pretext of a destination or purpose. They glanced curiously at the line of official vehicles which drove on the boulevard running along the lower ridges of the city, through a gateway, and down in a series of long lazy curves, dropping over two hundred meters to the valley floor. Shortly after passing the enormous domed basilica of Santa Maria degli Angeli, Palottino swerved across a patch of loose gravel into a side road. The land was dead flat, divided into large plowed fields almost devoid of trees. Modern brick and concrete duplexes squatted here and there along the road, each with a few rows of vines trained along wires suspended from concrete posts behind them. This would all have been uninhabited malarial marshland until the postwar boom made it worth draining. The road ran straight ahead, the telegraph poles passing at regular intervals to the right.

In the bright sunshine, the yellow splash of paint showed up hundreds of meters away. A farm track led off to the left opposite, flanked by deep drainage ditches. The fields appeared to have been abandoned, the broken stalks of the crop left to rot in a vast expanse of furrowed mud which the recent rains had reduced to a sticky mess. Could there really be a building site in the middle of this swamp? The possibility that the telephone call had been a hoax seemed to be getting more likely all the time.

The bleak landscape reminded Zen of something at once very recent and yet long ago, unreachably removed. Eventually he realized that the solution to this riddle was the dream he had had that morning. When the Germans invaded the Soviet Union in 1941, Mussolini thought the war would be over in a matter of weeks, and so that he could claim a share of the spoils for Italy he offered to send troops to the Russian front. The Germans had no illusions about the military effectiveness of their principal ally, and at first they agreed to accept only a few divisions of the Alpini, the specialist mountain troops who could hold their own with any in Europe. But that was not enough to give Mussolini the bargaining leverage he wanted. He insisted on sending more, and so 230,000 Italians were packed into trains and sent off to Russia.

Zen's father had been among them. But the war was not over in a matter of weeks, and the Italian conscripts had neither the training nor the equipment to fight a winter campaign in Russia. They suffered ninety thousand casualties. Sixty-six thousand more made the weary trek home again. As for the remaining seventy-five thousand, nothing more was ever heard of them. They simply disappeared without trace. The Soviet authorities had no reason to take any interest in the fate of a handful of foreign invaders when over twenty million of their own people had been killed; while as for the Italians, it had suddenly become clear that they had in fact been anti-Fascists to a man all along and could hardly be expected to sympathize

with the relatives of those few fanatics who had been rash
enough to fight for the despised Duce. In any case, the whole
country was in ruins and there were more urgent matters to
attend to.

"There it is!" Palottino burst out.

From a distance it resembled some piece of modern sculp-
ture: disjointed planes, random angles, a lot of holes. It was only
as they drew nearer that he began to make out that it was the
concrete skeleton of an unfinished three-story duplex. Half-
built walls, pillars, and floors rose out of a sea of mud. On one
side a staircase led up into thin air, breaking off abruptly on an
open landing about fifty meters above the ground.

They parked a short distance away. Zen got out, jumped over
the shallow ditch running alongside the track, and began to
work his way through the deep mud at the edge of the field
toward the back of the concrete structure. The building site was
surrounded by a token fence consisting of two slack strands of
barbed wire. Pietro Miletti was slowly making his way after him.

On the south side of the structure the concrete was cleaner
than to the north, where it was discolored with moss. Here the
stains were reddish brown, from the twisted-off ends of the
rusty reinforcing wire. It felt warm and sheltered. Plants had
already seeded in crevices around the foundations, preparing to
take over the instant man's will failed. A yellow butterfly loped
by with its strange broken flight. The unfinished concrete floor
was littered with cement bags, lengths of wire, nails and lumps
of wood, a lone glove. The upper stories had not yet been
floored and through the concrete joists and beams above the sky
was visible. There was no sign that anyone had been there for
months.

"Papa!"

Pietro Miletti appeared, his elegant shoes and trousers spat-
tered with mud.

Zen scraped some of the mud off his shoes on the bottom step
of the staircase. "I'm afraid it was a hoax."

"But why would they do that? What have they got to gain?"
Pietro sounded indignant, as though the kidnappers had broken the rules of a game and ought to be penalized.

"Perhaps it wasn't really the kidnappers who phoned you."

"It was them, all right. Do you think I don't know his damned
voice by now? Besides, who else would it be?"

"How should I know?" Zen snapped back, his tension finding

an issue. "Someone who hates your guts. There must be plenty of them around."

He turned away toward the outside of the building, veering to the right to complete his circuit of the structure. In the distance someone sounded a horn several times. The view ahead was obscured by a section of partially completed walling, but when he reached the corner Zen found that the only unpredictable feature of the landscape was a river which cut across the track about a hundred meters farther on. Once, no doubt, there would have been a bridge, since swept away by floods or war. Or perhaps it had never existed. It was hard to say whether the track continued on the other side.

It was only when he turned to the more immediate problem of finding a way back through the mud that Zen noticed the figure lying slumped against the wall.

The floor was made up of dark red hexagonal tiles touching at their points, separated by triangles of a deep chestnut color. Another way of looking at it was that the basic form was a large lozenge consisting of a red hexagonal core surrounded by four brown triangular tips, or again, diagonal strips of red hexagons kept in place by pairs of triangular brown wedges. The strips ran in both directions, creating a number of crosses. It should have been possible, theoretically, to work out how many there were. But it would have taken more than just time and ingenuity. You would have needed something else, some understanding of the principles involved, access to formulas and equations, a head for figures. Something he hadn't got, at any rate. As it was, an irrelevant image kept popping up in the corner of his eye, dragging his attention away: the image of an old man lying slumped in the mud against a wall of concrete blocks, turned away, as though death were an act as shameful as intercourse or defecation, an act which he had sought to conceal as far as possible, even in the bleakly exposed place where it had come to him.

Zen forced his attention back to the floor. But now a new pattern emerged as the red and brown shapes blocked together to form overlapping triangles all pointing across the room at the double doors opposite. These doors were now firmly closed, but they had opened several times since Zen's arrival, admitting a succession of visitors who had run the gauntlet of the mass of bodies and expectant faces in the corridor outside, sweltering under television lights and waving microphones in front of anyone who appeared.

It was six o'clock in the evening, four hours since the Deputy Public Prosecutor had summoned Zen to his office in the courthouse. When he arrived he had been told to wait, and he had been waiting ever since. He was being put in his place, softened up for what was to come. And what was that? "When they found a policeman at the payoff they must have panicked," Major Volpi had remarked to Di Leonardo when they arrived together at the scene in a Carabinieri helicopter. Yes, the death of Ruggiero Miletti was Zen's fault. He was completely innocent, but it was his fault. Even the tiles concurred, for now the arrows had all flipped over and were pointing at him, pointing out the guilty party, the incompetent official, the unworthy son. The pain that tugged at the muscles of his stomach and chest was so intimately hurtful that he knew it was nothing but useless, unspent emotion. What he needed was to break down and howl like a child, and it was the effort not to do so that was tearing at him. It was all his fault, his fault, his fault. He had never known the man, but it was his fault. He was condemned by an image which had haunted him for over thirty years: a poor defenseless body lying curled up in a vast flat dismal landscape, a father abandoned to his lonely fate. He must be guilty. There could be no excuse for such a death.

It was almost a relief when the door opposite suddenly opened and Di Leonardo appeared, immaculate as ever in a dark suit and sober tie.

"This way!" the Public Prosecutor called to him like a dog as he strode toward the door behind which a continuous threatening murmur could be heard.

Zen obediently rose and followed, wondering as a dog perhaps does at his stupidity in not understanding why they were going that way, where their enemies lay in wait.

The gentlemen of the press had had a fairly lean time of it so far. Di Leonardo's personal secretary had issued a statement shortly after midday, a masterpiece of prolixity that took about five minutes to say that Ruggiero Miletti had been found dead and that another statement would be issued in due course. Since then anyone who had been unwise enough to venture along the corridor had been pounced upon and picked clean. Magistrates, lawyers, various clerks, a court reporter, a telephone repairman, and even a number of ordinary human beings untouched by the grace of public office had been accosted, to no avail. So when the Deputy Public Prosecutor himself suddenly appeared in person, the assembled newshounds reacted like a gaggle of novices witnessing an apparition of the Virgin Mary.

Appropriately enough, Di Leonardo's first gesture, a hand raised to still the clamor, looked not unlike a blessing. When complete silence had fallen, he produced a sheet of paper from his pocket, folded it back on itself to remove the crease, smoothed it out a number of times, and then read a statement to the effect that inquiries were proceeding, steps being taken, fruitful avenues opening up, and concrete results expected within a short space of time. Having done so, he folded the sheet of paper again, replaced it in his pocket, and turned to leave.

The reporters protested vociferously. Di Leonardo looked flabbergasted, as though never before in his experience had the media failed to be satisfied by the reading of a prepared statement. But questions continued to be hurled at him from every side, and eventually, as an extraordinary mark of favor, he consented to answer one or two of them.

The first came from a man in the front row, a crumpled individual with the look of someone who has been dropped on his head from a great height at some stage in his life.

"Is it true that the magistrate investigating the Miletti case is to be replaced?"

Di Leonardo glared back in frigid indignation. "Certainly not! Dottor Bartocci is and will remain in charge of the investigation into the kidnapping of Ruggiero Miletti."

"And into his murder?" called a younger reporter on the fringes of the group.

"That is another and quite separate development, whose importance and urgency I need hardly stress. In addition to the kidnapping case, Dottor Bartocci is already handling the murder of Avvocato Valesio. My wish, the wish of all of us, is simply that we may as quickly as possible get to the bottom of the shocking and cold-blooded crime which has stunned and appalled the entire country, and arrest and punish those responsible. In order to avoid placing an impossible burden on the shoulders of my young colleague, it has been decided that the investigation of the events whose tragic outcome was discovered this morning will be directed by Dottor Rosella Foria."

"But the murder of Signor Miletti is evidently linked to the other two cases," pointed out a well-known interviewer with a television news crew. "Why is the same magistrate not investigating all three crimes?"

Di Leonardo smiled wearily and shook his head. "You reporters may spin whatever theories you choose. Our task is to weigh the evidence objectively and impartially. At the present juncture there is no evidence to suggest that this crime is necessarily linked to those you have mentioned, or indeed to any others."

There was a flurry of protest, which Di Leonardo once again stilled with a gesture of benediction.

"But it is too soon to pronounce on these matters with any certainty," he went on smoothly. "Should any such evidence come to light in the future we will of course be prepared to review the situation."

"You mean Bartocci may lose the other two cases as well?" asked the crumpled man. There was a ripple of laughter.

A tall woman with the chic, efficient look that spells Milan held up her notebook, and Di Leonardo immediately nodded encouragingly at her.

It's a fix, thought Zen, and he edged back against the wall. Mesmerized by the Public Prosecutor's performance, no one had yet noticed him, but he had a premonition that this was about to change.

"The Miletti family have made a statement in which they lay the blame for the murder squarely on the shoulders of the police," the woman began. "They have named a Commissioner Zen, whom they claim demanded to be present when the ransom money was paid, threatening to wreck the payoff by a show of force if they did not comply. They further assert that in the course of the payoff Commissioner Zen's identity was revealed and that the kidnappers were so incensed that they assaulted him. They conclude that the death of their father was a direct result of the kidnappers' instructions having been disobeyed, and demand that this official be subjected to the appropriate disciplinary procedures. Have you any comment to make?"

Di Leonardo smiled again. It was a beautiful smile, brimful of wisdom, understanding, and compassion.

"I don't think I need remind anyone of the tragic blow which the Miletti family, and indeed the whole of Perugia, has suffered today. Far be it from me to criticize comments made in the heat of the moment, which should be understood for what they are, cries of unendurable suffering, a passionate outburst of all-too-comprehensible anguish. I am sure I speak for all of us here when I say that our thoughts are with the Miletti family in this ordeal."

Di Leonardo paused for a moment, seemingly overcome by emotion. Then he looked up, brisk and businesslike again.

"Nevertheless, the fact remains that disciplinary action against officials who may have exceeded their duties or willfully abused the position of responsibility with which they have been entrusted is a purely internal matter which will be carried out, should the situation warrant it, by the appropriate authorities at the appropriate time. The views and wishes of private individuals, however comprehensible, cannot be permitted to influence whatever decision may eventually be arrived at."

"Do you accept the family's account of the events surrounding the payoff?" a reporter demanded.

"I have no further comment to make."

"But this Zen is still in charge of the case?"

Di Leonardo shook his finger as though admonishing a backward pupil. "As I have already explained, Dottor Foria is directing the investigation."

The crumpled reporter who had started the questioning now sighed theatrically and rubbed his forehead. "Let's see, have I got this right? As far as the police are concerned it's all one case and the same officer remains in charge, but when it comes to the judiciary it's a completely unrelated development and a new magistrate has been appointed."

"If you study the answers I have given I think you will find that they are very clear." Di Leonardo smiled. "Should you have any further questions, I suggest you put them to Commissioner Zen himself."

The Public Prosecutor pointed Zen out with one finger, and as everyone turned to look he slipped through the suddenly passive ranks to the safety of his office, closing the door firmly behind him. Immediately all hell broke loose.

"What's your reaction, dottore?"

"How did it feel finding Miletti's body?"

"Do you accept responsibility for his death?"

"A spokesman for the family has described your handling of the case as a quote disgraceful and disastrous example of official interventionism unquote. Would you care to comment?"

"Isn't it true that during the Moro affair you were transferred from the active list of the Rome Questura to a desk job in the Ministry following a disciplinary inquiry? Would you describe today's events as a further setback to your career?"

As the lights glared, the cameras whirred, and the microphones thrust and jabbed, Zen realized why he had been summoned to the courthouse.

"If you study the answers the Deputy Public Prosecutor has given, I think you will find that they are very clear," he told them. "I have nothing further to add."

The reporters didn't give up so easily, of course. But stolid stonewalling makes for poor copy and dull viewing, and eventually they let him go, although even then a few of the younger and hungrier among them followed him down the wide staircase and out into Piazza Matteotti, hoping for a belated indiscretion.

It was dusk, and the evening was as still and airless as the previous one when, impatient for news, Zen had gone out for a stroll. It was strange now, walking through the same streets, to know that by then it had already happened. But even on a cursory examination the dottore had been in no doubt.

"Rigor mortis is complete but there's no sign of it passing off. Body temperature almost down to the ambient level. He's been dead at least eighteen hours, more likely twenty-four."

At the time, Zen had barely heard him, shocked by the sight of the man he had been summoned to Perugia to save lying naked on a plastic sheet with a thermometer sticking out of his anus. Ruggiero Miletti had been killed the day before, on Monday morning, and yet the gang had waited until this morning to alert the family with a cruel message of hope! In all his experience Zen could remember nothing like it. Kidnappers could be violent, but in the easy, unashamed manner of men to whom violence was natural and legitimate. If they had killed their victim to teach the Milettis a lesson they would have said so, even bragged about it. But this crime, and above all the manner in which it had been mockingly announced, had a twisted sophistication, a kink in the logic, which Zen would have said was quite alien to a gang of Calabrian shepherds.

But he impatiently dismissed this line of thought. Little enough was left him now, but at least his dignity remained, even though no one but himself could see it. If he were to start clutching at straws, hoping against hope for a way out, then even that would be lost.

Back in his office he reached for the phone and dialed his home number. As usual, Maria Grazia answered and then yelled to his mother to pick up the extension phone by her chair, in the deep underwater gloom of the living room. The connection was especially good, almost as if they were face to face, and Zen found himself resentful that he should be deprived of the usual screen of interference on an occasion when he could find nothing to say.

"Happy birthday, Mamma. Did you like the present?"

"Is this going to take long? Crissie's having her baby and I don't want to miss that. Wayne will be livid when he hears. And that half-brother of hers, do you know what he's done? Sold the property over their heads! That couldn't happen to us, could it?"

"No, Mamma."

"Why not?"

Was she having a sly laugh at his expense, talking nonsense and then cornering him with a sudden question?

"Is it because you're in the police?"

"Yes, that's it, Mamma. They wouldn't dare do anything like that. You see, there are some advantages after all."

"What?"

"To being in the police. You know you're always telling me that I should have got a job on the railways. But if I weren't in the police they might kick us out."

"Kick us out? Who might? What are you talking about?"

Damn her!

"Never mind. If you're still watching when the news comes on, you might see me. I'm—"

"Oh I haven't time to watch the news. There's the dolphins on Six right afterward. They've kidnapped them, the bastards."

"Who, the dolphins?"

"Anyway, if you were on the railways we'd get free tickets wherever we wanted to go."

"I already get free travel, Mamma."

"I don't!"

"But you never even leave the apartment anymore!"

"That's what I'm saying. If you had a nice job on the railways maybe I could get out and about a bit."

There was a knock, the door opened, and Luciano Bartocci appeared. "May I?"

After a moment's hesitation Zen waved him forward.

"Look, I've got to go," he said into the phone. "Happy birthday. See you soon." He hung up.

"Sorry if I disturbed you," Bartocci said. "I was just passing, and I thought I'd . . ."

He took off the heavy overcoat he was wearing and laid it across the top of the filing cabinet.

"I won't stay long." The smile trembling to be born at the corner of his mouth was even more active than usual. "The thing is, you see, I realize that I've been rather stupid, and rather selfish, and I'd like to apologize."

Zen stood staring at the younger man. He had no idea how to deal with the situation. A judge apologizing to a policeman! What were we coming to?

"I asked you to collaborate unofficially," Bartocci went on. "That was irresponsible. You could have refused, of course, but it was a choice I shouldn't have forced you to make."

Zen watched the younger man circling the office, inspecting the fixtures and fittings as though they were evidence at the scene of a crime. He's not apologizing to me, Zen realized. He's apologizing to himself, for letting himself down.

"My entire strategy was incorrect from the start," the magistrate continued. "It's mere bourgeois adventurism to think that the conspiracies of powerful vested interests can be defeated by individual efforts. I should have known better. The ratking is self-regulating, as I told you before. The strength of each rat is the strength of all. Any individual initiative against them is doomed from the start. The system can only be destroyed politically, by collective action, a stronger system."

The distant smile was in place on Zen's lips. By a bigger and better ratking, he thought.

"Did you actually hear the recording of the message the Milettis received this morning?"

For a moment Bartocci appeared slightly confused. "Hear it? Why?"

"Is anyone sure it was really the kidnappers who phoned?"

There was silence while Bartocci thought through the implications of this remark. Then he smiled and shook his head. "I see what you're getting at," he said. "But I'm afraid it won't do. You've been away from active duty for a while, haven't you?"

Evidently the rumors about Zen's past were beginning to catch up with him.

"All interceptions are now subjected to voiceprint analysis as a matter of routine," the magistrate explained. "If the one this morning hadn't matched the pattern I'd have been informed. No, I'm afraid we must accept that Miletti was murdered by his kidnappers."

"All right, perhaps they pulled the trigger. But there's still the question of how they knew I would be there at the payoff. Ubaldo Valesio believed that someone in the family was passing on information. Isn't it possible that the informant deliberately told the kidnappers I would be there, knowing what the consequences were likely to be?"

"You mean that one of the family got the kidnappers to do their murder for them? I doubt very much whether you'll be able to interest Rosella Foria in such a theory!"

"Why? Is she . . . ?"

Bartocci shook his head. "No, no, Rosella's straight enough. But she does everything strictly by the book. She has to. There still aren't many women in the judiciary, so everything they do tends to get scrutinized by their male colleagues, and not only those on the Right, I'm afraid to say. If a woman makes the slightest mistake it's pounced on as evidence of her general incompetence. The result is a natural tendency toward caution. And after what's happened to me Rosella's going to be treading very carefully indeed."

For a moment Zen wondered whether he should tell Bartocci about the photocopy of Ruggiero's letter. Since the death of the writer, the insults and threats he had dealt out to each member of his family took on a new significance. But in the end he decided against it. That letter was a card up his sleeve, the last one he had.

"What *has* happened to you?" he asked instead.

"I'll have to look for a new posting."

"You're being transferred?"

"Nothing as simple as that. The judiciary only resort to disciplinary action in the most blatant cases, where the alternative would make us look even worse. All I've done is offend one or two of the wrong people. It's not the end of the world. I'm quite free to stay in Perugia for the rest of my life, as an investigating magistrate. But if I want to move up the ladder I'll have to go elsewhere."

"I still don't understand why the Milettis didn't try and stop you from handling the investigation in the first place if they feel so strongly about you."

"They did try! But they went about it the wrong way. It was Pietro's fault. He's been away too long, lost his touch, forgotten how things are done. When I was assigned to investigate Ruggiero's kidnapping, Pietro made a statement to the press drawing attention to my lack of experience and my political views and demanding that I be replaced immediately. After that I couldn't be touched, of course. This time they went about it correctly, which is to say incorrectly. A few discreet phone calls and suddenly I find myself shunted into a siding while the investigation into Ruggiero's murder passes me by."

As Bartocci took his coat, the crucifix which Zen had placed on the filing cabinet the previous evening fell to the floor.

"Where you're concerned the Milettis got it wrong again," the magistrate remarked to Zen as they stood at the door. "The Ministry would have been only too happy to have handed you over stuffed and pickled if they'd been asked in the proper way. But once Pietro started sounding off to the press, they had to stand by you to avoid charges of bowing to pressure."

"I expect it'll come to the same thing in the end," Zen told him as they shook hands.

The crucifix had broken in its fall. Zen picked it up and wandered over to the window, trying to push it back together again.

One effect of the years of terrorism had been to abolish night in the vicinity of prisons, and the scene outside was bleakly bright. Every detail was picked out by the floodlights mounted high up on the walls behind protective grilles. Remote control video cameras scanned back and forth, while up on the roof a nervous-looking teenager in gray overalls made his rounds, hugging a machine gun for comfort.

That was another slight anomaly about Ruggiero Miletti's death, Zen reflected. Like Valesio, he had been shot through the mouth, but this time the only sign of damage was a single discreet exit wound in the back of the neck. The bullets fired into the victim's cranium were still lodged there. When the projectile that had escaped turned up in the mud, all was explained: it was a 4.5mm, low-power ammunition for a small pistol. This choice of weapon seemed rather bizarre. The negotiating cell of the gang had brutally dismantled Ubaldo Valesio's skull with a submachine gun, while the hard men who had executed Ruggiero had done so with a small handgun, a bedside toy for nervous householders.

As Zen stood there fiddling with the crucifix, the end of the upright suddenly came away cleanly in his hand and he saw that it was hollow and that the lower part of the shaft contained a heavy rectangular pack about two centimeters long, connected to a wire running back into the shaft and disappearing through a small hole into the figure of Christ. This figure was painted in the same syrupy pastel shades as the rest of the crucifix, but when Zen tapped it the head resounded not with the dull thud of plaster but with a light metallic ring.

"*He's been away too long,*" Bartocci had said of Pietro Miletti. "*He's lost his touch, forgotten how things are done.*" He wasn't the only one. Zen clearly remembered the occasion when he'd felt that some detail in his office had altered. He'd thought that it was just the calendar which had been turned to the correct month, but something else had been changed too. The original crucifix had been much smaller, too small in fact to contain whatever it was he was now cradling in his hand. And to think he hadn't noticed! At this rate he couldn't even count on keeping his Housekeeping job much longer. People would be auctioning off whole police stations under his nose.

The broken fragments of the crucifix looked like some bizarre act of desecration. He laid them out on the desk, got a plastic bag out of the bottom drawer of the filing cabinet, and swept all the bits and pieces into it. Then he put on his overcoat and pushed the package deep into the pocket.

It was almost eight o'clock, and the streets were dead apart from a little through traffic. While he was still undecided as to what to do a bus appeared round the corner and slowed to a halt nearby. The doors opened and the driver stared at him expectantly, and Zen got in. The bus wound its way through the ring of nineteenth-century villas on the upper slopes and the postwar apartments below them, down to the modern blocks and towers on the flatland around the station, where it pulled up. The engine died and everyone got out.

He went over to the row of luggage lockers, laid the plastic package in one, dropped in three hundred-lire coins, locked the door, and pocketed the key. On the wall opposite there was an illuminated display listing the tourist attractions of the city. The word *Cinemas* caught his eye, and one of the names seemed familiar. He gave it to the driver of the taxi he found outside, who whisked him back up the hill again, back through time to a medieval alley smelling of woodsmoke and urine. A more unlikely situation for a cinema was hard to imagine, but the driver pointed to a set of steps burrowing up between two houses and explained that it was as near as he could get in a car.

The small piazza into which Zen eventually emerged had an eerie underwater look, due to a uniform coating of lurid green light from a neon sign mounted on a building otherwise no different from the others. CINEMA MINERVA, it read. Zen made no attempt to find out what was showing. He paid, walked down a dark corridor, and pushed through a curtain into a deep pool of sound and flickering light. The auditorium was almost empty. He walked without hesitation to the front row, sat down, and leaned back, gazing up at the screen. Enormous blurred masses swarmed into view and out again. An ear the size of a flying saucer appeared for a moment and then was whisked away and replaced by a no less monstrous nose and half an eye. Giant voices boomed at each other. He snuggled down in his seat with a blissful smile, battered by images, swamped by noise, letting the film wash over him.

It was the perfect mental massage, and when it was over he rose feeling slightly numb, but tingling and refreshed. In the foyer he paused to look at the posters, and learned that he had just seen a comedy called *Pull the Other One!* featuring a fat, balding middle-aged clerk, the slim glamorous starlet madly in love with him, the clerk's wily, roguish, ne'er-do-well cousin, and the cousin's battle-ax of a wife. As he stood there he felt a hand on his shoulder.

He would never have recognized Cinzia Miletti if she hadn't approached him, for she was virtually in disguise: a silk scarf entirely covering her hair, dark glasses, and a long tweed coat buttoned right up to the chin. She lowered the glasses for an instant so that he could see her eyes, then raised them again.

"Did you enjoy it? We did, didn't we, Stefania?"

They were the classic female twosome, mouse and minx. Stefania played her role to perfection, managing to give the impression of existing only provisionally, but being quite prepared at the drop of a hat either to become completely real or to vanish without a trace, whichever was more convenient.

Zen was so astounded at finding Cinzia there on that particular evening that he could think of nothing whatever to say.

"I think he's just fantastic, don't you?" she went on unperturbedly. "I've seen all his films except *Do Me a Favor!*, which funnily enough I've never managed to catch although it's on TV all the time. He's working in America this year, you know."

By now the foyer was empty. On every side images of love and violence erupted from glass-fronted posters advertising coming attractions. In her booth the cashier sat knitting behind a tank in which a solitary goldfish swam in desultory circles.

Cinzia looked at her companion.

"I must go," breathed Stefania, and was gone.

"Would you walk me home?" Cinzia asked Zen. "I'm staying here in town, it's only five minutes' walk, not worth calling a taxi, but I don't like to go alone. There are so many Arabs about now. Of course I'm not racist, but let's face it, they've got a different culture, just like the South."

Still he couldn't reply, his head too full of questions to which he didn't particularly want to know the answers. But he managed to nod agreement.

"Of course you think I'm shameless," Cinzia remarked as they set off, the windless, muffled night hardly disturbed by their footsteps. "Do you believe in a life after death? I don't know what to think. But if there isn't one then nothing makes any difference, does it, and if there is I'm sure it'll all be far too spiritual for anyone to get in a huff over the way the rest of us carry on."

The part of the city through which they were walking reminded Zen of Venice, but a Venice brutally fractured, as though each canal were a geological fault and the houses to either side had taken a plunge or been wrenched up all askew and left to tumble back on themselves, throwing out buttresses and retaining walls for support as best they could.

"I mean do you really think the dead sit around counting who goes to the funeral and how many wreaths there are and how much they cost? I just hate cemeteries, anyway. They remind me of death."

Her tone was even more strident than usual. Zen wondered if she was slightly high on drink or drugs.

"Going home to stick it up her, eh? Filthy old bumfucker! Squeeze it tight and you might just manage to get a hard-on, you miserable little rat!"

The voice was just overheard, but when they looked up there was no one there.

"Good evening, Evelina," Cinzia called up calmly.

"Don't you 'good evening' me, you shameless cunt! You

blow-job artist! I bet you beg for it on your bended knees! I bet you let him shove it where he wants! Whore! Masturbator!"

They turned a corner and the malignant ravings became blurred and indistinct.

"Poor Evelina used to be one of the most fashionable women in Perugia," Cinzia explained. "Nobody seems to know what happened, but one day during a concert she suddenly stood up, took off her knickers, and showed everyone her bottom. After that she was put away until they closed the asylums. Since then she's lived in that place. It's one of her family's properties, they own half the city. Sometimes you hear her singing, in the summertime. But mostly she just sits up there like a spider, sticking her head out the window to insult the passersby. It's nothing personal, she says the same to everyone."

For some time now Zen had been wondering where they were going. When Cinzia said she was staying "in town," he'd assumed that she meant the Miletti villa. But although the structure of the city still defeated him in detail, he had got his bearings well enough to know that this could not be their destination. Eventually she turned up a set of steps rising steeply from the street and unlocked a door at the top.

"You'll come in for a moment, won't you?"

Without waiting for an answer she disappeared, leaving the door open.

Zen slowly mounted the steps, then paused on the threshold. Ruggiero Miletti was dead and the family blamed him. What better revenge than to disgrace him by rigging a scandal involving the dead man's daughter, a married woman? But he told himself not to be crazy. How could they have known he was going to that cinema when he hadn't known himself until he saw the name at the station?

A narrow stairway of glossy marble led straight into a sitting room arranged around a huge open fireplace. There was no sign of Cinzia. The room had roughly plastered walls and a low ceiling supported on enormous joists trimmed out of whole trees. Everything was spick-and-span, more like a hotel room than a home. Zen was instinctively drawn toward the one area of disorder, a desk piled with leaflets, envelopes, magazines, newspapers, letters, and bills. He picked up one of the envelopes and held it up to the light: the watermark showed the heraldic hybrid with which he was becoming familiar, with the wings of an eagle and the body of a lion. Next to it lay a note from Cinzia to her husband about collecting their daughter from school.

"This is really Gianluigi's place," Cinzia explained as she breezed in. She had changed into a striped shirt and a pair of faded jeans that were slightly too large for her. "I only use it when he's away, there's no telling who I might find here otherwise. What do you want to drink?"

"Anything at all."

Her bare feet padded across the polished terra-cotta tiles to the bottles lined along a shelf in the corner. Zen sat down on the large sofa which occupied most of one wall, thinking about that last card which he'd fondly thought he had up his sleeve. Thank God he hadn't tried to play it! The trap had been beautifully set, and he'd avoided it only because, thanks to Bartocci's machinations, he'd already fallen into another one.

Cinzia brought them both large measures of whiskey and sat down astride the wicker chair in front of the writing desk, facing him over the ridged wooden back.

"I don't normally drink with strangers," she remarked. "It's quite a thrill. We do all our drinking in private, you see, in the family. Like everything else, for that matter!"

She reminded Zen more than a little of his wife. Luisella had also been the child of a successful businessman, owner of one of the most important chemist's shops in Treviso, and she too had had brothers who had dominated her childhood, driving her to defend herself in unorthodox ways. Life was a game like tennis, set up by men for men to win with powerful serves she would never be able to return. She countered by deliberately breaking the rules, exhausting her opponents, and winning by default.

"That's a clue by the way," Cinzia continued. "You're never going to get anywhere if you don't understand the people involved."

"I thought the people involved were Calabrian shepherds."

"Oh, well I don't know anything about them. You should have asked Stefania. Her brother's best friend is Calabrian, a medical student. But his family is extremely rich and I don't expect he knows any shepherds."

She got up abruptly. "Shall we have some music? Let's see, I can never remember how to work this thing."

She pressed a button and one of the hit songs of the season emerged at full volume, the tough shallow lyrics gloatingly declaimed by a star of the midsixties who had traded in her artless looks and girlish lispings for a street-wise manner and a voice laden with designer cynicism.

"I'd rather just talk," Zen shouted.

With a flick of her finger she restored the silence. "I thought you were bored. Well what shall we talk about? How about sex? Let's see how you rate in that area. What do you think we go in for, here in Perugia? Wife swapping? Open marriage? Group gropes? Singles' bars?"

"None of those, I should have thought," Zen replied with a slight smile.

"And quite right too. Bravo, you're improving. There's some of that around, of course, but it's not *traditional*. So what do you think is the specialty of the house? I'm talking about something typically Perugian, homemade from the very finest local ingredients only."

She finished her drink in one gulp. "No idea? I don't think you're a very good detective, I've given you loads of clues. It's incest, of course."

She banged her empty glass down on the desk, as though she had expected to find the surface several centimeters lower than it actually was.

"Don't look so surprised, it makes perfect sense. From our point of view marriage has one big drawback, you see. It lets an outsider into the family. Much safer to stick to one's close relations. There's no trusting cousins and the like, of course. No, we're talking mother and son, father and daughter. See what I mean? If you don't know these things how can you hope to get anything right? For example, you disapprove of my going to the cinema this evening, but what do you think I should be doing? Cleaving to the bosom of my grieving family? What do you think they're doing? Daniele will be locked in his bedroom watching the latest batch of video nasties. Silvio? He'll be stripping for action with Helmut or whatever his name is this week. And Pietro will have gone to bed with a nice English murder story. Not much in the way of company, you see."

"And your husband?"

Zen was still irrationally worried that Gianluigi might walk in at any moment, hunting rifle in hand. Or would he use the other gun, the little 4.5mm pistol registered in Cinzia's name? Where was that kept?

"He's still in Milan," Cinzia replied carelessly. "He couldn't get a flight back because of all the journalists wanting to get down here, or so he claims. Anyway, he has nothing to do with it, he's not family. Of course he didn't realize that when he married me. But you don't break into the Miletti family as simply as that! So he's been reduced to other expedients."

"And why did *you* marry *him*?"

Cinzia looked around vaguely, as if trying to remember. "Well, he's very handsome. I know men don't think so, but he is. That might almost have been enough."

"But it wasn't."

"No. I married him to spite my father."

Zen gave her a look of appraisal. "You're not being very typically Perugian yourself, are you, telling me all this?"

Cinzia's eyes suddenly flashed and she smiled, displaying an excessive number of rather dirty teeth.

"It's strange, isn't it? I knew his death would be a release, but I thought it would be terrible, that I would suffer. I thought he would always make me suffer, whatever happened. But it's not like that at all. All this time, all these years, I've been lugging this weight around with me, for so long now that I've forgotten what it's like to be free of it. I'd even begun to mistake it for part of my own body, an incurable growth that I've got to learn to live with. But it's not, it's not! That disease, that horror, that swelling, it was all *his*! I'm whole and healthy and light, I find. Sorry for his death? I feel like dancing on his coffin!"

But there were tears in her eyes. For a moment it looked as though she was going to break down.

"There used to be this old-fashioned clothes shop on the Corso," she went on more quietly. "It's gone now, they've turned it into a boutique. It was full of wooden drawers and cupboards and enormous heavy mirrors on stands and boxes of buttons and threads and trimming. All the clothes were wrapped in tissue paper. I can still remember the sound it made, a lovely special sound, as light and thin as the clothes were solid and heavy. Everything smelled of mothballs and lavender and cedar. That shop was like a dream world to me, full of secrets and wonders. My mother took me there occasionally, and we used to pass the window every Sunday after Mass. They always had beautiful things in the window. There was one I craved in particular, a pink nightdress with a lace hem and a frilly neck and a family of rabbits embroidered on the chest. I always stopped to look at it, although I knew it was much too expensive. But when my eighth birthday came I found it among my presents, with a little card from my father."

He saw that she was weeping, not for her father but for herself, for the child she had been.

"Well, I expect you can guess the rest! That evening he came to my room, to see how I looked in my new nightdress. He told me to sit on his knee. That was normal, I didn't think twice about it. But what happened next wasn't normal. I knew it must be wrong, because afterward he made me promise not to tell anyone about it, not even Mummy. What had happened was our secret, he said. That was the agreement we'd made. He'd kept his part by buying me the nightdress, now it was up to me to keep mine. I didn't remember making any agreement, but what could I do? Fathers know best, don't they? So although I didn't like him touching me the way he had, I decided not to tell anybody. I didn't realize that by keeping quiet I was walking into a trap."

She sniffed loudly and picked up her cigarettes.

"After that he came to visit me almost every evening. After he had gone I found that my nightie was covered in a horrible sticky mess with a strange sour smell. I'd go to the bathroom and scrub myself until I was raw. But I still didn't tell anyone. In the end he stopped bothering to make any pretense of cuddles, it became fucking, pure and simple. And his filth was no longer just on my skin, it was inside me."

Zen tried to think of something to say, but it was useless. Faced with this ordinary everyday atrocity, he felt ashamed to be a man, ashamed to be human.

"Finally I threatened to tell Mummy. I was older and more daring. That's when he finally sprang his trap. If you do that, he told me, we shall go to prison, both of us. Because it's really all your fault. You encouraged me, you led me on. You must have enjoyed it, otherwise you would have told someone before now! You're as bad as me, my girl, or even worse."

She lit her cigarette and smiled at Zen, inviting him to appreciate her father's cleverness.

"The worst thing about his lies was that they were partly true. Because although I hated it worse than anything, I *did* enjoy it too, once I got used to it. *Of course* it felt nice, what do you expect? And don't you think it was flattering, in a way, to be preferred to my mother? What a position to be in! On the one hand I could send us both to prison, shame my mother, beggar my brothers, scandalize the city, and blacken the Miletti name forevermore. On the other hand, I could do, I *did*, exactly the opposite, keeping my father satisfied and happy and my mother ignorant, helping to shore up their marriage, holding the family together, and preserving my unsuspecting brothers, who thought they were so superior to me, from disgrace. Half the time I felt like a vicious little whore and the other half like the heroine of a nineteenth-century novel. But mostly I just felt my power! My father used the carrot as well as the stick, of course, and that meant I got everything I wanted—clothes, jewelry, perfume. And when his friends and business associates came round, I would put on my finery and try out my power on them too. And it worked! Antonio Crepi, for example, used to give me looks that would have melted a candle. I was twelve at the time."

"Did your mother never suspect what was going on?"

After a long time Cinzia looked up. "That's a terrible question. At the time I was sure she didn't know. How could she know, I thought, and not do anything about it? Now I'm not so sure. She would have had every reason to look the other way. Besides . . ."

"What?"

"Sometimes I think she deliberately ignored what was happening. Perhaps it was her way of taking revenge. Perhaps she too thought that it was my fault, that I enjoyed it, that I was as bad as he was, or even worse."

She straightened up, her voice bright and brisk again. "Anyway, none of that matters now. There was a car crash, she died, he was in hospital for a long time, and when he came out everything had changed. He may have seen her death as a judgment. I don't know, we never talked about it of course. But he never came near me again, and I was left high and dry with all that power lying idle inside me. It didn't lie idle long, needless to say."

She gave him a wry smile. "So now you know everything there is to know about me! Not even my husband knows what I've just told you. A rare privilege, and one you didn't deserve, to be perfectly honest. But I needed to tell someone, after all these years, and it had to be a stranger of course. You just happened to be in the right place at the right time."

Zen finished his whiskey. "There's still one thing I don't know."

"What?"

"Why you sent me that copy of your father's letter."

She barked out a little laugh.

"I thought at first it must have been Ivy Cook," Zen went on. "But that doesn't really make sense. Take the envelope, for example. Did she carry it with her when she went to find that bottle lying in the gutter, or dash to a stationer's afterward and buy it? It's hard to believe, especially since it wasn't just any old envelope, but a special luxury brand with a griffin watermark. Like the ones on your desk."

She gave him a bored look. "It's not my desk, it's Gianluigi's. I expect he sent you the letter. You've no idea how resourceful he is. He just about owns poor Daniele ever since that business with the drugs, not to mention those photographs he has of Silvio—"

"No, it wasn't your husband," Zen interrupted. "It was you. You rewrote the letter after the original had been burned, had your version photocopied, and then sent me the copy. The handwriting is the same as that note on the desk asking your husband to collect Loredana from school."

"Well, supposing I did? It's not a criminal offense, is it, sending information to the police? You should be grateful! I may have changed a word here or there, but apart from that it's all exact. I wrote it while the text was still fresh in my mind. It was hardly the kind of letter that is easy to forget! When Pietro told us that you were going to the payoff I felt that you should know what you were getting yourself into."

Zen smiled skeptically. "I thought it might have something to do with the fact that when it emerged that I'd received the letter, Ivy Cook would become persona non grata in the Miletti family."

Cinzia giggled. "Well, why shouldn't I get something out of it too? That bitch has been a thorn in our flesh for too long. Help yourself to another drink, I'll be back in a moment."

She lurched off across the room, reaching for the wall to steady herself, and disappeared upstairs. Sometime later there was the sound of a lavatory flushing, but Cinzia did not reappear. Zen sat there thinking over what she had told him. Someone had said that nowadays doctors had to double as priests, offering general consolation and advice to their patients. But there are things you would be ashamed to tell even your doctor, things so vile they can be confessed only to the lowest and most callous functionaries of all. There were days when Zen felt like the Bocca de Leone in the Doges' Palace: a stiff stone grimace clogged with vapid denunciations and false confessions, scribbles riddled with hatred or guilt, the anonymous rubbish of an entire city.

There was still no sign of Cinzia, and suddenly a nasty thought cut through Zen's reflections. He got up quickly, walked to the foot of the stairs, and called out. There was no reply. He put his foot on the first step and paused, listening.

"Signora?" he called again.

The high marble steps curved upward, paralleling the flight leading up from the front door. Zen started to climb them. There were three doors in the passageway at the top. He chose the one to the right and opened it carefully.

"Signora?"

The room inside was startlingly bare, reminding him of his mother's flat in Venice. Two empty cardboard boxes sat on the floor, one at each end of the room. Between them a small window showed a blank stretch of wall on the other side of the alley.

The second door he tried was the bathroom. A quick search failed to reveal any suspiciously empty bottles of barbiturates, but of course she might have taken them with her. That left just one door, and he hesitated for a moment before opening it, bracing himself for some shocking rearrangement of everyday reality.

But the scene which met his eyes was perfectly normal. A large high old-fashioned bed almost filled the room. Cinzia Miletti was lying across it on her back, bent slightly to one side, fully clothed, her eyes closed. Her breathing seemed steady. For some reason Zen felt he should cover her up, but her body proved unexpectedly awkward and resistant. One arm kept getting entangled in the sheets, until he began to think that she was playing a trick on him. Paradoxically, it wasn't till her eyes opened that he knew he was wrong. Their unfocused glance passed over him without the slightest flicker of movement or response. Then they closed and she turned over and began to snore lightly. His last image before switching off the light was of her head lying on the pillow in the center of a mass of long blond hair, her mouth placidly sucking her thumb.

Outside, the night had turned clear and bitterly cold, and the stars were massed in all their intolerable profusion. The light cast by one of the infrequent street lamps glistened on a freshly pasted poster extolling the virtues of Commendatore Ruggiero Franco Miletti, whose funeral would be held the following afternoon.

8

By morning everything had changed: the sun shone on a new landscape. Immediately beyond the two churches visible from Zen's window the world abruptly ended, to begin again fifteen or twenty kilometers away, where the upper slopes of the yeasty mountain survived as a small island rising from a frozen ocean. A few other islets were visible on the other side of the valley, but apart from these patches of high ground and the stranded city itself, a glistening white mass of fog covered everything.

The Questura was barely fifty meters down the hill, but it was below the surface, and as Zen walked there from his hotel he felt the invisible moisture beading his newly shaved skin. When he looked up, the light was pearly and the sky a blue so tender he could hardly take his eyes off it, with the result that on several occasions he collided with people coming the other way. But everybody was in a good mood that morning, and his apologies were returned with a smile. He remembered a Chinese fable Ellen had once told him about a man who falls off a cliff, saves himself by clutching at a plant, and then notices that two mice are gnawing away the branch on which his life depends. There is a fruit growing on the branch, which the man plucks and eats. The fruit tastes wonderful.

"How did the mice come to be halfway down a cliff in the first place?" he had asked her. "And why didn't they eat the fruit themselves?"

He couldn't see the point of the story at all, but Ellen refused to explain. "You must experience it," was all she would say. "One day it'll suddenly hit you."

He had been skeptical at the time, but she'd been quite right, for he had suddenly understood the story. *"It'll come to the same thing in the end,"* he'd told Luciano Bartocci. His days in Perugia were clearly numbered, and he would spend them like the young magistrate, on a siding running parallel to the main line but going nowhere and ending abruptly. The process had begun the day before, at the scene of Ruggiero's death. It was Major Volpi who had been given responsibility for putting up roadblocks and carrying out house-to-house searches. The police had made one mistake too many in this case and would be given no further opportunities to demonstrate their incompetence. As for Zen, any day now he would receive a telegram from the Ministry summoning him back to Rome, and that would be that.

But in the meantime, how sweet the fruit tasted! And although the bureaucratic mice were invisibly at work, he still went through the motions of shifting hands and improving his grip on the branch. Thus, his first action on returning to the Questura the day before had been to send his inspectors out to question the people living in the houses along the road to Cannara and talk to the local farmers, just in case anyone had seen anything. When he arrived at work that morning the result of their labors was waiting for him in a blue folder.

Five minutes after entering his office Zen reappeared in the inspectors' room, where Geraci was watching Chiodini fill in a coupon for a competition promising the winner a lifetime supply of tomato concentrate.

"What *is* this?" he demanded.

Geraci looked warily at the folder Zen was holding up. "It's our report."

"I've never seen a report like this. What's all this stuff down the side?"

"Those are computer codes."

"Since when have we had a computer?"

"We haven't, it's at the courthouse. All packed up in boxes, down in the basement. But we'll be getting terminals here, once it's working. You see, this report isn't really meant to be read, it's meant to be put into the computer, which then displays the information any way you want it."

Zen regarded him stonily. "But there is no computer."

"Not yet, no. But they want to be ready for when it starts operating, you see. It's going to be wonderful! All the files from us, the Carabinieri, the Finance people, everything, is going to go straight into the computer. Anything you want to know, it'll be there at your fingertips. Say you've got a report about a small red car, and you want to compare it with all the other small red cars that have been reported in the area. With the old method it would take you hours looking through files, but with the computer you just push a button and it tells you right away. And the same for all the large red cars, or the red foreign cars of any size, or the small sports cars of any color . . ."

Zen passed one hand across his forehead. There were clearly various possibilities which the Chinese hadn't thought of. For example, the mice stop gnawing, scamper down your arm to perch on your shoulder, cock their legs, and piss in your face.

"Listen, you don't mean to tell me that everyone around here gets their reports in this form. I simply don't believe it."

"Of course they do! Isn't it the same in Rome?"

Zen looked away. Of course it was the same in Rome. It would be the same everywhere, that was how the system worked. What Geraci still didn't know was that Zen had no recent operational experience in Rome or anywhere else.

"Mind you, some of the older officers get us to do a backup report in the old way," Chiodini told him.

"But it's strictly unofficial," Geraci added hurriedly. "Can't be logged or filed."

Zen was leafing through the folder. He seemed not to have heard. "Did you speak to this witness?"

The inspector took the file and glanced at the entry pointed out by Zen's broad flat finger.

"No, that was Lucaroni."

"But it's marked G."

"That's right. G stands for Lucaroni."

"Really? I suppose you're L?"

Geraci frowned. "L? No, L is already in use by the system. For example, here in the same entry it says L-twenty-three, right? That means an unidentified foreign car."

"Where *is* Lucaroni?"

Geraci hesitated.

"Upstairs," said Chiodini.

That meant either the senior command structure or the Political Branch, whose rooms were situated on the top floor of every Questura. The fact that the same word was used for either reflected the general feeling that the distinction between the two was fairly hazy.

"Tell him I want to see him as soon as he gets back."

He closed the door behind him. So they were getting a computer, were they? Soon the intolerable mysteries of Mediterranean life would be swept away by the electronic wonders of real time and random access for all. And just to make sure that everything was fair and above board, the computer, like the facilities for wiretaps, would be located at the courthouse, safely out of the hands of the police. "They're doing to small-time corruption what the multinational corporations are doing to small-time business," a cynical Sardinian friend had once remarked apropos of the latest initiative to clean up the police. "It's not going to stop the abuse of power, it's just going to confine it to the highest level. Anyone can afford to buy you or me, Aurelio, but only the big boys can manipulate judges."

Zen stared at the wall, where the calendar now looked oddly unbalanced. Yes, it might be time to phone Gilberto. He couldn't leave the crucifix in the luggage locker forever.

Lucaroni appeared about ten minutes later, all apologies for the delay. "I was just having a word with Personnel," he explained. "My sister's getting married next week and I wanted to know whether there'd be any chance of a spot of leave."

Zen passed him a page of the report. "Tell me about this woman who claims to have seen a large blue car near the scene of the crime."

The inspector scanned the page. "Well, there's just what it says here. It was a large blue foreign sedan, she said, driven by someone with fair hair, going along the—"

"Tell me about the woman."

"The driver? But we don't—"

"No, the woman you spoke to."

Lucaroni made a conspicuous effort to remember. "Well, she

was oldish. Lives with her in-laws in one of those new houses along the road."

"How did she see the car?"

"She was out gathering salad leaves for the evening meal. There's very little traffic on that road and she knows most of the people, so when she saw this strange car she noticed it."

"She called it a 'strange' car?"

"Yes."

"So how did the idea that it was foreign come up?"

"I asked her about the make and she said she didn't know. I asked if it was foreign and she said that it was."

Zen nodded. The old woman wouldn't have known a Rolls-Royce from a Renault. "Foreign" just meant that the car was a large luxury sedan of a kind she'd never seen before.

"And there was only one person in it?"

"So she said. A woman with blond hair."

Zen took the report back again. "It says 'fair hair' here."

"Well, you can't put blond, can you?" Lucaroni pointed out. "The computer won't accept it. Hair is either fair or yellow."

"Yes, of course."

The inspector turned to go.

"Oh, there's one other thing," Zen murmured. He pointed to the wall. "You remember the crucifix that used to be there? You don't happen to know where it came from, do you?"

Lucaroni's tongue emerged to dampen his lips. He shook his head.

"I had a visitor in here the other day; there was an accident and the thing ended up in pieces. Most unfortunate."

"In pieces?" Lucaroni murmured.

Zen nodded. "Luckily my visitor was a Communist, so he's not superstitious about these things. I'd be happy to pay for a new one, but I have no idea where to go. Do you think you could get me one? I'd really appreciate it."

There was a long silence.

"Well . . ." Lucaroni began.

Zen tapped the man's chest with one finger. "But I want one that is the same. You understand? Exactly identical in every respect."

Their glances met and held.

"Identical," breathed the inspector.

"Absolutely. I was very fond of that crucifix. It had a certain something about it, know what I mean?"

Lucaroni's mouth was now completely out of control. His tongue shot out continually, dumping saliva on his lips, which barely had time to spread it around their shiny surfaces before the next load arrived. Zen hastened to dismiss him before he self-destructed.

A glance at the map revealed that there was a shortcut down to the Miletti villa, so instead of summoning Palottino he decided to walk. What he was thinking of doing was risky enough as it was. The less official he could make it, the better.

The shortcut was a lane which started abruptly at the bottom of a flight of steps opposite the Questura and ran straight down the hillside like a ruled line. It must have been one of the old medieval roads into the city, now closed to traffic by the concrete retaining wall of the ring boulevard. To either side old farmhouses and new villas stood in uneasy proximity. Beyond them, a narrow fold in the hillside was being filled with rubbish to provide space for a parking lot. Down below, lost in the mist, he could just make out the holm oaks and cypresses surrounding the Miletti property, a lugubrious baroque monstrosity built on a shoulder of land jutting out from the steep hillside.

Zen walked past it for another 150 meters to the separate entrance marked SOCIETÀ INDUSTRIALE MILETTI DI PERUGIA. At this depth the mist was still unwarmed by the sun, clinging glaucously to every surface. This was the site of Franco's original workshops, built just below the house. In those days captains of industry were not ashamed to live close to the source of their wealth. Since production had been moved out to Ponte San Giovanni, the buildings had been gutted and transformed into the administrative headquarters of SIMP. Zen expected tight security at the entrance, but the gates were open and unmanned, and a passing employee directed him along a concrete road leading to the garage, where a man in blue overalls was washing one of the Fiat sedans. Behind him a dozen or so more of the cars were lined up, their paintwork gleaming.

Zen flashed his identification with contemptuous brevity and then allowed a little time for the man's fear to be fruitful and multiply. Everyone has some reason to be afraid of the police, and fear, like money, can be spent on something quite unrelated to what has created it. When Zen judged that he had enough for his purposes he pointed to the Fiats.

"Are you responsible for these cars?"

The man nodded. Zen gave a satisfied smile, as though he had obtained a damning admission.

"Then what have you done with my cigarette lighter?"

"Cigarette lighter?" the mechanic stammered. "What sort of cigarette lighter?"

Zen's smile vanished. "Why, how many have you found?"

"None! I haven't found anything."

"Then why did you ask what sort, eh? Think you can keep anything you find, eh? Supplement your lousy wages with a little private enterprise, is that it?"

The man flung down his sponge angrily. "I've found nothing! I've just cleaned them all ready for this afternoon. There was no cigarette lighter in any of them."

"They're going to use the company cars for the funeral?" Zen queried in a tone of deep disgust. "Talk about cheap!"

"It's what Signor Ruggiero would have wanted."

"Don't try to change the subject! You claim not to have found any lighter, is that it?"

"I don't claim anything! I didn't find any lighter and that's all there is to it. Have a look for yourself if you want, I've got nothing to hide!"

"Oh, I'm going to! Don't you worry about that, I'm going to."

The mechanic watched him out of the corner of his eye as he went from car to car, making an elaborate pretense of examining the interiors.

The mud surrounding the building site where Ruggiero Miletti had been murdered had proved a rich source of impressions. A preliminary investigation, completed while Zen was still present, had yielded five different footprints and two distinct sets of tire marks. One of the two sets, which consistently overlaid the other, was distinctive, in that one of the tires did not match the other three. Zen had imagined that this would be a rarity, but in fact four of the cars in the garage had one odd tire. Only one configuration, however, matched that found at the murder scene.

"What the fuck do you think you're doing, Zen?"

It was Gianluigi Santucci. The Tuscan turned on the mechanic with barely suppressed fury.

"What has he been asking you, Massimo? If you've told him as much as the time, you're fired!"

"Nothing!" protested the mechanic energetically. "I've said nothing!"

"That's true," Zen confirmed. "He's been most unhelpful."

"I haven't found any lighter, I don't know anything about any lighter," Massimo went on indignantly. "I told him so, but he insisted on looking himself. But he didn't touch anything, Signor Gianluigi. I kept my eye on him the whole time."

Gianluigi Santucci glared at Zen. "Cigarette lighter my balls! What are you up to? Come on!"

"I've lost my lighter and I thought I might have left it in the car the other day. I didn't want to disturb the family at a time like this so I came to check in person. But I don't understand what you're getting so excited about. Is this garage a secret research area or something?"

Too late, Gianluigi realized his error. In an attempt to compensate he forced a smile.

"You haven't understood, have you?" he sneered. "You think you're still in the game, but you couldn't be more wrong. You're a foreigner here. No one wants you, no one likes you, no one needs you. If you haven't got your marching orders yet it just means no one can be bothered to tell you what's happening anymore! Now kindly fuck off out of here and don't come back."

When Zen reached the gate the security guard was back in his place, but he was so intent on the spluttering exclamations of his walkie-talkie, cradling it to his face and murmuring to it like a mother trying to calm a baby, that Zen's departure went as unremarked as his arrival.

He walked on down the hill to the junction of the lane and the main road, where the bottle containing Ruggiero's letter had been left. Opposite there were a bakery, an office-furniture showroom, a driving school, and a tobacconist showing the familiar public telephone symbol of a blue dial in a yellow circle. Zen went in, got two thousand lire's worth of tokens, and dialed a number in Rome.

"Gilberto?"

"*Who's this?*"

"Aurelio."

"*Aurelio! How's it going?*"

"Can you do me a favor?"

"*Such as?*"

"It means coming up here."

"*Where's here?*"

"Perugia. I've got problems."

"*What kind of problems?*"

"Can you come up this afternoon?"

"*This afternoon! Jesus.*"

Even at this depth the sunlight had finally started to filter down through the mist. There was a grove of olive trees opposite the café, on the other side of the main road. Above the rush and scurry of the traffic they stood in monumental stillness, each leaf precisely outlined against the deep blue sky.

"*What do you want done?*"

"Can we talk on this line?"

"*Listen, I'm in industrial espionage, you know. How long do you think I'd stay in business if I didn't keep my own lines clean? You worry about your own end.*"

Zen told his friend briefly about the murder and the large blue car that matched both the witness's description and the tire marks found at the scene. Then he told him what he wanted him to do. Gilberto said he would, although it might mean losing a contract to proof a leading Rome estate agent against electronic surveillance. They arranged to meet at half past four at a village a kilometer or so from the cemetery.

Zen rode a bus back to the Questura, where he checked out a pair of binoculars. Then he walked up to the center and wandered along the Corso. The steps of the cathedral were being used as a grandstand by some of the local young people and a few early tourists. A German youth whose exaggerated features looked as though they had been molded from foam rubber explained loudly to his companion how he *needed* the sun, the sun for him was not a luxury but a physical necessity. The two Nordic girls he had seen the day before were now basking like seals outside another café. One of them had even contrived to get sunburned. Her friend was delicately pulling little wafers of flaking skin off her chest, watched hungrily by a group of young men in leather jackets, narrow ties, and mirrored sunglasses.

All at once Zen saw a vigorous bulky figure in a dark gray overcoat with a black armband striding toward him across the piazza. It was Antonio Crepi. He prepared a greeting, but the Perugian passed by without a word or gesture, leaving Zen with his hand still uncertainly raised in salutation.

It was the first time that someone had cut him dead, and it was a shock. He had always thought of it as a superficial and outmoded gesture found only in old novels. But what had just happened had nothing to do with etiquette: Antonio Crepi had made it clear that for him, and by extension for the whole of the Perugia that mattered, Zen had ceased to exist. That's why ghosts wail, Zen thought, condemned to haunt a world which has no further need of them. He walked away quickly, trying to shake off the unnerving effect of the encounter.

The air was carved into blocks by the buildings, soft and warm where the sun reached, chill and unyielding in the shadows. Zen stopped at a small grocery and ordered a roll filled with anchovies sprinkled with vinegar and a little crushed chili, which he ate with a glass of white wine.

There was a newspaper open at the local pages on top of the freezer, and as he munched the roll Zen read an article describing the life and times of the late head of the Miletti family in such exorbitantly fulsome terms that Zen wondered in his dour Venetian way whether such a paragon would find Paradise quite good enough for him. He also wondered whether Ruggiero's daughter had seen the article, and if so what she thought of it. Cinzia had told him what kind of drinkers the Perugians were, and what kind of lovers. What he needed to know now was what kind of murderers they were.

When he had finished his lunch, Zen walked back to the center and caught a bus which deposited him, twenty minutes later, in an area with a name of its own but otherwise indistinguishable from the rest of the suburban sprawl. It was dominated by slablike apartment blocks, a concrete wasteland where children played among scrawny bushes planted in tubs cut from lengths of sewer pipe. Nothing else grew but the weeds, pushing up everywhere between the rectangular gray slabs.

Zen entered the farthest apartment block and started to climb the steps. After a week and a half in Perugia, steps no longer held any terrors for him, and despite the heavy binoculars he was hardly out of breath when he reached the flat roof of the building. Three washing lines were stretched from one end of the roof to the other, and Zen had to negotiate billowing sheets and rows of brassieres, corsets, and underpants. Once clear of this intimate jungle he made his way to the edge of the roof and looked down. A rare smile greeted the discovery that his calculations had been correct.

Perugia was in fact two cities, each on its separate hill. The city of the living was balanced by the city of the dead, which was laid out below him now like the stage of an amphitheater. The former might be larger, but the latter was arguably more attractive, with its gravel alleys and slim stately cypresses. And today at least it was livelier, as well. A vast crowd of people thronged the alleys, and the cars which had brought them were backed up from the entrance halfway to the apartment building from which Zen stood observing the scene through the binoculars. These were years out-of-date, like most police equipment, so they weighed many times as much as a modern pair of equivalent quality. That quality, however, was very high indeed, and for as long as Zen could stand the strain on his forearms and wrists—about three minutes at a time—his view of the proceedings was as clear as if he had been standing among the crowd gathered for Ruggiero Miletti's funeral.

That of course would have been unthinkable. The Milettis had blamed him publicly for Ruggiero's death, and, as Antonio Crepi had made clear, most of Perugia agreed with them. But Zen's present position offered all the advantages of attending in person, except for not being able to hear. With one of Gilberto's gadgets he could no doubt have listened in too, but that wasn't really important. Grand funerals are like grand opera: the gestures are exaggerated and stylized, and you don't need to understand the language to follow what's going on. And what *was* going on was of the highest interest. It was not the funeral itself. Zen, in fact, was barely aware of the progress of Ruggiero's coffin up the central alley to the Miletti family tomb. He was too busy studying the faces of the survivors to pay proper respect to the dead.

Cinzia was the first to draw his attention. Her outfit was almost identical to the one she had been wearing when she met Zen out shopping two days earlier, only a tone darker: the slacks were now black and the silver fox jacket had been replaced by one of sable. The occupant of this finery was gorgeously grieving. For once in her life no one could deny Cinzia the chance to go utterly and completely over the edge, and she was making the most of it, throwing herself into her husband's arms as though about to collapse, raising her hands to heaven in supplication, and wrenching her features into grimaces reminiscent of medieval statuary, to say nothing of a variety of vocal histrionics which Zen was spared. But apart from the intrinsic pleasures of this display, particularly given the exquisite contrast with Cinzia's real feelings about her father, might there not be another reason for her behavior? With all eyes on his wife, Gianluigi Santucci passed almost unnoticed. His wife's high-profile hysterics enabled Gianluigi to play the devoted husband so convincingly that no one stopped to wonder what manner of son-in-law he might have been.

On the other side of the Santuccis walked Daniele. The young man looked dazed. Faced with that fundamental event, the death of a parent, Daniele reacted as though his video player had jammed or a computer program refused to load. Something had gone wrong and he didn't understand what it was or how to put it right. But soon the mechanic would come and fix it and everything would be back to normal again.

Ruggiero's two eldest sons walked together at the head of the cortege, one either side of the priest. Silvio looked absolutely the same as always, as though his arrangements had been disrupted by an inconvenient function which he was obliged to attend but hoped would be over as soon as possible. But it was not Silvio but his elder brother whom Zen found himself watching most, like all the others for that matter. Oh yes, they were watching one another, the Milettis! But most of all, they were watching Pietro. Like Zen, they were perhaps thinking of what the man now lying in that elegant casket had written about his son just a few days earlier: *"You don't instigate plots, because you know that plots get discovered. Instead you manipulate the plots of others to your own ends, playing one off against the others, letting them waste their energies in fruitless rivalries while you look on from a safe distance, waiting patiently for the moment to make your move, the day when I drop dead and you can come home and claim your own."* That day had come sooner than anyone had expected. After the funeral Pietro would return to London to wind up his affairs there, but they all knew that he would return, and as head of the family. Now they were watching for some clue to his attitude, his feelings about them, his intentions. But Pietro was giving nothing away. His English manners served him well here. Where Silvio looked as though he couldn't care less, Pietro, while displaying no more emotion, contrived to suggest that this was not because he didn't feel any—on the contrary!—but because it simply wasn't done to let it show. Only once did he compromise. As his father's coffin disappeared into the tomb, Pietro raised one gloved hand to his cheek and wiped away a single tear, the strong man overcome by grief. The gesture was more effective in its economy than all Cinzia's ravings.

As the priest read the funeral service, Zen looked at the members of the family grouped around the tomb. He found himself thinking of what Luciano Bartocci had told him about ratkings: *"Evidently the creatures have evolved some way of coming to terms with their situation."* The Milettis were no more conscious of the priest's words than Zen was. They were watching one another, coming to terms with their new situation. And what was that situation? That Pietro was in charge, for one thing. But there was more to it than that, Zen thought as he watched the glances flickering back and forth among them like lightning.

He set the binoculars down for a moment to rest his arms and light a cigarette. When he looked back to the cemetery he found his gaze focused not on the main participants but the throng of friends and employees gathered around the family. There was Antonio Crepi. Ruggiero's death seemed to have triggered a gradual implosion in the old man's body. He was collapsing inward like a leaky sandbag. Next Zen picked out Ivy Cook, occupying a suitable position midway between the family and the employees. But where the others were restlessly searching one another's faces for clues and hints, Ivy's gaze was fixed steadily on Silvio. Her expression was caring yet efficient, like a good surgeon. Not far behind her stood Massimo, the garage mechanic Zen had browbeaten that morning, cap in hand and a look of genuine grief on his face.

Zen shifted the glasses to cover the road and the line of parked cars. A short sturdy man conspicuously not dressed in mourning had opened the hood of one of the company's Fiat sedans and was tinkering with the engine. A moment later he closed the hood, climbed inside the car, and drove away. Zen looked back at the family, and suddenly he understood the meaning of those glances they were giving one another. *The Milettis weren't absolutely sure that the kidnappers had murdered Ruggiero.* They would never dream of admitting it, even to one another, but the fact remained that it had crossed each of their minds that Ruggiero had been murdered not by the kidnappers but by one of them! It was a revelation, as instant and inexplicable as it was incontrovertible, and it made Zen glad. For as he watched the Milettis performing their funeral rites, he envied them bitterly the simple fact of having a father to bury.

By half past four it was getting dark. The cooling air was scented with the heady reek of diesel oil from the bus which had brought Zen to the village at the end of its route. The driver was sitting on the step, smoking and reading the sports pages of *L'Unità*. Zen stood leaning on a rusty metal railing watching the courtship of two pigeons on the tiled roof of a shed below. The gurgling male, alternately bowing down and rearing up, chased the female from one row of tiles to the next. Eventually he appeared to lose interest, disheartened by her lack of appreciation, and turned away. Instantly the female stopped too, so that both birds came to a halt like toys whose batteries had run down. It seemed the end. Relationships were just too difficult, the sexes would never see eye to eye, it was all too much bother. Something essential had broken down and next year there wouldn't be any pigeons. Then, just as suddenly as he had stopped, the male was off again, perking up his feathers and hopping after his mate with a meaningful glint in his beady eyes. Zen had watched this cycle a dozen times or more when he felt a touch on his shoulder and turned to find Gilberto grinning up at him.

Gilberto Nieddu was so small that it wasn't clear how he had ever managed to get into the police force. There were the inevitable rumors of bribery and favoritism, but since Gilberto's father was only a small-time locksmith from Nuoro this seemed unlikely. Zen preferred to think that some alert recruiting officer somewhere, realizing the appalling threat a disgruntled Gilberto would pose *outside* the law, had bent the rules to let him in. For four years they had worked together in Rome. The Sardinian had resigned a week after Zen's transfer, and was the only one of his former colleagues whom Zen still saw regularly.

"Any problems?" Zen asked him.

"Only getting back here after I dumped it. You *had* to choose a place in the middle of nowhere."

"Close to the scene. Local color."

Gilberto was as compact as a squash ball, sallow, ugly, and muscular, yet amazingly deft in his movements. For a bet, he had once broken into the flat where a certain Vice-Questore was entertaining a lady friend and removed the couple's clothes so stealthily that the Vice-Questore believed something supernatural must have occurred and turned religious for a while. No, Gilberto wouldn't have had any problems stealing an unguarded car from outside a cemetery.

"Is this all really worth it?" the Sardinian asked Zen, who merely shrugged.

"How much do I owe you?"

Gilberto Nieddu spat thoughtfully at the pigeons on the roof below. "Take me out to lunch when you get back. At the Pergola."

"The Pergola! Wouldn't it work out cheaper just to pay your normal rates?"

"Now don't try and wriggle out of it or I'll send Vittorio round to see you. He's my new enforcer. A great success. You may think you have problems now, but Vittorio can make them seem like fond memories."

Zen handed him a key with a number stamped on the shaft. "This opens a luggage locker at the station. There's something inside, wrapped up in a plastic bag. I'd like to know what it is."

The Sardinian looked at him long and hard, shaking his head slowly. "You know something, Aurelio? You aren't really cut out to be a cop."

"Imagine living in a country where the cops are all people who're cut out for the job."

"I'll phone you tomorrow morning."

Zen shook his head. "*I'll* phone *you*."

The Sardinian spat once more, narrowly missing the male pigeon. "Christ, you have got problems."

Zen just had time to cross to the phone booth, dial the police emergency number, and give the message he had prepared. Then he hung up without giving a name as the bus driver started his engine again. He boarded the bus just as the doors were closing. Moments later the bus passed Gilberto walking back up the hill to the place where he had left his own car, just below the massive wall of the columbarium in the cemetery where Ruggiero Miletti had been interred two hours previously.

The switchboard on the ground floor of the Questura was manned by a chubby youth who was holding a large roll, turning it from one side to the other and studying it closely like a wrestler looking for a hold. As Zen came in he suddenly saw an opening and lunged forward, so that for the next thirty seconds or so he was unable to reply to his visitor's question.

"He wouldn't give his name," he said finally, swallowing. "Probably a joke."

"What exactly did he say?"

"Just said he wanted to report a blue Fiat abandoned on the road to Cannara, near the scene of the murder."

The telephonist kept glancing warily at his roll out of the corner of his eye, as though it might attack him.

Zen leaned forward on the top of the switchboard. "Listen, this could be very important. I want that car brought in, turned over to the laboratory, and given the works."

"They'll need confirmation in writing."

"They'll get it."

The telephonist nodded. He was too eager to get back to his roll to ask how Zen had found out about the anonymous phone call.

Upstairs on the third floor Zen stopped in at the inspectors' room, but there was no one there. He was about to leave when he froze in an awkward position midway across the room. Then he heard it again, a slight but unmistakable sound from next door. Someone was in his office.

As quietly as he could, he moved toward the connecting door, grasped the handle, and with a single movement flung the door open.

"About time too! I was beginning to think I'd have to spend the night here."

"Ellen."

"Ah, so you remember my name!"

He leaned back against the door, feeling his body slowly untense. "It's wonderful to see you."

"Really? I certainly wouldn't have guessed it from the way you've been behaving. Why haven't you telephoned me?"

"I did," he lied automatically. "You were never there!"

"I was!"

"Not when I phoned."

"I've been home almost every evening. When did you phone?"

"Well anyway, let's not quarrel. The important thing is that you're here. How long can you stay?"

"I'll have to see. It depends."

He tried to kiss her, but she evaded him in a half-angry, half-flirtatious way, so they were in the middle of a clumsy clinch when Lucaroni walked in.

"Oh fuck!" he said, on his way out again.

Zen exploded. "Didn't anyone ever teach you to knock? You're not home on the farm now, you know!"

"Sorry, chief. Really sorry. I didn't think anybody was here. I was going to put it up for you."

"Put what up?"

Lucaroni pulled back the wrapping on the package he was carrying to reveal a brand-new crucifix, the wounds daubed with bright red paint.

"Just what you wanted, right?" the inspector prompted eagerly. "Just like the other one."

Zen glanced at Ellen, who was staring at him in horrified disbelief.

"I'll explain later," he told her wearily. "Don't worry. I'll explain everything later."

A small white plastic bag containing various packets of waxed paper marked FOR FOODSTUFFS lay propped against the gear lever of the little Fiat. The draft coming in through the ventilation ducts made it tremble continuously. What a crazy idea, thought Zen. Picnicking on a mountain at this time of year! They should never have come. A crazy *foreign* idea.

It had all started the night before, when Ellen asked, "Is that Assisi over there?" They were standing in front of his hotel window. In the distance a mess of lights were spread out across the face of the night like a shovelful of glowing cinders, flickering and scintillating in the currents of air rising from the houses in the plain between. "Let's go there tomorrow," she'd suggested, and then talked about her previous visits, enthusing about the place so much that he grew quite determined to dislike it. But it wasn't until Ellen had come to pick him up that morning that he discovered that she had already bought everything for a picnic lunch. One o'clock in Piazza dei Partigiani after a stressful morning at work was very different from eleven o'clock the previous night after making love, but Ellen was bubbling with such enthusiasm that he hadn't the heart to voice his reservations. But he still thought it was crazy, and he'd been right. Here they were, parked a thousand meters up the dough-shaped mountain, huddled in Ellen's Fiat 500 because despite the sun the wind outside was wicked. Even the view was all but invisible through a windshield coated with Roman grime. Foreign craziness!

Ellen started to unwrap the food: a mound of ricotta, slices of cooked ham, olives in oil, half a loaf of bread. On a warm sunny day in the open air it might have been idyllic. Eaten off sheets of wrapping paper balanced precariously on their shivering knees, the cheese looked a disgusting white excrescence, the ham pale and sickly, and the olives slimy. Even the wine, a heavy red, was a failure. Cold and shaken from the journey, thick with sediment, and drunk from a plastic beaker, it tasted like medicine. But it did him good, and the food tasted better than it looked, and after a while the silence grew less tense and they began to chat about the contrast between earnest, bloody-minded Perugia, just visible on its windswept ridge as a distant smudge of gray, and Assisi, symbol of everything nice and pretty and kind, whose pink stone made even its fortifications look as innocent as an illustration in a book of fairy tales. But as Zen pointed out, at least in Perugia you were spared the relentless commercialization of the pilgrim city, the three-dimensional postcards of a glamorous Saint Francis preaching to an audience of stuffed animals, the bottles of "Monk's Delight" liqueur, the ceramic prayer texts suitable for mounting over the toilet, the little figurines of lovable monks with round bellies and mischievous smiles.

"Yes, but despite all that there really is something special about the place, isn't there?" Ellen insisted.

It was the sort of comment, at once vague and gushing, that always irritated him. Sometimes he wondered whether that was why she kept making them.

"To me it's just another pretty Umbrian hill town," he retorted. "It's a shame it's been ruined."

He was going too far, pushing too hard, saying things he didn't really believe. It was quite deliberate. Something had gone wrong between them, and he intended to find out what it was. Normally he handed over responsibility for the routine maintenance of their relationship to Ellen, but today she was letting him down. He was going to try the only technique he knew: drop some explosive overboard and see what floated to the surface.

"How can you say that?" she demanded indignantly. "What about all the churches? They wouldn't exist if it hadn't been for him. The basilica is one of the greatest buildings in the world. Or would you dispute that?"

"On the contrary, I think it's so great that it should be put to better use. I remember when I was at university in Padua we went to see the basilica there. It's magnificent, one of my friends said, after the revolution we'll turn it into a sports center. The place here would make a good Turkish baths."

"You're showing your age, Aurelio. That sort of knee-jerk anticlericalism has been out-of-date for years."

"Or best of all, they could use it as an exhibition center. They could start with a display about the concentration camp at Jasenovac."

"Wasn't that in Poland?" she asked as she cleared away the food.

"Yugoslavia. No one's heard of it, it wasn't in the Auschwitz or Belsen class. They only killed forty thousand people there."

"And what's that got to do with Assisi?"

"The commandant of Jasenovac concentration camp was a Franciscan monk."

He opened the window a crack, but the wind made such a noise that he immediately closed it again.

"When the Germans turned Croatia into a puppet dictatorship, the Catholics there immediately got to work settling old scores with the Serbs, packing them into their churches and burning them alive, that kind of thing. The Church knew what was going on and they could easily have stopped it. But the Pope kept quiet and the atrocities went on, many of them supervised by the followers of Saint Francis. At the end of the war Eva Peron, the wife of the Argentine dictator, sent us a boatload of brown cloth. Guess why."

She shook her head.

"To dress the Croatian thugs up as Franciscan monks so that they could escape to Italy out of the clutches of Tito's partisans. They were fed and sheltered here in Assisi and in other monasteries and church buildings until they could get away to South America. They were good Catholic boys, after all."

"I don't suppose Tito's men were angels either."

"I don't suppose they were. But at least they didn't go around with beatific smiles mumbling about peace and goodwill."

"Well I'm relieved to see that you haven't changed after all," Ellen remarked as they lit their cigarettes. "I got a bit worried when I found you'd been sending your subordinates out to buy crucifixes."

Zen smiled too, but privately he heard Gilberto Nieddu's voice again, the Sardinian accent strong and clear-cut even over the bad line from Rome:

"Oh yes, Aurelio, I've identified it. No problem. For me, that is. You've got problems all right. Your crucifix contains a transistorized short-wave transmitter with a cadmium-cell feed. Korean job, cheap and

easy to obtain, four to five months continuous operation, use once and throw away. The mike concealed in the head of the figure is only medium quality, technically speaking, but it would pick up a flea farting in a smallish room. The transmitter would then beam that out about two hundred meters. Somewhere within that radius there'll be a receiver, probably rigged up to a voice-activated tape recorder. Once every so often someone comes along, swaps the cassette, and takes away the highlights of your day at work."

There was a long silence, during which the noise on the line seemed to become a third party in their conversation.

"What do you want me to do with it?"

"You'd better send it back."

"Do you have any idea who it belongs to?"

The silence lasted even longer this time.

"Upstairs, maybe," Zen finally murmured.

Gilberto's next words had shaken him more than anything that had happened so far:

"Watch yourself, Aurelio. Remember Carella."

Avoiding Ellen's eyes, Zen wrapped his coat more closely about him. "Anyway, let's look on the bright side. The way things are going I should be back in Rome soon."

"I still don't understand what all the fuss is about." Ellen's tone was slightly peevish. "Miletti's death was nothing to do with you, surely?"

"That remains to be proved."

"Oh, I see. It's the old story. You're guilty until proven innocent."

"Not necessarily. Sometimes you're guilty anyway."

They sat there listening to the wind buffeting the car.

"You didn't tell me the whole truth that evening at Ottavio's, did you?" Ellen asked at last.

He didn't reply.

"I want to know, Aurelio. I need to know."

He turned his pale grave face toward her. "When you were a child, did you have someone who used to tell you stories?"

She looked at him in surprise. "My father used to read to me."

"No, I don't mean that. If it comes out of a book you know it's not real. I mean someone who would just sit down and tell you things, as if they had just happened on the way home. I had an uncle who did that. For example, once he went to Rome on business and when he got back he told me about a building which was like the sky at night, so big that even when you stood

in front of it you couldn't believe you were actually seeing it. Yet
it was completely useless, he said. It had no roof and no floor,
just hundreds of huge brick arches piled one on top of the
others like a team of acrobats. He was describing the Colosseum."

He opened the window and tossed out his cigarette.

"Once he was late arriving at our house. He told me that when
the *vaporetto* arrived he had noticed something strange about it.
The boat was lying far too low in the water, almost level with the
surface, the decks awash. It made no sound, and even seemed to
absorb the sounds around it, like a sponge soaking up water.
The people who were waiting all boarded this strange boat, all
except my uncle. I asked him why he hadn't got on with the
other passengers. Because that was the ferry of death, he said.
He explained that the people who had got on that ferry would
get off in another world, and would never be seen in this one
again. There is another city all around us, he told me. We can't
see it, but there are ways into it, although there is no way back.
Anyone who boards a certain ferry or walks down a certain
street or enters a certain building or goes through a certain
door disappears forever into that other city."

Ellen was looking at him with an expression he had never
seen before. For a moment he wondered if he was doing the
right thing. But in some odd way the decision no longer seemed
to be in his hands.

"My uncle's stories sounded unlikely, but they always turned
out to be true. That parallel world really exists, and what
happened to me in 1978 was that I unwittingly blundered into
it."

The wind surged around the little car, streaking past across
the expanse of long brown grass still flattened from the snow
that had lain on it over the winter.

"In 1978 I was in the kidnapping section of the Criminal
Investigation Branch. I was considered to be doing well. Rome
Central is one of the three top postings in the country, along
with Milan and Naples, and I'd worked my way there through
a succession of jobs in various provincial headquarters. Promotion to Vice-Questore seemed certain and the general feeling
was that if I played my cards right I would make Questore in the
end. When the Red Brigades kidnapped Moro we were all
thrown into the investigation, under the direction of the Political Branch. The first thing we discovered was that there

seemed to be almost no information to go on. Despite all the money the Politicals had been siphoning off for years, they claimed to have no material on the terrorists beyond a few isolated descriptions and photographs. It was almost unbelievable. Here was Aldo Moro, an ex-Prime Minister, the leader of the Christian Democrat Party, and one of the most powerful and influential men in Italy, at the mercy of the best-known organization of political extremists, and the people responsible for combating political extremism told us there was nothing we could do except organize random house-to-house searches. So that's what we did, along with chasing after various red herrings which somebody provided to keep us busy. It was all we could do, until one day when one of my inspectors, a man called Dario Carella, phoned in claiming to have seen one of the suspected terrorists. Carella had followed the man to a chemist's shop in Piazzale della Radio and then to a bus stop. But the suspect must have noticed him, because he suddenly waved down a passing taxi and drove off. Carella had taken the number of the taxi and we discovered that it had dropped the suspect outside the San Gallicano hospital in Trastevere. Meanwhile Carella went back to the chemist's to find out what the man had bought. The result was very interesting. The prescription had been forged, and the medicines listed were all among those regularly used by Aldo Moro. Remember, besides suffering from Addison's disease, Moro was a bit of a hypochondriac and he used a lot of drugs. He had a supply with him when he was captured, but this would have run out by then. It looked as though one of his captors had been sent to get more. The Political Branch were informed and the hospital duly sealed off and searched, but there was no trace of the man. Next we did a door-to-door of the whole area. You probably remember that."

"I certainly do. They almost wrecked my flat."

"That wasn't any more successful. But Carella had an idea. The bus stop where the suspect had waited in Piazzale della Radio is served by three lines, the 97, 97C, and 128. And just around the corner from the San Gallicano hospital, in Piazza Sonnino, is the terminus of the 97 and 97C. Suppose the suspect had taken the taxi to get rid of Carella, got out at the hospital to confuse matters further, walked around the corner to the terminus, and then continued by bus to his original destination? In that case, this wouldn't be Trastevere but one of the districts to the south where those two lines go, Portuense or EUR.

Carella explained his idea to me, and I thought it was worth following up. It might not be much to go on, but it wasn't as though we had a wealth of other leads. So I went upstairs and proposed that we should do a house-to-house on those two areas. There was nothing very original in this. It was just routine procedure, playing percentages, and I was very surprised when I heard that the proposal had been rejected. When I queried the decision I was told that it had been made at the very highest level, as a result of information not available to me."

He tried to remove a smudge from the windshield with the tip of his finger, but it was on the other side of the glass.

"Well, all right, so I thought the decision was surprising, but I'd long since realized that if I allowed that sort of thing to keep me awake at night I was going to be a chronic insomniac. But Carella was not so phlegmatic. He was a Southerner and a devout Catholic, like Moro himself, and I think he felt guilty for not having made more of the best chance anyone had so far had to rescue his hero. In short, he got a bit obsessed with the whole thing and he couldn't accept the decision not to pursue it further. At least, that's what I assume. We didn't discuss it, and when he didn't appear at work the next day I thought he was just sulking. But that night one of my other inspectors phoned and told me that Carella was in hospital after being struck by a car in the Portuense district. It was the San Gallicano hospital, as it happened. By the time I got there he was dead."

He looked up through the clear patch of windshield at the clouds moving slowly and peacefully across the upper reaches of the sky. The wind up there must be a different quantity from the restless gusts where they were.

"This is where it gets difficult to explain. Because instead of just letting it go I allowed myself to get involved. I don't know why. I've been asking myself ever since. Dario Carella wasn't a relative or even a friend. I didn't actually like him very much. And yet I risked everything I had worked for, all the hope of what I might do in a position of real power, for something that was obviously doomed to failure from the start. That bothers me, it really does. I've always thought of myself as a sensible person, yet I allowed myself to do that. I can't understand why."

Ellen laughed, a short mirthless noise. "Oh Christ, Aurelio, I don't believe it!"

"You don't believe what?"

Her expression became opaque. "Nothing. Go on."

Apparently he'd got it wrong yet again.

"The next day I went to question the bus drivers. As I suspected, Carella had been there before me. One of the men I spoke to said that a colleague of his had identified the terrorist suspect from a photograph Carella had shown him. I got the colleague's address and went to have a word with him. As I was walking up to his house, two young bearded men in jeans and sweaters got out of a car and ran toward me. For a moment I thought they were terrorists, but I was wrong, they were Political Branch operatives. They drove me back to headquarters, where I was questioned by an officer I'd never seen before, a colonel. It was a small stuffy room, and yet I distinctly felt a chill in the air, like a draft, and I knew that it must be coming from that other world my uncle had told me about, and that the threshold to it was somewhere very close at hand. The colonel wanted to know what I had been doing and who I had talked to. It wasn't an easy hand to play. On the one hand I needed to stress the bus driver's evidence in order to bolster my case, which was that Carella had somehow stumbled on a clue to Moro's whereabouts. On the other hand I knew that if I made the driver sound too important he might end up under the wheel of a bus instead of behind one. In the end I was told to go home and to stay there. The next day I received a telegram informing me that my request to be transferred to clerical duties at the Ministry of the Interior had been granted. I hadn't submitted any such request, of course."

There was a long silence, broken only by the perpetual nudging of the wind, which seemed to be getting stronger all the time.

"Shall we go?" Ellen asked.

She started the engine without waiting for an answer and began to drive along the track winding down the mountain.

"The Red Brigades were holding Moro in Portuense, weren't they?" she commented suddenly.

"In a ground-floor flat in Via Montalcini. About four blocks from where Dario Carella was run over."

It wasn't until they reached the walls of Assisi that she spoke again.

"It's no good, I don't understand. I'll never understand. Why should they *let* him be killed? It doesn't make any sense! After all, he was one of them."

"Perhaps he was no longer really one of them. Perhaps they didn't know that until he was kidnapped. Perhaps once he'd gone they realized that they were better off without him. The ratking is self-regulating, it responds automatically and effectively to every situation."

She took her eyes off the road for an instant to glance at him. "What have rats got to do with it?"

"Oh, nothing. I was just trying to explain how Miletti came to be killed."

"Miletti?"

"I mean Moro."

"How much have you had to drink?"

"Enough to need a coffee."

They stopped in a village on the flat straight road from Assisi to Perugia. The air was still and it was pleasantly warm. The café was a brash new building full of old men playing cards.

"I'm going back this afternoon," Ellen said as they stood at the bar, watched by every eye in the place.

Her visit had not been a success. The basic material of their relationship, the DNA itself, seemed to have gone wrong. As long as that condition lasted, the time they spent together, instead of adding to their store of shared experiences, depleted the existing one, leaving them more apart than when they were separated.

"I'll be back soon myself," he told her, "and then we'll forget all this and have a really good time again."

Ellen nodded, but her face remained blank and unconvinced. When they reached Perugia she dropped him opposite the Questura. As he stooped to kiss her Zen noticed that her cheeks were wet.

"Why are you crying?"

She shook her head. "I'm afraid."

"Afraid of what?"

"Of everything."

"There's no need to be afraid. It'll be all right."

But he stood there watching until the little car had disappeared, as though Ellen were setting off on a long and dangerous journey from which she might never return.

9

One day toward the end of the
war five ships had appeared in the lagoon off Venice. For a few
weeks they lay moored together, like a new island between the
city and the Lido, and then one day they were gone. Later Zen
worked out that they must have been American warships of an
obsolete type, waiting to be sold or scrapped, but at the time
their slightly menacing presence seemed a pure challenge, and
when his friend Tommaso dared him to try to get aboard one he
naturally agreed. Close up they were as big as churches: great
solid slabs of crudely painted gray with black numbers too large
to read. Only the end vessel was manned by a token guard, and
it was easy though terrifying to slip into one of the narrow
channels between them, where the water slapped back and
forth, tie their skiff to the anchor cable, and then shin up it to
the deck. The rest of that day they spent in an alien world of
pipes and gauges and controls and levers and incomprehensible
signs, like the first explorers of a ruined city.

With most of the staff going home at two o'clock, the end of
the working day for employees of the State, the Questura had a

similar air of massive abandonment which Zen always found attractive. The rooms and corridors were empty except for a few elderly women cleaning up the male mess of scattered newspapers, stained coffee cups, overflowing ashtrays, and the odd half-eaten sandwich. They had not yet reached Zen's office, but someone else had been there, for there was a telegram on his desk.

Although he had been expecting it, it was still a shock. He put it away in his pocket unopened, and mechanically leafed through the report on the forensic tests he had unofficially requested on the Fiat sedan Gilberto Nieddu had stolen from outside the cemetery during Ruggiero Miletti's funeral and left abandoned near the scene of the murder. He had pinned all his hopes on this report providing him with some positive evidence to lay before the investigating magistrate, Rosella Foria, and when it had arrived that morning he'd been bitterly disappointed.

True, the three Pirellis and the odd Michelin on the car corresponded "in their general type and configuration" to the tire tracks found at the murder site, as he had confirmed when he checked the car at the SIMP garage. But in the absence of "specific individuating features" a positive identification was not possible, while the soil samples found were merely "consistent with types found throughout the area." As for the interior, it was clear that the mechanic had done his work well. The only items found were inconclusive traces of paint and dust, some cigarette ash, a few yellow nylon threads, and a fifty-lire coin which had fallen and lodged beside the seat support, whose metal base protected it from the nozzle of Massimo's vacuum cleaner. In short, nothing that would convince Rosella Foria that there was any case for pursuing this line of inquiry, when to do so would mean admitting that one of the Miletti family was under suspicion. To justify that you would need a lot more than the vague phrases of the report and the confused statements of a single witness. You would practically need a photograph of one of them pulling the trigger, and it had better be a damn good photograph, and even then the smart thing to do would be to tear it up, burn the fragments, and forget you'd ever seen it.

The door opened and a grizzled face bound in a yellow scarf appeared. At the same moment the phone began to ring.

"*May I speak to Commissioner Aurelio Zen, please.*" A woman's voice, cool and distant.

"Speaking."

"This is Rosella Foria, investigating magistrate. I should like to see you in my office, please."

The cleaning woman was already hard at work, banging her mop into the corners of the room.

"Now?"

"If that is convenient." Her tone suggested that he'd better come even if it wasn't.

"It stinks!" the cleaning woman remarked as he hung up.

"What?"

"He can't control his pee." Her accent was so broad that Zen could barely understand. "I rub and scrub from morning to night but it's no good, everything stinks."

She waved at the crucifix Lucaroni had provided. "He hangs up there doing sweet fuck-all and they expect us to feel sorry for Him! I just wish we could change places, that's all! Half an hour of my life and He'd wish He was back on his nice cozy cross, believe you me."

For once Zen accepted Palottino's offer of a lift up to the center of town. On the way he amused himself by constructing a prima facie case against Cinzia Miletti. The gun used to kill Ruggiero was the same caliber as the pistol registered in her name, and the old salad-gatherer had said that the driver of the Fiat had blond hair. Cinzia claimed to have gone to Perugia to meet Ivy Cook, but Zen had discovered that she'd lied about the copy of Ruggiero's letter, and that lie too had been intended to throw suspicion on Ivy. Cinzia could have arranged the appointment to fake an alibi, gone to avenge herself on the man who had abused her innocence, then driven into Perugia and made a point of accosting Zen in order to strengthen her story. She'd had the motive, the means, and the opportunity, and if her second name hadn't been Miletti they would have run a ballistic check on that little pistol of hers, questioned her in detail about the time during which she claimed to have been waiting for Ivy, and staged a line-up to find out if the witness who had seen the blue Fiat and its blond driver could pick her out. As it was, all that was out of the question. Luciano Bartocci might have risked it, which was precisely why he had been replaced. Rosella Foria wouldn't make the same mistake. If only one of those nylon threads they'd found on the floor of the SIMP Fiat had been a blond hair instead, Zen thought. *"Hair is either fair or yellow,"* Lucaroni had told him. It sounded like a line from a pop song, and he murmured it over and over to himself as the car bumped over the cobbles of Piazza Matteotti.

Rosella Foria turned out to be a fragile-looking woman in her early thirties. Although her manner was suitably authoritative, her face seemed to seek approval. Her office, although almost identical to Bartocci's, was impeccably neat and tidy.

"There are two matters which I wish to discuss with you, Commissioner," she began. "The first concerns a car belonging to the Miletti family which I understand has been impounded by the police."

Zen had been expecting something of the kind.

"Two days ago I was informed that a blue Fiat Argenta sedan had been found abandoned near the scene of the murder," he replied. "Since such a car had been sighted by a witness near the scene at the time of the murder, I followed normal procedure and sent the vehicle for forensic analysis with a view to eliminating it from suspicion."

"Yet you failed to notify the Public Prosecutor's office of this development. Why?"

Despite her uncompromising tone, she was still smiling. Zen was used to dealing with men, whose signals, ritualized over centuries of aggressive display, were clear and simple to follow. But Rosella Foria was unencumbered by such traditions.

"Because the correspondence with the car mentioned by the witness was only superficial, and I saw no reason to anticipate a positive identification."

The magistrate drew her well-plucked brows together. "I don't understand how you could fail to see the significance of your action for the investigation given that the car belonged to the Miletti family."

"I didn't know that it did."

Rosella Foria's frown deepened. "Do you mean to say that you failed to take the elementary step of tracing the registered owner of the vehicle?"

"On the contrary, that was the first thing I did. The car proved to be registered to a Fiat dealer. From what you have just told me, I assume that it was one of those leased by the Miletti firm and used by the family."

"It didn't occur to you to contact the dealer in question?"

"I certainly should have done so if the tests had produced any positive results. But in fact they were inconclusive."

She looked at him long and hard, but he noticed her

shoulders relax and knew that it would be all right. She might or might not believe him. The main thing was that he had given her a story she could pass on to Di Leonardo and the Milettis. She was off the hook.

"All the same, it's most unfortunate that this has happened. Needless to say, the family are extremely displeased."

Zen did not need to ask how they had learned of it. Like every powerful family, they would have a contact in the force.

"The car was apparently stolen from outside the cemetery while they were attending their father's funeral," the magistrate observed, watching him carefully.

Zen's gray eyes remained impenetrably glazed. "Probably some youngsters took it for a joyride and then dumped it."

"Possibly. In any event, we may consider the incident closed. But in the present situation misunderstandings of this kind are to be avoided at all costs. I should like your assurance that you will take no further initiatives without consulting me."

"Are you suggesting I have exceeded my powers?"

He knew very well that she wasn't, of course, just as he knew what she *was* doing: telling him to forget the legal niceties and please not lift so much as a finger without her consent, because the situation was so delicate, the moment so critical, and the stakes so high.

"I don't feel it's the letter of the law that we ought to be concerned with here," she went on in a conciliatory tone, fingering the single-strand pearl necklace which looped above the neck of her Benetton cardigan. "It's more a question of not hurting people's feelings by hasty or ill-considered gestures, of not wounding a family which has just lost one of its members in deeply distressing circumstances. Above all, it's a question of not doing this when it is demonstrably gratuitous and irrelevant to the purpose of apprehending those responsible for this crime."

"But it's not demonstrably anything of the kind," Zen protested. Although he lacked the hard evidence he'd hoped for, it was surely time to open this woman's eyes a little, give her some idea of the possibilities that were being swept under the carpet. "On the contrary, in my experience it's unheard of for criminals to phone a number they know is being monitored in order to give the location of the body of a man they have just killed. If they wanted to murder Miletti, why didn't they do so up in the mountains or wherever they were holding him? Why risk moving him to a spot close to Perugia only to shoot him dead?"

The investigating magistrate carefully rearranged the stack of papers on the desk in front of her so that the edges were perfectly aligned.

"If I chose, Commissioner, I could answer these objections with a much stronger one. You seem to forget that Dottor Miletti was murdered almost twenty-four hours *before* the call informing us that he had been released. During that period of time only the kidnappers knew where he was. So how could anyone else possibly have committed the crime? However, this is all beside the point. I said I had two things to tell you. The first concerned the Milettis' car. The second is that the Carabinieri in Florence have detained a number of men who are believed to be members of the gang which kidnapped and murdered Ruggiero Miletti. I'm going there tomorrow morning to conduct the formal interrogation, but I'm informed that they've already made a full confession."

This was different, this was real. He'd been wrong, terribly wrong. Zen felt like a child on the beach whose sandy battlements have melted beneath the first big wave. Appropriately, Rosella Foria's concluding words sounded almost maternal.

"Don't take it too hard, Commissioner. It's a pity that your efforts here have not been rewarded with success, but once you're back in Rome you will no doubt soon find other outlets for your energies."

As soon as he got outside, Zen took out the telegram which had been waiting for him that morning at the Questura. As he had thought, it was from the Ministry, informing him that his temporary transfer to the Questura of Perugia would terminate at midnight on Saturday and that his normal duties at the Ministry would resume at 0800 Monday.

For at least a minute he stood motionless on the curb, oblivious to the animated scene around him. Then he crumpled up the telegram and walked back to the Alfetta, where he made Palottino's day by ordering him to drive to Florence as quickly as possible.

The Neapolitan took Zen at his word, but even he couldn't cover the 150 kilometers in much less than an hour. But to Zen the journey seemed much shorter than that, for he fell asleep in the backseat and found himself with Ellen in what looked like the baggage room of a large railway station, although in fact it was a funeral parlor. The mortician kept making jocular remarks to Ellen about the carvings on the casket being "really tasteful," the implication being that they were actually tacky in the extreme. Finally Zen took him to one side and said, "Listen, show a bit of respect, can't you? This is her *father*." The mortician promptly whipped out a screwdriver and started to open up the coffin. Zen braced himself, because the body was bound to be pretty far gone after all these years. But the coffin contained nothing but a set of smaller coffins, stacked one within the other, identical except for the carvings, which the mortician kept opening one after another like a conjuror. They were down to the size of a shoebox by the time Zen went to the cashier to pay. The bill seemed very reasonable, only a few thousand lire, although they would apparently have to do the burial themselves. The cemetery was packed solid with some clan from the South who were exhuming the body of a long-dead relative, the women all dressed in their Sunday best, the young girls wearing garlands of flowers on their foreheads. There was foreboding music, and in close-up he saw one of the girls being initiated by the older women, professionals of death, who drew the cadaver's shiny brown withered arm across the child's face in a ritual caress.

It was a relief to be awakened by the siren as the Alfetta left the motorway and entered the southern suburbs of Florence. At Carabinieri headquarters Zen was received with just that air of polite suspicion that he had expected. When he announced that he had important information about the Miletti case he was taken upstairs and handed over to Captain Rivolta, a young officer with an aristocratic appearance and a languid manner who denied any personal involvement in what Zen referred to as "this magnificent coup."

"It was a tip-off, I suppose," Zen suggested.

Captain Rivolta gave a minimal nod. "From a Sardinian gang, I believe. The usual rivalry."

"So the kidnappers were based here in Florence?"

Rivolta repeated his fastidious gesture of assent. "Two brothers. They ran a furniture showroom and recycled the ransom along with takings from the business. They handled the negotiations themselves. It was they who had the Milettis' representative killed. Apparently he caught sight of one of them during the negotiations."

Zen nodded sagely. It was going quite well, he thought. The young captain was relaxing nicely.

"Anyway, I understand you have some information to pass on," Rivolta murmured.

"No, that's just what I told them downstairs."

Captain Rivolta appeared to wake up fully for the first time.

"I've come to see the prisoners," Zen explained.

"Well, that's a bit difficult, I'm afraid. As you are no doubt aware, requests for interrogation rights must be presented through the appropriate channels."

"That's all right, I don't want to interrogate them. I want to beat them up."

The young officer's superior smile froze in place, as though he wasn't quite sure what to do with it. "Beat them up," he repeated mechanically.

"Well, just one of them, actually. The one who called me a fuckarse and a cocksucker when they had me at their mercy during the payoff, up there in the mountains. The one who kicked me in the balls and in the face and then left me there to die. If your men hadn't come out and found me, God bless them, I *would* have died! Phone them, if you don't believe me!"

The captain held up his hands placatingly. Zen gave an embarrassed smile.

"Anyway, perhaps you understand now why I came straight here as soon as I heard that you'd laid hands on the bastards. Just fifteen minutes with him, that's all I ask."

"Well, I'm really not sure that I can agree to authorize you to, ah . . ."

"I won't leave a mark on him."

"Possibly not, but . . ."

"I've done this sort of thing before."

"Yes, I'm sure you have. Nevertheless, there is the question of—"

Zen shot out of his chair. "There's the question of teaching these fucking bastards to respect authority, Captain, that's what the question is! Next time it might be you out there, remember. Now that the politicians have taken away the death penalty, what have these animals got to lose? We've got to stick together, Captain, make our own arrangements. See what I mean? Just fifteen minutes, that's all I ask."

Rivolta stared up at Zen, seemingly mesmerized. "You're sure there won't be any marks?" he murmured at last.

Zen smiled unpleasantly. "Like I always say, it's the ones that don't show that hurt the most."

∎   ∎   ∎

The corridor was straight, evenly lit, and apparently endless, with steel doors set at equal intervals on either side. Zen had unconsciously adopted the same pace as his escort, so their footsteps rapped out a single rhythm on the concrete floor. At length the sergeant stopped, produced a set of keys, and unlocked one of the doors. Zen's nostrils flared at the smell which emerged, sheep and smoke and dirt and sweat all worked together, overpowering the antiseptic odor which he hadn't been aware of until it went under to this blast from another world.

There were two men in the cell, one lying on the bunk bed, the other standing near the window. They stared listlessly at the intruders. The Carabinieri sergeant produced a pair of hand-cuffs and snapped them with practiced ease onto the wrists of the man on the bed.

"On your feet, shithead," he remarked without animosity.

He grasped the man's left elbow between forefinger and thumb and pushed him toward the door. The man winced and said something in dialect to the other prisoner. Then the door slammed shut and they were walking again, three of them now rapping out the same rhythm along the corridor.

They passed through a set of doors like an air lock, separating the cells from the rest of the building. The prisoner didn't move fast enough for the sergeant's liking and again he made him wince, although the only contact between them was the two-fingered grip on the man's elbow. Then they turned left through a pair of swing doors into a small gymnasium.

"Jesus!" the Calabrian muttered.

The sergeant guided him over to a set of wall bars. "You'll fucking well speak when you're spoken to and not unless," he remarked.

"But we talk already!"

"You don't understand," the sergeant told him. "That was work. This is pleasure."

He spun the prisoner round, undid one end of the handcuffs, looped it through the wall bars, and locked it back on the man's wrist so that the handcuffs wrenched his arms up and back in the classic *strappado* position.

"Okay?"

Zen nodded appreciatively. "Very nice."

The sergeant chopped the edge of his hand down on the elbow he had been gripping earlier. The prisoner winced again.

"Hurt his arm," the sergeant commented conversationally. "He's all yours, then. Fifteen minutes."

The swing doors banged together behind him a few times and then all was quiet.

Zen lit a cigarette. "You remember me," he said, placing it between the prisoner's lips.

The man stared at him through the smoke which drifted up into his unblinking eyes.

"Was it you?"

The prisoner drew on the cigarette. His gaze was as absolute and incurious as a cat's. His head shook. "They come looking for him but he is not there. They take the brother instead and later he is dead. From then he hates all police."

For the Calabrian the Tuscan dialect called Italian was as foreign a language as Spanish, but Zen dimly perceived the general outlines of the story.

"We know this only after," the prisoner went on. "We phone them to get you. We don't want anyone killed."

"Except Ruggiero Miletti."

The man mouthed the cigarette to one side. "We don't kill Miletti!"

"You've confessed to doing so."

"Only talk, no writing. We don't want to end like the brother. When the judge comes we deny everything."

"I don't think she's going to be very impressed by that."

The prisoner looked sharply at Zen. "It's a woman?" This seemed to disturb him more than anything else.

"What of it?"

"They're the worst."

Zen sighed. "Look, you had the means, the opportunity, and a reasonable motive. Everyone is going to assume you did it, no matter what you say."

The prisoner let the cigarette drop from his mouth and crushed it out with the care of one from a land where fire is not completely domesticated.

"It's the same. At Milan innocent till guilty, at Rome guilty till innocent, in Calabria guilty till guilty."

Zen glanced at his watch. "I believe that you didn't kill Ruggiero Miletti."

"Prison for kidnap, prison for murder. Same prison."

He's always known this would happen one day, Zen thought, and now that it finally has he feels oddly reassured. And I'm cast in the role of a smart lawyer trying to make Oedipus believe that I've found a loophole in fate and that given a sympathetic jury I can get him off with a suspended sentence.

"Look, I've read the letter Ruggiero sent to his family," he told the prisoner. "He made it clear that you treated him well. As far as the kidnapping goes you were small fry, manual workers. You'll go to prison, certainly, but with good behavior and a bit of luck you'll get out one day. But if you're sent down for killing a defenseless old man in cold blood then that's the end. They won't bother locking your cell, they'll just weld up the door. And you'll know that whatever happens, however society changes, whichever party comes to power, you're going to die in prison and be buried in a pit of quicklime, because if any of your relatives still remember who you are they'll be too ashamed to come and claim your body."

The prisoner stared stoically at the floor. Zen consulted his watch again.

"Tell me about the day you released Miletti."

There was no reply.

"If I'm to help you I need to know!"

Eventually the deep voice ground unwillingly into action: "We drive him there and leave him. That's all."

"What time was this?"

"Before light."

"On Monday? Four days ago?"

A grudging nod.

"And when did you phone the family?"

"Later."

"Later the same morning? On Monday?"

Another nod.

"Which number did you phone?"

"The same as before."

"When before?"

"When we go to get the money."

He seemed bored, as if none of this concerned him and he simply wanted to get it over with as quickly as possible.

"And who did you speak to?"

"I don't speak."

Of course. The gang would have picked someone more articulate as their spokesman.

"You don't know anything about who answered? A man? A woman? Young? Old?"

"A man, of course! Not of the family. Like you."

"Like me?"

"From the North."

Zen nodded, holding the man's eyes. The time was getting desperately short.

"The man who hates the police because of what they did to his brother, how did he know who I was?"

There was no response. Zen repeated his question.

"He say he can smell them."

Zen's foot hooked the man's ankles and pulled him off balance so that he fell forward with a short cry of pain.

"That was very brave of you," Zen commented as the prisoner struggled back to his feet. "But we don't have time for bravery. Now I'll ask you again. Who told you I was coming on the payoff?"

The man stood motionless, eyes closed, breathing the pain away.

"Some people say Southerners are stupid," Zen continued. "I hope you're not going to prove them right. I can't help you unless I know who your contact was."

He moved closer to the prisoner, inside the portable habitat of mountain odors that surrounded him like a sheath.

"Was it one of the family?"

No response.

"Or someone in the Questura?"

The man's eyelids flickered but did not open.

"Someone called Lucaroni?"

There was no reaction.

"Chiodini?"

Behind him the doors banged open and boots rapped out across on the parquet floor.

"Geraci?"

Suddenly the eyes were on him again, pure and polished and utterly empty of expression.

"Everything go all right?" asked the sergeant, appearing at Zen's side. "Didn't give you any trouble, did he?"

Zen turned slowly, rubbing his hands together. "It went just fine, thank you."

The sergeant unlocked the handcuffs and the prisoner straightened his arms with a long groan.

Zen buttoned up his overcoat. "I'll be going then."

"Didn't know you were here," the sergeant remarked cheer-fully.

The Alfetta was parked on the pavement outside, forcing pedestrians out into a street jammed with traffic. Palottino was reading a comic book featuring a naked woman with large breasts who cowered in terror before an enormous spider brandishing a bloodstained chainsaw. It was drizzling lightly and the evening traffic was at its peak, but thanks to a judicious use of the siren and a blatant disregard for the rules of the road the Neapolitan contrived to move the Alfetta through it almost as though it did not exist. Meanwhile Zen sat gazing out at the narrow cobbled streets, teeming with quirky detail to an extent that seemed almost unreal, like the carefully contrived back-ground to a film scene. But it was just the effect of the contrast with that other world, a world of carefully contrived monotony, designed for twenty thousand people but inhabited by more than twice that number, of whom several hundred killed themselves each year and another fifty or so were murdered, a world whose powerful disinfectant would seep into the blood and bones of the violent gentle shepherds who had kidnapped Ruggiero Miletti until it had driven them safely mad.

Zen lit a Nazionale and stretched luxuriously. What the Calabrian had told him made everything simple. All he had to do was get in touch with Rosella Foria before she left for Florence and pass on the information he had received and he could return to Rome exonerated and with a clear conscience. The key was that the kidnappers had telephoned on Monday, not on Tuesday, and that the number they had called was the one communicated to them by the family before the payoff, as stipulated in Ruggiero's letter. Whoever had answered this telephone call was at the very least an accessory to Ruggiero's murder and could be arrested at once. The rest would follow.

As they hit the motorway, surging forward into the rain-filled darkness, Zen suddenly felt slightly light-headed, and he told Palottino to stop at a service area so that they could get something to eat. Ten minutes later they were sitting at a Formica-topped table in a restaurant overlooking the motor-way. Zen was chaffing his driver about the toy panda, which he had just bought for his brother's little daughter, a great favorite of his. Palottino produced a number of photographs of the child, which they both admired. Encouraged by his superior's good humor, the Neapolitan asked how things were going, and Zen felt so relaxed and obliging that he told him what had happened in Florence. Palottino laughed admiringly at the clever ruse Zen had used to gain access to the kidnappers, and at his description of the languid young captain who had fallen for it. But when it came to the prisoner's revelations he unfortunately got the wrong end of the stick.

"Called another number on another day!" he jeered. "Oh yes, very clever! What do they take us for, idiots?"

"Sorry?"

"Well, I mean no one's going to believe that, are they? Not when there's a recording, logged and dated, of them actually making the call on Tuesday. I mean it's a clear case of pull the other one, right?"

Zen stared at him. He seemed to be having difficulty focusing. "No. No, you don't understand. They called *another* number, not the Miletti house. On Monday."

Quickly reading the signals, Palottino did an abrupt U-turn. "Oh, I see! You mean you *know* they did. Oh well, that's different! Sorry, chief, I didn't realize that. I thought it was just their word against the official record. And like we say in Naples, only believe a Calabrian when he tells you he's lying!"

Zen gazed down at the surface of the table, gleaming dully under the flat neon light. He stood up abruptly.

"I've got to go to the toilet. I'll meet you in the car."

As Zen washed his hands he gazed at his face in the mirror above the basin. How could he have failed to see what was obvious even to a knucklehead like Palottino? How could he have imagined for a second that the kidnappers' unsupported assertions would be taken seriously by anyone? On the contrary, they would be indignantly dismissed as a feeble and disgusting attempt by a gang of ruthless killers to add insult to injury by smearing the family of the man they had just savagely murdered.

It was Thursday evening now. His mandate in Perugia ran until midnight on Friday. That gave him just over twenty-four hours. He phoned the night duty officer at the Questura in Perugia and then, since he had some tokens left, dialed Ellen's number in Rome. But as soon as it began to ring he pushed down the button with his finger, breaking the connection.

He must have dozed off, for the next thing he knew he was feeling chilled and anxious. Through the window he could see the upper limb of a huge planet which almost filled the night sky. The collision in which the earth would inevitably be destroyed was clearly only seconds away, for despite its appalling size the planet's motion was perceptible. It was even close enough for him to make out the lights of the hundreds of cities dotted across its monstrous convex surface.

"Son of a *bitch*!"

The world swerved, veered, straightened up.

"Fucking truckdrivers, think they own the road," Palottino commented.

When Zen looked again, the rogue planet had become a ridge blanked in darkly on the clear moonlit sky and its alien cities the twinkling lights of Perugia.

It was only ten o'clock, but the streets were deserted. Palottino pulled into the parking lot where it was never night, and they got out, watched by the guard on the roof of the prison. In the blank wall of the Questura opposite a light showed in Zen's office on the third floor.

Geraci must have heard his footsteps, for he was standing by the window with a respectful and curious expression when Zen entered.

"Evening, chief. What's up, then?"

The duty officer had told him to report to the Questura and await further instructions. Motioning the inspector to a chair, Zen went round behind the desk and sat down, rubbing his eyes.

"I've just got back from Florence. The military have taken the whole gang. All of them. Well, not quite all."

Geraci's expression shifted almost imperceptibly, like the face of someone who has just died. The silence re-formed. Zen felt himself starting to slip back into his interrupted sleep and he forced his eyes open, staring intently at Geraci until the inspector looked away.

"I would never had agreed if it hadn't been for the boy," Geraci said.

"How much did they offer you?"

"It wasn't for money," Geraci replied scornfully. "We're from the same place, from neighboring villages. They simply asked me to help them out. I would gain nothing myself, just the goodwill of certain people, people who are respected."

He shook his head at the impossibility of a Northerner understanding these things.

"Anyway, I said no. So they started to use threats, although they don't like doing that. To them it's a sign of weakness. But they had asked and I had refused. That isn't permitted."

He paused and sighed.

"Just before Christmas I heard from my sister. Her youngest boy, just three years old, a little darling, had been taken. A few days later a letter arrived for me. Inside there was a little scrap of skin and a tiny fingernail. They'd amputated his finger with a pair of wire cutters. I never thought fingernails were beautiful until I saw this one. It was like a miniature work of art. That evening they phoned me again. The boy still had nine more fingers and ten toes, they said. I agreed to do what they asked."

Zen pushed back his chair and stood up, trying to dominate the situation again, to rise above the pity that threatened to swamp him.

"And what was that?"

"Get myself transferred to the squad investigating the kidnapping and pass on any information which might be useful."

"And they gave you the tape recorder and the crucifix?"

"Not until you arrived. While Priorelli was in charge I didn't need it, he was very open about his plans. But no one ever knew what you were thinking or what you were going to do."

Zen allowed himself a moment to savor the irony of this. He had been uncommunicative with his staff because he thought they were all hostile to him and reporting back to the Questore, if not the Ministry or the Security Services!

"Where was the receiver?"

"In the broom cupboard at the end of the corridor, hidden under a pile of old boxes and papers. I played back the tapes at home and noted down anything important."

"And the contacts with the gang? Come on, Geraci! I want to get home, go to bed. Don't make me do all the work."

"I'd put an advertisement in the newspaper offering a boat for sale. The day the advertisement appeared I took a certain train, got into the first carriage, and left the envelope in the bin for used towels in the toilet."

Zen shook his head slowly. His disgust was as much with himself as with Geraci, but the inspector suddenly flared up.

"I wasn't the biggest shit in all this! One of the Milettis was in on it too! Can you imagine that? Betraying your own father! At least I didn't sink that low."

Zen waved his hand wearily. "Don't waste time trying to do dirt on the family. I'm not interested."

Geraci got to his feet. "It's true, I tell you! I had to pick up his messages at a service area on the motorway and leave them on the train, same as my own. Once I got there early and saw him."

"So who was it?"

"I don't know."

Zen snorted his contempt.

"He was all wrapped up in a coat and a scarf and wearing dark glasses, and I was watching from a distance. I didn't want to risk being recognized either."

"How did he get there?"

"In a blue Fiat Argenta sedan."

"Was there anyone else in the car?"

"No."

"Describe him."

"Quite short. Medium build."

"How do you know it wasn't a woman?"

"He phoned to let me know he was coming. It was a man, all right."

Zen turned to the window, fearing that his thoughts might be visible in his face. Daniele and Silvio were out. Pietro, too. Ivy Cook's voice was deep enough to be mistaken for a man's, but she was too tall. Cinzia was the right size, but her voice was almost hysterically feminine. No, there was really only one person it could have been.

"How many times did this happen?"

"Four altogether. I can give you the dates."

Geraci took out his diary and scribbled on a blank page, which he then tore out and handed to Zen.

"Where did he leave the messages?"

"At the Valdichiana service area on the motorway. The envelope was inside the last magazine in the top right-hand row."

Zen sighed. "So let's sum up. You claim that an unknown person in male clothing driving a Fiat sedan left four envelopes in a motorway service station. You don't know who he was, why he was doing it, or what was in the envelopes, and you can't prove any of it. Doesn't add up to much, does it?"

Geraci looked away in frustration. "Ah, what's the use! It isn't doing wrong that counts, it's getting caught."

The same was even more true of doing right, Zen reflected.

The wrongdoer arouses sneaking admiration, but if you want to be merciful or generous without making people despise you, then you have to be very careful indeed.

"Tomorrow is my last day here in Perugia," he told Geraci wearily. "My tour of duty hasn't exactly been a glittering success and a public disclosure that one of my inspectors was a spy for the gang I was supposed to be hunting would be the last straw. So you're going to get a break, Geraci. You don't deserve it, but I do."

The inspector gazed at him with immense caution, clearly not daring to understand.

"My conversation with the kidnappers was private. As far as I'm concerned it can remain private. On principle I'd infinitely prefer to turn you in, but luckily for you I can't afford principles."

Geraci's eyes were glowing with emotion. "Dottore, my mother will . . ."

"Stuff your mother, Geraci! It's me I'm thinking of, not your mother or anybody else. I want you to take indefinite sick leave starting tomorrow, and you can spend your free time writing an application for transfer to the Forestry Guards. You're not staying in the police, that's for damn sure! Now piss off out of here before I change my mind."

Geraci backed up to the door. "God bless you, sir." The door closed quietly behind him.

"God help us," muttered Zen.

Nine o'clock was sounding as he walked out of his hotel the next morning. Halfway along the Corso workmen were setting up a platform, the ringing sounds of their hammers unsynchronized to the movements of the arms which produced them. As he walked toward them the problem gradually corrected itself, as though the projectionist had finally woken up and made the necessary adjustments, and by the time he emerged from his favorite café, having consumed a good frothy cappuccino made with milk fresh from a churn, the foam stiff as whipped egg whites, the same process had taken place inside his head. But any impression that things were finally going his way did not last long.

"All that material has been transferred upstairs," the technician on duty in the intercept room at the courthouse told him.

"What about transcripts?"

The man shook his head. "All upstairs with the judges. We've finished with that one. The line's been disconnected and everything."

Zen hesitated for a moment. "May I use your phone?"

"Help yourself."

There was an internal directory pinned to the wall by the phone. He dialed Luciano Bartocci's number.

"*Yes?*"

"Well, it did come to the same thing in the end."

"*Who is this?*"

"I'm going back to Rome tomorrow. But first I'd like to have a word with you. About ratkings."

There was a silence. Then: "*I'm very busy.*"

"It's vitally important."

Zen spoke slowly, stressing every word, giving Bartocci time to think. The technician was busy fitting a new leader to a reel of tape. His work probably left him little interest in listening to other people's conversations, but Zen kept his voice low.

"It won't take more than a few minutes."

"*In about half an hour. On the roof of the market building.*"

Zen pushed past the women selling doughnuts and flowers and through a group of African students giggling at the photos they had just had taken in the machine. The terrace on the roof of the market was deserted except for a flock of pigeons and the two Nordic girls, one of whom was sketching while the other basked in the sun, her head on her friend's lap. Zen walked over to the parapet and gazed out at the view. The puddle under a leaky tap nearby had frozen overnight and had not yet had time to thaw, so that the pigeons slipped and skidded as they came to drink.

When Luciano Bartocci appeared, tense and wary, Zen wasted no time.

"I need to consult a document."

"Ask Foria."

"She's not here. It's urgent."

Bartocci shook his head. "Out of the question."

"I just need a copy of the transcript of the call the gang made to tell the Milettis that they had released Ruggiero."

"Why?"

"The Carabinieri in Florence have arrested the kidnappers. I've been to see them. They didn't kill Ruggiero."

"What's that got to do with you? Or with me, for that matter?

Rosella Foria is investigating the Miletti murder. Let her investigate. That's her job. Or do you think you're cleverer than she is?"

"I think I understand the situation better, thanks to you."

Bartocci smiled at this clumsy attempt at flattery.

"Remember what you told me about ratkings?" Zen reminded him. "How each rat defends the interests of the others and so the strength of one is the strength of all? Well, I think there's one case where that doesn't apply, where the system goes into reverse and the rats all turn on one another."

"And that is . . . ?"

"When they sense that one of their number is damaged."

The magistrate shook his head. "They would simply destroy the damaged rat."

"But suppose they don't know which one it is?"

Bartocci considered this for a moment. "It all sounds a bit theoretical."

"I agree. What I want to do is to test the theory. And that's why I need to see that transcript."

Two pigeons were already scrabbling about at the men's feet, their beady eyes alert for a handout. Bartocci would clearly have liked to tell Zen to go to hell, but he was trapped by the relationship which he himself had been at such pains to create, and which he wasn't quite cynical enough to disavow now that it served not him but the other person. A victim of his own scruples, it was less trouble in the end just to give in.

"You remember the bar we went to in Piazza Matteotti?" he asked. "Be there later this morning, about midday. If there's anything for you, read it there, and then seal it up and hand it back. If there isn't then go away. And stay away."

On the Corso the hammering had stopped and the platform was being decorated with flags and bunting and posters proclaiming a political address the following day. By then, Zen thought, I'll be back in Rome, whatever happens. He found this oddly comforting.

The civic library was staffed by the usual sullen crew, as though it were a branch of the prison service. Since Zen was not a registered member it took his police identity card even to get him past the door. He climbed up to the periodicals room on the second floor and announced to the female attendant that he wished to consult back issues of the local newspaper.

"Fill in a request form," she replied without looking up from her knitting.

There were no forms to be seen, but one of the other inmates explained that they were kept in the corridor on the next floor up.

"And the access number?" the woman demanded when Zen brought his form back. The tip of her steel knitting needle hovered over a space as blank as Zen's face.

"I don't know what the access number is."

"Look it up!"

"Can't you do it?"

"It's not my job to fill in the forms. You have to look in the card catalog."

The card catalog was in the basement. It took Zen twenty minutes to locate the section dealing with the newspaper he wanted. Since each month's copies had a separate access number he then had to make out six different forms, which meant going back to the third floor and copying out his name, address, profession, and reason for request twelve times.

By half past ten he was back. The woman's knitting was making good progress. She pushed away his forms.

"No more than three requests may be submitted at one time."

He handed back the forms corresponding to the last three months. The woman scrutinized them in vain for further errors or omissions, laid down her knitting with a reluctant sigh, and trotted off. As soon as she was out of sight, Zen took out his pocket knife and cut through a stitch in the middle of the work she had completed. He needn't have hurried. A further fifteen minutes elapsed before she returned, pushing a trolley bearing three large folders fastened with black tape.

"Keep pages in order edges straight corners aligned do not crease crinkle or tear leave at your position after consultation," she told him, picking up her knitting again.

As he began his search through the classified advertisements, Zen realized why the kidnappers had chosen boats as their cover. Perugia is about as far from the sea as any Italian city can be, and interest in buying and selling boats is low, particularly during winter. As a result, there was little chance of the kidnappers' overlooking one of the messages intended for them. The discovery of the advertisements which confirmed Geraci's story was gratifying, but what really excited Zen was an announcement which had appeared the previous Friday, the day after the Milettis received Ruggiero's letter giving the instructions for the final ransom payment. *"Two-way radio for sale,"* it read. *"Phone 8818 after 7."*

It looked innocuous enough, and yet Zen felt like an astronomer sighting a planet whose existence he had predicted from his calculations. This was the clincher, the thing that made everything else make sense. It was like a dream where, tired of beating your fists against a locked and bolted door, you step back and notice for the first time that there is no wall on either side. Of course! It was so simple, so obvious.

In the bar opposite the post office, a street sweeper was explaining how he would sort out the national football team.

"Too many solo artists, that's the problem. One of them gets the ball and sees a bit of open space, all he thinks about is going forward, the rest of the team might as well not exist. When it comes off it's magnificent, I grant you, but how often does that happen, eh? No, it's percentages that add up in the end, this is what they don't realize. What we need is more discipline, more organization, more teamwork."

"Well, this is it," the barman said, turning to the new customer with an interrogatory lift of the chin.

Zen identified himself and was handed a white envelope tucked between two bottles of fruit syrup. He opened it and took out a photocopy of a typed page:

> INTERCEPT: *Yes?*
>
> CALLER: *Verona.*
>
> INTERCEPT: *What? You've got the wrong number.*
>
> CALLER: *Okay, listen. We have released Dottor Miletti. Understand? But someone'll have to go and pick him up. It's his leg, he can't walk. Here's how to find him.*
>
> INTERCEPT: *Wait a moment! Turn down that music, Daniele!*
>
> CALLER: *. . . the road to Foligno. Just beyond Santa Maria degli Angeli turn right, the Cannara road. Go to the telegraph pole with the mark and turn left. Take the second right and go about a kilometer until you see a building site beside the road on the left. The Milettis' father is there.*
>
> INTERCEPT: *Wait a minute! The second on the right or the left? Hello? Hello?*

Zen looked up, his breath coming short and fast. He sealed up the photocopy in the envelope enclosed and handed it back to the barman. Then he got a telephone token and dialed the police laboratory. *"Hair is either fair or yellow,"* Lucaroni had told him. But all that's yellow isn't hair, the laboratory now confirmed. The yellow threads found in the Fiat they had examined were strands from a cheap synthetic wig.

He emerged into the bright sunlight, blinking like a mole. The last piece of the puzzle was in place. He knew who had done it and how it had been done, and with the exception of the murderer he was the only person who did know. For a few more hours the whole situation would remain fluid and he held the key cards in his hands. If he played them right then perhaps just this once the bastards wouldn't get away with it after all. He tried not to think about what might happen if he played them wrong.

10

Gianluigi Santucci sat at the head of the dining table, watching his family feed. Although he had hardly noticed his wife take a mouthful, her plate was already empty. He wondered how she managed to do it, given that she had been talking almost uninterruptedly since the meal began. His daughter, Loredana, had originally taken only four pieces of ravioli, subsequently increased to five under sustained pressure from her mother. But since she had eaten only half of them, this apparent victory revealed itself, like so many in the family circle, as illusory. Gianluigi didn't need to read Cinzia's trashy psychology magazines to know that Loredana worshipped the ground he trod on. One of the ways in which this manifested itself was her mimicking of the meager diet to which her father was reduced by his digestive problems. For though Gianluigi was proud of the good fare he provided for his family, that was about the only pleasure he could take in it since this vicious intruder had taken up residence in his gut.

How his mother would have triumphed! As a child, Gianluigi had resembled not fastidious Loredana but little Sergio there, his face cheerily smeared with tomato sauce, putting away the sticky pouches with a single-mindedness he would soon devote to masturbation. Gianluigi too had been a stuffer, eating as though he had a secret mission to devour the world. His mother had never left him in peace on the subject. "Don't eat so fast, it's bad for you. Don't eat bread before your pasta, it's bad for you. Don't put oil on your meat, it's bad for you." But she had never understood the secret source of her son's appetite: a gnawing envy of an elder brother who seemed so much bigger and more successful. Pasquale could dominate a room just by walking into it, and even his absence usually appeared to be of more interest than Gianluigi's presence. "If you don't eat you won't grow," his mother told him. Gianluigi turned this logic on its head and determined to eat his way into a future where he would be bigger and better than anyone around. But the only result had been a stomach condition which left him unable to do more than nibble a few scraps while this pain roamed his innards like a rat.

His hunger hadn't disappeared, however. It had just taken a different form. He could do nothing about his size, but on every other score he had beaten his brother hollow! Pasquale was now a dentist responsible for curing half the tooth problems in Siena and causing the other half, as he himself liked to joke. But his three children were all girls, his wife was a whore—Gianluigi himself had had her three times last summer—and although his earnings were respectable enough, his rival could already match him lira for lira twice over. And that was only the beginning. The events of the past week had opened up perspectives which even Gianluigi found slightly dizzying.

Not that he was by any means unprepared for the pickings that Ruggiero's death promised to bring with it. On the contrary, he had been working toward that very goal from the moment he met Cinzia Miletti seven years earlier. For in the end Pasquale had proved to be a disappointment. Like many early achievers he had soon gone into decline, growing fat and complacent, no challenge for the pool of unused ambition that ached and burned like the excess gastric acids in Gianluigi's stomach. He needed roughage, and his solution had been to marry into a family full of brothers and take them all on. He had been counting on this using up his energies for many years to come, so his pleasure at the way things had worked out was mixed with a certain amount of regret that it was all over so quickly.

The Japanese deal on which he had expended so much energy and cunning was irrelevant now. Ruggiero's will would hold no surprises. Each of the Miletti children would receive a 25 percent holding in SIMP. Cinzia's share was already in his hands, of course, and he could count on Daniele's too. It was not just a question of the money he had been advancing the boy ever since he got himself into trouble over drugs, although by now that amounted to almost a hundred million lire. Daniele was hooked on something quite as addictive as hard drugs and almost as expensive: a fashion market whose sole function was to flaunt the spending power of its wearers, or rather their fathers. To admit that he could no longer compete because his father had turned his back on him would have been the ultimate humiliation for the boy, so he had been glad to accept his brother-in-law's help. But what made Gianluigi quite certain of Daniele's support was the fact that the boy admired him. Pietro had never understood that, never been prepared to admit that his younger brother's hero was the outsider in the family, the pushy self-seeking Tuscan. Pietro would have to pay for that. One of Gianluigi's axioms was that one always paid for any lack of clarity and realism. Meanwhile he accepted Daniele's homage as he did his daughter's, and with as little thought of consummating the relationship. The fact of the matter was that the boy hadn't a hope in hell of ever amounting to anything, being spoiled, weak, vain, and without that bitter inner pain that drives a man on.

So here he was in effective control of 50 percent of SIMP. But even if Pietro knew that, he would still be counting on Silvio to balance things out. Which was a mistake, because when the chips were down, brother Silvio would support Gianluigi too. This was something that Pietro could have no inkling of, for the simple reason that Silvio didn't know it himself and indeed would have denied it strenuously if he'd been asked. Nevertheless, when the time came he would vote with Gianluigi, because of the photographs. Gianluigi had paid a detective agency in Milan five million lire for them, but like Daniele's allowance it was money well spent. Those photographs would make him undisputed master of the Miletti empire. It had been a nerve-racking business, particularly the last few weeks. He wondered what his family would think if they knew the risks he had been running. But now it was all over and he had come out on top. The Milettis had made it clear from the beginning that they played winner-take-all. And he would, he would!

The doorbell sounded and Margherita set down the dish of fried fish she was serving to go answer it.

"Who on earth can that be?" Cinzia wondered aloud. "What an idea, not even lunchtime is sacred anymore, no wonder there's so much tension and unhappiness in the world, finish your pasta, Loredana."

The housekeeper reappeared in the doorway. "It's the police, dottore."

Gianluigi was accustomed to living with pains, but the one that shot across his chest now was a stranger.

"Tell them to come back later," his wife told the housekeeper, as though it was as easy as that, as though there were nothing to worry about. "It's really too bad, a total chaos and intrusion."

"No, I'll sort them out."

He got to his feet, gathering his strength, his courage, his wits.

Margherita's words had conjured up visions of armed men surrounding the house, and when Gianluigi reached the door he was relieved to find only the slight figure of Aurelio Zen. But relief merely made him angry for having been given an unnecessary fright.

"What the hell do you want now, Zen? Don't you know it's lunchtime?"

"I'm sorry to disturb you, dottore, but it's a matter of the highest urgency."

"It had better be."

He was sure of himself again, in control of the situation. This sort of confrontation was the stuff of his life, for which he trained like an athlete. Once he had mastered that initial moment of panic it was a pleasure to exercise those considerable skills.

"According to our records," Zen began, "your wife is the registered owner of a Beretta pistol. I would like to examine it with a view to eliminating it from our inquiries."

"Let me see your search warrant."

"I'm not conducting a search."

Gianluigi allowed his eyebrows to rise. "Oh? Then what the fuck are you doing, may I ask, disturbing me without the slightest warning in the middle of lunch?"

"I'm conducting a preliminary inquiry in the sense of article two twenty-five of the Penal Code, the results of which will be communicated to the Public Prosecutor's office and a search warrant issued in due course, your refusal to cooperate having been noted. But what's the problem. You *have* got the gun, haven't you?"

"Of course."

This automatic reply was his first error, for it conceded the man's right to question him. But Zen's sudden change of tone had caught him by surprise.

"Then why not just show it to me?" Zen suggested mildly. "It'll save both of us a lot of unnecessary bother."

There was a shuffle of bare feet as Cinzia appeared.

"What's going on, Lulu? Oh, Commissioner, I thought you were back in Rome. Surely you must be."

She and Zen exchanged a lingering glance.

"Get on with your lunch," Gianluigi told his wife. "I'll handle this."

Realizing that after this interruption his earlier position of rigid intransigence would seem stilted, Gianluigi told his visitor to wait, went through to the living room, and opened the top drawer of the old desk where the pistol was always kept.

It was not there.

For thirty seconds he stood quite still, thinking. But, though the disappearance of the pistol was both mysterious and annoying, there was nothing whatever to be worried about. He returned to the front door.

"Look, the thing appears to have been mislaid," he told Zen, who was now leaning against the wall smoking a cigarette. "Probably the cleaning lady put it somewhere. We'll have a proper look this afternoon or tomorrow if you care to contact me later."

He was starting to close the door as Zen replied, "That's fine. I didn't really come about the gun at all."

The door opened again. "I beg your pardon?"

"There's been an unfortunate development, dottore. As the result of a tip-off, the Carabinieri have arrested most of the gang that kidnapped your father-in-law. Among other things, they've been talking about their contact in the Miletti family, the one who left messages tucked in a magazine at that service area on the motorway. The last magazine in the top right-hand row, I think it was."

The exotic pain returned to Gianluigi's chest.

"And what has this got to do with me?" Articulating these words was one of the hardest tasks he could ever remember performing.

"Well, it depends how you look at it. On the face of it, all this amounts to is an unsupported allegation by a gang of known criminals. On the other hand, it's hard to see what they have to gain by lying. We've suspected for a long time that there was an informer passing on the strengths and weaknesses of the family's negotiating position to the gang, but we didn't know who it was. Pietro was in London for much of the time. If the pickup point was on the motorway, that excludes Silvio, who can't drive. As for Daniele, the gang say that the person who left the messages was short and slightly built, so he won't do. In one sense it's just a question of who's left, really."

He tossed the butt of his cigarette out onto the gravel drive, where it continued to smolder.

"But there's more to it than that. Above all, the investigating magistrate is going to be looking for a motive. Now if he had just wanted to beggar the Milettis the informant could have revealed the true extent of the family's finances straight off, but instead he chose to pass on scraps of information so that the negotiations were drawn out as long as possible. The magistrate will therefore be looking for someone who stood to gain from a delay in Ruggiero's return coupled with the need for a massive injection of cash to prop up the Miletti company. Cash from a Japanese company, for instance."

The silence that followed was as long and significant as the words that had preceded it. Whatever was said now would have extraordinary resonances, and that knowledge was as inhibiting as the acoustics of a great church.

"I think that you are full of shit," Gianluigi finally murmured, slowly and distinctly. "I'm going to find out. And if you are, I'll make sure you drown in it."

He walked slowly through to his study, his heart a madhouse filled with the shrieks of despairing wretches, his head a cool and airy library where shrewd men debated tactics. Norberto was the best route to take. As a member of the regional council he knew almost everything that was going on and could find out the rest quickly and discreetly.

"Norberto? Gianluigi Santucci. Yes, me too. I'm sorry, but it can't wait. Someone's just told me that there's been a break in the Miletti case, that arrests have been made. Have you heard anything?"

Sensing a movement, he looked round to find that Zen had followed him and was now standing in the doorway. For a moment Gianluigi was tempted to send him away, but he restrained himself. The news was good. Much better to show himself unconcerned, a man with nothing to hide.

"Nothing at all?" he confirmed. "I thought as much!"

"Get him to check," Zen warned. "This happened in Florence and the military are keeping it quiet until the magistrate gets there."

Gianluigi bit his lip. "Would you mind just checking that?" he said into the phone. "You'll call back? Very well."

As he replaced the receiver, Loredana's voice rang out from the dining room. "Christ, not chocolate pudding again! What are you trying to do, poison me? You know I hate chocolate! It brings me out in spots."

While he waited for Norberto to get through to his contact, Gianluigi thought back to that other phone call, in the days shortly after Ruggiero was kidnapped. The gang had been given the Santuccis' number as a "clean" telephone line on which to communicate. At first Gianluigi had played it absolutely straight, but when the kidnappers' unexpectedly modest demands were swiftly met and it began to look as if Ruggiero would be released within days, it occurred to him how convenient it would be if the old man's return could be delayed. The whole question of the deal with the Japanese was hanging in the balance, and with it Gianluigi's future, for if it went through he was a made man. So when the kidnappers next phoned he'd expressed slight surprise that they'd asked for so little, given the family's ability to pay. If they needed more information on this subject, he'd implied, this could be arranged. It had been a risk, of course, but very carefully calculated, like every risk he took. The kidnappers could pose no threat unless they were caught, a possibility so remote that Gianluigi had discounted it.

The phone rang and Gianluigi snatched up the receiver.

"Well, you seem to be better informed than I am, Santucci! The gang have indeed been arrested. A magistrate went to Florence this morning to question them. Hello? Hello, are you there?"

"Yes. Yes, I'm here. Thanks. I'll be in touch."

I'll never see Loredana's children grow, he thought, never take Sergio hunting. But this uncharacteristic weakness lasted no more than a moment. Then he strode to the end of the room and opened the sliding door to the terrace, beckoning Zen to follow him.

The terrace was covered by a pergola whose vines were just beginning to put out shoots. It was sunny, still, and surprisingly hot.

"So you're accusing me of collaborating with my father-in-law's killers, is that it?" Gianluigi demanded point-blank.

Zen looked taken aback. "Not at all, dottore! I just wanted to warn you of certain developments which could potentially cause problems unless steps are taken now. That's all."

"What kind of steps did you have in mind?"

Zen held up his hand, shaking his head. "That's your affair, dottore. I don't need to know anything about it. But whatever you decide, it'll take time, and time is precisely what we don't have at present. Rosella Foria is questioning the gang in Florence at this very moment. We must act right away."

So that was the way of it, eh? Thank God for human nature, thought Gianluigi, rotten to the core!

"Excuse me, but what's in this for you?" he queried pointedly.

Zen made a small gesture of embarrassment. "About four years ago I had a misunderstanding with my superiors in Rome. They transferred me from active service and stuck me away in the Ministry doing bureaucratic work. At this stage of my career I haven't got much to look forward to except retirement anyway, but my pension will be pegged to my rank. Before this thing happened I was in line for promotion to Vice-Questore, but now . . ."

Gianluigi nodded and smiled. "And you'd still like that promotion."

Zen shrugged, his eyes discreetly lowered.

"You spoke of taking action," Gianluigi went on. "What sort of action did you have in mind?"

"Well, there's another factor involved. The kidnappers admit shooting Valesio, but they deny the Miletti murder. Moreover, one of the SIMP Fiats was observed near the scene of the murder, driven by a woman with blond hair. I identified the car that day you found me at the garage, and later I had it stolen and subjected to a forensic examination."

Gianluigi was silent. A display of outrage seemed a bit beside the point under the circumstances, and anyway, he needed to save his energy.

"Several long threads were found," Zen continued. "Threads from a blond wig. It almost looks as though someone was trying to frame your wife, particularly since Ruggiero was shot with a pistol similar to hers, which you now tell me is missing. But the point is that all this presents us with both a risk and an opportunity."

Gianluigi almost missed this last remark. *A blond wig*, he was thinking. A blond wig.

Feeling that the silence had gone on long enough, he murmured, "A risk for my wife, you mean?"

To Santucci's surprise, Zen laughed rather nastily.

"No, dottore! Look, Ruggiero was killed on Monday, twenty-four hours before the phone call saying he had been released. Only the kidnappers knew where he was then, so if they didn't kill him they must have told the person who did. And only one person was in touch with the gang."

"I didn't kill him!" Gianluigi's voice swooped from a scream to a whisper as he realized that he might be overheard.

Zen nodded earnestly. "I know, dottore. I wouldn't be here otherwise. I'm just pointing out that the investigating magistrate is bound to assume that the gang's informant and Ruggiero Miletti's murderer are one and the same person. That's a risk we shouldn't underestimate. But it also provides a way out of the original problem. Because if the informant and the murderer are assumed to be one and the same person, then providing we can convince Rosella Foria that one of the others committed the murder, she'll naturally assume that person was also the informant."

After a moment's silence Gianluigi burst out laughing, as if he had just been told a story about the bizarre customs of a foreign country.

"You know, Zen, I think I've been underestimating you."

"We have an unfair advantage in the police. Everyone assumes we're stupid."

Gianluigi's smile abruptly disappeared. "But it won't work! Do you think these magistrates are children? How can you hope to implicate one of the family in Ruggiero's murder? It's preposterous!"

"That doesn't matter. The point is just to create as much fuss and confusion as possible, to send the shit flying in every direction. And then while Rosella Foria is busy trying to clear it all up there'll be plenty of time to take whatever steps you feel are appropriate to bring about a satisfactory and lasting solution to the problem. But I don't need to know anything about that. What I *do* need are those photographs you have of Silvio."

Once again Gianluigi lost his head. "Who put you up to this, Zen? You're not big enough to be operating on your own. Who's behind you, eh? What's the game?"

A dark suspicion suddenly took form in his mind as he remembered the look Zen and his wife had exchanged. Yes, it had to be her. No one else knew about the photographs.

He stepped forward furiously. "Look here, you fuck off! Just fuck off out of here right now!"

But Zen stood his ground, gazing at him with the stolid confidence of a dog or horse that knows its owner will see reason sooner or later. And Gianluigi immediately realized that he was right. He would deal with Cinzia later, in private. He mustn't make it a public shame, still less allow it to compromise the successful resolution of the appallingly dangerous situation he found himself in. To do that would be the folly of an impetuous amateur, not the astute and hardened professional that he was.

"What are you going to do with the photographs?" His voice was as calm as marble, and as hard.

"Don't you think it might be better if I didn't tell you?" Zen replied. "They're going to question you, you know. I think it would be best for you to know as little as possible. It's amazing what people give away without even realizing it. When I mentioned the blond wig, for example, you reacted. A magistrate would notice that. As you said, they're not children. What was it about the wig, by the way?"

Gianluigi eyed him for a final long moment before deciding. "I'll show you."

He went back into his office and locked the door. There, he opened the wall safe and took out a yellow envelope. There were nine prints in all. He selected two, snipped the corresponding negatives from the strip of film, and attached them to the prints with a paper clip. The other prints and negatives, the pick of the set, he put back in the safe. They would still do their job when the time came. Indeed, this could be a useful try-out, to see how Silvio reacted to being blackmailed.

When he reemerged Zen had his back to the house, gazing at the view Gianluigi greeted exultantly each morning on rising with the thought, "I bought you!" He handed over the envelope

and watched with undisguised amusement as Zen studied the
first photograph. It showed Silvio, naked to the waist, dancing
in a crowded discotheque. His hairy chest and smooth shiny
belly were bare and a leather dog-lead dangled from each of his
pierced nipples. His head was covered in a startling profusion
of long blond locks.

"The wig," murmured Zen.

Gianluigi nodded.

"Where was this taken?"

"In Berlin."

"Ah yes, of course. Home of Gerhard Mayer."

Gianluigi decided that it was time to remind his new employee of the realities of their relationship.

"So you know about that too, do you? Very clever. But don't
get so clever that you forget what's what, will you? Because if
you do, I promise that you'll regret it for the rest of your life.
And I don't make empty threats, Zen."

Zen looked at him with an expression brimming with earnest
sincerity. "Dottore, please! I'm one hundred percent on your
side!"

Gianluigi nodded. "Then we'll say no more about it. Now let's
see just how clever you are. What do you make of this, eh?"

The second picture apparently showed Silvio leaning against
a tiled wall. But what was that gleaming white mass of vaguely
rumplike curves looming above his chest? And why did he have
that expression of ecstatic martyrdom?

Gianluigi turned the print on its side, observing Zen's puzzlement with a knowing smirk. It really was very difficult if you
hadn't seen some of the later and more explicit shots.

"Does that help?"

Now Silvio was seen to be lying supine on a white tiled floor
beneath the white structure. It might almost have been an altar
of some sort. Certainly the scene had a ritual air about it, as
though it formed part of a ceremony whose exact significance
was revealed only to initiates.

"What's this?" Gianluigi asked teasingly, pointing out the
white object.

Zen shook his head.

"Well what does it look like?"

He was having his fun all right, getting his money's worth!

"To be perfectly honest, it looks a bit like a toilet."

Gianluigi applauded ironically. "Bravo, my friend. It *is* a toilet. But a rather special toilet. It's not connected to a sewer, it's connected to Silvio. He's waiting for someone to come along and use it. One of the places our Silvio goes when he visits his boyfriend in Berlin is a club for people who like to be crapped on, and vice versa of course. Don't you wish you'd thought of it, eh? What a gold mine! They both pay for their fun, and you've got a flourishing little business in top-quality garden manure on the side."

Zen laughed softly and replaced the photographs in the envelope. Gianluigi clapped him familiarly on the back, pushing him into the house. Now he must get rid of him quickly. He needed peace and quiet in which to think. It was no use alerting his usual contacts. For them to be effective they would have to know the truth, and if they knew the truth they would abandon him. There were limits to what you could get away with, and he was well aware that he'd overstepped them. It was a pity the judiciary were already involved. Magistrates were so bloody-minded that they would often pursue their investigations even when it had been made perfectly clear to them that it was against their own best interests. That sort of stubbornness was something that Gianluigi absolutely despised. As far as he was concerned it was an aberration like religious or political fanaticism, something quite out of place in a modern democratic society.

"I need to talk to Silvio as soon as possible," Zen remarked as they reached the front door. "Could you get someone to persuade him to go to Antonio Crepi's house this afternoon? Crepi himself needn't know anything about it."

Gianluigi stared at him. Then his eyes narrowed shrewdly. "You're asking an awful lot and giving very little in return," he observed sourly.

"I'm doing it all for you, dottore!" Zen exclaimed with a hurt expression.

After a moment, Gianluigi laughed brutally. "All for me, my arse! You're doing it for your pension, my friend, and don't think I don't know it."

Zen shrugged awkwardly. "Oh well, that too, of course."

"What now?"

Silvio silently echoed his driver's exasperated murmur as he caught sight of the patrolman waving them down. What now, indeed?

As the taxi slowed to a halt beside the unmarked police car parked at a bend in the road, a massive sigh began its slow progress up from the bottom of Silvio's chest. For this was not the first vexation which the day had dropped on him, not by a long shot! In fact it had been nothing but trials and tribulations from the moment his clock radio had turned itself on at five o'clock that morning, shocking him into consciousness. It was supposed to have awakened him from a nap the preceding afternoon in time for an appointment with a young friend, but he must have set it wrong; having messed up his evening by failing to go off when he wanted it to, it then buggered up his sleep into the bargain. So there he was, wide awake at the crack of dawn, with no more chance of going back to sleep than of getting a turd back where it came from, as dear Gerhard used to say.

He really must get in touch with Gerhard soon. One of the most unpleasant features of the last few months had been having to suspend his little trips to Berlin, but now that everything was satisfactorily resolved he would be able to slip away again soon. As Ivy pointed out, Ruggiero's death was not without its consolations.

"Rubbish!" she'd retorted when he claimed to be grief-stricken.

"But my father's dead!" he'd cried. "I've got a *right* to be upset. It's only natural!"

"But you're not upset. On the contrary, you're quite relieved."

"Don't say that!"

But he had known that she was right. That was what was so amazing about Ivy, her ability to reach into his mind and show him things he had never dared admit to himself were there. It was terrible, sometimes, how right she could be.

The policeman, a rather attractive young fellow with an enormous mustache, was checking the driver's documents. Silvio thought he'd seen him somewhere before. And wasn't there something familiar about the spot where they had been stopped, too? The sun was high and it was stifling in the taxi. He felt grotesquely overdressed in his heavy underwear, thick suit, and overcoat, perspiring all over. Silvio consulted his watch. The patrolman was now walking in a maddeningly leisurely fashion around the taxi, inspecting it closely, taking his time. If this went on much longer he was going to be really late.

After his rude awakening that morning, he'd tried in vain to get back to sleep, but in the end he'd given up and gone downstairs, only to find that Daniele had eaten all his special organic goat's yogurt rich in the live bacilli which Silvio's homeopathist was adamant he needed to maintain the precarious equilibrium of his health. The goaty taste was what attracted Silvio, though.

After that his day had gone from bad to worse, the last straw being this lunchtime call from that creep Spinelli at the bank, insisting on meeting a representative of the family at Antonio Crepi's villa that very afternoon to discuss some urgent problem that was too sensitive to discuss on the phone. Silvio had been hoping to treat himself to an afternoon of listening to Billie Holiday records and leafing through that auction catalog of rare Haitian issues which Pietro had sent him from London, no doubt hoping to keep him sweet for the future, now that he represented 25 percent of the company! Yes, there were certainly consolations to Ruggiero's death, just as Ivy had insisted. She should have been here to drive him, but by the time the call came she'd already left to keep an appointment. So he'd had to take a taxi, which of course had been late arriving and then got stuck in the traffic. And now this! It really was too bad.

An official in plain clothes climbed out of the police car.

"How's it going?" Silvio heard him ask the young patrolman.

"Not too good. Fucking thing's in excellent shape."

Suddenly Silvio realized why this spot seemed familiar. It was at this very bend in the road that his father's car had been forced off the road by the kidnappers.

"You planning to be much longer?" the taxi driver demanded.

"We're just noting the defects we've found on your vehicle," the official told him.

"Defects? What defects?"

The patrolman consulted his notebook. "Insufficient tread depth on near-side front tire. Rear window partially obscured by sticker. License plate light defective."

The driver laughed sarcastically. "The cigarette lighter doesn't work, either."

"Really?" queried the official. "*Two* faults in the electrical system, then. May I see your snow chains?"

"Snow chains?" the driver replied incredulously. "What the hell are you talking about?"

"All vehicles using this road between the beginning of November and the end of March are required to carry snow chains on board. Didn't you see the sign back there on the hill?"

"Can't you feel that sun? It's over seventy degrees!"

"That's the law."

"Then the law's crazy!"

"I wouldn't say that if I were you. You could end up facing a charge for contempt."

"For fuck's sake!" the driver murmured.

Silvio wound down his window. "Excuse me!" he called testily. "I'm already late for an appointment and—"

The official looked round. "Why, Signor Miletti! Please forgive me, I had no idea it was you."

Silvio squinted up, blinded by the sunlight. "Oh, it's you, Zen. I thought you were back in Rome."

"Not yet, dottore. Not yet."

"They've put you on traffic duty, have they?"

As someone often accused of lacking a sense of humor, Silvio liked to draw attention to his jokes by laughing at them himself. Zen duly smiled, although this might have been at the sound of Silvio's squeaky laughter rather than the joke itself.

"Anyway, will you please fine the driver or whatever you intend doing, and let us proceed. As I say, I'm already late for an appointment."

"Out of the question, I'm afraid. On a cursory examination alone, this vehicle has been found to have five defects. As such it is clearly unfit to ply for hire as a public conveyance. However, I'd be delighted to offer you a lift."

"I have no wish to travel with you, Zen."

"Suit yourself. But it's a long walk."

"Snow chains!" muttered the taxi driver disgustedly.

Silvio sat there stewing in the stuffy heat in the back of the car, thinking over what had just been said. A thrilling sense of peril had taken hold of him, and it was this that finally moved him to open the door.

"A long walk to where?" he murmured dreamily as the taxi screeched round in a tight turn and headed back to the city.

Zen opened the rear door of the Alfetta. "To where you're going."

"But you don't know where I'm going."

"Oh, but I do, dottore, I do."

"Where, then?"

It had been intended as a challenge, but Zen treated it as a real question.

"You'll see," he replied complacently. The patrolman revved up the engine and they sped off down the hill. In the distance, perched up on its ridge, Crepi's villa was already visible. The countryside flashed by at such an insane rate that in no time at all they had passed the driveway.

"You've missed the turning!" Silvio told the driver. "I'm going to Antonio Crepi's! He's expecting me."

"Wrong on both counts," Zen replied without turning round.

"You'll lose your jobs for this," Silvio stammered, almost incoherent with excitement. "This is kidnapping! You'll get twenty years, both of you!"

They had reached the flatlands near the Tiber, whose course was visible to the right, marked by a line of trees whose lower branches were festooned with scraps of plastic bags and other durable refuse.

"This one," Zen told the driver, pointing to an abandoned track burrowing into a mass of wild brambles and scrub. The entrance was marked by a pair of imposing brick gateposts in a bad state of disrepair. A cloud of red dust rose all around the car, almost blotting out the view. The driver braked and Zen got out. He removed his overcoat and threw it on the front seat. From the dashboard he removed a clipboard and a large yellow envelope. Then he opened the rear door of the car.

"Get out, dottore."

Silvio got out.

As the dust settled, he could see the massive piles of bricks all around the clearing where they were parked. They still preserved the vague outlines of the barracks, ovens, and chimneys they had once been, now fallen out of rank and order like an army of deserters. It reminded him of the old factory below the house which had been his private playground for many years, despite his mother's dire warnings about venturing into it. He had been a solitary child, and those deserted warehouses, yards, and alleys provided the perfect environment for his fantasies to flourish. They were fantasies of war, for the most part, or rather of suffering. His victims were Swedish wooden matchsticks, which he arranged behind bits of wall or in trenches scooped from the dirt and then bombarded mercilessly with bricks, from a distance at first but gradually closing in until you could see the sharp edges of the missile gouging into the ground. But the best bit was afterward, picking through the bent and broken splinters, picturing the appalling injuries, the grotesque mutilations, the agony, the screams, the pathetic pleas to be finished off. He played all the parts himself, his voice mimicking shells and explosions, sirens and screams. In that secret playworld he was transparent, secure in the knowledge that the gates of the abandoned factory were locked and guarded, the walls too high to climb and topped with shards of broken glass.

Then one day he looked up and found a pair of eyes on him.

The man was lean and hard and dirty, his clothes greasy and torn. Silvio had never seen a Communist before, but he knew instinctively that this was one. His father had told him how the Communists were going to take over the factories and kill the owners and their families. Silvio fled, and for weeks he stayed away. Then, gradually at first, he found that the danger was no longer a reason for avoiding the factory but rather an irresistible temptation to return. He had no further interest in his innocent games. They were lost to him forever, he knew, part of something he now thought of for the first time as his childhood. If he were to go back it would be in exploration of a new dimension he felt opening up within himself. He felt wrenched apart internally, split and fractured like one of his matchstick heroes. But there was no denying it, and he already knew he would be its willing slave for the rest of his life.

The second time he saw the man, it was Silvio who had the advantage of surprise. He had rounded a length of wall, moving stealthily, and there in a corner he saw the figure, back toward him, head bent, intent on some furtive task. He knew he should run for his life, but instead he found himself moving toward the man, who remained quite still, apparently unaware of his presence. Then, when Silvio was almost close enough to touch him, he suddenly whirled around and sent a high spray of urine flying through the air, splashing Silvio's clothes and face, his lips, his mouth.

Afterward he had drenched himself with the garden hose and told his parents that the rough boys near the station had thrown him in the fountain. His clothes came back unspotted from the laundry, but the obscene warmth and acrid taste of the bright yellow liquid had marked his flesh as indelibly as a tattoo. He never returned to the factory, which shortly afterward was converted into offices and parking space for the management of what would soon become SIMP. But those barren desolate landscapes were now a part of him, like that stain which no water could wash off. Whenever he touched himself in bed at night he was there again, at risk from merciless mocking strangers, drenched in their stink and slime, both cringing and exultant.

"You see, dottore?" Zen remarked ironically, bringing him back abruptly to the present. "I told you I knew where you were going."

It was suffocatingly hot. Silvio could feel little rivulets of sweat running down his body, trickling through the hairy parts and soaking into his underclothes.

"Naturally I didn't just happen to be waiting at that bend in the road by pure coincidence," Zen went on.

"It's a plot!" Silvio muttered.

"Yes, it's a plot. But you're only the means, not the end. All I need from you is your signature on these papers."

Zen handed him the clipboard. The sun made a dazzling blank of the page, and Silvio was forced to turn so that the clipboard was in his shadow before he was able to make out anything except the crest printed at the top. Even then it took him an eternity to see what it was about, because of the florid formulas and the stilted tone of the text. When understanding suddenly came, he almost cried out with a pain as different from the gaudy agonies of his fantasies as a gallon of makeup blood is from a drop of the real thing.

He had never forgotten his mother's strict orders not to venture into the site where he had first experienced those horrid thrills, and when she was taken from him a few years later he knew that he was being punished for his disobedience. Not that this stopped him; on the contrary, guilt made his forbidden pleasures taste still sourer and stronger. But the gentle hurt of her absence was something else. Nothing could assuage that, until Ivy came. And now . . .

"You must be out of your mind!"

"It's nothing to do with me, dottore," Zen assured him with a placatory gesture. "I'm only following orders."

"Whose orders?"

"Well, I can't really tell you that, now can I? But surely you can work it out for yourself?"

Silvio struggled to summon up the small residue of cunning which he had inherited from his father. This man had known that he would be passing that spot on the road. Therefore he must have known that he was going to Crepi's. In other words, the summons from Spinelli had been nothing but a ruse designed to draw him into an ambush. So the banker must be part of the plot. But he was only a minor figure, like this man Zen. Who controlled them both? The obvious answer was his own brother-in-law, Gianluigi Santucci, the banker's patron. But Gianluigi wouldn't waste his energy on petty personal vendettas of this type. No, it could only be Cinzia.

He flung the clipboard at Zen's feet. "You can go fuck yourself!"

"We don't expect you to do it for nothing, of course," Zen said mildly, bending to pick up the papers.

"You're trying to *bribe* me?"

Although eminently unworldly in his way, Silvio was enough of a Miletti to resent the idea that anyone would presume to patronize him financially.

Zen didn't look up, occupying himself with dusting off the papers. "No, it's a question of a few souvenirs, that's all. Souvenirs of Berlin."

Slowly, Zen withdrew two photographs from the large yellow envelope and held them up.

Instantly Silvio's real pain and righteous anger were overwhelmed by stronger sensations. To think that all the time this beast had *known*, had *seen*!

"No, I won't do it!"

He knew quite well that this petulant refusal wasn't worth the paper it was wiped with, as dear Gerhard would put it. But Zen was apparently taken in.

"In that case," the policeman declared, his tone heavy with hypocritical regret, "I'm afraid that prints of these photographs will begin to circulate among the friends and enemies of the Miletti family in Perugia and elsewhere. Just imagine the scene, dottore! There they are, early in the morning, still dewy-eyed over that first cup of coffee, when *bang!* Hello! What's this? Good God! It looks like Silvio Miletti waiting for someone to come and take a dump on him! What do you think their reaction is going to be, dottore? Oh well, it takes all sorts, different strokes for different folks, don't knock it till you've tried it?"

Silvio was speechless. The idea of those images being seen by people who inhabited a quite separate zone of his life, whom he met at receptions and conferences, at dinners and concerts, who

greeted him on the Corso every day! The revelation of his secret
pleasures to the whole of Perugia would be a humiliation so
monumental, so absolute, so *perfect*, that he knew he would
never survive the excitement it would generate.

But at the thought of what he was about to do, these thrills
faded and the real pain returned.

"But it's all lies! Filthy obscene lies and nothing else!"

To his amazement, Zen winked conspiratorially.

"Of course it is! That's why it doesn't matter. In fact the
kidnappers are already under arrest in Florence. They've
confessed to the whole thing. Believe me, dottore, if I thought
for a single moment that these allegations would be taken
seriously, I'd never have agreed to be a party to this! But it's just
a question of stirring up a bit of scandal, a bit of dirt. Quite
harmless really."

The man's protestations made Silvio queasy, but what he said
made sense. If the gang had already confessed, then the papers
he was being asked to sign were totally worthless except
precisely to someone who would stoop to any trick to sully the
honor of the woman he loved and whose love sustained him.
Someone like Cinzia, in fact. But they would deal with her later.
Meanwhile he must get this over with and warn Ivy immediately. It was awful to think how she might suffer if she was
suddenly confronted with his apparent treachery.

"Just put your name on the dotted line at the bottom,
dottore," Zen prompted. "Where it says that you made the
statement freely and voluntarily."

Silvio took out his pen and signed. When the yellow envelope
was safe in his hands he turned to Zen.

"I may be dirty in superficial ways," he remarked, "but you're
dirty through and through! You're a filthy putrid rancid cesspit,
a walking shitheap."

The final proof of the official's total degeneracy was that he
didn't even try to defend himself. He merely climbed into the
waiting car, his despicable job done. Silvio followed, but more
slowly. Despite the varied splendors and miseries of his existence, the pleasure of moral superiority was one that very rarely
came his way. As a connoisseur of exotic sensations he was
determined to savor it to the utmost.

11

She almost changed her mind at the last moment. It was the place itself that did it, the smell of cheap power, making her realize just how far she had come since those early days, the days of secretarial work and English lessons. The world Ivy lived in now was drenched in power too, of course, but quite different from the low-grade kind that pervaded places where you came to post a parcel or cash a check or renew your residence permit. How she'd always hated the bitter envious midgets who patrol these internal boundaries of the State, malicious goblins wringing the most out of their single dingy magic spell. Her Italian friends claimed to feel the same way, but Ivy had never been convinced. The opium of these people was not religion but power, or rather power *was* their religion. Everyone believed, everyone was hooked. And everyone was rewarded with at least a tiny scrap of the stuff, enough to make him feel needed. What people hated in the system was being subjected to others' power, but they would all resist any change which threatened to modify or limit their own. The situation was thus both stable and rewarding, especially for those who were rich in power and could bypass it with a few phone calls, a hint dropped here, a threat there. At length Ivy had come to appreciate its advantages, and to realize that she could make just as good use of them as the natives, if not rather better in fact. In the end she'd come to admire the Italians as great realists who saw life as it really was, free of the crippling hypocrisy of the Anglo-Saxon world in which she had been brought up.

She'd learned her lesson well. Gone were the days when she had to hang around under that sign with its contemptuous scrawl FOREIGNERS, waiting for the Political Branch officials who would wander in and out as it suited them, or not turn up at all, or send you away for not having enough sheets of the special franked paper which could be bought only at a tobacconist's shop, which meant another half-hour's delay and then starting from scratch again having lost your place in the queue. Nowadays she dealt directly with the people with real power. The snag, of course, was that they wouldn't speak to you unless you had real power too, or knew someone who did. Only since her association with Silvio Miletti had she been able to make full use of the lessons she had learned, to put her newly acquired skills to the test. Yes, she had come a long way.

"You looking for something?"

Hesitating there at the foot of the stairs, she'd attracted the attention of the guard, who fixed her with a supercilious stare.

"I have an appointment with Commissioner Zen," she replied coldly.

"Never heard of him."

"It's all right, I know the room number."

She tried to move forward to the stairs, but the man barred her with one arm and yelled to a colleague, "We got a Zen?"

The man consulted a list taped to the wall. "Three-five-one!" he yelled back.

"Three-five-one," the guard repeated slowly. "Third floor. Think you can make it on your own?"

"Just about, I should think, thank you very much."

Her attempt at irony did not make the slightest impression on the man's fatuous complacency. You couldn't beat them at their own game, of course; the mistake had been agreeing to come in the first place.

Normally she would not have done so. In the circles in which she now moved, one did not call on policemen unless they were on the payroll, in which case the meeting would be on neutral ground, in a café or on the street. But when Zen had phoned, just before lunch, Ivy had agreed with hardly a moment's thought. He was going back to Rome that evening, he said, and he'd like to clear up that matter they had discussed on the phone at the beginning of the week, did she remember? She remembered all right! Not the subject of the phone call, which had been rather vague in any case, something about a letter he had received. But she wasn't likely to forget the way he'd quizzed her about her appointment with Cinzia that morning. At all events, today he'd suggested that she stop by his office in the afternoon, and to her surprise she had agreed. The problem, she was forced to admit, was that her reflexes had not yet adjusted to her new position. Silvio would have got it right instinctively, but you had to have been born powerful for that. In her heart of hearts Ivy still feared and respected the police as her parents had taught her to do. She might have come a long way, she recognized, but there was still a long way to go.

Her sensible rubber heels made hardly a sound as she walked along the third-floor corridor. With some surprise she noticed that her palms were slightly damp. The place was having its effect. That shiny travertine cladding they used everywhere, cold and slippery, seemed to exude unease. Get a grip on yourself, she thought, as she knocked on the door.

The occupant of the office was a rough common-looking individual of the brawn-and-no-brain variety. She thought she must have made a mistake, but he called her in.

"The chief'll be back directly. He says you're to wait."

Ivy glanced at her watch. She was by no means certain that it had been a good idea to come and this provided the perfect excuse for leaving.

"I'm sorry, I've got another appointment."

But the man had taken up a position with his back to the door. "Take it easy, relax!" he told her in an insultingly familiar tone. "You want to read the paper?"

He picked a pink sports paper from the wastebasket and held it out to her. There was a long smear of some viscous matter down the front page.

The man's body was bulging with muscle. His nose had been broken and his ears were grotesquely swollen. He had an air of ingrained damage about him, as though his life had been spent running into things and coming off second-best. The effect was both comical and threatening.

Ivy consulted her watch again. "I shall wait for fifteen minutes."

Why hadn't she insisted on leaving immediately? It had something to do with the man's physical presence. There was no denying it, he intimidated her. But if she wanted to leave this oaf couldn't stop her, of course. He was staring at her with an expression which, to her alarm, she found that she recognized. She had discovered its meaning back in the days when she was working at the hospital, where she'd been secretary to one of the directors, an unmarried man in his midforties. He was distinguished, witty and charming, and seemed intrigued by his "English" secretary, amused by her, concerned about her welfare. He gave her flowers and chocolates occasionally, helped her find a flat at a rent she could afford, and once even took her out to eat at a restaurant outside Perugia. He had never made the ghost of a pass at her.

One weekend there was a conference in Bologna which he was to attend, and at the last moment he proposed that Ivy accompany him. When she hesitated, he showed her the receipt for the hotel booking he had already made, for two single rooms. She could assist him in various small ways in return for a little paid holiday, he explained. He made it sound as though she would be doing him a favor. He appealed to her as an attractive vivacious woman, a fellow conspirator against life's drabness, the ideal companion for such a jaunt as this. Nothing quite like it had ever happened to her before. The experience seemed to sum up everything she loved about this country where people knew what life was worth and understood how to get the best out of it.

They stayed in a luxury hotel and dined out that evening at one of the city's famous restaurants. Ivy's pleasure was dimmed only by a slight anxiety as to what would happen when they got back to the hotel, or rather as to how she would deal with it. Ivy was not physically attracted to her employer, but she had long ago been forced to face the fact that the men she found attractive did not feel the same way about her. They were younger than she, for one thing, handsome reckless types who didn't give a damn about anything. Unfortunately they didn't give a damn about her, even as a one-night stand, so she had learned to compromise. And when someone had been as attentive and thoughtful as her employer, taking such pains to ensure that the weekend was a success, not to mention the various practical possibilities for the future this opened up, well why not, she thought.

Only it didn't happen. It didn't happen that night, when he simply kissed her hand and wished her a good night's sleep, or the next, when they went out with a group of his colleagues to a restaurant in the country outside Bologna. The men all talked loudly and continuously and so fast that Ivy wasn't always able to follow the conversation. There were even moments when she doubted whether they meant her to. After the meal a bottle of whiskey was brought to the table. As it circulated through the fog of endless cigarettes, Ivy watched meaning coming and going like a landscape glimpsed through clouds from a plane. She felt lost, discarded. Her boss had moved into the world which men inhabit with other men and where women are not at home. From time to time he glanced at her, made some comment or smiled, but he was no longer there, not really. She was alone in spirit, and later quite literally, for in the confusion of leaving the restaurant she ended up in a car with four men to whom she hadn't even been introduced, and had to spend the whole forty minutes of the drive back to Bologna fielding crassly insensitive questions about her private life, her family, why she was living in Italy, and whether she liked spaghetti. Back at the hotel her employer was nowhere to be found. She made her way alone to her room, cursing herself for a stupid sentimental bitch.

The next morning a waiter awakened her with a bouquet of roses and a handwritten card covered in fulsome apologies and inviting her to take coffee on the terrace. There the apologies were repeated in person. He had drunk too much and become confused, the group he ·was with had wanted to go on to a nightclub despite his objections, and so on and so forth. Later he drove her back to Perugia. Nothing seemed to have changed.

But something *had*. She noticed it immediately in the eyes of the other men at the hospital and in the way they treated her. But she had no idea what it meant until about a week later, when she overheard two administrative assistants chatting on the stairs.

". . . for the weekend with that English piece."

"But he's a pansy!"

"That's what everyone thought! Looks like he gets it coming and going, eh?"

"Crafty old bugger!"

It was so cruel, so nasty! Above all it was so unfair! "But we didn't do anything!" she felt like screaming. "He *is* a pansy! He didn't lay a finger on me!" But of course no one would have believed her. "Where I come from," an Italian girl had once told her, "if a man and a woman are alone together in a room for fifteen minutes it's assumed that they've made love."

Her employer had managed to salvage his reputation with the other men at the hospital—and how much depends on that reputation!—at no cost to himself. How very clever. Even in the intensity of her hatred and hurt at the way she had been used, Ivy remained coolly appreciative of how cleverly it had been done. Having realized at an early age that stupidity makes a poor sauce to plain looks, she had always sought to give cleverness its due.

And now, incredibly, this brutal policeman was looking at her in the same way as those men at the hospital, the way a man looks at a woman he knows to be sexually available. But that didn't make sense! The situation was utterly different in every respect. What was going on?

Ivy felt immensely reassured when Zen finally arrived. He didn't look at her in that vulgar impertinent way. His expression was detached, calculating, and morose, as if to say that he would do his job to the best of his ability even though he was not deceived as to its value. His gaze was dull and opaque, like the surface of water where the last traces of some violent shock lingers on.

"All right, Chiodini, that'll do," he said, summarily dismissing the man who had been guarding the door like some mastiff. As he walked over to his desk, Ivy noticed that his shoes and trousers were coated with a fine red dust.

"Is this going to take long?" she asked a little irritably. "You said two o'clock and I'm in rather a hurry."

Without replying he took a sheet of paper from his pocket and passed it to her. It was covered in the same fine red dust as his clothing. Was this the letter which he'd referred to? But she could see from the printed heading POLIZIA DELLO STATO that it was official. The typed text began with one of those formulas which the judicial system employs to eliminate the ambiguities of normal human utterance.

I, the undersigned, depose as follows.

On the morning of Monday, 22 March at 9:20 approximately I observed Cook, Ivy Elaine, outside the garage
below our family residence at Via del Capanno 5, Perugia.
She was carrying a small green plastic bag. She got into one
of the Fiat sedans kept there for the use of the family and
drove away. Since Cook is entitled to the use of these cars I
thought no more of it at the time.

Later the same morning, at 11:45 approximately, I saw
Cook walking upstairs to the room she occupied in our
house during this period. She was carrying the same plastic
bag as before. I wished her to type some letters for me and
called to attract her attention. When she did not respond I
followed her upstairs. Her room was empty and I could
hear the sound of the shower from the bathroom next
door. The plastic bag she had been carrying lay on the
table. To my surprise, I found that it contained a blond wig
which I had bought the previous year to attend a Carnival
party and a small automatic pistol which I recognized as
belonging to my sister Cinzia.

Ivy noted the effect this text was having on her body: the
thudding of her heart, the swelling pressure of her blood, the
dryness of her mouth, the moisture erupting in patches all over
her skin, the weight on her chest against which she had to
struggle to draw breath, the numbness and trembling, the urge
to break out in short sharp howls like a hyena.

When Cook returned to the room I asked her about the
wig and the pistol. She appeared confused, and then said
that she had just been playing a joke on Cinzia. I was
appalled that she could contemplate such a thing at a
moment when we were all anxiously awaiting news of my
father's release and demanded further details, but Cook's
replies were incoherent and when I pressed her she became
hysterical.

I assumed at first that this episode was due to the
tremendous strain under which we were all living at the
time. But when my father was subsequently found dead,
and it emerged that he had been shot during the period
that Cook had been absent from the house and with a pistol

similar to the one I had observed in her possession, I began
to suspect the horrifying truth.

As it got worse, it got better. This is a pack of lies, she
thought.

Appalled by the idea that I had been responsible for
introducing a viper into the bosom of the family, I threw
caution to the winds and decided to confront Cook. To my
astonishment, she claimed that I had imagined the whole
sequence of events described above. She admitted going
out at the time in question, but asserted that my sister had
telephoned and asked Cook to meet her at the Santucci
house, outside Perugia. On arriving there, she said, she had
found Cinzia absent, and after waiting for some time, had
returned to the city. As for the plastic bag containing the
wig and the pistol, she denied all knowledge of them.

When I questioned my sister about this I discovered that
the truth was that Cook had phoned Cinzia and asked for
a meeting in Perugia, at which she had failed to appear.
Clearly her motive in decoying my sister away from home
had been to obtain entrance to the Santucci property,
where she was admitted by the housekeeper and left
unobserved for some time, in order to take the pistol which
I had subsequently observed in her possession.

Upon searching the house, I discovered that my wig had
been replaced in the chest of drawers where it is kept. Of
the pistol I could find no trace. Faced with Cook's angry
denials and the assurance of the authorities that my father's
murder had been committed by his kidnappers, I decided
to keep my doubts to myself. But I now feel that this
decision was mistaken, and have decided to come forward.

The above statement has been made freely and of my
own volition and my legal rights were fully respected
throughout.

Silvio Agostino Miletti

Perhaps in an attempt to counter its reputation for gross
inefficiency in everything that matters, the State is a stickler for
precision when it comes to trivia. The legal system which takes
so long to bring people to trial that they are often released after

being found guilty, having already been imprisoned longer than the period of their sentence, insists that statements to the authorities record not only the date on which they were made but also the time. Thus it was that Ivy noticed that Silvio's statement to the police had supposedly been made at 12:42 that day. That was very interesting, because Ivy remembered quite clearly that Silvio had spent the half hour before lunch whining about the selfish behavior of his brother Daniele in eating the Bulgarian yogurt which he, Silvio, went to considerable time and trouble to obtain from a supplier in Rome. The time on the statement meant that the whole thing was a transparent forgery. But this knowledge failed to reassure Ivy. Quite the contrary. Because that big loopy signature at the bottom was genuine all right, so that Silvio had to be a party to whatever monstrous conspiracy was afoot.

She looked up at Zen. "I don't know what to say. I feel like asking if this is some kind of joke. But it quite obviously isn't."

The gray eyes regarded her cryptically.

"So what *is* it?" she demanded with a nervous laugh.

"It's a statement made to me by Silvio Miletti."

"It's a pack of lies!" she cried. "It's rubbish, sheer invention, as you must know very well! And not even clever invention! Do you really think that if I'd committed a murder I would bring the gun back to the house in a plastic bag and leave it lying in my room in full view while I went to have a shower?"

"The witness describes you as hysterical. Hysterical people do irrational things."

"I was *not* hysterical!" She sounded it now, though. "I wasn't even there! After I got back from Cinzia's I went home to my flat, for heaven's sake."

"What time was that?"

"I don't know, late morning. I remember I had to do some shopping, to get something for lunch. Yes, that's right, and then I ran into a friend on the Corso. We had an aperitif together. There, that proves it. He'll verify my story!"

"What about earlier, before the appointment with Cinzia? Where were you then?"

She was about to reply, but checked herself. "If you're going to question me then I'm entitled to the presence of a lawyer."

Zen acknowledged the point with a fractional inflection of his lips, not so much a smile as the memory of a smile. "But this isn't an interrogation," he said.

His words were such an unexpected relief that Ivy felt quite faint. "I really must go," she murmured.

Zen stared at her in silence, and his expression was even more alarming than Chiodini's, although quite different. He looked at her as though she were dead.

"I'm afraid that's not possible," he replied courteously.

"What do you mean?"

"Signora, an eminent citizen has come forward and made a statement implicating you in the murder of his father. Now I don't know exactly what conception you have of the duties of the police, but I can assure you that I wouldn't be performing mine if I simply ignored this allegation on the grounds that the person accused claims that it's all a pack of lies."

"Are you saying I'm under arrest?"

"Not exactly. You're being held on suspicion of having committed a crime punishable by life imprisonment. This will be communicated to the Public Prosecutor's office, who will in turn inform the investigating magistrate, Dottor Foria. She will want to question you, I imagine. But that won't be for a day or two. She's in Florence at the moment. The kidnappers are under arrest there."

So far Ivy had been proud of her control, but now a manic giggle escaped her. Dear Christ, how much more could she take?

"Obviously she's got her hands full with that at the moment," Zen continued. "The Public Prosecutor is supposed to be informed within forty-eight hours, and the magistrate is bound to interrogate you within a further forty-eight. In practice that tends to get run together to suit everyone's convenience, of course, but at the worst it shouldn't be later than Tuesday."

"Tuesday." The word seemed meaningless. "And until then?"

"Until then you'll be held here, I'm afraid. Chiodini!"

The bruiser came back in.

"Take Signora Cook down to the cells."

The word was like an electric shock, and Ivy sprang to her feet. "Just a moment! I'm entitled to make a phone call first. It's my legal right!"

Zen ignored her.

"Now listen to me, Chiodini," he said. "I won't be here to supervise this, so I'm depending on you. Until Rosella Foria gets back from Florence, Signora Cook is out-of-bounds, in quarantine. Understand? She speaks to no one and no one speaks to her. And I mean no one."

"Right, chief. Come on, you!"

Chiodini made a grab at Ivy's arm, but she evaded him and walked out, deliberately repressing all thought. There'll be time for that when I'm alone, she told herself.

As it was, she had to fight even for the small privilege of solitude. The cells were in the basement of the Questura, which clearly predated the rest of the building by several centuries. Their doors had an air of total impenetrability, which Ivy found oddly reassuring. Her privacy was very important to her, and she saw the doors not as shutting her in but as keeping others out. What had always terrified her most about prisons was the overcrowding, four or five people shut up together in a cell intended to be barely tolerable for two. Italians seemed to be able to stand such enforced intimacy, but Ivy knew that it would drive her mad. She simply couldn't function adequately without a space she could call her own, and she was acutely aware that in the hours ahead she was going to need to function not just adequately but quite extraordinarily well.

So it was a nasty shock when the cell door swung open to reveal a strange-looking woman with a smell on her and a wild look in her black eyes.

"I'm not going in there," Ivy said firmly.

"Oh, you're not, eh?" Chiodini replied.

"No."

He stared at her in some confusion, unsure how to proceed. If she had been a man he would have hit him. But with women things were different; you could only hit them if they were married to you.

"There are lots of other cells," she pointed out.

"They're being painted."

"For God's sake, man, she's a *gypsy*! How would you like it?"

With a bad grace, Chiodini locked the cell up again and installed Ivy in the one next door.

She slumped down on the bed. To think that on her way to the Questura, just an hour ago, she'd been worrying about whether to splurge on that slinky but hideously expensive Lurex trouser suit she'd had her eye on for some time. The contrast between that reality and this cell, this mean pallet bed, that door as massive as the slab over a tomb, was so disturbing that she felt black waves of panic lapping up at her. But she refused to give in. To do so would be sheer self-indulgence. After all, she had managed before. When she discovered the reason why she had been invited for that weekend in Bologna she had calmly set about reviewing the options open to her. They fell into two categories, revenge and reward. There was no question that revenge was a very attractive option, but in the end Ivy had rejected it in favor of reward. Damaging your enemies is satisfying, but doing yourself a favor is more important in the long run. Only in exceptional circumstances is it possible to combine the two.

Like everyone else, Ivy had envied those who had a secure job, one guaranteed by the State, which could not be taken away no matter how lazy or incompetent you were, and whose admittedly meager salary could be supplemented by tax-free moonlighting in the afternoon. Her position at the hospital was, as they said, "precarious." To keep it she had to please, which meant everything from picking up one man's suit from the cleaners and buying fresh pasta for another to queuing for over an hour in the pouring rain to get theater tickets for one of the patients, quite apart from being expected to do the work of an entire typing pool single-handed. But she didn't dare complain. "Don't give yourself airs!" the old Fascist who served as porter remarked when she'd made the mistake of letting herself be provoked by his rudeness. "The day the director decides he doesn't like the color of your knickers you'll be out on the street." He might have added, "On the other hand I'm here forever, whether he likes it or not." That was implicit in everything he did, or more usually failed to do.

Ivy didn't necessarily want to work at the hospital forever, but she did want to be the one who would decide if she would, and that meant getting a secure position. The director could grant such posts, but he knew what they were worth and wasn't going to hand them out to some foreigner when the telephone was ringing off the hook with locals offering him this that and the other if he would see to it that Tizio or Cosetta was fixed up. So Ivy bided her time and kept her eyes and ears open, waiting for events to take her where she wanted to go.

Then one day her employer came storming into the annex where she worked and grilled her for over half an hour about some documents which he said had disappeared. From a man who habitually paraded his velvet gloves, this display of iron fist was disconcerting, especially since Ivy knew nothing of the existence of the documents, never mind their disappearance. But now she did, and she also knew that he half-suspected her of having taken them. All of which added up to the opportunity she had been waiting for, because despite this the porter's prophecy was not fulfilled. Her job hung on a whim, but it was not indulged. The conclusion was obvious, and brought with it the reflection that her employer was not as clever as she had previously thought.

That afternoon she returned to the hospital after lunch, supposedly to catch up on her work. Just to balance things out, the other porter was a Stalinist, who responded to her request for the key to the supply cupboard as she had known he would, by tossing her a huge bunch which would open every door on the top floor of the building. Identifying and labeling the keys was a task which the porters considered too onerous to undertake, and since their jobs were not precarious no one could make them do so. So if anyone wanted the spare key to a particular room they were given the bunch for the entire floor in question and had to find the key themselves.

It took Ivy twelve minutes to do so, but that was the hardest part of the whole business. Men did not hide things very well, she knew. Their minds ran in predictable ways. Once inside the director's office she quickly found the spare key to the filing cabinet, taped to the back of it. A few seconds later, the missing documents were in her hand. They had been where she had known they must be, lying on the bottom of the metal drawer. They had been carelessly placed between two files and had then worked their way down as the drawer was opened and closed. It was obvious, it happened all the time, and yet her employer had not thought of it. Part of the reason was that predictability of the male mind she had already noted, but it was also due to a structural defect of the system under which they all lived. The great weakness of paranoia is that it cannot take chance into account. Because the documents might be damaging to him if they fell into the wrong hands, the director had assumed that their disappearance must have been due to a deliberate act on someone's part. To think otherwise would have been to run the risk of being exposed as gullible and unrealistic, the very things that a man in his position could least afford to be.

Back home in her little flat Ivy examined the documents at her leisure. They looked innocuous enough, mere lists of figures and dates and initials, but the next morning before work she dropped into her bank, rented a safety deposit box, and placed the documents in it. She did well, for when she got home that afternoon she found that her flat had been ransacked.

The next day she phoned her employer, rambling on incoherently about how she couldn't go on living in an atmosphere of insecurity and lack of trust, of groundless accusations and the perpetual fear of losing her job. If she had a secure position perhaps she would feel differently, but as it was . . . well, she didn't know what she might do. Really, she felt capable of almost anything.

A month later her post was made permanent.

She'd done it once, and if she could do it once then couldn't she do it again? But it wasn't as simple as that. The situation was quite different this time. She didn't know whether to laugh or to cry when she remembered Zen's panicky orders that she be kept "in quarantine." As though anyone was going to lift a finger to save her! Didn't he understand that she had no support whatever apart from Silvio? Her relationship had always been exclusively with him. That was the way he had wanted it. Evidently there was something about her that attracted homosexuals, perhaps the same thing that repelled the young men she would have much preferred to attract. But you had to make the best of things, and Silvio Miletti was a pretty good catch, all things considered.

Ironically enough, it had been Ivy's boss at the hospital who had introduced her to Silvio. That was before the two men fell out over their mutual infatuation with a young German called Gerhard Mayer. Never one to do things by halves, Silvio had deprived his rival not only of Mayer's services but of Ivy's as well. For three years now they had been a couple in all respects but one. Ivy's only stipulation had been to insist on keeping her job at the hospital, although the work was actually done by a succession of temporary secretaries paid through a Miletti subsidiary. It was partly a form of insurance to hold on to the salaried position and the promise of a pension that went with it, but it was mostly spite. The director had not been very happy about the arrangement, to say the least, but with the Milettis leaning on him from one side and the fear that the missing documents might one day surface gnawing at him from the other, he had ended by agreeing.

Silvio and Ivy had proved to complement each other perfectly. She had the vision, the will, the patience; he had the power, the contacts, and the influence. So far their exploits had been relatively modest. The anonymous letter she'd sent to Bartocci, alleging that the kidnapping was a put-up job, was a typical example. Ivy's method was to seize the opportunity when it arose, and meanwhile to stir things up so that opportunities were more likely to arise. The letter to Bartocci had in fact succeeded beyond her wildest dreams, for it had indirectly created the circumstances leading to Ruggiero Miletti's death, which had in turn removed the one remaining impediment to the brilliant future which beckoned to her and Silvio.

Or rather had seemed to beckon, until just a few hours ago. For now the unthinkable had occurred, the one eventuality which Ivy had left out of her calculations. Cautiously at first, but with increasing confidence as she recognized his utter dependence on her, she had sacrificed all her minor allegiances to this one relationship, which offered far more than all the others put together. It was often a considerable effort to remember that despite his fecklessness and petulance, his timidity and sloth, Silvio was a man of considerable power. And that power was now completely at her disposal, to use as though it were her own. It was a dizzying sensation, like finding yourself at the controls of a jet after a lifetime of flying gliders. Only at this moment did she appreciate the more sinister implications of this image. Gliders rode the buoyant winds, versatile and questing, finding alternative currents if one failed, but when jets went wrong disaster was swift and inevitable. But it had never seemed possible that anything *could* go wrong. Silvio needed her as he needed food and drink, not to mention more esoteric satisfactions. He could no more deny her than he could deny himself.

At least, so she'd always supposed. But apparently she'd been mistaken, with catastrophic results. Zen could relax. No one would be pulling strings on her behalf, for she had deliberately cut them all except for those which bound her to Silvio. And he—even now she could hardly bring herself to believe it!—had not merely abandoned her but turned viciously against her, perjuring himself in the vilest way so that she could be thrown into a common lockup like some gypsy beggar. No, Zen had nothing to worry about on that score!

Then an even more terrifying thought occurred to her. The discrepancy in the time of the statement proved that Zen and Silvio were hand in glove. He must *know* that the Milettis were not going to intervene to save her. Was he perhaps worried that their intervention might take a quite different form? A cup of coffee, for example, laced with something that would have her flopping about the cell like a landed fish, gasping out the classic last words, "They've poisoned me!"

That deposit box at the bank now held much more than her employer's precious documents, as Silvio well knew. There were photocopies of letters, account books and papers of all kinds, and above all the tapes, boxes of them. The answering machine had been a stroke of genius. For some reason answering machines were always regarded as slightly comical annoyances. No one liked having to deal with them, so they were always relieved when you answered in person, too relieved to remember that the machine was still there, still connected and possibly recording every word they said. For some reason that never seemed to occur to anyone. But it was a meager consolation, not nearly enough to keep the sickening tide of panic away. She might take a couple of the bastards with her, or at least scratch up their pretty, rich faces a bit, but that would not save her. Nothing could save her now.

When the door of her cell opened she hoped it might be a familiar face, but it was only the hard man who had brought her down there.

"Come on," he said, beckoning impatiently.

Ivy felt as reluctant to leave her cell as a condemned prisoner being led away to execution. "Where are we going?"

The man just stared at her in his insolent way, like those bastards at the hospital when they thought they had her where they wanted her.

Ivy got to her feet. "You're called Chiodini, aren't you?"

"What about it?" the man demanded, suddenly on guard.

"Nothing."

But if I ever get out of here, she thought, I'm going to call a certain number I know and pay whatever it takes to have one of those arrogant eyes of yours sliced in two like a bull's testicle, my friend.

Chiodini led her away along a narrow passage constantly switching direction, like a sewer following the turnings of the street above. The walls here were a world away from the shiny polished façades of the Questura—rough grainy slabs of stone beaded with moisture, studded with chunks of brick and rubble. Here and there diminishing islands of plasterwork still clung, but most of it had disintegrated into a gritty porridge that scratched and slithered underfoot. It felt like part of the complex system of tunnels and passages underlying the ancient city, into which it was rumored that children occasionally strayed and were never seen again.

At length they turned a corner to find a man who seemed to have been waiting for them. He was short and fleshy, with a melancholy face and heavy eyebrows, dressed in a heavy-duty suit of the kind farmers wear on Sundays. To Ivy, he was the image of an executioner.

"What are you doing here, Geraci?" Ivy's escort demanded. "They said you were ill."

"I'm all right. I'll take over now, you run along."

"But the chief said—"

"Never you mind about that! I'll look after her."

Chiodini looked at Ivy, then at the other man.

"Go on, beat it!" Geraci insisted.

When Chiodini had gone, Geraci led Ivy silently along the passage to a metal door. So lost was she in evil dreams that she expected to see a whitewashed stall inside, with a dangling noose, the wooden shutters of the trap and the lever that springs them back to reveal the pit beneath. But in fact the room was large and high ceilinged, bare of any features whatever except for a crucifix on one wall and a small barred window high up on the other. Through the window Ivy could just make out a section of exterior wall, bright with sunlight. The fact of its being outside in the real world where life was going on in its reassuring humdrum way imbued those stones with infinite fascination for Ivy. She wished she could see it all more clearly, admire the tiny plants sprouting from its crevices, watch the insects coming and going, study the shifting subtleties of color and shade. She longed to lavish a passionate attention on that poor patch of wall, to astonish it with her unwearying love.

Then she heard a sound behind her. Someone had spoken her name. On the other side of the great naked space a figure stood gazing at her with imploring eyes. *Silvio, it's Silvio*, she thought.

"I'll give you as long as I can," Geraci murmured.

Silvio nodded impatiently. "Yes, yes. Thank you."

The policeman bowed slightly as he backed toward the door. "Thank *you*, dottore. Thank *you*."

Despite his impatience, once they were alone Silvio seemed unable to speak.

"What are you doing here?" Ivy demanded.

"That man telephoned me and told me what had happened. I'd been trying to get hold of you all afternoon! I had no idea they would move so quickly."

At his words, something Ivy thought had died forever flickered into life again.

"But how did he get you in?" she asked guardedly. "They said I was to see no one."

"He's one of them. Apparently he's in some trouble, wants me to put in a word for him. But let me explain what happened, you have no idea—"

"Excuse me, I know *exactly* what happened! I've seen the whole thing, read every one of the lies you put your name to."

Silvio rubbed his hands together in anguish. "You don't think I signed that thing willingly, do you? Ivy, you must understand!"

"I don't much care how you signed it! It's quite sufficient that you did. Do you know how I've spent the last few hours? Sitting all alone in a stinking cell, totally humiliated and despairing! And you have the gall to try and interest me in your state of mind when you signed the libelous rubbish that made that possible? You expect me to *understand*? No, no, those days are over, Silvio. I don't feel very understanding anymore. I don't have time to worry about your problems. I've got problems of my own."

"But you haven't! It's all meaningless!"

He blundered blindly toward her. "Ivy, you must understand! It's all just a trivial vendetta by Cinzia. It doesn't amount to anything. You'll be out of here by this evening, I promise. I'll retract the whole statement, deny everything. They'll have to let you go."

She turned toward him, a new light in her eyes. "Cinzia?"

"That's right. She got hold of some photographs taken in Berlin and gave them to that bastard Zen. They threatened to make them public unless I signed. What could I do? I was taken completely by surprise. I thought I'd have time to warn you, at least. But it doesn't amount to anything, that's the important thing. She just wanted to stir up a bit of scandal, to give you a bad time for a day or two. But we'll soon sort her out, won't we? We'll make her sorry!"

Ivy was silent. The nightmare was beginning to fade, but

something still remained, some real cry of distress which the dream had taken up and used for its own purposes. What had it been?

Silvio told her the whole story, starting with the call from the banker which had set him up to be waylaid by Zen. It was all Cinzia's fault, he repeated. But Ivy knew better. Long ago she had recognized Gianluigi Santucci as her most formidable opponent. Like her, he was an outsider; like her, he had a personal hold over a single member of the family; like her, he was ambitious and unscrupulous. Indeed, in different circumstances they might have been natural allies. As it was they were deadly rivals. Ivy had always known that sooner or later she would have to deal with Gianluigi. Evidently he'd had the same idea, and had struck first. It should have occurred to her that he would have had Silvio followed to that club and his indiscretions photographed. In his position, she would have done exactly the same thing.

But there was still that other thing nagging at the back of her mind. It was something Zen had told her almost casually and which she had immediately forgotten, not because it didn't matter but because it mattered far too much, because coming on top of Silvio's apparent treachery it was just too hideous to contemplate. But now that she wanted and needed to deal with it, Ivy found that repression had done its job too efficiently. Try as she would, she simply couldn't recall what it was.

"By the way, do you know that they've arrested the kidnappers?" Silvio asked her eagerly.

They had often remarked on the fact that one of them would mention something that had been on the tip of the other's tongue, as though they were able to read each other's minds. Now it had happened again. And now Ivy understood why she had deliberately forgotten. This was the worst news in the world.

There was only one way. She dreaded it as one might dread a painful and risky operation, even knowing that there was no alternative. It would have to be very quick, before she could change her mind.

"Silvio, the kidnappers didn't kill Ruggiero."

He tossed his head impatiently. "But they've confessed!"

"They didn't do it."

"How do *you* know?"

It was his scornful, cocksure tone of voice that tipped the balance in the end, that made it possible for her to tell him.

"Because I did."

It took him a moment to react.

"That's silly." He frowned. "Don't say things like that. It's horrible. It frightens me."

"It frightens me too. But if we face it together it won't be so frightening. You know that nothing can frighten us as long as we're together." She moved toward him. "And now we'll never have to be apart again."

His mouth opened a crack. "But . . . you . . ."

"When they phoned to say he'd been released I suddenly realized what that would mean. We've been happy these past months, haven't we? Happy as never before. And that happiness is precious, because people like us know so little of it. The others are rich in happiness, yet they want to take away what little we've got. You remember the letter he sent. You remember what he said about us. Why should people be allowed to say things like that? You know it's unfair, you know it's wrong. And it was all about to start again. We would have been separated again, kept apart from each other. You would have been trapped at home, having to listen to his cruel obscene gibes. You couldn't stand that. Why should you be expected to stand it?"

Although she was very close to him now, she still did not touch him. He turned away, and for a moment she thought that she'd lost him, that he was about to rush to the door, scream for the guards, denounce her.

"Perhaps I've done the wrong thing," she went on, almost whispering. "Perhaps I've made a terrible mistake. Even mummies aren't perfect, they make mistakes sometimes. But babies have to forgive them, don't they?"

After an interminable moment he looked back at her, and she knew she was safe. That dash to the door would never happen, for it would be like running off a cliff.

"What are we going to do?" he moaned.

"We must plan and act, Silvio. That statement will be used against me."

"But since it's all lies . . ."

"It's all lies, yes. But it's not all untrue."

Just as she had once paid tribute to her employer's cleverness, she now gave Gianluigi Santucci his due. It was very cunning, the way he had woven details like the wig and the pistol and the fake appointment with Cinzia into a tissue of lies. Yes, there was enough truth there to give the investigators plenty of material to get their teeth into.

"Besides, if they've arrested the kidnappers then sooner or later they'll find out that it was my number they called on Monday morning to announce Ruggiero's release."

"But that's not true! They called us at the house on Tuesday! I remember that perfectly well. Pietro took the call."

Ivy shook her head wearily. "No, that was a recording I made when they phoned me the day before. The gang was given my number before the ransom drop, because it wasn't being tapped by the police. Don't you remember?"

Silvio gestured impatiently. "Who cares what they say? It's just their word against yours. I'll get you the finest lawyers in the country. . . ."

"That's not enough. The judicial investigation is secret, don't forget. However good a lawyer you get, there's nothing he can do initially. Besides, the Santuccis will be working against us, and there's no telling what line Daniele and Pietro will take. No, it's going to be a struggle, I'm afraid. We must prepare to fight on a much wider front, and that means we're going to need friends, all the friends we can get. Russo, for example, and Fratini. Possibly Carletti. I'll send you a list later. We must think flexibly. We might make it seem all a grotesque plot which Gianluigi is orchestrating in order to compromise the Miletti family. The new investigating magistrate will remember what happened to Bartocci. Hopefully she'll think twice about venturing too far on flimsy evidence in the teeth of sustained opposition. And if she does, we'll put it about that her zeal is not wholly inspired by a fervor for the truth, tie her in to Gianluigi's interests in some way."

She had been thinking aloud, her eyes gleaming with enthusiasm as she began to see her way clear. But Silvio just moved his big head from side to side as though trying to dodge a blow.

"I can't do all that!" he wailed.

This brought her down to earth with a bump. She gripped his arms tightly, pouring her strength and determination into him.

"Nonsense! Remember what happened with Gerhard, after they arrested Daniele. You managed then."

"But you were there too!"

"And I'll be here this time, to help you and tell you what to do.

But you must do it, because I can't. Don't you see that? You must! No one but you can."

But his look remained vague and distracted. She took his head in both her hands, forcing him to look her in the eyes.

"You know what happened to your real mummy, don't you?"

He bridled, but her grip was firm, holding him steady.

"She died, Silvio. She died because you didn't love her enough. Because you were too tiny, too weak. Do you want that to happen to me, too?"

He twisted away, a look of unspeakable horror on his face, his eyes screwed tightly shut, blocking out the unspeakable truth. Tears squeezed out between the straining eyelids. At length, he sighed compulsively.

"All right, then. I'll do whatever you want. Whatever has to be done."

Ivy drew him down, tucking his nose into the hollow in her shoulder blade where it loved to nestle.

As they embraced, she gazed up at the crucifix on the wall. The figure on the cross was oddly distorted, suggesting not the consolations of the Christian faith but the realities of an atrocious torture. It looked as though the crucifix had been broken and then crudely glued together again, she thought idly.

"There, there," she murmured. "Everything's going to be all right."

"*By the way, do you know that they've arrested the kidnappers?*"

"*Silvio, the kidnappers didn't kill Ruggiero.*"

"*But they've confessed.*"

"*They didn't do it.*"

"*How do you know?*"

"*Because I did.*"

"*That's silly. Don't say things like that. It's horrible. It frightens me.*"

"*It frightens me too. But if we face it together it won't be so frightening. You know that nothing can frighten us as long as we're together.*"

"Right, that'll do."

Geraci pressed a button on the tape recorder and Chiodini clapped his enormous hands together.

"We got the bastards, didn't we? We really got them!"

Zen looked at them both. "You can never be sure, can you? But on balance, yes, I would say that this time we've got them."

12

It was raining in Rome. People said Venice was wet, but it seemed to Zen that it rained even more in the city of his exile. Perhaps it had something to do with the way the two places coped with this basic fact of life. Venice welcomed water in any form, perfectly at home with drizzle or downpour. The city was rich in cozy bars where the inhabitants could go to shelter and dry out over a glass or two, secretly glad of this assurance that their great ark would never run aground. But Rome was a fair-weather city, a playground for the young and the beautiful and the rich, and it dealt with bad weather as it dealt with aging, ugliness, and poverty, by turning its back on it. The inhabitants huddled miserably in their drafty café, gazing bleakly at this dapper passerby with his large green umbrella and his bouquet of flowers, taking the rain in his stride.

Two weeks had passed since Zen's return from Perugia. His working days had been dominated by the readjustment to the humdrum world of Housekeeping and his personal life by the apparent impossibility of getting together with Ellen. Whenever he tried to arrange to see her it seemed to be the wrong day or the wrong time. In the end he'd begun to suspect that she was putting him off deliberately, but then this morning she had phoned out of the blue and invited him round to her flat for dinner.

"I'll get us something to eat. It won't be much, but . . ."

He knew what she meant by throwaway phrases like that! She had probably been planning the meal for days.

Ellen was given to dressing casually, but the outfit in which she came to the door seemed fairly extreme even by her standards: a sloppy shapeless sweater and a pair of jeans with paint stains whose color dated them back more than two years, when she'd redecorated the bathroom. The flowers he presented her with seemed to make her slightly ill at ease.

"Oh, how lovely. I'll put them in water."

"There's no hurry, I expect they're wet enough."

She led him into the kitchen.

"I really meant it about the food being simple, you know," she said, holding up a colorful shiny packet.

Findus 100% Beef American-style Hamburgers, he read incredulously. Was this one of her strange foreign jokes, the kind you had to be a child or an idiot to find funny?

"I imagine you ate well in Perugia, didn't you?" she continued with restless energy. "Tell me all about it. What I don't understand is how the Cook woman ever thought she could get away with it. Surely it was an insane risk to take."

He sat down at the kitchen table.

"It only seems like that because the kidnappers were arrested. Of course, once I knew what had happened, then I started to notice other things. For example, in the phone call to the Milettis which we recorded on Tuesday, the gang's spokesman gave the name of a football team, Verona, as a code word. Pietro should have responded with the name of the team Verona were playing the following Sunday, but he didn't understand and simply assumed it was a wrong number. Yet the kidnapper, instead of insisting or hanging up, said that's fine and went ahead as if the correct response had been given. Which it had, of course, in the original conversation with Ivy. Also the spokesman referred to 'the Milettis' father,' because he knows that the person he's speaking to is not a member of the family. If he'd been phoning the Milettis direct he'd have said 'your father.'"

Ellen ignited the gas under the grill.

"Go on!" she told him as she peeled away the rectangles of plastic which kept the hamburgers separate. But she seemed more concerned that he might fall silent than interested in what he had to say.

"Well, you know most of the rest. The kidnapper I spoke to in Florence told me that they'd phoned the same number as was used to arrange details of the kidnapping. The family had never revealed what this was, and I obviously couldn't approach them directly. But I knew that the kidnappers had used advertisements in a local newspaper as a way for people to get in touch with them. I went to the library and looked through the paper until I found an advertisement that was supposedly for a two-way radio. Phone 8818 after 7, it said. There are no four-digit telephone numbers in a big city like Perugia. But if you read the instructions literally you get a five-digit one, 78818. That was Ivy Cook's number."

There was a crinkling sound as Ellen tore off a sheet of aluminum foil to line the grill pan.

"What confused the issue slightly was that the kidnapper told me that the person who answered was a man with an accent like mine. For a moment I thought it might have been Daniele. But Ivy's voice is deep enough to be mistaken for a man's, and to a shepherd from Calabria her foreign accent sounded like someone from the North. She recorded the kidnappers' call on the answering machine attached to her phone, edited the tape to cut out her own voice, then telephoned the Milettis the next morning and played it back to Pietro."

Ellen laid the patties on the foil and slid the pan under the grill. "I'm surprised she and Silvio weren't more cautious. Talking freely like that in a police station."

"They weren't in a police station, just an anonymous room in an annex of the prison. But what really put them at their ease was that it all seemed to have been rigged in their favor. I arranged for one of my inspectors to call Silvio and offer to get him in to see Ivy in return for various unspecified favors. It's the sort of thing that happens all the time to people in Silvio's position, so he found it completely natural. When he arrived, the inspector got rid of Ivy's guard and made a big point of the fact that he was leaving the two of them alone together. They both simply assumed that the Miletti family power was working its usual magic. After that it never occurred to them to watch what they were saying. They felt they were on their home ground, as though they owned the place."

The patties were sizzling away loudly. Ellen kept busy slicing up buns and laying them on top of the grill to warm.

"Can I do anything?" he asked.

"No, you just take it easy."

Normally she would have asked him to set the table, at least, but this evening he was being treated as an honored guest, except that she'd hardly bothered to cook at all. Zen had once seen a film in which people were taken over by aliens from outer space. They looked the same and sounded the same, but somehow they weren't the same. What had Ellen been taken over by? No sooner had he posed the question than the answer, the only possible answer, presented itself, and everything made sense. But the sense it made was too painful, and he pushed it aside.

"All the same, so much scheming just to bring one guilty person to justice!" she exclaimed. "Do you always go to this much trouble?"

"Not usually, no. But I was practically being accused of responsibility for Miletti's death myself. Besides . . ."

"What?"

Zen had been going to say that he had personal reasons for wishing fathers' deaths to be avenged, but he realized that it might sound as if he were fishing for sympathy.

"It's not that I'm criticizing you, Aurelio," Ellen went on. "I'm just staggered, as always, at the way this country works."

"Oh, not that again!"

It was intended as a joke, but it misfired.

"I'm sorry," she said in a tone that was half-contrite and half-defiant. "I won't say another word."

She served the hamburgers wrapped in paper napkins and brought a liter bottle of Peroni beer from the fridge. The hamburgers were an unhappy hybrid of American and European elements. The meat, processed cheese, and ketchup tried to be as cheerfully undemanding as a good hamburger should, but were shouted down by the Dijon mustard, the pungent onions, and the chewy rolls.

Zen began dismantling his hamburger, eating the more appetizing bits with the fork and discarding the rest. Ellen had wolfed hers down as though her life depended on it. After a few minutes she lit a cigarette without asking. He took the opportunity to push away his plate.

"Don't you like it?" She sounded almost pleased.

"It's delicious. But I had to eat something with my mother. You know how it is."

Ellen laughed quietly. "I surely do."

The conversation stalled, as if they were two strangers who had exhausted the few topics they had in common.

"Anyway, what have you been up to?" he asked.

She refilled her glass with beer. "Well . . ."

She broke off to puff at her cigarette. But he already knew what she was going to say. She had met someone else, these things happened, she'd been meaning to tell him for some time, she hoped they would remain friends. This was what he had glimpsed earlier, the answer to the question of what was making her act in this odd way, of what it was that had taken her over. The only possible answer was another man.

"The thing is, I'm going home, Aurelio."

But you *are* home, he thought. Then he realized what she meant.

"For a holiday?"

She shook her head.

"You're joking," he said.

She walked over to the glass jars where she kept rice and legumes, pulled out an envelope tucked under one, and handed it to him. *"Whether you travel for business or pleasure, MONDITUR-IST!"* it read. *"Our business is to make traveling a pleasure!"* Inside there was an airline ticket to New York in her name.

"I decided one night last week. For some reason I had woken up and then I couldn't get back to sleep. I just lay here and thought about this and that. And it suddenly struck me how foreign I feel here, and what that was doing to me."

She paused, gnawing a fingernail until she realized what she was doing and stopped abruptly.

"People who have been exiles too long tend to end up as either zombies or vampires. I don't want that to happen to me."

There was a roar from the street outside as a metal shutter was hauled down, then a gentler rumble as it was eased into position and the lock attached. The greengrocer opposite was closing up and going home to his family.

"I think we should get married," Zen said, to his total astonishment.

Ellen gave a yelp of laughter. "Married?"

One of the other tenants had put on some rock music whose bass notes penetrated to where they sat as a series of dull thumps. Somewhere else, seemingly quite unrelated to them, a tinny melody line wailed faintly.

Ellen sighed. "You don't know how many times I've imagined that you might say this, Aurelio. I always thought that it was the one thing needed to make everything right."

"It is. It will."

But his voice lacked conviction, even to himself.

He looked around slowly, conscious that all this was about to join his huge gallery of memories. *The latest addition to our collection. A significant acquisition.* "They're turning the whole city into a museum," Cinzia Miletti had complained. But it wasn't only cities that suffered that fate.

"I'd better go."

She made no attempt to stop him.

"I'm sorry, Aurelio. I really am."

The rain had almost stopped. Zen stood waiting at the tram stop, his mind completely blank. The shock of what had just happened was so severe that he found it literally impossible to think about. The last thing he could clearly remember was eating the hamburger and telling Ellen about the Miletti case. He had not mentioned the most recent development, which had occurred just the day before.

The arrest of Ivy Cook had had the unusual effect of uniting both sides of the political spectrum. On the one hand there was talk of a carefully orchestrated attempt by the forces of the Left to undermine the Milettis, on the other of a typically cynical solution by the Right to the embarrassing problem of the family's involvement in Ruggiero's death. In short, whatever your political leanings, Ivy Cook appeared as a humble employee who was being made to take the rap for others, a foreigner without influence or power, the perfect scapegoat. Di Leonardo, the Deputy Public Prosecutor, contributed to the debate with some widely quoted off-the-record criticisms of the "serious irregularities in the procedures adopted by the police," Senator Gianpiero Rossi publicly expressed the opinion that the tape recording was inadmissible evidence since it had neither been authorized by the judiciary nor made on official equipment, while Pietro Miletti flew back from London to demand an end to "the continual harassment of the Miletti family and our dependants." The net result had been that Rosella Foria had finally granted an application for Ivy Cook's release on bail pending a full investigation. The case still hung in the balance, but Ivy was free.

The tram arrived and Zen was rumbled and jolted across the Tiber, over the Aventine hill, and past the Colosseum to Porta Maggiore. He then walked three blocks to the street where Gilberto Nieddu lived with a dark-haired beauty who treated him with bantering humor, as though Gilberto's clumsy attempts to woo her aroused nothing but her amusement. In fact they had been married eight years and had four children, who sat open-mouthed and wide-eyed as Uncle Aurelio announced the dramatic end of his relationship with "*l'americana*."

Rosella Nieddu diagnosed a lack of proper food and made Zen eat a bowl of spaghetti, while Gilberto opened a bottle of the smooth and lethal rosé made by a relative of his. Then the children were packed off to bed and the adults spent the evening playing cards.

"Unlucky at love, lucky at cards," Gilberto joked to his friend, but as usual Rosella Nieddu easily beat both of them, even with one eye on the television. Then the phone rang, and while the Sardinian went to answer it Rosella changed channels for the late movie, catching the end of the late-night newscast. There were stories about the seizure of a shipment of heroin by the Customs in Naples, a conference on the economic problems of the Third World due to open in Rome the following afternoon, and a trade fair promoting Italian agricultural machinery which had just opened in Genoa.

"*And finally the main news again. In a dramatic development in the Miletti murder case, Signora Ivy Cook, the foreign woman formerly being held in connection with this crime, today failed to report to the Questura in Perugia as laid down in the conditions of her release. According to as yet unconfirmed reports, she may already have left the country. Investigators are attempting to trace the person who chartered a light aircraft from Perugia to an airfield in Austria late this afternoon. And now for a roundup of the weekend sports action here's . . .*"

"I have to go," Zen said as soon as Gilberto came back. "Mamma will get anxious."

It had finally stopped raining. He started to walk home through the deserted streets. Ivy's plans would have been laid for days, carefully worked out in the course of her meetings with Silvio. The chartered plane to Austria would no doubt have been followed by an international flight to South Africa, from which she could not be extradited. Her passport had been impounded, so Silvio must have obtained false papers for her as well as putting up the bail money and arranging the flight. Money would have been no problem. All sorts of people would have been happy to contribute financially to ensure that the contents of the famous safety deposit box vanished with Ivy.

So she was in the clear. For Silvio the consequences were likely to be more serious, at least in the short run. The fickle public mood was about to turn very ugly indeed. Important people had been made to look foolish. The Miletti name would no longer be enough to protect Silvio. Her hands freed, Rosella Foria would have him arrested and charged with conspiring to pervert the course of justice. The case would drag on and on, getting bogged down in tedious details until everyone had lost interest, and then in a year or so, when the whole thing had been forgotten, Silvio would be quietly released for lack of evidence.

Suddenly Zen felt something give way inside his chest. It's my heart, he thought, I'm dying. The pain was excruciating. He bent over a parked car, fighting for breath. And then he realized what was happening to him. For the first time in years, he was weeping. It was a brutal and convulsive release, as painful as retching on an empty stomach.

"Waiting for a bumfuck, grandpa?"

Hands gripped his shoulders, pulling him round.

"Rim job you're after, is it? Up from the provinces for a bit of fun, or are you local? I can fix you up, no problem. Not personally, you understand, but for the right money up front I can lay on a kid who went down on Pasolini. Meanwhile let's check your financial standing. Wallet, fuckface! Wallet!"

A torch flashed in his face. Then he heard a gentle chuckle.

"Well, well, dottore, what a coincidence! Don't you remember me? That time on the train a few weeks back, with the old fart who tried to act tough."

The youth looked more closely at Zen. "But what's the matter?"

"Nothing."

"What have the bastards done to you?"

"I'm all right."

Unconvinced, the youth tugged his arm. "Come and have

something warm to drink, dottore. There's a place open just round the corner."

"No, I'm all right, really."

But his whole body was trembling uncontrollably, and he allowed himself to be led away.

"You shouldn't hang around here at this time of night, you know," his companion remarked casually. "This is a very tough neighborhood."

The only other customer in the all-night bar was an old prostitute sitting in the corner talking to herself and obsessively shaking out her hair with both hands. The youth greeted the barman familiarly and ordered two cappuccinos. He produced a packet of Nazionali from his jacket.

"Smoke, dottore?"

"Thanks."

"Fucking bastards. Don't ever let them get you down, though. You let them do that, it's the end."

As their coffees arrived there was a screech of tires outside. The door slammed open and two patrolmen walked in.

"Evening, Alfredo."

"Evening, lads. What can I get you?"

"For me a *cappuccio*, really hot, lots of froth on it."

"And a hot chocolate."

"Right away. Cold out there?"

"It's not warm. See the game last night?"

"That Tardelli."

"Beautiful."

The patrolmen stood looking round the bar, rubbing their hands together and stroking their mustaches, staring with insolent directness at the other customers. The muffled squawks of their car's shortwave radio could be heard outside.

The youth looked down the room to the door at the end, beyond the video machine and the pinball table. Then he glanced at the barman, who shook his head almost imperceptibly.

"Had any trouble lately, Alfredo?" asked one of the patrolmen.

"No, no. We never have any trouble here," the barman assured him, a shade too hastily.

"Glad to hear it."

Time passed, marked by the slow coiling of smoke from their cigarettes.

"Was that us?" one of the patrolmen finally remarked.

His colleague ambled to the door and held it open, listening to the radio. He turned and nodded.

"Domestic altercation, Via Tasso."

"Someone giving the wife a bit of stick," the patrolman guffawed to Alfredo. "What do we owe you?"

"You joking?"

"Thanks. See you, then. Don't work too hard."

"No fear."

The patrolmen went out, leaving the door wide open. A moment later their car roared away.

The barman started toward the door.

"I'll get it," the youth told him, gulping down the rest of his coffee.

He gave Zen a little nod. "Take care now, dottore."

He sauntered to the door and disappeared.

"How much do I owe you?" Zen muttered to the barman.

"It's already taken care of."

"How much?"

Something in his voice made the barman look at him more carefully.

"Cappuccino's eight hundred lire."

As Zen took out his wallet he came across the internal memorandum he had received that morning and had put away unopened. It was bound to be bad news, probably disciplinary action of some kind resulting from his irregular handling of the Miletti case. But he had nothing left to lose now. Let's know the worst and have done with it, he thought, as he tore open the envelope.

> *To: Chief Commissioner Zen Aurelio*
> *From: Enrico Mancini, Assistant Under-Secretary*
>
> *You are hereby informed of your promotion to the rank of Vice-Questore with effect from the 1st of May and consequent on this your transfer from inspection duties to the active rosta of the Polizia Criminale.*

It took him a moment to realize what had happened. His deal with Gianluigi Santucci had only been intended to disguise his real purpose, which was to arrest Ruggiero's murderer. But the Tuscan's involvement with the kidnappers had gone undetected, and here was Zen's reward.

I'm back in the pack, he thought. A functioning member of the ratking once again.

Outside, the sky was clear and littered with stars. Zen began to walk home through a silence broken only by the thin, insistent ringing of a distant telephone.